THE COMPLETE SERIES
KEEPER OF DRAGONS
BOOKS 1-4

The Prince Returns
The Elven Alliance
The Mere Treaty
The Crowns' Accord

J.A. Culican

Edited by: Cassidy Taylor

Cover by: Covers by Christian

Paperback
ISBN: 978-1-725192-57-7

www.dragonrealmpress.com

Contents

The Prince Returns

The Elven Alliance

The Mere Treaty

The Crowns' Accord

J.A. Culican

THE PRINCE RETURNS

KEEPER OF DRAGONS

BOOK 1

For my youngest daughter, Eva and her love of all things magical.

Prologue

I slammed the front door behind me and kicked my shoes toward the closet. My mom constantly yelled at me for not putting my shoes where they belonged, but I couldn't be bothered today. My job search had come up empty once again. I'd graduated high school a month ago and had searched day in and day out for anything I could do to occupy my time. College was out of the question—my grades were barely mediocre and I had little talent elsewhere, so no schools knocked on my door when scholarship time came. All in all, I was close to hating life these days. I had sat back and watched all of my classmates talk about their grand post-high school plans and how excited they were to attend colleges. On my side of things, I had nothing going. And while all through high school, nothing was glorious and free, right now, "nothing" felt like a black hole where I would fall in and disappear forever.

"Cole, come have a seat. Your mother and I have something important to talk to you about," my dad directed from the other room. His voice sounded serious.

I wasn't in the mood for whatever my parents had to talk to me about and wanted to ignore my dad's command, but something in his voice had me concerned. I stepped into the living room and plopped down on the old recliner. Sooner or later, I thought for sure I would plop too hard and hit the floor with all the groans and creaks the chair made. My dad had refused time and time again to get rid of it. I looked up at my parents as they sat across from me on the similarly old, rickety couch. They looked...scared? What could they possibly be scared about?

"Cole," my mom started and hesitated. She looked at my dad, lowered her head, and started to cry.

"Mom, dad what's going on? Is everything okay?" I started to shake as I spoke, unsure of what was about to happen. I had never seen my mom so frightened before. "Is everything okay?"

My dad took a deep breath. "Cole, the last few days have been hard for your mom and me." He paused and grabbed my mom's hand. "I'm disappointed in myself. We let our fear lead us as we raised you. We were so worried someone would find out about you that we never pushed you to do anything. We completely sheltered you from everything." He let go of my mom's hand and put his arm around her shoulders. He squeezed as she continued to cry.

I was confused. I'd known I wasn't doing great but hadn't realized they were that disappointed in me. "I'm sorry, Dad, I really..."

My dad raised his free hand in my direction in an attempt to wave off my response. "No, Cole, just listen, let me finish. Your mother and I always wanted a family. Unfortunately, we weren't able to have children. That was, until you." He paused and took a breath, while beside him, my mom nodded her head in silence. "You were our miracle, our chance at being whole," he explained.

"Dad, I don't understand." I shook my head in confusion. "I know all this, so why do you both look so frightened?" I had heard the story a million times about how thankful they were for me, how they had tried for years to have children and been unsuccessful.

My dad continued. "Cole, you came to us...when you were just a small baby." His voice wavered as he stared at me with a look of uncertainty.

Wait, what? I felt uneasy. A nervous sensation engulfed me like a dark, gloomy cloud that lurks in the sky on a rainy day. But a rainy day I didn't question. This I questioned.

"Are you saying I was adopted?" I began to fidget in my seat as I digested what my parents were trying to tell me. I clasped my hands on my lap to stop the tremble that had begun to take over my body. "Why wouldn't you tell me this before? I mean, kids are adopted all the time." I started to ramble, but I couldn't help it, an unexpected anger making me flustered. Why would they keep this a secret? How didn't I know? Okay, I was adopted, but why did they both look so scared as they told me this fact? Did they think I would leave or go look for my biological parents? That was a thought I was not ready to deal with.

Letting go of my mom, my dad held his hands up to stop my rambling. "Your mother and I love you as if you were our own. To us, you are ours and always have been and always will be."

This I knew, since I had no clue they weren't my real parents until now. They had proven their love for me over and over throughout the years, but this thought didn't stop the anger I felt toward them. I couldn't grasp why they would keep this from me.

"We honestly never thought we would be given the chance to have a baby, but then your parents came to us." My dad looked at me, waiting for it to sink in.

"Wait, you met them?" I couldn't believe it. My hands began to lose circulation from the grip I had on them. I released my hands and shook them out as my mind raced further. "Do you know them? Do I? Why'd they give me up?" I started to babble again. It was like I couldn't get my thoughts straight. My mood jumped around just as much as my thoughts. I was mad one second and scared the next.

"Your biological parents love you just as much as we do. That's why they gave you to us. They trusted us to raise you and love you as our own."

Now I was so confused that my brain couldn't even ramble this time. Even the nerves that shook my body stopped. I was frozen as I sat there and stared at the two people in my life who had always been my home.

"We made a promise to them. We promised..." My dad paused and looked at my mom. She hadn't taken her eyes off me, almost like she thought I was going to just up and disappear. My dad finally turned back to me. "We promised to give you back when you turned eighteen."

"But, but that's like... in two days," I stuttered as I gaped at my parents. I was so confused and a little

12

alarmed by the short notice. They were just going to what, hand me over to two people I had never met? Then what? I began to panic.

My dad stood up and came over to me. He grabbed me under my chin, which forced me to look him in the eyes. "It was part of our promise, that we couldn't tell you until it was time. You're special, Cole, and your family, they're protectors, just as you will be," he stated. "I know your mother and I have just dumped a lot of information on you, and I am really sorry. We had hoped we would have more time, but we don't."

Protectors? How am I supposed to be a protector? And a protector of what? I could barely take care of myself. My mom did everything for me. She cooked my meals, cleaned my laundry...she even made my bed for me each morning. My mind raced with questions, but I couldn't get a single one out. I was confused, frightened, and even angry. I wasn't sure which emotion was most dominant at the moment. I could only imagine what kind of expression I had on my face. We sat in silence as the minutes passed by, our thoughts kept to ourselves.

Finally, my dad broke the silence. "Cole, it's getting late. Why don't you head to bed and we will talk more tomorrow? Let everything sink in, get your thoughts straight. I know this is hard, but I promise it will be alright." My dad reached for my elbows to pull me to standing. As soon as I was on my feet, my mom rushed over and threw her arms around me. My body stiffened from her contact.

"I love you, Cole, no matter what," she whispered in my ear as my body began to relax in her hold.

After she let me go, I turned and ran up the stairs to my room. I shut my door, ambled over to my bed and sat down. My thoughts were still all over the place, an internal uproar flurrying in my head. I only knew one thing for sure: there was no way I would get any sleep that night.

Chapter One

Two hours and thirty-one minutes. That was all the time I had left before my real parents were scheduled to arrive. I sat on my bed, the bed where I'd slept for the last eighteen years, and tried to imagine a different life for myself. Unfortunately, my thoughts weren't any clearer now than when my parents had sat me down two nights ago. I'd received no answers to the questions I'd asked. It seemed my *parents* took me in on faith and faith alone. They never questioned why I was given to them or why I had to be given back at eighteen.

I'd attempted to talk with my mom the next morning at breakfast after news broke of my imminent departure.

"Coley, we wanted you so badly that it didn't matter the why. We loved you immediately." That was the only response I got from my mom and I didn't push her further. As soon as she'd called me Coley, a name she hadn't used since I was little, I knew she was hurting. Her voice trembled as she spoke, it made me think she was scared, which, in turn, made me scared. I stopped with the questions and went back to my room.

I spent the last two days holed up in my room with my cell phone turned off. My friends wouldn't understand. How could they? I didn't even understand what was going on. What would I say to them? Everyone was busy getting ready to leave for college anyway. Me, I had no plans, but *I guess I did now.*

I figured that once I got settled at where I was headed, I'd give them a call and we could all have a good laugh over it. At least that's what I banked on. My closest friend, Eva, had left for college a few weeks earlier to attend summer classes. She was the only one who tried to get me to apply to college or at least make some type of plan. She was unsuccessful, though, so here I sat. I hadn't heard from her in a few weeks and could only hope the distance didn't pull us apart. She'd been my one and only friend I could always count on.

Eva was the one person I had always trusted. Since the day she moved in with her grandparents next door almost eight years ago, we were inseparable. Besides my parents, she was the only other person who got me and accepted me. I guess I just never fit in anywhere. I wasn't athletic or smart, just average. Average in everything, right down to the way I looked. I had never been anything special, which was fine by me. It kept me out of the spotlight and behind the scenes, right where I felt comfortable. Eva, on the other hand, I had no doubt would do great things. She was beautiful and smart. The girl could talk circles around me. I was definitely going to miss her.

Of all things I didn't know, the whereabouts of my new home had bothered me the most; my imagination and maybe my lack of sleep hadn't helped. Whenever I dared to close my eyes, outrageous visions of a place I had no name for filled my head. It made me feel like I was flying in an airplane. All I could see were clouds, but there was something special about them. They almost looked like they were painted onto the blue sky, too perfect to be real. The vision was so close, I felt like I was there.

A noise outside my door startled me out of my daydream.

"Cole?" My Dad's voice sounded strange. "Can I come in?" He seemed worried, like I would actually tell him "no."

I got up off my bed to walk across my room and open the door. There stood my dad, shoulders hunched over. He looked...defeated? Instantly, my panic came back. I stepped back to let him in. He entered and took my spot on the bed I'd just vacated. Only then did I notice my bed was unmade, my plain blue comforter smooshed at the foot in a ball. My mom hadn't been in today to make it like she always did.

My thoughts quickly moved to my dad after I realized he hadn't said anything yet. He held his head in his hands and stared at the ground. He looked like he was going to say something, but changed his mind. Finally, after what felt like minutes though really just a few seconds, he looked up at me. "Cole, no matter what, I just want you to know you always have a home here. You will always be our son." He rushed all this out on one, single sob.

He continued to stare at me as tears fell from his eyes. I had no idea what I was supposed to say to that. I was confused about, well, just about everything, but I never questioned their love for me.

Now that I had heard it straight from my dad, it hit me hard. I would always see him as my dad, but I now had another dad. A man I didn't know at all, who gave me away as a baby, who I was just supposed to...accept? It seemed like I basically had no choice but to accept this fate. But I did have a choice. *Right*? I mean I was eighteen, a legal adult; I could stay. How did this thought never cross my mind the last two days?

My Dad continued to stare at me, waiting for some sort of reply. My thoughts had taken over again and I forgot for a moment he was there. "Dad, I don't have to leave. I'm an adult now. Tonight, when my biological parents come by, I can meet them and send them on their way. Nothing has to change." I was holding my breath, awaiting his reply. Whatever he said next could change everything.

I could barely hear him when he responded, "I wish that were true. Your mother and I would want nothing more than to have you stay here with us forever." The pain in his voice was almost unbearable. "Yes, you're now a legal adult, but I fear where you're going, your age won't make a difference." He stopped and sucked in a breath, almost like he wasn't supposed to tell me any of that.

Wait, did he say my age wouldn't matter where I was going? "What do you mean?" My father flinched. "I thought you didn't know where I was going?" Nothing else could come out of my mouth. I just looked at him while I waited for a response. *Maybe I heard him wrong*?

He looked uncomfortable. "I'm so sorry, Cole. I just— I just need you to trust me. Promise me you will go with them tonight without a fight. Keep an open mind. Your mom and I love you so much. We want nothing but the best for you, and this is the best." I could tell each word that passed his mouth was more painful than the last. He looked like he was in complete agony.

I was more confused now than before he came up the stairs. I just wanted this all to be over. For someone to answer my questions. Nothing made sense at all.

My dad interrupted my inner debate. "Please, come downstairs and have dinner with your mom and me. Please, we..." He couldn't finish his thought. I could tell he felt beaten.

"Yeah...I'll be down." For some reason, I couldn't be mad at him. It was clear he didn't want any of this to happen. I just wished he would answer my questions. He seemed to know more than he initially let on.

He stood up to leave my room and looked back at me when he reached the doorway. "I love you, Cole, no matter what. Remember that." With that, he walked out and quietly closed the door behind him. An ominous feeling was left behind with his parting words.

I wasn't sure how dinner was going to go, but I decided if I had to leave tonight, I didn't want to leave on a bad note. My parents, even with everything that had happened in the last two days, had always been the best parents anyone could ever ask for. That was one thing I could be grateful for. At least my birth parents had left me with a couple who loved and cared for me better than any other parent could. They had always supported me in everything. I never would have thought I wasn't biologically theirs. It was this thought alone that propelled me from my room to head down for dinner. My parents deserved everything I could give them. Everything in my life was because of them, and I wouldn't let them down.

As I made my way down the stairs and into the kitchen, I could hear my parents as they talked in hushed voices to each other. I wasn't sure if I should wait a few minutes and let them finish their quiet conversation or just head in. I guessed my dad was letting my mom know how his talk had just gone with me. I wondered if he thought it was successful. To be honest, I wasn't sure what to think about anything anymore.

Finally, I found the courage to walk into the kitchen. As soon as I walked in, both of my parents turned and looked at me. My mom had a relieved expression on her face. *Did they think I wouldn't show?* It took me a second to collect my bearings; I walked over to the table and took a seat in the same chair I had sat in almost every night for dinner for the last eighteen years. Rarely did we eat anywhere else except this table. My mom always insisted we eat as a family every night. *This might be our last family dinner.* That thought alone depressed me.

My parents headed over to the table carrying various dishes of food. When I looked at the assorted plates on the table, I noticed my mom had made my favorite dinner, corned beef hash. Eva once told me this was a favorite meal among Texans, but I guess I wouldn't know. I had never left the great state of Texas, and had only left the small town of Clover a few times. It was the town where everyone knew everyone. The kids here were dying to leave, and college was one of the few ways out, but I guessed I never had the need to flee like everyone else. *Again, my mind rambled.*

My mom interrupted my racing thoughts. "Happy Birthday, Cole."

I could tell she was trying to sound cheerful when she said this, but I had completely forgotten today was my birthday. Usually, turning eighteen was all teens could think about. I guessed the whole "being sent back to wherever I came from on this day to protect something I didn't know," took away the happy excitement I should have felt. I finally looked up at my mom and mumbled a thank you. I could tell she wanted to say more but stayed quiet, gesturing for me to eat. I did, not tasting anything. I was sure it was all wonderful, like it always was. My mom was one of the best cooks I knew. But then I wondered if my real mom knew how to cook. *I guessed I would find out soon.*

Once I cleared my plate, my mom brought out an apple pie, again one of my favorites. I knew it was my birthday and my last day with them and she just wanted to make me happy, but it was getting to be too much. It made me think of all the things I was going to miss.

"I don't want to go!" I blurted out, my eyes on the steaming pie in the middle of the table.

My parents looked at me with regret and pity. All of these emotions in the last few days overwhelmed me. My dad came around the table and kneeled next to me.

"We know son, and we don't want you to go either, but it's what has to happen." He took my hand and pulled me up. "Come on, let's go watch some of that horrible reality

TV you like so much. We have a little bit of time before your parents arrive." His voice caught on the word parents, but he continued to pull me to the living room as though nothing he just said hurt him at all.

Thanks for the reminder, Dad. I knew he just wanted to get my mind off everything. Maybe he was right; mindless TV sounded okay. But I made it about two steps before I began to feel strange. It was like my whole body was pulsating with some kind of energy. I tried to look to my dad for some kind of confirmation that he was feeling it, too, but he looked blurry, like I was seeing him through a film. The vibration intensified, and I wasn't sure how much more I could take. I attempted to say something, but all I could manage was some kind of whimper. I thought my parents were speaking to me but I couldn't be sure, nothing made sense. My legs gave out, and a crazy energy started to devour me. And then, just as suddenly, everything went silent.

Chapter Two

A loud bang echoed through my head. All I wanted to do was cover my ears but my arms weren't cooperating. My parents were next to me; I could feel them grabbing my arms. *Were they moving me?* A loud, terrified shriek rang out, but everything was foggy so I couldn't make out the words or who was yelling them.

Without warning, the energy that pulsed through me stopped, catching me off guard. I couldn't catch my breath for a moment. Everything that had just happened came back to me. I looked up to find my mom staring down at me where I lay on the old green couch in the living room. "Mom?" I squeaked out.

She looked at me with concern; she was just as confused as me about what had happened. "Just stay still, I'm sure everything is going to be okay."

She glanced over the couch at something behind me. *Maybe my dad?* I looked closer at her face and saw that she looked pale. The last few days had been rough on everyone, not just me.

My mom took a deep breath and looked back down at me. With a look of astonishment, she whispered, "Your parents are here. Your dad is in the other room with them. I'm not sure how long he is going to be able to keep them out."

How long had I been out of it? It had felt like mere minutes, so we still had a good half hour until my parents were supposed to arrive. I tried to sit up but was unsuccessful, so my mom helped me. She sat next to me with her arm around my shoulders. Neither of us said a thing but I was glad she was there. Without her support, I would've gone completely crazy.

The door that separated the living room and foyer banged open behind me and I twisted on the couch toward the noise. In walked a massive man who looked to be about thirty-five. He was well over six feet tall and had to duck his head as he passed through the doorway. I'd never seen a man as large as him and became instantly alert. Behind him was a beautiful woman about the same age. She had long, golden hair and a perfect complexion, and wasn't much shorter than the enormous man standing in front of her. My dad stood behind them. He looked so small and seemed a little intimidated by our visitors.

The man was the first to speak. "My son, how are you feeling? I did not expect our power to affect you in the manner it did." He walked closer to us as he spoke, regarding me in a predatory manner. It took everything I had not to get up and run out of the room. He stopped in front of my dad's recliner and looked down at me, waiting for a response.

I couldn't get my mouth to work, but thankfully my mom saved me. "Rylan, Sila, please come in and have a seat." She pointed to the recliner across from us. "The two of you haven't changed at all since the last time we saw each other. Hard to believe it's been eighteen years already."

There was no way these two could be my parents. They looked way too young, and the more I studied them, nothing like me. The man's hair was a dark shade of red, which I knew only a few people could get away with; on him, dark red looked strong and powerful. The woman had an impressive head of golden blonde locks, which I found odd because my own hair was a dull shade of brown. Not to mention their eyes. They both had the same shade of jade green. I was completely mesmerized; the color had a calming effect as they shined like emeralds. My eyes were the wonderful shade of mud. How was any of this even possible? *I did pay attention a little in biology class.*

Rylan, my *father*, looked from my mom to me, nodded his head, and advanced towards my dad's favorite recliner. He plunked down on it and the predictable creaks and groans ensued. I held my breath as I waited for the chair to crumble to the ground under the behemoth sitting in it. Sila, my *mother* joined him. She stood behind the recliner and faced my mom and me. I was thankful when my dad joined us on the couch, sandwiching me between him and my mom. I sent a silent prayer of thanks up for the support they had continued to give me.

All the attention was now on me. I hadn't uttered a single word throughout the whole exchange, and I had nothing to add, even now. I sat nestled between my parents while I stared at the two people who wanted to take me from my home.

"What's the plan from here?" My dad's voice rang through the silent air. It seemed extremely loud after the intense silence. He cleared his throat and looked around. "I mean, Cole just found out that the two of you existed. He has a lot of questions we haven't been able to answer."

"There will be time later to answer all your questions." Rylan looked only at me as he spoke. "We must be going. We only have the cover of night for so many hours, and we have quite some distance to cover. Do not worry, Michael," said, finally turning away from me and focusing on my dad. "You will be compensated for taking care of our son. Our people will forever be grateful for you and Ella."

Well, that news got my adrenaline to spike. This guy was crazy if he thought I was just going to get up and walk out without so much as an introduction from him or the woman standing behind him. Especially after the mention of "our people." What people?

In true Cole fashion, I blurted out the first thing that came to my brain. "No way, I don't want to go anywhere with you."

This time, the woman, Sila, answered. "Son, we know you don't understand what is going on, but everything will make sense once we get you home," she assured me. "We will have all the time in the world to answer your questions. But, like your father said, we don't have the luxury to sit here and discuss this further." Just like her eyes, Sila's voice seemed to soothe my nerves. I started to stand without a thought and got all the way to the door before my brain started to kick in again. *What had just happened?*

I turned and looked at everyone in the room. Rylan had already stood from the recliner. I was so confused. I mean, there was no way I was going with them! Why did I just leave the comfort of my parents? I wanted nothing more than to run back over and jump between them and stay there forever. But now that I was up, I needed to play this just right. Maybe I could make a run for the front door? Or run up to my room and lock the door? I was beyond frightened, but something told me it wouldn't make much of a difference what I tried to do. I would still be leaving with these two strangers tonight.

Rylan interrupted my internal debate. "Very good my son, you are stronger than you know. By your reaction earlier to us, I thought there was something special within you, and now I know for sure." Rylan started to walk toward me, but I was completely rooted to the spot near the living room door. I wasn't sure what to think of what he had just said to me but knew one thing for sure: strong and special were two words I wouldn't use to describe myself. He stopped right in front of me. I had to tilt my head completely back just to look at him.

"Get your things, son. Bring only what you can carry. We can send someone later to gather the rest of your belongings." His voice sent a vibration through me that frightened me to my core. No way could I say no to this man, not when he stared at me with such intensity. Visions of being sacrificed, or worse, flashed through my mind, but my body betrayed me, doing as he instructed.

I turned to walk up the stairs. As I hit the top step, I heard my mom behind me, offering to help me pack my things. I'm sure my dad was thrilled to be left behind with my biological parents, *or so they claimed.*

As soon as we turned into my room, my mom shut the door and looked at me. I had a feeling of déjà vu; not too long ago, my dad stood in exactly the same spot for what I was sure a similar conversation.

"I love you, no matter what." She paused as she walked toward me, then grabbed and held my hands between us. "You can always come home, you can always call us. No matter what, we are here for you, for the rest of our lives," she whispered.

I could tell she was doing all she could to hold herself together and keep her tears from streaming down her face. Unfortunately, I wasn't as strong, no matter what Rylan said, so my tears flowed freely. I didn't even have the strength to pull my hands from my mom's and wipe them away. I was still angry—furious, in fact. But that took second place to the reality that this was goodbye.

We pulled apart and stared at each other for a bit. Only then was I finally able to get something rational out. "Thank you, Mom. I love you and dad, too. I'll visit, I promise; I already miss you both." I choked out my words but was glad I got them out before I had to leave. I realized that I didn't have a choice. I'd be leaving my home soon with two people who had done nothing but intimidate me.

I mustered up the strength to remove my hands from my mom's and grab my stuff. I pocketed my dead cell phone that hadn't left my dresser in the last two days, as well as my wallet. I turned to grab my red backpack off my bed but my mom had already grabbed it and walked to my door. I took one last look around. I had already packed most of my stuff into boxes, and my fingers were crossed that I would be able to get them sent to me soon. I'd left a few belongings behind in hopes that I would be able to come home and visit soon, you know, *like tomorrow.*

I left my room and shut the door behind me. Taking a deep breath, I wiped my face roughly to get rid of the wetness, trying to find as much courage as I could gather to walk down the stairs. I needed to be strong, just as Rylan suggested I was. In an effort to do just that, I stood tall and looked straight ahead as I headed back down to the living room. While I walked, I made a promise to myself. I promised I would make my mom and dad proud. They had given away the last eighteen years of their lives to take care of me, to love and support me. And no matter what biology said, they were my real parents and I wouldn't let them down!

When I made it to the bottom of the stairs, I noticed everyone stood in uncomfortable silence as they waited for me. *Maybe my pep talk took longer than I thought.* I took my backpack from my mom and gave both my mom and dad a hug, holding each of them longer than I normally would have. Rylan and Sila as they stood by the front door waiting on me, clearly in a hurry. I wasn't sure what to say, but maybe there was nothing left to say. So, I kept it simple as I turned back to my parents.

"I'll call you when I get there." I thought about how I needed to charge my phone on the way. They both nodded and grinned through teary eyes.

I pulled open the door and gestured for Rylan and Sila to walk out ahead of me. They nodded to my parents and walked out. I took what felt like my millionth deep breath in the last few days, then stole one last look at my parents before walking out the door into the night.

Chapter Three

Crickets were chirping outside as I shuffled behind my new parents. The crickets didn't seem to care that the world as I knew it had come to an end. I followed behind Rylan and Sila to the driveway, which was on the side of the house. I'd grown up in the old farmhouse, spending the better half of my life fixing it up with my dad. It still needed quite a bit of work, but it was home nonetheless. I wasn't sure what kind of vehicle I expected to find in the driveway, but no vehicle at all was not something I had considered. *Did they take a taxi here? Maybe that means they lived close. Except I knew pretty much everyone in this tiny country town.* Neither of them stopped when we arrived at the driveway. Without so much as a pause, they continued to walk toward the road. *Where were they going?* They couldn't live that close. As we approached the end of the driveway, I stopped and looked both ways down the road in search of a car, but nope, nothing for as far as I could see.

I broke the silence "Where are we going?" I asked. "No one has told me."

Sila paused and looked back at me. "We're taking you home. Everyone is excited to meet you." She turned back around and continued down the street.

We lived in the middle of nowhere, like, literally in the middle of nowhere. The closest house was Eva's grandparents', and that was almost a mile away. *Did they really plan to just walk, in the pitch black dead of night, to wherever we were going?* "Umm, where exactly is home? Do you plan to walk there?" I started to have visions of being led to some remote location where "their people" would tie me up and torture me or something. I began to wonder, again, who these two strangers were, and what had propelled me to follow them into the night.

This time they both stopped and turned completely around to face me. They looked confused, like I should have known the answer to both of those questions. Rylan's voice boomed in the silent night as he answered. "We're taking you to Ochana, where you were born. I'm sure Michael and Ella have told you all about Ochana. And of course we don't plan to walk. There's only one way to get there and it is way too far from here to walk." He shook his head at me and smirked, as if I had made a joke.

I was more confused now than before. My parents had never mentioned this place called Ochana, and it definitely didn't even sound familiar to me. I had no idea where it was, and if it was that far away, and we weren't going to walk, how were we getting there? I couldn't take it anymore; I needed them to answer my questions. I planted my feet on the dirt road and refused to move. It took them a few seconds to realize I was no longer behind them.

Rylan turned back around again and looked at me like I was a rebellious teenager. "What is it now? We're in a hurry," he huffed.

I gave him the best glare I could under the circumstances. But since I stood in the dark, in the middle of nowhere, with two humungous strangers, I'm sure it looked more like a grimace than a glare, but I went with it. "I've never heard of Ochana, I have no idea where it is, and I have no idea how we are getting there. Now, can someone give me honest answers to my questions?" Because, let's face it I was starting to freak out again, but luckily, I was smart enough to leave that part out.

Rylan and Sila looked from me, then to each other, and an expression I couldn't decipher floated across their faces. "What exactly do you know?" Sila's voice had a cautious tone to it.

Dumbfounded, I just glared at her. I knew nothing; I felt like I was being kidnapped or something. "Well, you gave me up as a baby. My mom and dad adopted me, which I am still having a hard time grasping. They just told me this a few days ago. Oh, and you guys are some kind of protectors and I am expected to be one as well." *What else was there?* The two of them had been so cryptic with me when I asked them questions that I was under the impression they weren't allowed to tell me anything, but here I was, stuck with two strangers who thought I knew everything that was going on.

Neither of them said a thing for a long while. I guess they wanted to choose their words with care. "We are protectors and you will be, too," Rylan stated with confidence. "As for the rest, maybe we should show you. We were under the impression that Michael and Ella had already told you everything. Well, what they knew, anyway." Rylan tacked that last bit on a bit smugly. "Now I understand your confusion with how you reacted to our power," he added. Again, with the lack of answers. I guess they were worried about scaring me. Little did they know, I was way past scared.

"Then show me," I demanded, finding my courage. "No more of these meaningless answers." I hoped that was the right thing to say—no more secrets. It's what I'd wanted all along.

Rylan looked around, but I wasn't sure what he was looking for. It's not like there was anything nearby, being the middle of nowhere and all. We were surrounded by trees, but I could still see the lights from my house—*my parents' house.* The sky was clear except for a few stars that were out, and the moon hung high, casting an eerie glow onto the ground. Rylan took off toward the tree line. Sila stayed quiet next to me, but did not follow. I wasn't sure if I was supposed to stay with her or follow Rylan into the trees. Curiosity won and I took a step toward Rylan, but Sila stopped me with a hand on my shoulder. This was the first real contact I had with either Rylan or Sila, and her touch sent a shiver through my body.

"Stay here, open your senses, and stay calm."

Stay calm? Was a pack of werewolves or something going to fly out of the woods? I almost asked her as much but held my tongue at the last minute, not wanting her to see that side of me. I could no longer see Rylan. *What was he doing?* Finally, I heard a rustling, like someone, I assume Rylan, was coming toward us from the trees. I squinted into the darkness but saw nothing. Sila looked down at me with a face of comfort and ease. She waited for me to see. See what, I wasn't sure.

Finally giving up, I looked at Sila and asked, "Where did Rylan go?" I paused after my question, realizing that I had called Rylan by his name and not Father, or Dad, or whatever I was supposed to call him. No introductions were officially made yet.

Sila said nothing, but gestured with her hands for me to continue looking at the trees. What was it she had said to me? *Open my senses?* I concentrated on opening my senses, though nothing seemed to be happening. I turned back to Sila and she again gestured toward the trees. I growled in frustration but looked back at the trees, squinting once again.

Sila's voice echoed around me almost melodically. "Relax. Feel it, deep within you. I promise, my son, it's there inside of you."

I closed my eyes and took my millionth and one deep breath, then relaxed. I opened my eyes and looked at the trees. I felt different, more in touch, with what I wasn't sure yet. I could also feel something within me, something I had never felt before, something no words could describe. I felt whole, like I had been missing something and never knew.

I continued to relax as I stood next to Sila in the dark, with nothing but the moon and a few stray stars for light. Out of nowhere, I saw something. It blended with the trees, like camouflage. It looked to be some kind of animal, but much larger than any animal I had ever seen. My eyes were playing games on me; what I thought I saw couldn't exist. Didn't exist. It was impossible. I started to shake, forgetting to relax and stay calm. It seemed Sila must have seen I was about to lose it.

"My son, it is alright. What you see is real, but he would never hurt you. That, my son, is your father." She grabbed my shoulders in what seemed to be an attempt to stop my shaking.

I knew it was Rylan the second my eyes landed on him. Somehow, I knew, I felt it, but that didn't take the fear away. If anything, it amplified it. If that thing was my father, then what was I? My eyes stayed on Rylan. "What is he?" I whispered, not wanting to startle the creature.

I could feel Sila as she looked at me, somehow sensing her *energy* toward me. "I think you know, my son. I need you to answer that question. Dig deep within you and do not be afraid. What is it you see?"

Of course she couldn't just answer my question. Why make anything easy for me? I blew out the breath I had been holding and answered her hesitantly. "He...is he a dragon?" I questioned. Thinking it in my head and saying it out loud were two completely different things. Saying it out loud made it that much more real.

Sila squeezed my shoulders. I hadn't realized she still held me. "You are correct. No need to question what your eyes see." She let go of my shoulders and stepped to my side. She continued, "Your father and I are green dragons, or Leslos as we call them in Ochana. Born of fire and made with earth, Leslos are the leaders of Ochana." Sila turned toward Rylan.

Unbelievable. My parents were dragons. I continued to stare at Rylan, the dragon. I wouldn't have believed it if I hadn't seen it with my own eyes. I guessed that's what he'd meant by it being best to show me, because there was no way I would have believed them otherwise. I hesitated a second as I attempted to get my thoughts straight. Questions raced through my head, but I wasn't sure where to start. I finally tore my eyes away from Rylan and turned to Sila.

"Why couldn't I see him at first? Now that I see him, I don't see how anyone could miss him." He was gigantic, like a tyrannosaurs rex. He almost reached the tops of the old pine trees.

Sila ignored my question. "We need to leave. The only way we are going to make it back to Ochana tonight is if we hurry." She walked toward Rylan.

I still didn't know where Ochana was or how we planned on getting there. It seemed my questions were endless as of late, and wholly unanswered. I started to follow Sila across the road toward the trees where Rylan still stood as a Leslo, as Sila had called him. The closer we made it to Rylan, the more my eyes were able to pick up the details of the magnificent creature in front of me. It was like nothing I had ever seen before. Rylan was brilliant, a spectrum of glistening green hues radiating the sky dust around his figure, and even though the darkness made it almost impossible to see the exact shade of green he was, I could tell it was miraculous.

A thought popped into my head and before I could stop myself, I blurted it out. "Wait, if you both are dragons, then what am I?" I halted in the middle of the road, thoroughly disturbed by the thought. Luckily this part of Clover was deserted, with just a few houses spread miles apart.

Sila paused ahead of me and turned slowly until she faced me. I could see the wheels turning in her head as she thought about her next words carefully. "My son, you are more than just a dragon." She paused to read my expression on my face, then continued. "You are the son of two very powerful Leslos and our expectations for you are high. We have expectations for who and what you'll be."

After that last bit, she smiled like I should be happy about her declaration. I began to wonder if they had even picked up the right kid. I mean, I was just ordinary Cole. I was never good at anything, just a normal kid. Any expectations they had for me were bound to be unrealistic. This scared me more than the dragon standing less than twenty feet away.

Chapter Four

We caught up to Rylan a few moments later. I was still confused about the plan to get to Ochana without a mode of transportation, though Sila and Rylan didn't seem concerned at all. I watched as Sila walked behind Rylan. I began to follow, but got a huff from Rylan, which I assumed meant to stay put. Sila had left me alone with a massive green dragon, something that shouldn't exist, who also happened to be my father. My mind raced over everything I had learned in the last five minutes. When I'd been wondering about who my parents were and what they would be like the last two days, I never even came close to reality.

Suddenly, another disconcerted presence jolted me from my internal thoughts. I looked up to see another green dragon, or Leslo, standing next to Rylan. Well, at least I knew where Sila had gone. They both gazed at me, waiting for something. I knew they couldn't answer me, but I asked anyway.

"Now what? How are we getting to Ochana?" I waited a few seconds for a response. Nothing. Not that I had expected one. I looked around at the trees and the vacant road, then back up at Rylan and Sila, waiting in silence for some kind of signal as to what to do next.

Then, Sila's lyrical voice echoed in my head—literally, in my head. "Son, you'll ride on your father's back. There's no other way to get to Ochana but to fly. Unless you're able to shift into your dragon?"

Startled, I tried to process the fact that Sila's voice was inside my head, then I thought about what she said. I had no idea how to even begin to turn myself into a dragon. Swallowing my hesitancy, I walked as close to Rylan as I could. He bent down so I could climb onto his scaly back. The feeling was awkward without a saddle or harness. I positioned myself between two *spikes*—I'm sure there was a technical name for them, but I didn't know it. I wrapped my arms around the one in front of me and sent a prayer up to my guardian angel that I wouldn't fall. Rylan's skin felt rugged and dry, not slimy like I had expected.

Rylan walked out into the middle of the road and spread his wings. He was even bigger than I had first thought; his wings touched the trees on each side of the road. There was no way this wasn't going to end without me falling to my death. My arms shook with the strength I was using to hold on and we hadn't even left the ground yet. I heard a snort behind us and turned around in time to see Sila step behind Rylan and spread out her wings just as Rylan had. The sight amazed me.

Rylan took my distraction as an opportunity to scare the heck out of me. He hastily crouched his legs and hurled me into his front spike. I refastened my hands around it just in time as he pushed off the ground and climbed into the sky. Squeezing my eyes shut, I sucked in a breath; I'd never been more terrified then I was at that moment. I hoped my ride on the back of a dragon would be a short one.

We ascended for just a few minutes, then leveled off. I took a large breath and cracked open my eyes. The sight that met me was shocking—a dark sky with just the moon as our guide. I relaxed a bit around Rylan and looked around more with ease. I had never been in an airplane, so seeing the ground from the air was all new to me. The lights from the ground blinked up at me just as the stars had looked down on me so many nights before.

The excitement began to wean and I felt exhausted. My adrenaline had worn off as the whole night finally caught up to me. The last thing I needed was to fall asleep and plummet to my death. I still had a lot of questions, and seeing as Sila was able to answer me before in her Leslo form, I went for it.

"Sila, how long until we arrive in Ochana?" My question was met with silence for a few minutes, and I decided that maybe she couldn't hear me. I thought animals had better hearing then humans, but I didn't know anything about dragon hearing.

"We will arrive in about two hours, son. You'll find that our time is remarkably fast considering the distance we will be traveling."

Two hours? It would be a struggle to keep my eyes open, but it was better than the alternative. It would give me the time to think through everything, and maybe Sila would be open to answering some more of my questions since all we seemed to have was time.

"Where is Ochana located?" It was a question I'd had for the last two days, though not specifically about Ochana, but about where my new home would be.

It took Sila a few minutes again to answer. "Ochana is high above the clouds, off the coast of Greenland."

Wow, we planned to fly all the way to Greenland? Sila had said it would only take a couple of hours, so I could only imagine the speed we were traveling at for that to be true. It felt like we were merely floating, not speeding through the air. My mind raced as to what it must be like there, though my knowledge of Greenland was limited. I knew it was cold, like, really cold, but that was it. That thought made me wonder about my present situation. I should be cold now, but I wasn't; if anything, I was warm.

Sila interrupted my thoughts. "Very good, son, your thoughts are loud and clear. You aren't cold because I don't will you to be. You will learn about this will. We call it mahier. Mahier is an old Ochana word. It is what makes us dragons. You will learn later what that entails."

Sila's unexpected disruption only gave me more questions. She could read my thoughts? I was sure she'd gotten a real laugh out of all my inward jibber jabber since we met. I hoped I hadn't completely embarrassed myself. Mahier, eh? It would take some time to be able to say it like Sila had with her harmonious voice, but I wondered about it. Was it like magic? A few hours ago, something like magic would be laughable to me, but now anything was possible.

Since she was willing me to be warm, was she willing me to feel like we were floating as well? I wondered what else she was capable of. I had almost forgotten about Rylan. He didn't seem to be able to talk to me while as a

Leslo, like Sila, or he didn't want to talk to me, which could be a real possibility too.

We had to have traveled quite far by now, though time was a strange concept while flying on the back of a dragon. There was no way I was letting go of Rylan to check my watch. As I looked around, I noticed what looked like snow on the ground. I had seen little snow in my time in Texas, though I had always wanted to try snowmobiling or skiing. Maybe with my new life, I finally could.

The ground grew closer as Rylan began to descend toward an empty field. It astounded me how I could barely feel any of this, not even the cold. Everywhere I looked, all I could see was snow. *Surely this wasn't Ochana?*

Rylan's clawed feet hit the ground with a quiet thud. I squeezed him tighter, afraid I would fall off from the impact. Thankfully I was able to hold on and stay put. Rylan leaned down as a signal for me to climb off. I leaped off and turned to Sila, who had already transformed back into her human form. She really was stunning; it was hard to believe she was my mother. I was relieved to see she'd transformed back with clothes on. It had to be part of the mahier she talked about earlier. She turned to me and beamed a knowing smile my way.

"How do you feel? Your first flight seemed successful." She winked at me and gave a slight chuckle.

"Well, I didn't fall so I would call that a success. I'm starting to feel tired, though. Are we there?"

Instead of Sila, it was Rylan who answered. "We're close," he said, stepping toward me. He was back in his human form, also clothed. "This is Ellesmere Island,

Canada. We're resting for a bit; we have traveled quite a distance."

Geography was something I'd never paid much attention to, and all I knew about Canada was that it was in the north. I regretted not paying more attention in school.

"However, we need to get you in touch with your dragon in order to continue our trip and enter Ochana," Rylan continued.

I should've guessed it wouldn't be as easy as just hitching a ride on the back of a dragon. How was I supposed to get in touch with my dragon? I didn't even know if there really was a dragon to get in touch with. I looked at Rylan and Sila with an expression that I hoped showed my true distress on this matter.

Rylan chuckled. "Relax, son. You've already proven your strength to us. You're able to control our mahier. It's how you were able to take control back after your mother ordered you to leave the house." Rylan nodded toward Sila as he said "mother." He continued, "Only a very strong dragon, especially one with no experience, could accomplish that."

Rylan's revelation didn't make me feel any better. I wasn't thinking about dragons. or mahier, or much of anything back at the house. My only concern then was not wanting to leave. How would I explain to Rylan that I wasn't as strong as he thought I was, that it was just a mistake? Something I never had control over.

Sila grabbed my shoulders, much like she did when I first saw Rylan as a Leslo. Her green eyes pierced me. "But you are strong, son, I can feel it. When we landed at your house tonight, your father and I were both in our Leslo forms. It is why your body reacted the way it did. You haven't been in the presence of such power since you were a baby. Your body was recalling that power, the mahier. You will find your dragon. I can promise you that." Sila dropped her arms and walked to Rylan, who had gone about two hundred yards from us to set up some kind of makeshift camp. Where did he find all those supplies? Sila angled herself toward me and mouthed the word "mahier." I would have to remember that Sila could read my thoughts. It was definitely something I would have to get used to.

As I got neared the camp, I noticed he had already set up two tents, started a fire, and was already cooking something over it. I was impressed; he had set up camp in the middle of a frozen desert. I hoped they were right about me. I'd love to be able to do the things they were able to. I took a seat next to Sila in a chair that seemed to appear from thin air, peering over the fire as Rylan cooked.

"Where do I start? I mean, with finding my dragon. How do I do that?" I wasn't asking either of them in particular, just hoping one of them would answer.

"It's different for everyone," Sila said. "Everyone has a unique relationship with their dragon. It also depends on your type of dragon. Rylan and I are Leslos, but there are other types. Each type has its own responsibilities and purpose." Sila took a breath and looked at me. "Just concentrate, son. Reach out to your dragon. Let him know you're ready to accept him. He will appear, in one form or another."

Concentrate on my dragon. It seemed much easier than it was. Once I found my dragon, would I just shift into it? To be honest, I was terrified, and I bet it hurt a whole lot to shift. I wondered what it would feel like. Would we be separate or become one? I was so confused that my focus was not on finding my dragon, but scattered in thoughts.

Rylan waved a plate of food in front of me. I wasn't sure exactly what it was, though it was definitely some sort of meat that smelled delicious. I grabbed the plate from him. Rylan sat back down and started to eat, and I stared at him in wonder. He had already scarfed down more food than I could eat in a whole day, and he didn't seem to be slowing down. If he always ate this way, I had no idea how he was in such good shape.

A chuckle came from beside me. "It takes a lot to shift, son, and your father is not only feeding himself, but his dragon. Usually we would feed while in our Leslo forms, but we didn't have the time tonight to do so. Now, eat. You will need your strength. Then we will leave you alone to connect with your dragon. Your father will need about an hour to rest and gain all his mahier back."

That was interesting; Rylan lost some of his mahier and needed to rest, yet Sila seemed just fine. Maybe Sila was stronger than Rylan, though by looking at the two of them, I'd thought for sure Rylan was stronger.

"Your father had to use his mahier more than I did. Rylan protected us as we flew so that no human was able to detect us. My job was much simpler. All I had to do was protect you." Sila pointed at me with that last bit.

It made sense now, why Rylan didn't speak as we flew. He was focused elsewhere. At least some things were starting to make sense. Now I just needed to find my dragon.

I finished eating and watched as Rylan stepped into one of the tents. Sila took my plate and placed it on top of hers, setting them by the fire. She nodded at me and stepped into the same tent as Rylan. I sat there alone, and as they left, I suddenly felt relief. Finally, just one thought was in my head—how to find my dragon.

J.A. Culican

Chapter Five

Finding my dragon wasn't going to be easy. If I had a dragon, wouldn't I have already found it in the last eighteen years? Taking a deep breath, I closed my eyes and pictured what I wanted my dragon to look like. The dragon I pictured was strong and powerful, and a Leslo like Rylan and Sila. It stood taller than both of them, its wingspan at least twice theirs.

I concentrated hard on the image in my mind, but nothing happened. I opened my eyes and kicked at the sticks by my feet that Rylan had left for the fire. I still felt nothing except disappointment. My first request by my biological parents had been to turn into a dragon, and I was about to fail them.

I thought about my mom and dad and how they would've reacted to my situation. It was obvious to me now that they knew what I was or what I was to become. Even with that knowledge, they'd loved and supported me. They were always proud of me, no matter what little I actually succeeded in. I remembered the promise I made to myself before I left home. I wasn't going to let them down! With this new encouragement, I took yet another breath and tried again.

This time, I didn't picture what my dragon would look like, as I remembered what Sila had said about different types of dragons. Instead, I thought about the traits I would want my dragon to have. Strong, fair, kind, and smart. These traits made me think of my friend, Eva. Apparently, I wanted my dragon to be like her. I shook my head and cleared my mind of my friend. I again focused on my dragon.

My breath evened out, almost like I was asleep. Everything around me faded away. It was just me. There, deep within, I felt it. Almost like I was being pulled toward something. I concentrated on it, trying to grab onto the pull I felt and reel it in.

My breath caught in my throat. Something was happening. I was no longer in control. My body started to shake and my vision blurred around the edges. I looked down at my hands in time to see my fingers turn into claws, ginormous and sharp. My body pitched forward until I was on the ground on my stomach. I tried to stand back up but had no control of my arms. Shimmering scales burst through the skin of my hands and feet, progressing until they covered my whole body. I looked behind me in time to see spikes emerge from my spine. A tail covered in thorns grew out of the bottom of my back, sprouting from my tailbone. I gasped, my breath stolen from me as, on either side of the spikes, gigantic wings ripped through my back. My head started to expand and two horns pierced through each side of my head.

Then everything stopped. I tried to take inventory of my new form, but my movements were awkward. I no longer had complete control of myself. I stood on all fours, right where our makeshift camp used to be. Even though

I knew what had just happened, and had even asked for it, I was terrified.

"Breathe, son," Sila commanded, "your dragon is in control. You mustn't be afraid. Reach out to your dragon, become one."

For the first time, I was thankful she could read my mind. I did as she had said, beginning breathe slower while I tried to reach out to my dragon. I focused my thoughts and felt a twinge in the back of my mind. It felt like I was being connected to something or joined. A feeling of peace surrounded me.

Rylan's voice startled me. "Very good, son, your transformation was quicker than I had expected. Many dragons in the past have been stuck right where you stand for months as they wait for their dragons to appear."

Months? I was frustrated with the few minutes I couldn't find mine. I was unable to imagine the toll a wait that long would cost someone. The thought alone made me shiver.

"That thought, son, is what will make you special among our race," Sila said. "Empathy is not a feeling many Ochana's possess." She paused to examine me. "Your color is one I haven't seen before." Sila and Rylan exchanged a curious look.

Until that comment, I had felt confident in my new dragon state. A color they hadn't seen before? What did that mean? I had hoped to just blend in when we arrived at Ochana.

"Our council will be able to explain your color. I'm sure it's a sign of strength. For you, son, will be strong." I had waited for Rylan to smile about this, but instead he gave a little nod and walked away.

I watched intently as Rylan shifted into his dragon, the process much smoother than mine had been. For me, it had been difficult and chaotic, though, now that I thought about it, painless. Rylan was so sure I would be strong, and I hoped I didn't disappoint him.

Sila placed her hand on my shoulder—well my dragon shoulder. "You could not disappoint your father in any way. You have no idea how proud he is of you." She turned to approach Rylan and shifted as she walked toward him. Her shift was even more fluid than Rylan's. If I had blinked, I would've missed it.

I stood behind them as I waited to see what to do next. Not surprisingly, they hadn't told me anything. I could barely walk as a dragon, and couldn't even imagine trying to fly. I looked over at them as we walked. They were so much larger than me. I wondered if it was because of my age or the type of dragon I was.

"Do not worry, you will grow." Sila angled her head toward me as her voice flowed through me. "It is time to learn to fly."

Rylan kicked off the ground and flew into the sky. The sight amazed me. The powerful green dragon circled us from above. I watched how his body moved, trying to memorize his movements. He continued to circle us as he ascended further up into the sky until he looked like nothing more than a bird flying above us.

"Your turn."

I was so engrossed in watching Rylan that Sila's voice startled me. My turn? I had no idea how to start. Rylan had just kicked off the ground, making it look simple.

"There's your answer, son. Once you get up, your dragon instincts will take over." Sila gestured for me to get on with it.

What's the worst that could happen? *Falling, crashing...dying.* I tried not to think of the real possibility of this ending horribly, so instead, I shifted my focus on moving my dragon body the way I needed it to. I walked a few feet away from Sila, but I found the simple task of walking difficult, which didn't leave me much confidence in my ability to fly. I squatted as low as I could, digging my clawed feet into the snow, and then pushed myself off the ground with all my might, spreading my wings. I made it about twenty feet from the ground before I fell back down to the earth. I hit the snow with a loud thud and my whole body shuddered. I shook the snow off and turned to Sila for guidance.

With a quiet chuckle, Sila's smooth voice filtered through my dazed brain. "Do not fret, son, I have never met a dragon who flew on their first try. It may take some time. Once you're up, stay there and follow Rylan and I. We will guide you to Ochana." With that, Sila took off toward Rylan, and they both circled me from above.

They hovered in the air with their eyes focused on me. Rylan seemed to be in such a hurry to get back to Ochana that I knew I needed to get myself together and up into the air. I was so worried about Rylan being disappointed in me. He was so sure I was going to be this super strong dragon. I wanted to be that for him even though I didn't understand my need to make him proud. I dodged that thought and tried to clear my mind, except for one thought—fly.

I shook the snow off once again, leaned down until my chest almost touched the ground, pulled my wings back, and kicked as hard as I could off the ground. Once I was about thirty feet up, I took a deep breath and spread my wings out. I started to glide, and the feeling was incredible. Then I started to descend. I needed to fly, not glide. I flapped my wings up and down. My dragon instincts began to take over as I flew higher and higher. My movements were choppy and clumsy, but it was enough to get me close to Rylan and Sila.

Rylan took off toward the clouds while Sila stayed back with me. We followed behind him at a much slower pace. I started to fly without thought; it felt like my body just knew what to do. With this new freedom, I could focus my attention on my surroundings. It was still night, but the moon and stars seemed brighter than before. I could see the clouds as we weaved through them. The sight took my breath away. I thought I would be scared, being so far off the ground. Instead, I felt unafraid, almost fearless, like nothing bad could happen to me. At least not in my dragon form.

I couldn't see Rylan anymore, so I stayed close to Sila. She didn't seem to pay any mind to me as she flew. Everything that happened in the last few hours still left me stunned. How could this possibly be my life? A dragon. Imagine that. Not in my wildest dreams did I ever think dragons existed or that I would be one. Sila veered right and I followed her over the water. It was beautiful; frozen patches covered the majority of it.

"This is the Lincoln Sea. It is part of the Arctic Ocean. Human population in this area is near extinction, which is why this location was chosen for Ochana. We are free to come and go undetected with ease. The water here is frozen quite thick, so the vibrations from our wings go unnoticed with the support of our mahier."

That knowledge ignited many questions about my future home; however, I wasn't sure how to communicate with Sila as a dragon to ask. I hadn't heard Rylan speak as a dragon, so I figured it wasn't a skill all had.

Sila's laugh pulsed through my head. "Son, I hear you loud and clear through your thoughts. It is how I am communicating with you. I am projecting my thoughts. Your father can do this as well, but his focus is elsewhere. Your father has already made contact with Ochana, so the council will be ready to receive you when we arrive."

I wondered about them. Who was the council? Would they have answers about my color? Were they the dragons in charge? I focused on Sila. "How long until we arrive?" I hoped I was able to project like she had explained.

"We're almost there. Don't be nervous. The council is very excited to meet you. They have been waiting eighteen years for you. It may seem like an insignificant amount of time in a dragon's life, but we have waited for you for much longer than your short life thus far."

Before I had a chance to comprehend what Sila had just told me, she darted upward. The angle was difficult to follow, and just when I thought for sure I couldn't continue, Sila leveled out and began to descend. I looked out in front of her and noticed what looked like an island, only instead of being surrounded by water, it was surrounded by clouds. A large waterfall fell freely off the side, disappearing into the clouds. Ochana. It had to be.

Rylan landed effortlessly next to the magnificent waterfall, and then Sila followed suit. I braced myself for my first landing. I hit the ground hard and stumbled forward with a crash. I picked myself up in time to find Rylan and Sila as they observed me in their human forms. Behind them were four individuals who looked to be just a few years older than my parents. I inspected them as thoroughly as they inspected me. They each had a very distinctive trait that separated them. The characteristic that stuck out most were their eyes, each a different color; but still, like Rylan and Sila, they stood out like gems.

This must be the council.

Chapter Six

We all stared at each other for some time. My nervousness was beginning to show as my hands trembled. I couldn't get a good read on the council. They showed no emotion but their eyes never left me. I wondered what they thought about me as they studied me. This would be a great time to know how to read minds like Sila. I needed her to teach me that next.

Rylan broke the silence as he commanded the attention of the council. "It is my honor to introduce my son, Colton, Prince of Ochana."

I looked at Rylan after he finished. *Prince?* I had to have heard wrong. No one had said anything to me about being a prince or royalty. This can't be right; I'm just Cole, not Colton, not Prince. I can't be a prince.

A woman with long black hair bowed to me in respect before she spoke. "King Rylan, Queen Sila, we are glad to see you have returned so quickly. Your stay at Ellesmere Island must have been a short one. That is a very good sign of things to come." Finally she tore her stare from me, shifting her bright blue eyes to Rylan.

"Jules, you will find that my son is quite remarkable, as you can see even his color is unique." Rylan gestured toward me then turned towards the other councilmen. "Let's take this conversation inside; we have much to discuss now that the prince has returned." Rylan turned and walked about a hundred feet. He stopped beside the waterfall, and with a wave of his hands the water ceased. He continued to walk until I could no longer see him.

The council followed behind him. One councilman with calculating red eyes shot me a look over his shoulder before he disappeared with the rest. Sila came over to me and placed her hand on my shoulder. I could tell she was trying to relax my fear. It worked; her calmness cleared a bit of my anxiety.

"I need you to change back to your human form. The council will want to speak with you," she informed me.

"How do I change?" I hoped she could hear me.

"Just as you found your dragon, you now need to find your human."

I pictured myself as I knew me to be. My mop of brown hair that constantly fell in my face, my dull brown eyes, lanky limbs and thin physique. I felt a now familiar twinge in the back of my head and grabbed on to the feeling, like I did with my dragon. My body jerked for long moments until I found myself sitting on the ground by Sila's feet, human again. A smile had formed on her face as she looked down at me. She reached her hand down to help me up. I grabbed on and lifted myself off the ground. Once up, she continued to hold my hand as we walked through the waterfall. Once through, Sila looked back at the entrance and the water began to fall once more.

We walked through a series of caves. On the walls, there were pictures painted and words I didn't understand. The pictures showed dragons and humans alike throughout history. They were hard to decipher without knowing the history behind them, but I could see that humans and dragons had been connected since the beginning of time based on the evolution of man in the drawings. I couldn't wait to take a closer look. Whoever had painted them was very talented, and I was amazed by the drawings.

Sila squeezed my hand. "Soon you will learn all about our history and relationship with the humans. Some of it will be hard to hear and will anger you. Keep an open mind as you listen." She looked over at me as she spoke. "First, we need to get your training schedule prepared. Then, I will show you around Ochana and our home."

We finally arrived in a large square room. The first thing I noticed was that the room didn't have a ceiling. When I looked up, the evening sky looked down on me. My eyes shifted to the four walls. Each wall displayed a picture of a different colored dragon. The first wall showed a huge red dragon with fire shooting out of its mouth while it appeared to be in combat against a black, shadowy figure. The word "Woland" was carved near the bottom of the wall. The second wall exhibited a blue dragon who stood next to what appeared to be a large bird's nest full of eggs. This one was labeled as "Galian." The third wall showed a "Sien," a silver dragon who pulled a cart of fruits and vegetables behind it. Finally, the last wall showed a dragon I was familiar with. The large green "Leslo" stood at the top of a cliff, its head raised high.

I turned away from the last image to face my parents and the council. They had all taken seats around the huge, round table in the middle of the room. Rylan and Sila sat next to each other, but I noticed there were two empty chairs next to Sila and three next to Rylan, while the council occupied the remainder of the seats. Sila commanded I have a seat as she pointed to the spot next to Rylan. As I sat, I wondered who would fill the other empty seats.

"Son, I would like to introduce you to your council. The Keepers, as they are known, is formed of elders who represent the four founding dragons. As I'm sure you have noticed, dragons are distinguished by their color. Your mother and I are green dragons, or Leslos, as is Allas." Rylan gestured towards an African American woman with shining green eyes. "We are the leaders of Ochana. Our family has been in command for many generations. You will find that Leslos are the rarest dragon and the only dragon equipped to lead."

"Prince, it is an honor to see you again." Allas bowed her head slightly toward me. *Again?* I didn't remember meeting her.

"Blue dragons, or Galians, are our guardians and nurturers." Rylan pointed at a woman with brilliant blue eyes and black hair. "You met Jules when we first arrived."

"I will guide you in any way you need, Prince." Jules then bowed to me too.

"Seins, or silver dragons, are our workers. They keep Ochana running in its day-to-day operations." Gesturing at a man with gray eyes and a strong exterior, he said, "Luka is a Sein."

"My Prince." Luka bowed deeply to me.

"And lastly, red dragons, or Wolands, are warriors who protect everything you see. Jericho is one of the strongest of these warriors."

The last unknown occupant at the table glared at me, saying nothing. He made me nervous, with his eyes glowing red eyes and his dark hair that concealed most of his face. His eyes tracked each of my movements. Silently, he filed away his observations.

Rylan ignored Jericho's reaction toward me. I hoped this was his usual disposition with others, not just me. I broke eye contact with him and glanced around the table at the rest of the council. Rylan stated these were the elders, which was odd. The oldest appeared to only be in their late thirties. The four councilmen regarded Rylan as they waited for his next directive.

"As you all have noticed, the prince has a matchless color of our four founding dragons, and he is strong, stronger than any newly hatched dragon I've met. Do any of you have an explanation for this?" Rylan searched the faces of each councilman as he spoke.

I observed the reaction each member of the council had to Rylan's question, and each was different Jericho continued to glare at me, unbothered by the question, as the other three looked around at each other with a look of bewilderment. Jules seemed the most on edge by the question, so I was surprised she was the first to answer.

"Your Highness." Jules looked at Rylan with a fearful expression on her face. "We have seen rare dragon appearances many times before." She paused and looked around the table as if hoping someone else would finish her thought, or at least support its significance. "The dramons, My King, have never fit just one Ochana." Her eyes dropped to the table when she finished.

"Jules, don't be absurd! You are talking about the Prince of Ochana. No way could he be a dramon. That thought can never leave this table. The backlash would destroy Ochana." Luka looked furious at Jules as he refuted her idea.

The room went silent for a minute as everyone reflected on what was just discussed. What was a dramon? Was I some kind of mutant? I looked over at Sila and caught her assessing me. She nodded her head at me with encouragement, a small smile on her lips. She wanted me to ask my question out loud.

I coughed into my hand to clear my throat. Every eye in the room focused on me. "Umm, what's a dramon?" My voiced cracked as I spoke. I had hoped to sound certain of myself, but that wasn't happening.

"Son, a dramon is a half-human, half-dragon. They are rarer than Leslos. You need not worry; you would not be at this table if you were one. Only true-blooded dragons are able to enter Ochana." Rylan shifted and glared at Jules, his voice reverberating loudly. "Do you accuse our queen of treason with the accusation of Prince Colton's parentage?" His question carried the promise of a threat.

The statement lingered in the air before Jules responded, her voice shaking in distress. "King Rylan, Queen Sila, my intention was never to question the prince's parentage. I was only—"

Rylan cut her off with a wave of his hands and a look that froze her to her seat. "I am the King of Ochana. Prince Colton is my son. Do not ever question my claim again." Rylan released Jules from his hold and turned to Sila. "My Queen, accept my apology. I am confident my council never questioned your faithfulness."

Sila seemed unbothered by the accusation. She placed her calming hand on Rylan's. "My King, Jules has a responsibility to all of Ochana, and it is her due diligence to explore all possible reasons for the prince's color. Jules is right. A dramon's color does not fit into one of our four."

"My King." Allas bowed her head as she waited for permission to continue. "When the prince arrived, I closely observed his unique color. The remarkable hues do in fact fit into our four founders. If my recollections are correct, each of the Prince's scales show one distinct color, but each scale was different from the next.

"What do you mean, Allas?" Rylan gave her a look of impatience.

"My King, each one of Prince Colton's scales were one of four colors. Red, green, blue, and silver." Allas seemed unsure as she looked to each councilman for assurance. "Woland, Leslo, Galian and Sein," she explained.

The long silence was interrupted by Rylan's enthusiasm. "Amazing, you truly are remarkable, son, as I knew you would be!" Rylan pounded his fist on the table as he persisted. "Jericho, I expect you to personally train the prince in combat." He looked to Jericho for his confirmation even though he left no room for objection.

Jericho, for his part, continued to show no emotion as he nodded once in agreement. I still hadn't heard a peep from the man's mouth. Rylan continued to give orders to his council. Each member would be responsible for training me in one way or another. His last order was to meet again in the morning. Each member would be held responsible for conducting historical research on dragons who resembled me and was to be prepared to have an in depth conversation about it.

The council showed respect to their king and queen once more before they left for the night. Rylan and Sila faced me. Rylan still seemed elated with the news of my color. I didn't understand his delight, since we had no real answers as to what my color meant.

"You must have many questions, son. Let's go for a walk. We can talk as we show you your new home. The people of Ochana are excited by your return." Sila walked toward the cave we had entered from earlier.

Rylan waved for Sila and me to go ahead of him. As I passed by, he grabbed my arm. "Prepare yourself, son." With that, he let go of my arm and waited for me to walk behind Sila.

Once back in the cave, Rylan began to explain some of the images on the walls as we passed them. Most of the pictures depicted historical milestones for Ochana. Rylan stopped in front of one and waited for me to turn and give him my full attention.

"I have waited for you to ask." He paused. "Do you not wonder why you were not raised here on Ochana?"

I absorbed the contents of the painting he had stopped in front of. A green dragon, or Leslo, had a large, speckled egg held tight within its claws. A human woman stood in front of the dragon with her hands held out toward the egg.

"Dragons are protectors. We protect all that is true. However, there was a time in our history when we forgot our purpose. We hid away on Ochana from all that surrounded us." He looked at another painting on the opposite wall.

For the first time, he looked anxious, even apprehensive. The painting was much different than the others. In all the other images, the dragons were the strong, clear winners in whatever was going on at that time. However, in this particular drawing, a large, black-hooded figure hovered over humans, who cowered in its presence. The humans looked scared, many of them crying. A large fire was in the background. There weren't any dragons in this picture.

"A powerful Woland named Jago came to our council one night. He was fatigued and panicked. He had just finished his checks around Ochana." Rylan paused, taking a deep breath. "He was halfway back to his command center when his mahier started to wane. He went straight to our council and explained what had happened. He had just finished his explanation when he fainted. Our healers rushed to his side, but they were unable to stabilize him; his mahier had completely diminished. Without mahier, a dragon is unable to survive on Ochana."

Rylan looked at the ground. His shoulders shook, almost like he had just relived the whole experience firsthand. I had not yet seen Rylan like this. The Rylan I knew was strong and powerful; the man who stood in front of me now was not.

Rylan looked up and placed both of his hands on my shoulders. "Jago was my eldest brother. He was one of the strongest, most powerful Wolands ever. We were reminded that day of our purpose. We had neglected our responsibilities as protectors, and as punishment, our strongest warrior perished." Rylan dropped his hands and turned to the image on the wall. "Soon after that, our council decided that we needed a constant reminder of what we protect and why. It was proclaimed, all dragon infants would be handed over to humans until their eighteenth birthday."

Sila grabbed my hand to catch my attention. "The relationships you formed with the family who raised you and the friends who stood by you will stay with you always. Keep those memories close, because your future as a protector will not be an easy one."

Sila took Rylan's hand and began to walk toward the waterfall that would lead us to the rest of Ochana. I stood and stared at the black-hooded figure in the painting and wondered just what my life would entail here on Ochana. I wanted nothing more than to be faced with my boring life back in Texas. I wished my mother was here. I didn't know these people; they weren't my family. I knew I was about to cry, so I closed my eyes and took a breath.

Chapter Seven

I jolted awake from my slumber, overwhelmed by a feeling of uncertainty. I'd had one of the most vivid dreams of my life. As I lifted myself up and absorbed my surroundings, I realized it wasn't a dream at all. The more awake I became, the clearer the night before came back to me. Rylan, Sila, and I had decided to just head to bed after story time. I hadn't been able to take in much of my new home as we headed to Ochana Castle. The three of us had stayed silent as my mind raced with everything I had learned the previous twelve hours or so. Rylan's parting words to me were to be ready first thing in the morning. Jericho was to train with me before the council met. Jericho, the silent, menacing Woland, scared me to the core.

I threw my legs over the side of my bed, stood up straight, and stretched. The view out the huge, floor-to-ceiling bay windows was breathtaking. The brilliant stone castle was built at the apex of three mountains. It was one of the few things I remembered from my walk here last night. The sun was barely over the mountains yet and the sky portrayed a pattern of purple shades. My room opened up to the side that overlooked the main town, which seemed to be bustling with activity already. Even from my height and distance, I could see others start to prepare for their day. Some kind of market appeared to line the main street. Assorted carts and stands were filled with a variety of items for sale. As the dragons below continued on with their daily life, a feeling of home sickness washed through me. How I wished I was home with my mom and dad, sitting in my familiar seat at the table as my mom cooked and dad watched the news.

Suddenly, a knock on the door got my attention. As I turned to answer, the door slammed open. I jumped back in surprise. In walked a young woman with Jericho on her heels.

"My Prince," the young woman bowed to me. "My name is Mira. I have been assigned to you. Anything you need or want, please let me know." She tilted her head to acknowledge the looming man behind her. "Councilman Jericho has arrived. He insisted in joining me to wake you." She pursed her lips. "And Queen Sila has ordered clothes for you. They shall arrive later this afternoon."

Assigned to me? Like an assistant? At least she seemed to feel the same way toward Jericho as I did. I would have to pick her brain later about the ins and outs of Ochana. I watched Mira set up a bedside breakfast for me, the trays laden with more food than I could ever eat by myself. I glanced at the large variety of nourishment; every bit looked amazing, and the delicious smells made my stomach growl. She was a quick little thing, darting around the table to get things situated for me. Out of my peripheral vision, I noticed Jericho watching me as I observed the scene before me. He made me uncomfortable. I needed a distraction, so I looked around the room for my backpack; I needed to get ready for whatever Jericho had in store for me.

I spotted my bag in a nearby chair. The chair looked to be ancient, probably worth more than a car. I went over to grab my bag and searched for a place to change. Mira must have noticed my confused expression when I found no other doors within my spacious bedroom. She walked over to a bookcase and pressed her hand to the side of it. The bookcase opened into what looked like a bathroom.

"My Prince, you will find most doors in the castle are hidden. It was designed that way to keep the royal family safe."

Safe? This seemed like a pretty extreme security measure. Was I in danger? Mira must have noticed the look on my face, or could read minds like Sila.

"We no longer have a need for such security measures, do not worry. However, the Woland guard has insisted we leave the measure in place." Mira glanced over at Jericho as she spoke. She turned back to me, giving me her full attention. "Your breakfast is ready. Is there anything else I can help you with?" She bounced on her toes as she waited for my response.

I shook my head. I hadn't had a chance to fully wake, and the man in the room made me nervous. I just wanted to get this morning over with. Mira bowed before she let herself out. I looked at Jericho over my shoulder to find the man's eyes boring into me.

"Oh, um, I am just going to change real quick. Umm, feel free to have some breakfast," I mumbled. Not my finest moment, but it was all I could muster around the man.

Once in the bathroom, I turned to close the door when I realized I had no idea how. I heard a sigh, then what sounded like a tap on the wall. The bookcase closed with a thud. I changed and cleaned up as fast as I could. I needed to take a shower but the last thing I wanted was to make Jericho wait. When I was done, I stood in front of the wall where the door should be and contemplated my next move. He already thought I was incompetent, so why not confirm it? Sighing, I knocked on the wall and waited. Almost instantly, it opened, and Jericho stood in the doorway with his red eyes that seemed to have the ability to glare into my soul.

With a mumbled thanks, I scooted around him and went straight for the table. I scanned the assorted foods; it was more than one person could possibly eat, many of the foods strange to me. I grabbed a mug of coffee even though I detested the stuff—that's how badly I needed a jolt to wake up. I piled a plate high with foods that I knew—pancakes and bacon smothered with syrup. As wonderful as it all smelled, I wasn't in the mood to try something new. I shoveled the food in my mouth as fast as I could, aware of the silent man with a permanent scowl behind me. I finished in record time and turned to look at Jericho. He raised his eyebrows at me, his first sign of emotion. I had no idea if he was amused or frustrated with me.

"So, what's the plan this morning?" I asked cautiously.

Jericho shook his head and walked to the door. "You failed your first lesson." The sound of his voice surprised me. I had started to think he was mute.

He pinned me with his eyes as I registered what he had just said. *Failed?* What was the lesson? "I don't understand? How could I fail? We haven't done anything yet." My voice was laced with confusion.

"I have been charged with the responsibility to prepare you to be a protector. Do you understand the importance of that role?" His brows drew together and his mouth twisted in disgust. "You let a strange woman into your bedchamber, you asked no questions, and ate the food she left behind, food you left unattended with a man you do not trust. Your list of transgressions is endless." He cocked his head. "You are the Prince of Ochana. First lesson: everyone is your enemy." Jericho took one last look at me and stormed from my room.

My second impression of the man was no better than the first. I sat back down on my bed and contemplated Jericho's words. I hung my head and rubbed the back of my neck with my hand. Well, two things stood out the most to me: my new role as Prince of Ochana, and the importance of being a protector. As an alleged prince, I knew nothing about royalty or duties, and certainly not enemies. Was I in danger? I dropped my hands and fisted them in the sheets beneath, trying to quell my fear. Then there was the whole protector thing. I had no idea how to be a protector and wasn't sure exactly what I was supposed to protect. Rylan told me a protector protected all that was true, but it made no sense to me. It seemed I had much to learn and many questions to ask.

But first, I needed to find Rylan or Sila and meet with the council. I'm sure they assumed Jericho was escorting me there since I was supposed to be with him. I let out a harsh breath. Then again, Jericho probably ran right to Rylan and told him all about my failure. *More proof of my weakness.*

I shook my head. I needed to get out of this funk and start being the dragon Rylan was so sure I was. I picked myself up off the bed and walked to the door, which thankfully had been left open after Jericho's hasty departure. I peeked out the door and looked both ways down the hall. The castle was so huge that I couldn't see an end on either side. I went with my gut and turned right. After just a few minutes, I ran \ into Mira as she emerged from one of those hidden doorways.

"My Prince, you scared me." She grabbed at her chest and let out a gasp. "Do you need anything?" She straightened her back as her wide platinum eyes studied me.

"I am looking for my parents," I said cautiously as I remembered what Jericho had said about everyone being my enemy.

"The king and queen are in the throne room meeting with Ochanans as they do each morning. I can show you there." She smiled at me as she twisted her hands. It seemed the girl couldn't stand still.

"That would be great." I held my hand out for her to go first. "Lead the way." As I followed behind her, I thought about what Jericho had told me. I didn't know this girl at all, and even though she seemed harmless, I didn't know anything about dragons, or Siens, as I deduced she was based on Mira's eyes. With that thought, her silver eyes turned towards me, making me wonder again if she could read my mind like Sila.

"My Prince, I have waited many years for your arrival. It is an honor to be placed with you." She paused and twirled her almost black hair. "You arrived just last night, so you must have many questions." She turned back around and continued down the never ending hallway.

"Can you show me how to open the doors and maybe how to find them?" I knew there were much more important questions I should ask, but I had begun to feel trapped.

Mira stopped and looked at the wall, hesitating a moment before she replied. "Of course, My Prince." She placed her hands on the side of a fancy light. "Look here." She pointed at some kind of small picture beneath the light fixture. "This is the royal insignia; they are hidden quite well. Once you get the hang of it, though, you will see them everywhere. They symbolize an exit or entrance." She pushed on the image and the wall shifted, opening up to another hallway. "Press down lightly on the insignia, ask your mahier for entrance, and the wall will open."

She made it sound simple. Only problem was, I didn't know how to ask my mahier anything. I didn't want to explain my weakness to Mira, so I shook my head in acknowledgement and continued to walk behind her. I would practice later when I got back to my room alone.

Finally, we turned and entered a room with tall double doors, a great hall of sorts. The room was much larger than the council room and much more decorative. It also seemed more formal. Large crystal chandeliers were suspended from a tall, gold-leafed ceiling with pristine tapestries that covered each archway. On the far end of the room, a long line of people stood below three thrones. Rylan and Sila occupied the mounted space near the impressive gold and gem covered thrones. They seemed to be in a deep discussion with Allas. This, I felt, must be the throne room.

Mira paused and looked at me. "Here we are, My Prince. Is there anything else you need?"

"I'm good now. Thanks, Mira."

She bowed to me and walked away. I hesitated a moment before walking toward Rylan and Sila, keeping to the outskirts of the room in hopes no one would notice me. I passed suits of perfectly polished armor. Grasped in the hands of each knight was a different weapon. As I grew closer to the thrones, I could hear murmurs reverberating around me. I wasn't sure if no one had expected me to join, or if they hadn't known I'd arrived in Ochana at all.

Sila noticed me first. She walked over and held her hand out for me to grab. I glanced at her hand and wavered a moment, wishing it was my mom Ella's hand, realizing then how much I wanted to go home. Finally, I reached out and clasped her hand, letting her pull me to the front of the room. "Good morning, my son, what a pleasant surprise. I wasn't expecting to see you until after morning rounds." She looked over her shoulder at me with what looked to be a genuine smile.

I was so distracted by the murmurs and stares that I almost forgot to respond to Sila. "I, uh, didn't know where the council room was. Mira, she, um, told me you would be here." I looked around the room and caught more than a few surprised looks at my presence.

"I'm glad you found us. We just finished here. We will take the scenic route there so you can see Ochana during daylight." She waved to the crowd that had formed near us in just the past moment and guided me through another door behind the thrones. Rylan followed with Allas.

Rylan's large hand fell on my shoulder. "Son, I hope you slept well. How did your morning go with Jericho?" When I said nothing, Rylan continued. "I have been anticipating his report."

I had no idea what to say to him. Rylan sounded sure that my lesson with Jericho would be nothing but successful. He already sounded proud of me. Jericho had informed me that I failed, but I couldn't tell Rylan that. I started to give an excuse for my failure when we were interrupted. Two men barreled frantically toward us. I was instantly on alert.

"King Rylan." Two Wolands who wore military uniforms appeared before us, bowing before they continued. "We need you in the command center."

"We've had a breach!" Both Wolands looked at each other then back to Rylan as they attempted to catch their breath.

Before Rylan could respond, we were surrounded by guards shouting orders out to each other. They demanded we get to safety immediately. I had a guard on either side of me, and they pulled me toward the castle. Rylan and Sila were being pulled in the opposite direction. *What was going on?*

"Wait, I need to go with my parents...hold up." I tried to remove the guards hands from my arms, but my efforts were useless; they just held on tighter and moved faster.

A loud whistle pierced the air. Everyone went silent and turned to find Jericho. "Rylan and Sila, you need to go to the bunker now, I will make contact when it's secure." He pushed a bag into Rylan's arms and nodded, a serious look passing between them. "Prince, you will be escorted to a different bunker. We need to separate our two successors for the protection of Ochana." He gave me a no-nonsense look and turned to my guards. "Stay with the prince. Do not leave his side for any reason." Then he turned to me and said in very concise words. "Trust these three. None others."

With those orders, we were off.

Chapter Eight

We rushed toward the castle. As we were just about to reach the front, the guards pulled me to the right. It looked as though we were going to run right into the side of the mountain. I closed my eyes tight right before impact, but the collision I had braced myself for never happened. Instead, I found myself inside a cave at the foot of the mountain. I looked over my shoulder a little startled just in time to see the mountainside close, trapping us inside.

"This way, My Prince, we must hurry," one of the guards insisted as he pulled me along.

We began to run. It felt like forever. After we turned a corner for the tenth time, I lost count. If I had to do it alone, there would be no way I'd find my way out of this cave. Not that I could even open the doors that opened and closed as we darted past them to some unknown destination. The first thing I had to do when we got out of here was to figure out how to use my mahier, then I needed to find myself a map of Ochana.

Finally, we stopped in a small room that I assumed was somewhere in the middle of the mountain given the amount of time we traveled to get here. Two small chairs sat around a small square table, while a cot was set up along one of the rock walls. At the foot of the cot, I noticed a box that seemed to house some basic supplies. One of the guards pushed me toward the cot. I sat down and kicked my feet on the dirt floor.

"I'll take the first shift," the oldest of the three guards affirmed with the other two before he stepped out of the room. The door slammed shut behind him before either of the other two could respond.

I looked over at the two Wolands that were left with my care and found them watching me in silence. I instantly felt unnerved by the attention and I broke eye contact with them. My eyes drifted around the room, but there was nothing to see.

I looked back at the guards. "How long do you think we will have to stay here?"

"Until it's safe," guard number one responded.

"Yeah, I know that. But how long does it normally take? I mean, I'm sure you guys have security breaches all the time." Once Jericho gave the orders, the guards had acted immediately. They all knew where to go and what they had to do. This was obviously something they were used to.

"The last breach was almost ten years ago and it was a false alarm. You may as well get comfortable, My Prince. My guess is we will be here awhile. For security reasons, you will be the last one released." The two guards looked at each other, then turned to face the wall where the door was. They looked to be in serious guard mode, standing ramrod straight, chins held high, their hands behind their backs. I guess that was my cue: talk time was over.

***

I counted the crevices in the rock ceiling above the cot about a hundred times, wishing all the while that I knew what was going on. My guards hadn't said a single word to me since our earlier conversation. The oldest guard returned a while ago and another guard took his place outside our room.

Suddenly, a knock echoed through the room. The two remaining guards stood up even straighter and reached for the door. The wall slid open to an imposing figure. I couldn't see over the guards' heads to see who was there, but assumed since no weapons were drawn and no dragons appeared that our visitor was a friendly. The guards stepped to the side and Jericho moved into the room followed by my other guard.

"We need to go, My Prince," Jericho commanded. Before I could react, he was out of the room.

I jumped off the cot and raced after him. No way was I letting him out of my sight. Jericho rushed through the caves, and I had to speed up my usual pace double-time just to keep up with him. He seemed more uptight than normal. His jaw was clamped shut and his eyes focused directly ahead. His normal glares towards me were surprisingly missing. I wondered what had happened. Had we really been breached? If so, by who?

"Answers will be given in due time," he said, surprising me. "We are meeting with the council now." His steely eyes finally turned to me, and I thought I saw relief there for just a slight second. "Second lesson, pay close attention to each and every person in the room. Do not let your guard down for anyone. You and I will debrief afterward with your thoughts." With that, he turned away from me and picked up his pace even faster.

After some time, we arrived at the council room, entering through the iron doors which were flanked by two new Woland soldiers. Everyone was already seated around the table. Huge screens that I had not seen when I was there last were placed in the middle of the table, while still others lay flat on the elegant table. I couldn't see what was on the screens, but everyone's attention was focused on them. No one even noticed our arrival. It gave me a chance to take in the new faces that had joined us. It looked like two more Wolands and one Leslo.

"Micah, Nico, why are you away from command?" Jericho glowered at the two Wolands, awaiting a response.

"Sir, we have news. We knew you would want the information immediately."

"Why did you not call to me, Nico?" Jericho's temper was starting to show.

"Sir, we did, you did not respond." Both Wolands looked at Jericho with caution.

Jericho's body stiffened, but only I could tell due to my proximity to him. No one else around would have any idea as his expression never altered. I looked back at the Wolands in anticipation, awaiting their news. They stayed silent.

"Get on with it, we have much to discuss," Jericho spat.

The blond-haired Woland, Nico, cleared his throat, obviously affected by Jericho's tone. "Sir, we know who the Woland was." He paused and looked over at his partner for help. Jericho's eyes followed his line of sight.

"It was Cairo, sir. He had a dramon girl with him." Micah looked down before he finished his sentence, obviously uncomfortable.

Rylan's voiced boomed from across the room. "Impossible! No dramon can enter Ochana." His fists pounded on the table.

Nico bowed toward Rylan. "My King, our surveillance video caught his attempt at entering. The dramon girl was in a shift I have never seen before; she was flying on her own."

"How is that possible? Dramons don't possess mahier. Are you sure she was a dramon?" Rylan sounded unsure, his gaze settling on the council for answers.

"Never in our history has a dramon been able to wield our mahier. They just aren't strong enough," Allas stated as she looked around the table, shaking her head in surprise.

"Before we go any further, Micah, pull up the video. We need to determine if the girl was indeed a dramon." Jericho strode across the room, placed his hands on the table, and leaned over one of the monitors that was built into the table. He looked up at Micah. "Now!"

Micah scrambled over to another monitor. His hands flew across the screen in search of the video in question. I wandered over to where Rylan and Sila stood, placing myself on Sila's right side and looking down at the screen in wait. Sila place her hand on my shoulder in a sign of comfort. Everyone stayed silent.

The screens came to life after just a few moments. At first, all I could see were the clouds that concealed Ochana. Then, in the bottom right corner of the screen, a huge red dragon became visible. I heard Sila whisper the name "Cairo," but no one else made a noise as we continued to watch. Cairo's whole body became visible in the screen just as a reddish orange dragon-like creature flew into view behind him. The girl had scales that covered a human-looking body, with large goldish-red wings that flapped from her back. As she flew closer, it became obvious that her eyes glowed gold.

My breath caught in my throat. I couldn't believe it. I knew that girl. I looked around the room to see if anyone else had the same revelation as me. She looked so different from the last time I'd seen her not more than six weeks ago. My eyes were glued to the screen as I begged them to see something different, someone different. Both Cairo and the girl's heads suddenly looked up. They were regarding something over the camera, out of view. Quickly, both of them spun around and took off in the other direction. I continued to watch as what looked to be around twenty Wolands took chase after them.

Everyone continued to stare at the screen, but there was nothing left but clouds. I inhaled a deep breath and looked up. Jericho stood across from me, his eyes pinning me in place. He hastily shook his head at me and looked away. I was confused. Did he want me to stay quiet about what I saw? How would that even be possible with at least two dragons here who could read my mind?

"Dramons can't fly or shift. What was that?" Rylan looked around. "Have we made contact with Cairo?" No one answered.

"Answer your king!" Jericho roared with a slam of his hands on the table.

Micah's eyes swung to Rylan's. "We lost them, My King. We have been trying to call for him, but he hasn't answered yet."

"Get back to command, I will speak to you both later." Jericho dismissed them without looking up from the screen.

The wall slammed shut with their departure, shaking everyone awake from their stupors at what they'd just witnessed. Everyone started to speak at once. I tried to keep up with the conversations around me, but it was impossible. My own mind raced with what I had just seen. I took a step back and observed everyone, just as Jericho had instructed me to do. Everyone seemed on edge except for Sila. She was still focused on the screen.

When she finally looked up, her eyes scanned the faces around the table. Everyone paused as her eyes hit them until she had the room's full attention. "Something feels wrong; Cairo is one of our most loyal Wolands," she said. "For him to bring that creature to Ochana, he's either in trouble or she is important. We must find him. He must know we do not intend to harm him or the girl."

"Why would they run if they weren't here to harm us?" Jules' blue eyes looked worried as she addressed the table. "And the girl, she was no dragon. We should not concern ourselves with her wellbeing."

"Regardless, we need to talk to her. She was able to get too close to Ochana for us not to be concerned by her. As for what she is, we don't know if she is a dragon or not. We need to find them both. Jericho, make sure every available Woland understands the importance of finding Cairo and the girl, and bringing them back alive." Sila punctuated the word *alive*, leaving no room for a misunderstanding.

An unknown voice broke the trance between Sila and Jericho. "My Queen, My King." The new Leslo bowed to Rylan and Sila. "I am concerned with the wellbeing of Prince Colton. He has been in Ochana less than twenty-four hours and we have already had a breach. It could very well be unrelated, but we cannot be sure of it."

Every eye turned to me as if I would have the answer to that. I tried with all my might not to think what was really going through my head. I mean, I knew the mysterious girl. I've known her for what seemed like forever. It couldn't be a coincidence even though I prayed it was.

"Little brother, good point." Rylan nodded toward *my uncle?* "Jericho, step up security around the prince. He is to never be alone. We must not underestimate Cairo and the girl. We need to find the two now." Rylan looked at the rest of the council. "As for the rest of you, we must proceed with inducting Prince Colton to Ochana. We will not let this breach discourage us. His training will continue as planned. I expect my son to be ready in four weeks to start with the new protectors."

That caught my attention. It had been brought to my attention a few times the importance of being a protector and that I would be one. I was still unsure as to what I would be protecting, however. An induction was news to me. Induction into what, I wondered. I needed time with Sila, mostly because she seemed the least threatening of my two parents and the most willing to answer my questions. I had yet to have more than five minutes alone with either of my parents since we arrived, though, so it was important I found time soon.

"I agree, My King." Jericho looked at each council member. "We need to pick up our schedule with the prince. Each of us must work with him every day. As for security, I will bring our prince with me to command and select two personal guards. It will be a good opportunity for the prince to see our Wolands in action."

"Good, we will meet again tomorrow. I expect we will have news on Cairo by then." Rylan's words came out more as a threat than a command. "Also, I expect reports from each of you on your plans to train the prince."

Rylan stood and walked to the door with Sila close behind. They left me with the council and my apparent uncle. I looked to Jericho for direction. He stood and glared at my uncle, locking eyes with him. "Prince Zane, a word."

He nodded and the two walked to the other side of the room. I was unable to hear what they talked about, but it seemed by the looks they gave each other, it was not a pleasant conversation. Both men were wound tight, glaring at each other as they spoke. Jericho left the conversation and walked towards me.

"My Prince, let's go."

Jericho never broke stride as he walked right by me. It was clear he expected me to follow him without question, and by the man's expression, there was no way I wasn't going to. To the two guards who stood outside the main council room entrance, he said, "Watch him," before he headed toward the command center.

Chapter Nine

We walked to the command center in complete silence. Mere steps in front of me, Jericho vibrated with anger. I had so many questions but was afraid to utter a sound at the irate man ahead of me. The walk ended quickly. We reached a set of stairs. Jericho bounded up and I followed. We arrived in a circular glass building that didn't seem to fit in with the rest of Ochana. I stared at it in wonder until I realized Jericho had a glow in his eyes as he glared at me. He looked down at me over his shoulder.

"The lesson continues. Don't say or touch anything." He didn't wait for me to reply. Instead, he turned and stomped through the doors.

As we entered the building, the chatter and murmurs in the background completely fell silent. Every eye turned toward Jericho. I shrank away from him, not wanting the attention placed on me. I gazed around the ginormous room, which was made to feel even bigger by the glass walls. There looked to be around fifty men and women scattered about as they completed their duties. The two Wolands closest to me typed away on one of the most high-tech looking computers I had ever seen. They were almost completely surrounded by monitors that depicted a series of numbers and letters I had no idea how to read. A few of the people looked familiar. I noticed the two men who left the council room earlier and my three guards from our lock down.

"My office, now," he addressed a fellow Woland, who seemed unaffected by Jericho's sour mood. The Woland was taller than Jericho, with almost white hair and oversized red eyes. "I want every bit of information we have." He turned to leave, but right before he entered what I assumed was his office, he turned and addressed everyone. "We will get Cairo and that girl by nightfall. Alive. No excuses."

I ran after him and the other Woland before he closed the door. I still had no idea if I would be able to open it once it closed. As I entered, Jericho pointed to a chair while he scowled at the man in front of him. I took my cue and had a seat. No way did I want those eyes trained on me.

"When did he return?" The glass walls vibrated with the strength of his voice.

"He arrived right before the breach, sir. With all that was going on, he slipped right past us." The man never took his eyes from Jericho's.

"Unacceptable. He is a threat. You know that. How many eyes do we have on him?"

"Four, as you commanded."

"Full reports, every hour. Do you understand?"

"Yes, sir. I will check in with the team now."

Jericho waved the man out and impaled me with his eyes. I had no idea how the other man was able to stare him in the eyes without fear. I tried to understand what I had just witnessed. I figured they were talking about my

Uncle Zane; however, I had no idea why and knew nothing about him. I hadn't even known he existed until a few minutes ago.

"Speak, tell me everything." His voice came off so much calmer that it took me by surprise.

I wasn't sure what he wanted me to speak about. There seemed to be an endless amount of things we needed to discuss. The breach, Cairo, the girl. Then there was the topic of my alleged uncle. Not to mention the hundred or so questions I had about everything else. I looked at Jericho for guidance. Could he be more specific?

"We will speak of all of it. First, the girl. Who is she?" He remained unnervingly still.

"I think...I think she is my best friend." I stared at the ground as I spoke. I wasn't sure how much to tell him. I didn't want him or anyone to hurt her. "She doesn't have a mean bone in her body. There is no way she was here to harm anyone." I finally looked up at Jericho, hoping he could see how honest I was being.

"Do you know what she is?"

"No, I've never seen her that way. I don't know what happened to her." As I thought about it, she would be just as surprised to know what I had become.

"This girl, your best friend, attempted to enter Ochana just a few hours after your arrival. Only the council was aware of your arrival until this morning. Think, Cole, what could she want?"

I was caught off guard. It was the first time he had called me by my name; actually it was the first time anyone had called me Cole. I had no idea why she would be here. She never said anything to me about being different, but neither did I to her. Wait, I didn't know I was a dragon until just last night, so maybe she just found out about herself, too. As the thought sprouted in my head, I looked to Jericho. He nodded his head in agreement.

"You could very well be right. But that doesn't answer the question as to why she was here and why she was with a loyal Woland." He stood and started to pace the length of the room.

Again, I wished I could read minds like most of the other dragons. I could only imagine the thoughts that were inside Jericho's head at the moment as I watched him pace from one side of the room to the other. He stopped by the large glass wall that overlooked the edge of Ochana. The view was a picturesque setting of endless clouds as far as I could see. He stood there in silence for what felt like forever.

"Your friend, what is her name?" His words were quiet, thoughtful.

I didn't want to tell him, I was scared for her. "I—"

He turned to face me. "Her parents, what are their names?"

"Umm, I don't know. I met her when she moved in with her grandparents. I was only ten or so." Truth is, she never spoke of her parents. I don't even know what happened to them, if anything.

Jericho was quiet for a bit as he processed this bit of information. "Do you know where she would go? Some place she would feel safe?"

I knew exactly where she would go, somewhere we both had gone many times whenever we needed to get away. It was our place. But if she knew I was here, would she go there? The thought popped into my head before I could stop it. I still didn't trust Jericho completely and I didn't want him to hurt her. I peered up at him and held my breath as I waited.

"Good, trust will be earned. I will not hurt your friend. I want her alive. I am very curious about her and need to know why she came here. Now, tell me about this place." Again, his eyes pinned me to my seat.

"It's silly." I paused to look at the wall over Jericho's shoulder. I knew I didn't have a choice, but I didn't want to tell him. "When we were around ten, we found an old hunting cabin between our houses. It looked like it had been abandoned for years."

"Tell me more. Why would she go there?"

"It was our safe haven of sorts. Whenever we needed a break from the real world, we would go there. No one else but the two of us knew of it—at least, no one ever let on that they knew about it." Memories sped through my mind. When we were younger, we spent all our free time there. Once we got older and busier, we would still go, but not usually together.

"We will leave within the hour. You will bring me to this cabin of yours."

Jericho left no room for argument. I just hoped she was smart enough not to go there. If she knew I was here, she would know that was the first place I would look for her. Unless she wanted me to find her. I paused with that thought and peeked over at Jericho. He tapped on some sort of screen on his desk, completely engrossed and paying no mind to me. Did she want me to find her? Maybe she was in trouble.

Another question popped into my head and before I could stop my mouth, I spit out the question to Jericho. "Why don't you trust Zane?"

His eyes flashed from his screen to me. "You will find that there is much for you to learn. Like I told you before, everyone is your enemy."

"You included?" Darn my mouth, though Jericho didn't seem phased by my question.

"Everyone."

He punctuated the word in a way to end my questions. His eyes once again found the screen, putting a halt to any further conversation. What would happen when we got to the cabin? What if she wasn't there? Based on Jericho's expression, he seemed sure she would be.

Jericho stood from his desk, throwing the screen he had in his hand down onto his desk and walking to the door. He paused and looked over his shoulder at me. "I don't believe in coincidences. She will be there. If she is truly as close to you as you claim, she will know that is the first place you will have thought about. She wants us to find her and she knows you won't hurt her." He walked out the door and headed toward the same Woland he had yelled at before.

I followed behind him. In my head, I replayed what he had just said to me. Did she really want me to find her? He was right, I would never hurt her, no matter what she was or what her reason for coming here was. I had tuned out everything around me until I heard a loud crash and Jericho's voice as he yelled at a group of Wolands.

"What do you mean, gone? Where were you?" He turned to the poor Woland that he seemed to always be mad at. "Garrik, find him. Now." He took off toward the door we had come through earlier, and at least five Wolands chased after him. Once outside, Jericho raced toward the castle, the Wolands hot on his heels. I ran after them, not knowing exactly what was going on. I guessed they had lost track of Zane. He seemed to get the most heated when it came to him. Jericho stormed through the front entrance, the guards parting in his wake without hesitation. He continued down the long hall. Unlike me, he knew his way around the castle. I was lost.

Finally, we turned into a familiar room—the throne room. Jericho continued to stomp his way to the front where Rylan and Sila were seated. He had no care for the dragons around him. His entourage of Wolands stayed close behind him. When Jericho reached the front of the room, he bowed to Rylan and Sila. I was too far away to hear what was said, but Rylan stood suddenly and stormed to the exit behind the thrones, followed by Sila and the Wolands. I ran to catch up with them.

Once the door shut behind me, Rylan bellowed with anger, "What do you mean gone?" He looked between everyone present. "Find him."

"My King, I can promise you we will find him." Jericho held Rylan's attention. "We have a lead on the girl. Prince

Colton is needed in order to capture the girl securely. I ask that you allow him to join us on our mission."

Rylan swung his eyes in my direction. I could see the indecision there. "His safety is in your hands, Jericho. Bring my son back unharmed."

"You have my word, My King, I will protect him with my life." He bowed to Rylan and Sila and gestured to the rest of us to follow him.

As I passed by Rylan, he stopped me, "Be safe, my son. Trust Jericho and do as he says."

I nodded as I trailed behind the Wolands. Once outside, Jericho started to bark orders at everyone. It seemed these were the Wolands who would join us on our journey. He expected us to arrive in Clover by nightfall. I thought about the trip I took with Rylan and Sila. I hadn't flown the whole way, hitching a ride on Rylan's back. It was the only time I had flown, and it was a much shorter trip than the one Jericho had planned.

We headed to the exact spot we had landed my first night in Ochana, when the council had accepted me. The Wolands around me started to transform into their dragons. I stood still, evened out my breathing, and attempted to call for my dragon. I was way too nervous around the others to change and didn't even feel a twinge.

"Men, go ahead, we will follow behind," Jericho shouted to his men as he walked toward me. He looked down at me with a slight frown. "You need to shift, the men are gone. They are aware that you have just found your dragon. There is no reason to be nervous." He turned and shifted rapidly into his dragon. If I had blinked, I would've missed it completely.

Jericho was massive, even bigger than Rylan though much leaner. His scales were a dark red, almost black, and his eyes were the same menacing red that glowed when angry. Right now, they glowed deep red my way. I took a deep breath and closed my eyes. I needed to find my dragon and fast. I pictured myself in my dragon form, with my colorful scales, wide wings, and frightening claws. The shift started unexpectedly, it seemed much quicker than before, but still much longer than Jericho's. The breath was taken from me as my wings broke free, pushing me to the ground. I looked up to see Jericho's eyes had dulled; he seemed unsettled.

"Stay close," he said finally.

The vibration from Jericho's voice shook me as I watched him propel from the ground and take off. I exhaled as I followed his lead, praying I'd make it to Clover in one piece, and that Eva would be found safe when I got there.

J.A. Culican

Chapter Ten

The wind whooshed around me as we flew over the Lincoln Sea toward Ellesmere Island. Thanks to the light and the time of day, I was able to take a better look around me than I had the last time I took this journey. The scenery was something out of a fairy tale. The clouds were smooth and crisp as they floated around me unbothered by the mammoth-sized dragons speeding through them. The sea was a light shade of blue, almost white, and frozen in most areas. I had never seen anything like it.

Jericho stayed close to me as we flew, though I could feel the impatience radiating off him with how slow our pace was. I tried to fly as fast as I could; however, no matter how much I was able to pick up my speed, they all flew faster. It was clear by how easy the flight seemed to be for everyone else that they were used to much quicker speeds. I finally got into a good groove when I realized the Wolands ahead of me had started to descend. I followed their lead. As I neared the ground, I sent up a silent prayer that I wouldn't tumble when I landed like the last time. The dragons around me were fierce warriors. I paled in comparison. Even though I was new to being a dragon. If I crashed and burned, there'd be no way they'd think high of me.

Finally, my feet hit the ground with a powerful thud, and my firm claws dug into the snow which kept me upright. I exhaled in a sign of relief. The Wolands all gathered around Jericho and me, some had shifted to their human counterparts, while others stayed as dragons. Jericho was in his human form, and luckily, he didn't seem angry anymore.

"You have fifteen minutes. Eat and meet back here." With no question, the five Wolands took off in search of food with Jericho's words. "Have you hunted in your dragon form?"

I was the only one left so it was clear Jericho was speaking to me. I'd done a whole lot of nothing besides fly to Ochana in my dragon form.

Jericho shook his head. "This ought to be interesting. Let your dragon lead. Use your instincts. Follow me."

Jericho swiftly morphed into his Woland. It amazed me how fluid and inherent his shifts were. He pushed off the ground with ease and started for the tree line. I was able to follow, but my moves were much more chaotic. I swayed back and forth, and had no handle on my position. I began to wonder what we were going to hunt. Last time I was here, I didn't see any animals, but Rylan did feed us some kind of meat. Back when I lived with my actual dad, he would take me hunting every year, deer season being his favorite.

"Muskox, to your right."

I shifted my head and saw a herd of something. The animals had thick black coats, curved horns that bulged from their heads, and a horrible odor even at this distance. Muskox. I had never seen anything like them. We definitely didn't have these back in Texas.

"Descend quickly, grab one, and keep going. The oxen expect to be hunted by dragons, so they will run if they catch sight of you."

I watched as Jericho swooped quickly toward the herd. He snatched one of the muskox with his large jaw and kept flying, circling back around to where we had originally landed. Somehow, I thought my experience with hunting would be helpful in this situation, but I couldn't be more wrong. Hunting with a bow and hunting with my mouth were two completely different tasks.

I braced myself for the inevitable and took off toward the herd. One muskox was off to the side alone, occupied as he nibbled on a piece of plant sticking up through the snow, so I targeted him. Just as Jericho had, I swooped down toward the muskox. Right before I reached him, his head popped up and he looked directly at me. He took off at full speed, moving much faster than I had expected. His rapid movement caught the attention of the rest of the herd and they all took off. Out of my peripheral, I saw what looked like the biggest muskox of the group. Abruptly, he started to charge in my direction. I wasn't in the mood to fight him off, so I swooped back up and headed back to Jericho empty-handed.

The five Wolands stood by Jericho and watched me return. I could see the laughter in their eyes as I approached, but none of them said anything to me about what they just witnessed. My feet hit the ground.

"Good," Jericho said. "I've never met a dragon who successfully caught a muskox their first time. You were close." He gave a quiet chuckle, a sound so faint, I am pretty sure I wouldn't have even heard it in my human form. "Help yourself to the leftovers, we are leaving in five minutes."

I wished he had warned me about that little tidbit of information before I attempted to catch a muskox; maybe then I wouldn't have felt like such a failure. It seemed these dragons were all about making the new dragons feel foolish, or maybe it was just me. I walked over to the remains of the leftover muskox. It smelled putrid. I wrinkled my nose and gave it a go anyway. I'd never had raw meat before, but I guessed a dragon always ate that way based on what I saw of the other dragons around me. It actually tasted good. So good that I finished off the rest of the scraps.

The Wolands began to snicker at me. I was just about to open my mouth in defense, but they briskly shifted into their dragons. It was probably better off that way. I felt the rumble of Jericho's voice before I actually heard it.

"There is always a first time, so why not get it out of the way? Next time, you'll be ready." Without waiting for a response, he took off into the sky.

I guessed he had a point. With that thought, I took off immediately after him. I felt a little better. The longer we flew, the more in control of my dragon I felt. It was like my dragon and I just needed time to bond and get to know each other. It was such a strange feeling, my dragon. I thought it would be like two separate beings, me and my dragon, but it wasn't like that at all. He was a part of me, like an arm or a leg. I noticed the snow was gone and there were city lights not too far off. Darkness began to creep toward us.

"Stay close, my mahier is protecting you from humans." He paused. "I feel something else watching us."

I flew as close as possible to Jericho, and the other Wolands surrounded us in a protective circle. What could possibly be watching us that would make them all act this way? My eyes searched the space around me, but all I could see were clouds and the city as we approached. We started to fly above the clouds, in an attempt to conceal us further. We flew the rest of the way in silence.

My nerves were completely fried by the time we arrived in Clover. Surprisingly, the familiarity of home did nothing to soothe me. As we descended, I realized I didn't fear my landing as I had in the past. It was clear that the longer I was in my dragon form, the more comfortable I was with trusting its instincts. We landed quietly and shifted back into our human forms right on the outskirts of Eva's grandparents' property. The cabin wasn't far from here, about a five-minute walk. The Wolands seemed to be scoping the area out.

"Cairo is here. Let's go."

Jericho took off into the woods. I had no idea how he knew where he was going or that Cairo was here. I felt nothing. The only sounds were the wildlife that encircled us. I could hear a pack of coyotes off in the distance howling at the moon, the sound matching the fear that I felt. The Wolands walked in complete silence. My steps were the only ones loud enough to hear as they crunched on the brush under my feet.

Our arrival to the cabin was swift. We stopped about twenty yards from the front door. Without words, the Wolands encircled the small cabin. Once my haven, this one-room, rickety cabin with no electricity or plumbing was the only thing that stood between six powerful Wolands and my best friend.

The front door swung open with a loud creak, and out came a large man with long brown hair well past his shoulders and fiery red eyes. *This must be Cairo.* He walked straight up to Jericho and lifted his hands up in a show of peace. He stopped about three feet in front of him and bowed his head.

Jericho spoke slowly and evenly. "Who is she?"

"She is the one."

"Be more specific!" Jericho's hands rolled into tight fists. "I will charge you with the endangerment of all dragons who call Ochana home—"

"She is the one from Aprella's premonition. The second will show himself soon."

Jericho broke eye contact with Cairo and gaped at me. "Are you sure?" His eyes were still fixed on me but he wasn't talking to me.

"Yes, I spent two hundred years studying the book of Aprella before you recruited me to the guard. It was luck I came across her when I did. And you know neither of us believe in luck. I was meant to find her. No other Woland would have known what she was. They would have killed her on sight." Cairo looked over his shoulder just as Eva poked her head through the door.

Jericho looked past Cairo to get a glimpse of her. "Why not come to us with this news? You knew how we would react to your breach."

"That was my plan."

Cairo stepped closer to Jericho and whispered something in his ear. I watched as Jericho's body stiffened. Like a set of dominos, the rest of the Wolands' bodies stiffened as they looked to each other. I figured some kind of clairvoyant communication had transpired between them.

"We must get back to Ochana immediately. It is not safe for the girl or the prince to be out here," Jericho stated with certainty.

"The prince? I was unaware he had returned. Why would you bring him with you?" Cairo seemed confused. "I agree, we need to leave. I had hoped you would come sooner."

Jericho stepped back and assessed Cairo. "Why would you come here, to an unfamiliar place I know nothing of, if you did not know the prince was back?" Jericho stepped in front of me in a protective stance as he spoke.

"I called to you and told you where I was. What does the prince have to do with my location?" Cairo shifted his body until it completely covered the cabin door, effectively blocking our view of Eva.

Jericho cocked his head to the side, "The prince knows the girl. He identified her to me and brought me here."

Cairo eased up a bit, "Is he—"

Boooom. A loud crash interrupted Cairo. It came from the east, in the exact direction of my parents' house. I started to move to where the explosion occurred but was stopped short by a hand on my shoulder. I turned to see Jericho, who nodded to his guards. They all took off in the direction of the crash.

"We must go. Now. Get the girl."

Jericho pulled me forward and together we bolted toward the main road. Faintly, I could hear Cairo and Eva not far behind us. Finally, we broke through a line of pine trees. Jericho and Cairo promptly morphed into their dragons. I followed their lead. This time, the shift into my reptilian state was brisk. I barely thought about it. I rotated my head to look at Eva. She had already shifted too. My initial glimpse of dragon Eva was only through security cameras back at Ochana. Now, I could see the intricate details of her golden scales. They gleamed a magnificent gold and practically covered her entire body. She was a vision with her golden wings and amber-gold feathers.

"We must fly fast, straight to Ochana. Do not stop for anything."

Jericho's eyes blazed as his voice bounced around in my head. I think he expected a fight from me, and I almost put one up until I heard another loud crash that sounded nearby. It felt like the large pine trees were being uprooted from the ground and catapulted into the distance. Whatever was causing the noise, I knew I was no match for it. I hoped the Wolands ensured my parents were safe and kept them that way.

"Their first goal is to keep you safe. Only then will they check on your parents. They aren't here for them, they want the two of you. Let's go."

I hoped Jericho was right. If I brought any troubles to my parents, I couldn't live with myself. Eva stood close to me and placed one of her golden-scaled hands on my shoulder, almost like she didn't believe I was real. I knew how she felt. Everything felt surreal.

Jericho led us into the sky as Cairo fell into position behind us. We traveled fast, much quicker than we did on our way here. Eva seemed to have no problem keeping up with us. She was so small next to us, almost like a pixie amongst giants. Only, we were dragons, and she was...?

J.A. Culican

Chapter Eleven

I landed on Ochana with a bang. As soon as my feet hit the ground, my entire body thrust forward and my upper half smacked full force into the hard terrain. I was exhausted. In a show of delicate grace, Eva made a light-footed landing next to me. I was jealous at her ease. Almost immediately, we were encircled by over twenty Wolands. Jericho and Cairo puffed out their chests, ready to defend the decision to bring Eva here. Their dragons were much larger than the Wolands that surrounded us. Jericho and Cairo's dragons frightened the guards, who took a few steps back in horror. Jericho crouched low, ready to pounce at the slightest threat. Every time any of the guards made any kind of movement, both dragons bellowed a deep warning growl.

As exhausted as I was, I scrambled to my feet and stood as tall as I could muster. I shielded Eva with my wings, but she stepped out from my protection. She spread her wings and prepared herself to fight. Without notice, the two guards parted in front of me. Rylan stepped through. He gave me a quick glance, then turned to the Woland guards.

"Your Prince has returned. His mission was to bring Cairo and the girl back. He has completed his first mission with success. Is this the greeting you meet him with?

Show your respect. Now." Rylan growled at the guards until they relaxed and bowed their heads my way.

The guards started to shift back to their human forms. Once the Wolands had morphed back, Jericho and Cairo did also. They had waited for all threats to banish first. Cairo stepped to Eva's other side, sandwiching her between us. Once Cairo was in place, Jericho turned to Rylan.

"We need to meet with the council immediately, and have Councilwoman Jules bring the book of Aprella." Jericho turned and gestured to the three of us. We morphed back into our human states and followed Jericho through the streaming waterfall.

I was surprised Rylan let Jericho speak that way to him. He didn't ask, but rather told him what needed to be done, and Rylan had accepted it with no question. It either showed that Rylan trusted Jericho, or feared him.

"Both."

Jericho's deep voice caught me off guard. He nodded his head at me and turned to Cairo. He didn't say a word to him, just glared. I wondered if Jericho was probing through Cairo's mind as he often did with me. I thought about what he'd just said to me, and wondered how Jericho had earned his trust when he was always telling me not to trust anyone.

The four of us took a seat around the large, polished stone table as we waited for the council to arrive. I watched Eva inspect the carved images on the wall. We had yet to speak to each other about what was going on. I assumed she was just as confused as me the first time I sat at this table.

Suddenly, a commotion erupted outside the council room. Both Cairo and Jericho stood as the whole council barreled into the room. Everyone took their assigned seats. I was already in my seat next to Rylan's, with Eva next to me and Cairo on her other side. Jules, the Galian with sapphire eyes, placed a large book in the middle of the table. The room fell silent as each attendee gazed at the old, bulky book.

Rylan interrupted the silence. "Explain to me what is going on." His eyes pierced Jericho, then Cairo in turn.

"I believe the golden dragon prophecy is coming true, My King." Cairo nodded toward the book.

"Why now?" Sila asked. "The prophecy was to come at a time of great fear."

"What makes you think this girl is the golden dragon?" Rylan challenged as he tilted his head at Eva and squinted.

"Aprella's prophecy affirmed that the golden dragon would encompass humanity, therefore they would not take the true shape of a dragon, but one of a human..." Cairo paused and turned to Rylan. "My King, she can wield mahier as only dragons can, but her shape is that of a human."

Jules cleared her throat to get everyone's attention. "It would explain the prince's coloring." She nodded at me. "A warrior that is comprised of the four dragon founders would fight by her side." It sounded like Jules was reciting the prophecy from heart.

"We must know for sure." Rylan looked at Jules. "Your Galian, Meka, is the Keeper of the Book of Aprella. There must be a way to know for sure."

"It has been many years since I studied that prophecy. If it is true, it means we are in a time of fear. I will speak with Meka."

"You must look into it now and report to the council tomorrow. If it is true, we need to act fast. The last time we were in a time of fear, we lost a great warrior as punishment." Rylan's voice wavered a bit. "Jericho, check in with each Woland guard. We must know if they have encountered anything during their rounds that will back this book's claim."

"Yes, My…"

Cairo interrupted Jericho. "Tonight, My King. We were under attack. The Woland guard that was with us, have we heard from them?"

The whereabouts of the other Wolands had completely escaped my mind. Between the prophecy, and Eva being the golden dragon, I was distracted. I'd heard the part about the loss of the great warrior during the previous time of fear and became completely sidetracked. I looked over to Jericho, who had somehow found a tablet, which he pressed at irritably as he tried to discover the fate of the other Wolands.

"My King, they are on their way back. The attack had come from a pack of"—his eyebrows scrunched in confusion—"carnites." He turned the tablet screen toward Rylan so he could see the video that played.

Jericho looked up from the tablet, a muddled look on his face. I had never seen that much emotion from him. Everyone looked around the table in disbelief. *What were carnites?*

"You would know them as a mix of trolls and giants, my son," Sila answered my unspoken question. "Large beings, highly destructive, though not too bright. We haven't had a sighting of them in many years." She seemed perplexed by the news.

Eva abruptly stood, causing her chair to skid behind her and tumble to the floor. "Can someone please start from the beginning? I am having a really hard time following all this. What is the Book of Aprella, what is the prophecy about, and what am I?" She stared confidently at Rylan as she spoke.

Cairo chuckled beside me. "This one is a spitfire; no fear whatsoever."

Sila gestured for Eva to sit back down as she herself rose and began to pace around the room. "Let's start from the beginning. Not your beginning, but the beginning of all." Sila paused and gazed at the images on the wall. "Aprella was the first ever known dragon. No one knows where she came from or how she came about."

"Most dragons believe she was born from the four elements, with fire being the most dominant," Rylan added.

"My King, this is true," Sila confirmed. "Aprella carried the mahier of all the dragons of today. You could imagine the amount of strength it gave her. She bore four dragon sons, and legend has it, she broke off some of her mahier in order to create them. A Galian, a Sien, a Woland and a Leslo, the four founding dragons." Sila gestured around the room at the images that surrounded us as she spoke. "She shared her mahier with her sons in a way that each dragon born would also carry her mahier."

"We all descend from Aprella," Jules said, picking up the narrative. "She created Ochana. Aprella was gifted with sweeping prophetic visions. She is the only known dragon to possess such power. She could see what would be." Jules seized the book from the center of the council table. "Everything she saw is inside our book of prophecy. It has yet to be wrong."

"So, what did she write about me?" Eva still sounded strong and sturdy, though quite eager.

"If you are who we think, you are a dramon," Sila explained. "But a true dramon. Other dragons have been described as such, but they are not. They are not like you." A smirk spread across Sila's lips. "You are the golden dragon, the one who will stand by a great warrior and save all that is true. Aprella wrote about you, a girl who was half dragon and half human. She would come in a time of great need, and soon after, a special warrior would be born who embraced the essence of the four founders. Together, the half-dragon girl and great warrior would become the Keeper of Dragons. They would save us all." Sila sat back down with that last sentence, her voice much softer.

I could picture Eva as the girl from Aprella's prophecy. She had always been strong and confident, and picked up new skills with ease. In school, classmates from various groups and cliques flocked to her. She had such a way with people. They all trusted her. I never understood how we became friends, or why she chose to stay my friend through the years. I was nothing like her.

Eva studied me as my thoughts rambled. Her eyes seemed to smile at me even though her mouth didn't move a muscle. "You are much stronger than you think, Cole. When I first moved to Clover, you took me in as a friend. I was an outsider. No one moves to that small Texas town, they are born there. But you accepted me from the beginning. That took a lot of guts, a lot of heart, and a lot of true care." She placed her hands on my forearm and smiled. She then turned back to Sila. "What are we saving you from?"

"Everything." Sila looked to Jericho.

"We have been protecting this world from the beginning. Creatures always want to conquer and capture Ochana. For some time, it has weighed heavy on the dragons' shoulders to protect the land and all that is true. If you both are now in Ochana, our two key fighters, and the prophecy is coming to light, there must be uncovered forces working in darkness. Creatures like the carnites are preparing for war." With each word, Jericho's voice grew stronger, as if he became more confident as he matched prophecy to the recent events. "Since the beginning, it has been the Wolands' job to protect the land." Jericho bowed towards us. "We will stand alongside the two of you. We will protect you as you protect us."

A warrior. They think I'm the warrior who will save them. Who will protect humans from creatures I don't know anything about. I felt like the time was now to explain to them how weak I was. I failed Jericho's first test. How was I supposed to protect anyone when I couldn't even protect myself?

I also wondered how Eva had deciphered my thoughts earlier. Suddenly, I heard a loud giggle. It was Eva. I turned to her. "How?"

"I don't know, it felt like you were screaming it to me. It resounded in my head." She shrugged. "Also, you're wrong about being weak. I promise you."

"She's right. You come from a long line of warriors," Rylan reassured me. "One day, you will see what we all know, what the prophecy has revealed to us." Rylan exhaled, then addressed Jericho and Cairo. "We must meet with all the Wolands who have fought the carnites as soon as they land. Stop them." Rylan then turned to face the rest of the council. "As for the rest of you, you need to rest. We will meet first thing after rounds in the morning. It seems dire times are ahead."

Everyone nodded to Rylan's command and filed out of the council room. I stayed behind with Eva. I wanted to know if my parents back in Texas were alright, and more about the carnites. Jericho walked over to me. From over my shoulder, he began to press along the screen. On it, a creature as tall as a tree and made from stone ran through the woods near my house. With slight ease and great strength, he pulled trees from their roots and chucked them at the Woland guards. I wondered how a creature with such a colossal size could go unnoticed. It would surely be all over the news the next day.

"No one will remember a thing tomorrow. The Wolands are not only trained to fight, but to protect all life. It is their job to ensure no human witnesses our dragonic trials. They would have made sure that no human saw anything, and if they did, they would use their mahier to cast a spell over the humans so they would forget." He took the tablet from me. "Your parents are safe. The carnites were not there for your human parents. They came for the two of you."

I didn't understand. "How would they even know we were going to be there?"

"It seems they know more than we thought. I—"

The Woland guards stormed through the council room doors and interrupted Jericho. It was clear they had arrived back safely. They trudged over to where Eva and I stood. They each lowered to one knee and bowed their heads to us. I looked around the room at the remaining dragons. My gaze stuck on Rylan, who had a proud look on his face. The guards then stood and moved to Rylan and Sila. They bowed their heads again and took their seats at the table.

"I will escort you both to your rooms. It's best to get some sleep, tomorrow will be a big day," Sila said to Eva and me.

I almost wanted to insist I stay and learn about the carnites, but Sila was right. I was exhausted, and who knew what tomorrow would bring.

J.A. Culican

Chapter Twelve

Bannggg. Bannggg.

A loud knock at the door woke me abruptly. The only difference from the last time I awoke from an unexpected thud was the absence of one red-eyed Woland. Mira quickly helped me get ready, and five minutes later, we were out the door to pick up Eva and head to the council room. By the time we entered the council room, it was completely packed and the air was filled with loud, deep discussion. I resumed my seat from last night and attempted to catch up on the conversation.

"Disappeared? In the middle of the fight?" Rylan roared at Jericho. "How does that happen?"

"My King, they must be working with another being, one that can wield mahier or another magical element. We know carnites do not hold any magic." Jericho pondered for a moment. "It would explain their disappearance. They could have been planning this for the last ten years. I'm concerned about how they knew the prince and the girl were there." He turned to me. "Do the Keepers know what we are facing?"

"You speak as if you are sure that they are the Keeper of Dragons," Allas said.

"I've seen with my own eyes that they are. I've felt the energy radiating off of them. Prince Colton is the warrior who will save us, and this girl"—Jericho pointed to Eva—

"is the golden dragon who will assist him on his journeys. I am convinced they are the Keeper of Dragons," Jericho stated with a confidence I didn't feel.

"If you're right, then we are all in danger, dragons and humans alike. Our existence is in a state of imbalance." Allas wiped a puddle of perspiration from her forehead. Beside me, Rylan looked to be in a state of disbelief. "What you're saying is, the time of fear is now." Troubled by her own words, Allas peered around the table.

"We hadn't seen movement from a single carnite in years. I'd thought perhaps they were extinct." I could tell Rylan's error had now caused him a great deal of distress. "We must find out who is aiding them before it's too late." Rylan studied the room until his eyes met mine.

"Son, good to see you have arrived. As I am sure you've caught up by now, we lost the carnites last night. We are not sure where they went." My heart sunk. I wasn't sure what all this meant for Eva and me. "You will shadow Jericho until we know more. Do not go anywhere without your guards." He turned to the Wolands. "Do not let him out of your sight."

He then turned his attention to Eva. "Today, you will meet our Keeper of the Book of Aprella. She will verify if you are indeed the dramon of Aprella's prophecy."

Eva nodded. Instantly, Jules came forward and brushed Eva's arm, gesturing her to follow. Eva looked back at me and grinned. "I'll see you soon."

Let's hope. I wondered what would happen if she wasn't the golden dragon. Surely they would let her stay; she could fly, read minds, and had a host of other magical talents. She had to be a dragon of some kind. I lifted my eyes and saw a sad smile spread on Sila's face as she listened in on my internal dialogue. I turned away from her gaze and stared at the door through which Eva had just exited. I wanted to run after her and get her to safety. A hand on my shoulder brought me back to the other people in the room. It was Rylan.

"You need to focus on your training. If you are the warrior from Aprella's prophecy, the lives of every dragon and human are on your shoulders, son." Rylan squeezed my shoulder one last time before he turned his focus on the remaining council. "You all have jobs to do, get to them. And stay alert."

Rylan left the room. Sila followed, but stopped to get one last glimpse of me over her shoulder before disappearing down the tunnel. In desperation, I sent a prayer up. As scared as I was about being this grand warrior of all of Ochana upon whom the entire world depended, I was more scared about possibly losing Eva.

"Let's go," Jericho commanded, clearly displeased with my train of thought.

I nodded and followed after him, but my mind still raced. What would happen now? How was I supposed to protect everyone? As we strode through Ochana, I looked around at the other dragons, mostly Siens, who had no idea they were in any danger. The dragons laughed and chatted like it was any old day and any old time, not one of fear. They continued on with their usual activities; setting up and running their open-aired market stands, puffing out large flames of fire with their mouths to cook meals for each other, flying low in pods as they soaked up the glory and beauty of Ochana. And each of these dragon's lives were in my hands. I needed to get my head on straight.

"Finally," Jericho stated.

It was only one word, but it was enough to blaze a fire inside me. If this were all true, I had to find strength. I needed to train. I needed to know what I was up against. "What other creatures can wield mahier?" I asked.

"Only dragons. But there are other creatures that wield different forms of energy. Depending on the creature, each have their own names, but in human terms, I guess you would call it magic." He shook his head as if he detested human words for dragonic considerations.

"These creatures, what are they?"

"We need to focus on the others that would help the carnites. There aren't many; carnites on their own are easily defeated and not easy to form an alliance with. But two creatures come to mind, farro and elden. We need to make contact with them. Get a sense for what they're worth."

He grew quiet when we arrived at command, giving me a chance to think about what he'd said. I had never heard of farro or elden, ever. I concocted all sorts of images for what they could look like. Maybe large brown beasts with razor sharp teeth and monster claws, the kind of evil creature that would haunt a small child's nightmares and make them too frightened to rest their head on a pillow ever again.

At least we knew where to look for these magical imps, but what would happen when we found them?

We entered the glass building on the edge of Ochana and found it much busier than the last time I was here. Wolands rushed back and forth, mumbling to themselves or to colleagues, working busily at their tasks, and completely ignoring Jericho and me. We walked straight to Jericho's office. I took a seat in front of his large desk as he pulled a tablet from his side drawer and perused its contents. His eyes widened.

Crack!

Jericho slammed the tablet on his desk so hard it completely shattered, its glowing screen turning into black bits and pieces. Immediately, Jericho and I looked up as we could we feel someone watching. Garrik stood in the doorway.

"The farro? Are you sure?" He pierced Garrik with one of his terrifying looks.

"Looks that way. We've been tracking an increased movement from the Grove. No sign of the carnites, but you know how tricky the farro are." Garrik paused to look at me. "Should we attempt contact?"

Jericho began to pace around his office. I focused my attention on him with the hopeful notion that maybe, just maybe, I could read his mind. There must be more to it than just focus, though maybe not, and it came back to me that I still couldn't open doors. My mahier seemed slow, almost impaired. So far, all I could do was shift into my dragon and fly. I began to laugh at myself—*all I could do*.

"Do you find this amusing?" Jericho stopped his pacing and sneered at me. "The farros are involved. Those tricky little beasts are too smart for their own good. I'd bet my life they know exactly who you are. Somehow they are two steps ahead of us." He resumed his restless back and forth. "Two steps ahead," he mouthed to himself, though loud enough for Garrik and me to hear and ponder for ourselves.

"How? We didn't even know." Garrik stared at me, brows furrowed in thought.

"We've missed something. We've missed a lot of somethings."

Jericho slammed his hands against one of the glass walls of his office, and I was shocked they didn't shatter like his tablet. Smoke started to billow out from behind his ears and shoulders as he shook in anger. I jumped out of my seat and began to say something, but the words left me.

I stood against the opposite wall in complete astonishment. His eyes glowed as he took in my expression, then he stormed out of his office and into the glass building's main entrance. In the time it took me to flinch, he shifted into his dragon and took off.

"I haven't seen that in many years," Garrik remarked. "Jericho has been in control for a long time, but your arrival has changed all that." He turned and looked out the glass wall, watching as Jericho soared through the clouds, a line of smoke trailing in his path.

"How many years?" I was barely able to pay attention to Garrik, I was too focused on Jericho. When I was met with silence, I looked over at Garrik, who continued to follow Jericho's enraged movements in the sky.

He sighed. "I'd say close to two hundred years."

Was he kidding?

"I remember it like it was yesterday. It was the night Councilman Jago died. Jericho was extremely close with him, so it came as no surprise when the council voted Jericho in as his successor." A look of sorrow crossed his face. "It's one of the reasons Jericho is so serious—he vowed to never let something like that happen again. He's devoted his life to the Woland guard." He moved to Jericho's desk and started to clean up the remains of the broken tablet. "He'll be back soon. I'm surprised he left you at all. I'll be right out that door"—he pointed to Jericho's office entrance, the only door in the room—"if you need anything. Two guards will patrol outside the room until Jericho returns."

Garrik bobbed his head and left, leaving me alone. I watched as he summoned two guards and placed them right where he said he would. The two Wolands instantly went into guard mode, ignoring my presence. I sighed and turned back to the glass wall. I could no longer see Jericho, but I hoped he would be back soon, especially after hearing that he had been alive for two hundred years! That news astonished me. I wondered how old he was and how old dragons lived to be.

A loud bang from the command center caught my attention. I walked to the door but was stopped by two arms spread across the doorway. I looked at the two Woland guards, who shook their heads at me. *I guess I'm not allowed to leave.* I poked my head out to see what the commotion was. I could still hear thuds and all visible Wolands appeared frazzled. *What was going on?*

"Sir, we've lost all communication, in and out." The Woland sounded anxious as he spoke quickly to Garrik. "Everything is black."

"Micah, get ahold of King Rylan, and someone find Jericho." Garrik banged on one of the computers with no luck.

The door swooshed open and Jericho walked in with a look of confusion on his face. He looked right at Garrik. "What in Aprella's name is going on? I was gone five minutes." I sensed aggravation in his voice.

"We've lost communication. We are troubleshooting now." He knocked on the computer again for good measure.

"What do you mean?" Jericho looked around the command center; he noticed all the blank screens and frantic Wolands. "How is this even possible? It's all powered by our mahier." His brows scrunched as he continued to gaze at the chaos.

"Explain." I jumped at the sound of Rylan's voice. I hadn't heard or seen him enter. It seemed Jericho and Garrik hadn't either. Rylan stood stock still in front of the main doors. Everyone froze for a moment as they looked about the black screens of the monitors. Jericho walked to the large glass wall that overlooked the clouds. He searched the sky, for what, I didn't know. He turned and addressed the Wolands.

"Everyone, get in your positions. We will know soon what is going on." He turned my way. "My Prince, stand by me." His eyes fumed. "Garrik, release the first realm and set up a perimeter around Ochana."

I raced over to Jericho, whose presence eased my fear a bit. Rylan stepped up beside me. We stared together out the large glass window, but the sudden chirp from the screens coming alive made me jump. Everyone in the room turned to look at the large screen in the middle of the room. A young, white-haired woman stared back at us. She looked small, like a pixie. She smiled slowly to reveal sharp pointy teeth. In mere seconds, she went from seemingly innocent to a dwarf-sized demon.

"Good morning, dragons." Her raspy voice reverberated from the speakers. "Ah, it seems I am in the presence of royalty. My King, My Prince." The woman sneered as her whole body shook with laughter.

"Who are you and what do you want?" Rylan demanded.

"How rude of me, My King. I am Queen Tana of Farro Grove. I would like to meet with you to discuss an alliance." She was serious.

"We do not give coalition to fallen creatures like the farro. Now, tell me what you really want."

"Very well. I offer you a trade." Her midnight eyes roamed the room as if she was really able to see everyone in the room, even those out of her peripheral view.

"Continue."

"We will stop the war that has already begun if you give us the Keeper of Dragons."

"I know nothing of war or the Keeper of Dragons," Rylan spat.

"We must be honest with each other, King Rylan. You met the first wave of our attack just the other night. Those dumb carnites are just the start. As for your denial of the Keeper of Dragons, I see one half of the pair as we speak. The other half isn't far off, in the Temple of Aprella. I will give you twenty-four hours to decide. Good day, My King." She roared maliciously until the screens cut her off to resume standard function.

"How?" It was the only word Rylan seemed able to utter as he monitored the room and looked over the stunned faces of the Wolands.

Jericho and Garrik punched at the screens. "The Woland guard sees nothing. No one has breached Ochana." Jericho looked back at Rylan.

"That is where you are wrong. That farro broke through our mahier and took control of our communication networks. She had eyes in this very room and all around Ochana. Find out how she succeeded. Now!" Rylan stormed from the command center. As soon as he was outside, he shifted into his dragon, mounted his wings, and took off.

Chapter Thirteen

"We need eyes on the Grove," Jericho barked. "Garrik, I want you to lead the mission." He turned from Garrik to face the rest of the Wolands. "Keep realm one on the perimeter, and send guards to the Temple of Aprella." He paused to examine his shattered tablet. "Find me a new tablet, and bring me the golden dragon."

Jericho continued to shout orders around the command center as he stormed from one computer to the next. I watched the Wolands jump at his orders and race to complete his commands. I stayed put, still shocked by what had just transpired. The Queen of the Farros had just taken complete control over the communication at Ochana's command center. If we were back home, I wouldn't be too impressed with the hack, but it seemed everything here ran off mahier, and only dragons were able to wield it. *Maybe they have a dragon on their side?* A chill ran up my spine as I considered it. Would someone really betray their own kind? And for what reason? Or, maybe they have learned how to manipulate it somehow? The more I thought about it, the more questions I had, and my fear escalated with each one of those thoughts.

"My Prince, it is best that you stay in Jericho's office. It is the safest place in the command center. We need to keep you and . . ." Garrik trailed off as his eyes wandered to the door. Eva had entered, and was accompanied by two guards. "Ah, the golden dragon has arrived." Garrik beckoned Eva over and led us into the office. He nodded to the guards, who took their spots at the door.

I turned to face Eva. She didn't say a word to me. Her eyes were wide in wonder as she gazed through one of the glass walls. The view was especially breathtaking; a mist of clouds glided slowly through the sapphire sky as the waterfall streamed down from Ochana, making its way to earth. Eva's wonder made me realize that I hadn't had time enough to revel at the beauty of Ochana. I hailed from a land that floated high above the earth, almost like a hot air balloon, while beautiful gleams of purples and turquoises poured from a glorious waterfall. It looked like a liquid milky way with magical powers. And the mountains, the mountains! One of the points was so high it peaked above the haze. I spotted patches of colorful trees and flowers laden along the smoother surfaces of the mountain edges. What a view. What a place to be born. It was hard to believe we were in the middle of, well, a war. That was the word Queen Tana had used. We were at war and didn't even know it. My thoughts then turned to Eva. I wondered what she was told, and if they were able to verify who or what she was.

"What did they say to you?" I asked hesitantly.

Eva turned to me, her eyes shining a light gold. They were no longer the usual bright blue I expected them to be.

"Are we really the Keeper of Dragons?" I asked when she didn't speak.

"Yes, it is true. And there is no need for you to worry about my fate." She gave me a small grin and turned back to our glass view. "Meka had begun to tell me what this all means but the guards came rushing in." Her body stiffened. "I had no idea what was happening; I still don't."

I didn't know where to start. It took me a few seconds to figure out what I should tell her. I didn't want her to see how scared I was about it all, but before I knew it, I began to explain everything to her, about the Queen of the farros and how she was able to break through the mahier. I nodded to Jericho, who was still barking orders to anyone in his ear space. "He's been like this since the computers came back on."

Eva watched Jericho bounce from one guard to the next. "Has that ever happened before?" Her eyes remained on Jericho.

"I don't think so. Everyone seemed surprised. Rylan was furious. He shifted and took off as soon as we were back online."

Eva turned my way. I could tell she was struggling to say something. "You know, it will be our job to take on the farros. I mean, we are the Keeper of Dragons. We are fated to save them all, from all enemies." She glanced to the ground then back up to me. "Meka showed me the prophecy. The more time we spend with each other, the stronger our powers will become. I don't think it was a coincidence that I moved next door to you when I was ten. I have a feeling our fate has been laid out for us long before we were born." She paced over to the window and gazed at the clouds in contemplation.

I knew what she said was true. I didn't believe in coincidences. I just wondered what force had brought us together as children, and why. How were we supposed to take on the farros? Let's face it, the farros were not going to wait for Eva and me to complete our training before raging insufferable war on the dragons of Ochana. We would have to figure out a way to defeat them in our lowly dragonic states.

"The Woland guards will back you throughout this journey, and every journey in the future. The farro are only one class of evil that you will face in your life," Jericho explained as he walked into his office. He stood next to Eva and mirrored her stance. Silently, they both gazed out the window as the clouds drifted by.

Even the calming beauty of the scenery could not comfort me. "How many creatures are out there?" I asked.

"The number is endless. You will defeat one and more will appear. It is the way of the world, especially the life of a protector. The life of being the Keeper of Dragons." Jericho never turned in my direction.

"How will we defeat them? We don't even know what farros are, let alone any of the other creatures." My mind raced on this endless loop of my imminent life.

"You have dragonic support. We will aid you in your fight." Jericho turned to face me. "You have the knowledge of the council at your whim; all you need to do is ask and you will have all that you need." Jericho's head tilted to the side as he scrutinized me. "Your biggest challenge will be with yourself. You feel as though you are not strong enough for the challenges you will face." Jericho sighed. "Time will be your proof." He turned to Eva. "You have a strong ally in the golden dragon. I can feel the mahier pour from her. You will learn to share the burden with your partner."

He turned and walked back out to the command center. At least he seemed to be back in control. He was right. I had resources at the tip of my claws. All I needed to do is utilize them. Not to mention Eva. I needed to draw from her strength and lead by her example. Finally, my confidence began to build up. But then...

"My Prince," Garrik bowed his head through Jericho's office doorway. "I need to escort the two of you to the council room. It seems an emergency council meeting has been called. The Keeper of Dragons is needed to discuss our stance with the farro." He gestured for us to follow him.

Eva and I followed Garrik. The two guards at the door followed, with Jericho taking up the rear. I took a moment to internally appreciate Garrik, who always surprised me with his show of respect. I was just a kid he had just met, and yet he bowed to me as if I had proven to him my worth as his prince.

The walk to the council room had quickly become familiar. Now, it seemed the only two places I could successfully find on Ochana were the command center and the council room, but only as long as I was in one when going to the other. I really needed to find myself a map.

Just as Garrik said, the entire council was in attendance. I took my designated seat next to Rylan. They were recapping the breach from Queen Tana. Disbelief swept the room. Looks of astonishment crept over the faces of each man and woman.

"How is this possible?" Luka questioned. "Farros are powerful, but not as powerful as us."

"The fairies have either evolved in strength and supremacy, or they are getting help from an even more powerful creature."

"Who can be more powerful?" A few dragons murmured in the council.

"Another dragon," Jericho remarked, astounded by his own speculation.

"Dragon?" Rylan bellowed at Jericho. "Impossible! Who would dare aid a sworn enemy of ours and place their own kind in danger?" He examined Jericho closely.

Jericho didn't seem bothered by Rylan's fury. "We must investigate all options, My King. If the farros have evolved to this degree, we may have to call in some of our allies."

"Not yet. Let's wait until we get the reports from the second realm." Rylan's glare softened a bit as it shifted my way. "We now have the Keeper of Dragons to help in our fight." He raised his eyebrows at me with a small smirk.

"Indeed, My King," Luka answered. "But they have yet to be trained. We must be hesitant about sending them out to fight just yet..."

Jules interrupted him. "They wouldn't have been sent to us now if they weren't meant to be used in this war. The prince and the girl are not here by chance. We must utilize them in the manner for which they were created."

I sensed that Jules was ready to send us off to war in an instant. At the moment, I found myself thankful for Luka, who understood our lack of skills and our need to train. Beside me, Eva was lost in thought. I watched her as she scanned the council. Periodically, she would stop and hold one's attention before moving on to the next, until her eyes landed on Allas's. I realized she was sizing them up.

"What about you?" Eva addressed Allas. "You have stayed quiet through this whole exchange. What do you think we should do?" Eva challenged.

Allas exhaled. "Queen Tana says we are at war. If she wants a war, then I say we give her one. Jules is right. These two Keeper of Dragons were sent to us for a reason. I believe this impending war is that reason. We are at the time of great fear, and a battle is to be fought." Allas' green eyes locked with Eva's golden ones. Tension grew amongst the room.

"We will vote," Rylan declared. "All in favor of sending the Keeper of Dragons out with the Woland guard to the Grove, place their insignia in front of the Leslo in Allas' name. All in favor of keeping the Keepers of Dragons here in Ochana to train, place your insignias in front of the Sien in Luka's name."

Rylan and all four councilmen stood. In some kind of ritual, they circled the room and bowed to each founder's image. They then placed their hands on what looked to be the heart of the dragon of their choice and recited a phrase

I could not hear. Rylan went first, and when he removed his hand from the wall, he left a small symbol imprinted on it. The other three councilmen walked to the Leslo and did the same. Once everyone had voted, they returned to their seats.

"The council has spoken. Once the second realm has verified the farros are at the Grove, the Keeper of Dragons will accompany the Woland guard and defeat the threat of war." Rylan nodded in consent and stood. He looked directly at Eva and me. "The lives of all are now in your hands, Keeper of Dragons."

No pressure.

Chapter Fourteen

Word came first thing the next morning. The farros were at the Grove. The second realm had stayed to observe their activity. My guess was that the farros knew they were there, but were waiting for Eva and me to arrive. Queen Tana had made it clear who she was after—it was us she wanted. The Queen of the Farros saw us as a threat, the ones who could defeat her and her wicked tribe, but I knew what our fate would be if she was successful in capturing us. The question was, how did we defeat them?

"You seem so sure the queen considers us a threat," Eva observed from reading my mind. "She thinks we are the way to defeat all dragons, to use us against our own kind."

"It seems she already has a way to defeat us. Look what happened yesterday." I still considered what Eva said. Did Queen Tana really think we would betray our own?

"I think she has a different plan for us." Eva's voice was strong with conviction.

With our guards in tow, we walked to the command center. As we neared the glass building, I could see the high-story walls beaming as they reflected around Ochana. The beautiful sight did nothing to calm my nerves, though. My anxiety peaked as I pondered what would happen after we entered.

As we arrived at the command center, I could see that a hundred extra guards had been called in. In complete soldier mode, they stood with their backs straight, their eyes unflinching and staring directly ahead. They didn't move a muscle as we walked past. Eva and I entered the office to find Jericho and Cairo in a deep conversation. Neither of them paused their discussion with our arrival. The two guards left the room to reoccupy their positions at the door. Surprisingly, Jericho seemed calm, in total control. I had expected the smoke-puffed hothead from yesterday.

Finally, they ended their conversation, and Cairo acknowledged us. He gestured to the two chairs near Jericho's desk. We sat in silence as we waited for instruction. Cairo seemed tense, but it was no surprise. The council had voted for two eighteen-year-old, untrained dragons to defeat a race of malicious fairies. I considered the fact that we didn't even know where the farros lived or what they were capable of.

"Ask your questions, I thought I made this clear yesterday," Jericho said grimly. No one expects you to know all the answers when we, who have lived hundreds of years, do not."

"How old are you?" *Hundreds of years?*

Jericho chuckled and shook his head. "Well, I wasn't expecting a laugh this morning. I am relatively young at around five hundred." Jericho put his hands up to pause my next question. "Before you go any further, each dragon is destined to live a different life; however, most live to be well over a thousand."

That bit of information intrigued me, especially since Rylan had referred to Jericho and the rest of the council as elders when I was first introduced. In reality, Jericho was more middle aged than an actual elder.

"Enough of all that, we need to focus on our mission. Hold your questions about dragons for when you return."

"How do we defeat the farros?" Eva interrupted.

Jericho nodded his head. "The farros were the first beings to ever challenge a dragon. They have been around since almost the start." Jericho paused and picked up a remote, and with the push of a button, a large hidden monitor came down from the ceiling. "These," Jericho said, "are the farros."

The monitor came to life with a depiction of what looked to be around a dozen small creatures. Though they mostly had human characteristics, each farro had a head of platinum hair and small, flaxen wings that fluttered from their scrawny backs. Sharp, piercing teeth protruded from their thin-lipped mouths, and menacing, pitch-black eyes that seemed bottomless. If it weren't for their razor-edged teeth and sinister eyes, they would have looked just like the fairies children see illustrations of in fairytales. The farros moseyed around a dreadful looking garden that was covered in dead plants, wilted leaves, and broken stems.

"This is the first known picture that we have of the farros. You are right in your thinking. They are directly related to fairies. There is just one main difference." Jericho paused and looked directly at me. "These fairies are the Fallen."

"Fairies?" I asked.

"Fallen?" Eva's query followed mine.

"You are a dragon, you've heard the carnites, and now you are questioning fairies?" Jericho asked.

His point made me feel ridiculous, I would need to get used to the fact that things I didn't believe existed, actually existed.

"Fairies are innately good; however, a select few weren't happy with their role in creating peace in nature. They wanted more, and so they allowed their greed to consume them. Back then, all creatures were bonded together as a tight, cohesive unit, and a war amongst us never seemed possible." Jericho shook his head and walked to the glass wall. "The good fairies banished the Fallen from their home in belief that they were poisoning their duties."

"The farros searched for a home of their own. They finally landed in Sikkim, India, and it's where they have been ever since, where you will be going in just a few hours." Cairo finished Jericho's story.

"How do we defeat them?" Eva asked. I could see as her wheels turned with possibilities.

"It's not that easy. Their mere existence is proof we haven't ever been successful in exterminating them. We thought after our last battle they had finally realized they were over-matched. That no matter how many times they tried to stop us, we would continue to protect all that was true." Jericho turned from the wall to Eva. "I wish I had a real answer for you. We have been successful in diminishing their numbers, but they are still here and may never be banished for good."

Cairo interrupted Jericho. "Let's focus on our mission. We need to stop this war. Queen Tana said it was only a start with the carnites, which means we need to assume they have commandeered other allies." Cairo scrunched his brows in thought. "We need to break up these alliances. Together, they may be strong, but apart, they know we can overpower them, especially now that we have the Keeper of Dragons."

"Do you know who their other allies are?" Eva asked.

"No. Realm two hasn't seen any other being but the farros at the Grove. Not that I expected it to be that easy. The farros are smart; never underestimate them." Cairo walked to the door and shut it.

"Thank you, Cairo," Jericho uttered. "We don't know the role you both are going to play in this mission, mostly because we aren't sure what the two of you are capable of. But I agree with the council—you were sent to us for a reason, and I believe this was it. Now, you will be guarded at all times by realm five of the Woland guard. Realm five consists of five highly trained Wolands who will protect you with their lives. They have already been briefed. They understand the Keeper of Dragons is what the farros want, and that we believe the two of you are the only ones who can end this," Jericho stated.

"We will leave soon, setting us to arrive at nightfall," Cairo further explained. "The farros gave us twenty-four hours to hand the two of you over. Pull yourselves together, let's go meet realm five."

We walked through the doorway back into the command center. I expected a flurry of activity, but everyone was calm, like today was any other day. The guards looked like they hadn't moved an inch since we last saw them. I was impressed with their discipline. We stopped in front of five imposing Wolands who towered over Jericho and Cairo, each with a similar scowl on their faces, red eyes burning in my direction.

"Wolands were created for battle, My Prince. Warriors." Cairo looked at me over his shoulder. "These men here are realm five."

Each Woland looked in my direction and bowed in respect. I always felt uncomfortable when someone showed their respect to me, more so now. These men deserved my respect, not the other way around. I could tell just by the look of them that these Wolands had been to war many times and had always been victorious.

"It's an honor to meet you all." Eva's strong voice carried to the Wolands, and their attention shifted to her.

"The Keeper of Dragons, we devote our lives to you. It is an honor to go into battle with you. Our lives are in your hands now." The largest Woland of the group addressed us.

"This is Jude, High Guard of realm five. He will be in charge of your safety. You both do as he says." Jericho looked right at Eva as he spoke.

I wondered why he pegged Eva as the troublemaker, or maybe he just pegged me as the scaredy-cat too terrified to step a toe out of line, which I was. Eva always challenged authority, though not in a disrespectful way, more in a knowledgeable way. She was quick, able to survey and make sound decisions with little problem. She was going to make the perfect golden dragon for Ochana.

"Let's move out. As soon as we land in Sikkim, take your positions. Everyone keep your senses open and be prepared. The farros know we're coming." Jericho took off toward the door, the Woland guard followed close behind.

Eva and I trailed behind them with realm five. I watched as all the Wolands began to shift until Eva elbowed me and gestured for me to follow suit. I inhaled a deep breath and began my shift. I couldn't wait for my shifts to become as fluid as everyone else's. By the time I finished, I looked up to see that the Wolands and Eva had lifted into the air already, their wings flapping as they gawked at me, urging me to catch up.

I exhaled and pushed off the ground. As I ascended into the aquamarine sky, realm five encircled Eva and me. They were to stay in this formation for the entire flight. The sight truly amazed me, a hundred or so Wolands flying through the sky, their red scales shining through the clouds. I prayed everyone's mahier was strong; I couldn't imagine what a human would think of this sight. That thought made me think of the farros. They'd proved to us that they could control our mahier once, so what would happen when we arrived? Would they be able to control it then, too?

Eva's voice floated through my head. "Stay alert. I have a bad feeling. Something feels off."

"What do you mean?" I projected.

"They know we're coming. It feels like a trap."

I laughed at that. Of course it was a trap. We had no idea what we would find when we arrived in India. We didn't even know who the farros had convinced to help them with this war besides the carnites. Not to mention, we had no idea what they wanted with Eva and me.

My pulse raced with the knowledge that tonight would cement our fate.

Chapter Fifteen

I was exhausted. My wings were sturdy and kept me afloat, but all I wanted was to curl up in a ball and go to sleep. As we whipped through a thick cloud, one of the Wolands in realm five turned to Eva and me. He pointed down toward the earth with his claw and made a huffing noise with his fire-breather, which signaled the other Wolands to descend. In synchronicity, we lowered slowly, and, as the clouds parted, a land of green pastures emerged beneath us. Horned beasts roamed on all fours. Some were chomping on grass while others were lying on it. As we got closer, I realized they were elk. Suddenly, one of the Wolands sent a gust of fire directly into the chest of an elk that stood munching on a plant. It let out a loud cry and all four of its legs collapsed. Alarmed, I looked to Eva, who giggled. The Wolands had caught us dinner.

We set up a picnic along the green field, though Eva turned her nose up at the thought of consuming raw meat. One of the guards reached for a large branch of a nearby tree, lit a fire, and began to cook a piece of meat for Eva. The guards sure knew how to accommodate us.

After dinner, we rose back into the air to finish our trip to India. Luckily, my portion of elk had endowed me with enough energy to finish the journey.

We flew a little bit longer until one of the realm five Wolands motioned again for us to descend down to earth.

The clouds parted once more, and small patches of green land, miniscule trees, and a charming lake appeared. Each dragon came in for a landing, with mine being surprisingly smooth. A faint thud was all that could be heard. Satisfied with my landing, I looked around to see that the other dragons were shifting back into their human forms. It would make our trip around the lake a bit easier.

Jude had explained to us the importance of Mitra Lake in Sikkim. We had to walk around it in order for the Grove to appear. The farros had a magical element they wielded called tillium, which was similar to mahier, but less potent. They used it to protect their home and shield it from humans. At the end of the trek, the farros would lift the shield and allow us entrance, if they chose to.

"How was realm two able to see the Grove?" Eva asked, giving voice to my own thoughts. "I mean, we figured the farros knew they were there, but it shouldn't have been a question if they had to lift their shields to allow entrance."

"Our mahier is much stronger, and we are able to see through their shield. We are unaware if the farro know of this, hence our nature walk now," Jude replied.

"Can you see them now, through their shield?" I asked.

"No, my focus is on keeping the two of you safe. Other Wolands in other realms are tasked with keeping an eye on the farro's activity," he stated as he maneuvered over a large boulder.

If it weren't for the battle we had flown all this way for, I would have been in awe of the scenery. We were in Northern Sikkim, and the population here was very low, almost nonexistent at our exact location. We walked along the shore of a mighty lake in a valley between mountains. The mountain peaks were frozen and scattered with patches of snow. The lake was calm but seemed to be free of any wildlife. Either they could feel the presence of dragons and fled, or this was part of the allure. Boulders and rocks were scattered about the shore, which made our trip difficult as we stepped over rocks and dodged the uneven surfaces. I had to give it to the farros—they were smart. Any enemy of theirs who wished to meet with them would be exhausted by the time the shield was lowered. Not to mention it gave them time to prepare. Speaking of which, I could already feel the eyes of the farros on us. They knew we were here. I wondered if we could drop their shield and catch them off guard.

"Can our mahier lower their shield?" I asked Jude in a tentative voice. I was no soldier so strategy was not something I excelled in.

"We have never tried. Again, we do not want the farros to know the extent of our abilities. Even if we could, our goal is to stop a war, not initiate one. We will attempt a diplomatic solution before we progress to war."

"But they attacked us, twice. War has already started," I objected

"That was not war, those were battles. We have had great wars in the past, and many creatures and humans lost their lives. It is not something we want to repeat. Unfortunately, creatures like the farros do not care about the wellbeing of humans or even the loss of their own kind. They only care about one thing."

"What's that?"

"Power. To be at the top of the food chain," Jude explained.

"Then what? I mean, if they ever got there?" I asked, my voice starting to shake.

"My guess, they would fight each other until only one remained. Creatures like the farros are selfish. Yes, they'll work together now. But once they've won, they will fight each other in order to have complete control and power over the entire kinship," Jude said.

"But nothing will be left," I whispered.

"That is why we have been tasked with the job as protectors. We protect all that is true from beings like the farros so that nothing like that will ever happen"

"I'm starting to understand just how important the dragons are." Even if the idea terrified me.

"Ah, and you haven't even seen everything." Jude locked eyes with me. "When you do, you must stay strong. We all need you."

***

We made it around a good portion of the lake when the ground began to shake. Everyone stopped to look around. I could see the snowcaps on the mountains start to move and slide down the mountainsides. The Wolands threw their hands up in an attempt to stop the snow with their mahier, but the snow continued as if the dragons had done nothing.

"Shift, get into the air," Jude commanded of realm five.

"I can't."

"Something's wrong."

"My mahier..."

No matter what we tried, none of us could shift. The Wolands looked around, lost. They didn't know what to do without their mahier. I grabbed Eva's hand and started to run into the lake. We braced ourselves as we dived in. The water felt like ice, but if we remained on dry land, the avalanche would sweep us away. The Wolands noticed our escape, and followed. We swam out as far as we could, my teeth chattered and my body shivered. The snow barreled down the mountainside toward us, but right when it was about to hit the edge of the water, it disappeared.

Suddenly, we were no longer in the water or even in the valley. All hundred or so of us dragons seemed to have been transported to a remote region. A moment ago, we were in one of the most beautiful scenic areas I had ever seen, but now, we stood in what looked to be a frozen tundra. The ice-cold temperature distressed me. I held on to Eva's hand as realm five closed in around us and searched for any clue as to what happened. I looked up and saw the farros peppering the sky.

"Welcome," Queen Tana's voice echoed around the open space, "to Farro Grove." Her arms went wide in welcome.

I wasn't feeling very welcomed. I felt trapped. Scared. No one moved or replied to the Queen. Every Woland stood in attack mode, ready for the fight I was sure to come. I gripped Eva's hand tighter. She turned in my direction, and I could see it. Scales began to cover her face, but she held her finger up to her mouth for me to be quiet, then tilted her head toward the farros above us.

"I see you found our entrance without a problem." Tana clapped her hands. "Bravo! I'm hoping you brought my old friends with you?" she inquired as she gazed around the Wolands.

Tana found Eva and me and graced us with a fear-inducing smile that showed off her razor sharp teeth. "Ah, come here, my Keeper of Dragons, I have missed you so." With a wave of her hands, Eva and I started to levitate off the ground. Jude and the other Wolands attempted to grab onto us and pull us back, but their efforts were useless. The farros circled them and released silver sparks at the realm five Wolands until they fell to the ground. Queen Tana floated over to us and examined our features with her midnight eyes. She reached out to touch the scales on Eva's face, but Eva swatted her hand away.

"I have to thank you two. You have kept me and the rest of the farros quite entertained the last eight years, and given us much time to prepare. It is time to officially adopt you into our tribe."

"We're not interested in joining you or your tribe," Eva shouted at her.

Tana chuckled. "You, my dear, are just like me. Beautiful. Strong. Cunning. Fearless. You belong with us. Together, we can rule all." Tana smirked at us and then turned to the Wolands. "You all look confused. Shall I tell you a story?"

I searched the crowd for Jericho and Cairo. I knew they were there somewhere but it was hard to see the faces of the Wolands. The sky was dark with only a few visible stars and the farros zipped around us in an excited frenzy. I could make out some of the Wolands on the other side of Queen Tana. I attempted to angle my head to get a better view, but Queen Tana interrupted my search with a cold, bony hand on my chin.

"Pay attention, Coley," Tana mocked. "This is important."

How did she know about my mom's nickname for me? No one but her ever called me that, and she never said it in front of anyone, almost like she knew I wouldn't be able to live down that embarrassment.

"We found you when the two of you were young. We were drawn to the energy that surrounds you. We have watched you grow through the years. At first, we had no idea what it meant or who you were and spent the first few years searching for answers. Until we found it. You were the Keeper of Dragons, and we, the farros, were the only ones who knew. Not even the dragons or that arrogant King Rylan knew." Tana sneered as she spoke of Rylan the King.

"How did you know?" Eva asked. "We didn't even know."

"Answer this, my girl. When is the last time you were sick? Broke a bone? Needed stitches?" Tana just shook her head at us. "It was obvious something was special about the two of you. You fed off each other's energy, an energy that shined to us like a beacon in the sky. The day you met, we felt it."

"Enough! Do you honestly think we are going to let you take the Keeper of Dragons from us?" Jericho shouted from below us.

"What do you think you can do about it, dragon? I'm sure you've noticed your mahier is of no use here. As I said, we have been preparing for this day for many years." Tana snickered. "Today shall be your last."

"How?" I choked out.

"How what, my boy?"

"How did you take our mahier?" I was confused.

"Did you think we would be unprepared to take on the mahier? Without it, dragons are nothing but human. It's ironic, really. Dragons have devoted their lives to protect humans and other fragile creatures, but today, they will meet their end as powerless, helpless beings, just like a human."

The farros started to laugh. It sounded more like a hive of angry bees preparing to strike. I looked over at Eva. We had to do something. The Wolands counted on us; we were the Keeper of Dragons, after all. If we were defeated tonight, it would be the end of all dragons.

"Oh, I almost forgot. I have a surprise for you, a little family reunion." Queen Tana leered at us. "You asked how, and this may give you the answer you desire."

She nodded to a group of farros who took off behind a large boulder. The boulder split open, and a figure appeared through the dust. I squinted my eyes to get an unblemished view. Immediately, I could tell this was no farro. This was much larger than a farro.

It was Zane.

Chapter Sixteen

I couldn't take my eyes off him. The rest of the dragons back in Ochana were displeased with Zane, and a little worried about him, but this? Would he really betray us all? And if so, why?

"How's it hanging, nephew of mine?" Zane chuckled as he walked closer to us. "Tana, let them down. I'd like to see my nephew's eyes when he learns the truth."

"Why?" was all I could choke out as Tana released me and I tumbled to the ground.

"The Grove is all yours, Zane." Tana swung her arms around. "And look, you have the full attention of the Woland guard. I'm always up for a story!"

Zane looked around at each Woland, his eyes stopping on Jericho and Cairo. "Ah, look, you brought some of my closest friends, thank you Colton." He laughed as he turned back to me.

"These dragons are your family, and Cole is your nephew. Why would you do this?" Eva asked.

"The golden dragon, it is an honor to be formally introduced." He put his hand out to shake Eva's.

She glared at his outstretched hand. "Like I would shake the hand of the enemy," she sneered.

"You were right about her, Tana, I like her." He laughed and turned back to me. "However, let's get back to why we're here. You've already heard the story about my big brother, Jago, but what you don't know is what happened after. Answer me this, Prince Colton. Have you had the honor to meet your grandparents yet?"

I thought about the question, surprised to realize that my grandparents had never been mentioned. I just assumed they had passed. "No, I didn't know they were still alive," I replied.

"Oh, they are most definitely alive, banished from Ochana for the death of their son." Spittle flew from his mouth as he spit out those words. "And of course, being the dutiful son that Rylan was, he agreed to this punishment as his first ever ruling as king." Zane stressed the words to drive his point home.

"Liar!" Cairo shouted. "How could you?"

Jericho placed his hand on Cairo's shoulder to calm him down, but his eyes never left Zane. He said nothing. A look I didn't understand passed between them. Jericho stood tall and lifted his chin. His eyes shifted to mine and he nodded his head. It happened so fast I wondered if I had imagined it.

"Revenge or jealousy? Which is the real reason you betrayed your race?" Eva asked.

Zane shook his head at her. "Don't you see? I'm justified in my actions. The dragons turned their back on their own race, scared creatures that they are."

"Which we gladly used to our advantage," Queen Tana interjected. "Zane here has been helping us gain control of your mahier for years. The Keeper of Dragons couldn't have come at a better time, for we control your mahier, which means we control you!" she proclaimed with a sneer.

"Actually, I control the mahier," Zane clarified. "See, the farros gave me the use of their tillium, and together with how potent my own mahier is, I was able to manipulate your mahier any way I wanted."

"Now that you have it, what's your plan?" Eva asked.

"Lucky for you, you haven't been around long enough to form any true friendships," Tana replied with venom.

"First, another story," Zane interrupted. "This one is my favorite. It's a new story just for the farros. Gather around." He gestured with his hands for the farro to join him. The other fallen fairies scampered around Zane as they squeaked out high-pitched snickers.

"Make it quick, Zane, I am getting antsy!" Tana requested.

"Of course." He looked over to her and smirked. "Jago and I were very close before his death. I often accompanied him on his rounds, as a way to understand the Wolands, for I was trained as a Leslo."

"That experience has aided us on our journey," Tana added.

"I agree." He cleared his throat. "I was with him during his final round. We were circling Ochana, checking the perimeter."

"What?" Tana interrupted.

Zane put up his hands to stop her from questioning him. "We saw something stuck on the ice. We thought it was an animal of sorts. As we flew closer, we noticed it was a boat, but humans hardly came that far north, and when they did, it was because something was wrong. Being a protector, Jago flew over to the boat, hoping he could save the humans aboard. He took off ahead of me, and by the time I got to him, it was too late." Zane looked to the ground, his pain was evident.

"I don't understand," I whispered. None of this made sense.

Zane pierced me with an intense glare. "He was attacked. The boat wasn't full of humans like he thought. It was a trick. The boat was full of farros." Zane looked to Tana with an odd expression on his face.

"That's ridiculous. You lie!" Tana shouted.

"Jago was the strongest warrior of all the Wolands. Did you honestly think an attack with just the use of your tillium would leave him for dead so quick?" he shouted back. "He told me what happened, made me promise him that I would find the farros and end them." He sneered.

Zane bent back and shifted into his dragon in the blink of an eye. Instantly, fire flew from his mouth and his mammoth claws thumped along the ground, right where the farros had gathered. They scuttled around in madness; some fluttered off the ground, others dashed into the mountains. I felt my mahier creep back through my fingertips. I turned to the Wolands; their mahiers were returning too. Eva grabbed my hand and squeezed. I looked over in time to see her scales shelter her skin. I looked around in fear; the farros and Wolands were in a fight to the death. Eva's squeeze of my hand reminded me that she was still with me, and it was time to fight.

"We can end this. It's why we're here," Eva whispered for my ears only.

"How? Look around, we're standing in the middle of a war."

"Grab my other hand and hold on tight. Focus all your energy on the farros."

"Why? What will that do?" I asked.

"Use your instincts. I am."

I lowered my head and rested it on Eva's forehead; her eyes fluttered shut, and mine followed. I blocked out the fight that raged around us and focused all my energy on the farros. All I could feel were Eva's hands clasped with mine, and her soft breath every time she exhaled. I felt and heard nothing else. My focus was completely on the farros. A vibration started at my toes and crept through my entire body until it pulsed with a new energy. A light shot from the tips of my fingers and separated into tiny strings. Each string attached itself to a farro. By now, each fairy had taken flight and was suspended in mid-air. I yanked my hands back, pulling the tillium out of each farro. When the tillium was completely sucked out, the strings released, and, quite amused, I watched as each farro dropped to the ground.

When the light went out, my body began to tremor and my breaths became strenuous. My body hit the ground hard as the tremors continued. I could hear Eva saying my name, the panic evident in her voice. Moments later, the quakes stopped, and I could finally take a breath. I opened my eyes to see Eva gazing down at me with a look of terror.

"Cole, what happened? Are you alright?" she stammered.

I attempted to sit. "I... don't know what just happened," I said with confusion.

As I looked around, I noticed all the Wolands had shifted back into their human forms, and most of the farros were rigid on the ground. Even as humans, the Wolands towered over the farros. They looked different, but I couldn't quite figure out what it was that made them appear dissimilar to their previous characteristics.

Jericho and Cairo had Queen Tana cornered between them. They looked ready to stomp her out.

She turned to me. "What did you do to me? Just wait until my tillium returns!"

"Awfully courageous words for someone in your position, Tana. I do wonder what your fate will be," Jericho stated with a smirk. He looked my way. "My Prince, are you okay?"

"Yeah, I think so," I answered, taking stock of how I felt. I had an increased amount of energy zipping through my body, but it was different than the mahier I was used to when I shifted into my dragon. I had no idea what it was.

"It's tillium," Zane answered my thoughts. "You stole all the farro's tillium with that little trick you just did. It now lives in you. You are very powerful, more so than I gave you credit for." Zane finished with what sounded like pride.

"Give it back, it's not yours to take. You're breaking the rules of our treaty!" Tana roared.

"You broke that treaty the night you killed my brother," Zane said, whirling on her. "It has taken me over two hundred years to fulfill my promise. It seems bittersweet that the new Prince of Ochana was the one who defeated you. It is how Jago would have liked it." Zane turned to me. "It has cemented your right as the prince, Keeper of Dragons." Zane bowed to me, and the rest of the Wolands followed, much to my dismay.

"What about the rest?" Eva pointed to the farros. "What are we supposed to do with them?"

It was a good question. Even without their tillium, we couldn't leave them here. They could always figure out how to get more or recreate it, or worse, come up with something stronger. And they couldn't come back to Ochana with us. I looked over to Jericho and Cairo for an answer. Neither said a word.

"The decision is Prince Colton's," Zane answered. "He speaks for the king when the king is not present."

"Me? Why not you, you are also a prince," I objected.

"You rank higher than me as the king's successor, not to mention the Keeper of Dragons," Zane explained. "And let's be honest, not many dragons trust me these days." He winced.

"Zane is right, My Prince, the choice is yours," Jericho stated. "As for you," he said, looking to Zane, his voice stern. "You have earned quite a bit of trust back; however, you will have a lot of explaining to do when we get back to Ochana."

I felt a hand in mine and turned to see Eva. In silence, she squeezed my hand to show her support for whatever choice I made. I turned tos the Wolands. All of their attention was on me, awaiting a decision. I was about to ask for suggestions when I noticed what looked like a herd of butterflies in the horizon. I squinted as I tried to make out what was there. The Wolands turned around and followed my line of sight.

"Is that...?"

"The fairies," Zane finished Jericho's thought.

Fairies! I prayed they were nothing like the farros. None of the Wolands moved or shifted into their dragons, and I took that as a sign of comfort. Maybe they were here to help? As the fairies came closer, I noticed the similarities between them and the farros. Their size was the same, and so was the stiff platinum hair and spastic silvery wings. Now that I thought about it, that's what was different about the farros; their wings weren't flapping around in rage. However, that was where the similarities ended. The fairies' eyes were full and bright, each a different neon color, and their smiles flaunted straight teeth and dimples. The fairies landed with gentle grace around us.

"My Prince." The fairy bowed. "I am Queen Annabelle, Queen of the Fairies."

"Annabelle, you have perfect timing," Zane commented.

"I see that. I pray none of your dragons were hurt?"

"No, Your Highness, all are fine." Zane smiled at Annabelle.

"What is your plan with the farros?" she inquired as she gaped at Tana.

"We haven't decided yet," I responded. "They cannot come back to Ochana with us and I don't feel comfortable leaving them."

"I see. May I offer a suggestion, Prince Colton?"

"Of course."

"It is more of a request, truly." Her round eyes widened as she spoke. "The farros are ancestors of the fairies. Over the years, we have tried many times to stop the hateful transgressions they have committed. Unfortunately, we have been unsuccessful. I ask that you give the farros over to us, so we can make right on our name and end the farros for good."

I thought about her request. If I handed over the farros to the fairies, it would solve the problem, and I wouldn't need to make any further decisions on the matter. Even with all their wrongdoings, I felt I couldn't be responsible in deciding their fate, not with the little knowledge I had. And technically, the farros were the fairies' responsibility; they were the ones who expelled them in the beginning. I looked at Eva and she nodded her agreement with my decision.

"I grant your request, Queen Annabelle. The farros are your responsibility, and I will put their fate in your hands."

"Thank you, Prince Colton, Keeper of Dragons." She bowed her head and made a hand gesture to the other fairies. "We will take them back to our home. I will send word to King Rylan when a judgment has been made in regards to their fate."

I nodded in consent as I watched the fairies grab the farros with invisible ropes which seemed to come from their fingers. The farros flailed their scrawny bodies and shouted to no avail. Tana looked furious as Queen Annabelle grabbed hold of her and flew off. Once the fairies were out of sight, I turned back to the dragons.

"Now what?" I asked.

"Now we go home, My Prince," Zane replied, preparing to shift into his dragon. "You have a coronation to attend."

Chapter Seventeen

Hours later, we arrived in Ochana. My first inbound glimpse of the magical kingdom was the stunning waterfall, which greeted us with luminous charm as we soared in. I managed to land gracefully in the center of Ochana. The castle lay to my right while the mountains peaked straight ahead. Dragons from every direction hurried over to welcome us back. Some dragons flew in, while others had waited nearby for our entry. The trip home had been uneventful; no one spoke much on the way, completely lost in their own thoughts about what we'd witnessed. The biggest surprise of the night had been my Uncle Zane. I was full of curiosity and anticipation for the story he would have to tell soon. My uncle had waited two hundred years for the events that happened mere hours ago to finally unfold.

Rylan and Sila were front and center as I landed. They both rushed over to me. Sila enveloped me in an unexpected hug, while Rylan gave me a firm pat on the back, a beaming smile on his face. He walked over to Zane and Jericho while Sila stuck around to greet Eva.

"I am eager to hear everything that happened with Queen Tana and the farros. Come let's gather in the council room. We will have time to celebrate later!" Rylan exclaimed.

Along with the council and a few extra dragons, we followed Rylan to the council room. We stepped through the waterfall, and, for the first time since arriving at Ochana, I allowed my senses to enjoy my surroundings; I marveled at the flowing waterfall and the blue, cloudless sky . The council room looked exactly the same as it did last time I was here, the night the council voted on the destiny of Eva and me. It seemed like so long ago, but in fact it was only last night. I took my assigned seat and waited as everyone shuffled in and got comfortable.

"Everyone find a seat, we have much to discuss." Rylan turned to Zane. "Let's start from the beginning. The floor is yours, brother."

Zane nodded and stood, pacing from one end of the room to the other. He fought to find the words to start. Finally, he looked up from the ground, took a deep breath, and exhaled.

"It all began the night of Jago's death." His eyes stopped on Rylan's. "He was murdered by the farros."

"How do you know this? The healers they said his mahier was drained." Rylan sounded skeptical.

"It was. The farros used their tillium to do exactly that. They wanted us to think we were being punished. They used our absence from the outside world to their advantage." Zane pulled at his hair. "They hadn't expected a Woland as strong as Jago. It was dumb luck for the farros to be able to get their hands on the prince when he was alone." He paused and I felt the shame radiating off of him. "I was with him, but I was too slow to keep up. If he had waited just a few seconds for me..." He trailed off as he looked back to the ground.

"You'd be dead as well," Jericho stated. "The farros would have gotten their hands on two princes and we would have been none the wiser."

"Why didn't he call for backup when he saw the farros?" Rylan asked.

"He didn't know. We saw a boat out in the sea. We figured some humans were lost or hurt. You knew Jago." Zane shook his head. "He would give his life for the humans. He didn't even stop to question it, just flew off to help them." Zane looked back up. "By the time I got there, the farros were gone and Jago was barely alive."

"Why didn't you tell us all this the night it happened? So much would have been different." Rylan interrupted as he glared at Zane.

"Jago made me promise. He didn't want the farros to know he had survived for even a second. If either of us had told you that night, you would have declared war and flown off to battle." Zane glared right back at Rylan. "Right?"

"Of course I would have. It would have been the right decision."

"No. Jago knew we'd been ignoring our duties as protectors. He wanted his death to mean something, something more than war. He wanted us to remember who we were." He pointed to himself as his voice started to rise. "We are dragons, protectors of all that is true." He paused to let his words sink in to all that were listening. "We had forgotten our responsibilities, our obligations to all. He knew what was happening to him and he knew the conclusion our healers would come to."

"It's been two hundred years, Zane!" Rylan shouted. "Look at the sacrifices our dragons have made." His arms went wide. "All over a lie."

"He was right, it was the only way. If we'd been doing our jobs, we would have seen the farros coming a mile away. Instead, we were living in our bubble, ignoring all that was going wrong with the world. Think of all the tragedies we could have prevented." He shook his head and sat back in his chair.

"What happened next?" Rylan asked. "After his death you kept your distance from everyone. You were seen leaving Ochana at odd hours. There were many rumors."

"I started forming relationships with many ill-fated creatures. My goal was to befriend the farros and convince them I wanted to destroy the dragons as vengeance for the way I was being treated." He laughed, "It was easy to come up with a plausible story. And of course they bought it. It took many years, but eventually I was brought into their inner fold, let in on many secrets." He turned to Jericho. "You need to get the Woland guard ready. The farros were able to create many allies. Once these creatures get wind of the farros' fate, they will come after us and fight in their place."

"Wait," Rylan interrupted. "Why did it take so long? You must have been given many opportunities to end them."

"I did. But one thing led to another. The information they were able to get their hands on was staggering. Every time a situation arose where I could finish them, something would happen. A different creature would approach them, asking to help them in their war. Creatures I thought long extinct were coming out of the woodworks."

"The carnites?" Rylan asked.

"Were only one of many. We had our guard down for too long, and it gave them time to hide, find new homes, and make new friends." Zane exhaled loudly before he continued. "We are sitting in the middle of a war. A war none of you knew was even going on."

"Must not be much of a war if we know nothing of it," Rylan stated.

"That's because the war is against you. How many years before Jago's death did we keep our heads in the sand?" Zane asked. "Around a hundred. For a hundred years, these creatures were building an army, an army to defeat us. The farros may have started it all, but they had just a small part in the grand scheme."

"Where were these creatures tonight?" Jericho asked. "The farro knew we were coming. Their army should've been raring to go."

"Some were there—the carnites and the eldens." He ticked them off his fingers as gasps went off around the table. "Remember, the farros weren't expecting me to turn on them." He paused. "My guess, they saw what our Keeper of Dragons did to the farros and took off."

"Eldens? Are you sure?" Jules whispered, clearly startled by the news.

"Positive. I spoke with King Eldrick myself. They are very much involved in this war," Zane affirmed.

"What happened to the farros?" Rylan asked. "How were you able to defeat them?" He turned my way with an expectant look.

"I don't really know. Somehow I was able to steal their tillium from them." I looked over to Eva, who gestured for me to continue. "I can still feel it running through my body."

"With your mahier?" Rylan asked.

"I don't know. I mean I haven't even mastered opening doors. But somehow I was able to suck all the tillium out of the farros."

"I've tried many times to do what Prince Colton did," Zane added. "I was unsuccessful every time. Even when the farros transferred some of their tillium to me, I wasn't able to do much with it. All it did was make my mahier stronger."

"I would bet it has something to do with the pair of them." Allas pointed to Eva and me. "Being the Keeper of Dragons and all. There is much we don't understand about them. I will have to speak to Meka again, see if the prophecy says anything about their powers."

"They are another reason my plans were put off." Zane nodded at us. "Somehow, the farros figured out who they were. Tana attempted to explain it to me; she said they were drawn to them, the power within them. She had a constant watch on them for the last eight years. The farros were waiting until they fully came into their powers, then they planned on turning the prince and golden dragon against you to aid them in their war," Zane explained.

"That would've never happened. We would have never trusted them," Eva stated with conviction.

"Dark creatures have a way with persuasion," Sila added quietly.

"The sun has already risen; you must all get some sleep. Rest and relax. It sounds like we won't have much time in the future for either." Rylan gestured for everyone to stand.

A few murmurs sounded in the council room as everyone filed out. Eva and I waited by the door for Rylan and Sila. My mind raced with the future. More creatures were coming our way, all with the same goal—defeat the dragons and take control.

"We'll figure it out," Eva stated. "We were able to defeat the farros. I have confidence we will be successful again."

"I'm glad you have so much faith in us. Maybe it was dumb luck? We had no idea what we were doing," I stammered.

"You will train," Jericho interrupted. "We have a program for all new dragons when they return to Ochana. Of course, they are usually placed in one course based on their founder. Seeing how you take after all four, we'll have to combine the four courses just for you." He paused. "Well, the two of you."

Rylan and Sila walked up beside Jericho, and the five of us turned and walked toward the caves that would lead us to the castle. There was one question that still bothered me. Zane had told a story about my grandparents to the farros, but it couldn't be true, could it?

"What story is that, my son?" Sila asked.

I turned to Rylan, who stood in close proximity to Sila. "Zane said you banished them from Ochana after the death of Jago. That it was your first ruling as king."

Rylan chuckled. "Part of that story is true. I did take over as king after Jago's death. But as for your grandparents, they are still here in Ochana. I believe the human term is retired. After what happened to Jago, your grandfather stepped down. He held immense guilt for his death."

"Wait, Zane also said something about a coronation. You're not stepping down, are you?" There was no way I was ready to be a king. Rylan could retire in, say, five hundred years, and I might be ready then. Maybe.

"No, son. But we will be holding a coronation for you in two days' time. You will be the first prince to have one. It will be your formal introduction to the dragons here on Ochana." He paused as we stepped into the castle. "The preparations for your return have been going on for a few years now. I expect it will be one of the grandest events ever to be held here."

"Eva, darling, come with me. I will show you to your room." Sila gestured for Eva to follow her. "Goodnight, son, get some rest." Sila squeezed my hand as she walked by and Eva gave me a small wave over her shoulder.

"I'm very proud of you, son. Your actions tonight prove you are the true Prince of Ochana. I see great things in your future. Goodnight." Rylan nodded to me and walked down the hall away from me but not before I heard a small chuckle.

I turned to face my door and laughed out loud. Now was as good a time as ever to practice opening the door.

J.A. Culican

Chapter Eighteen

I woke up to the sun shining in my eyes through the open curtains in my room. It was the day of my coronation, or my royal debut, as I'd rather it be called. I stretched and looked to my door, which was closed, the new, polished wood shining in the sun. It seemed my mahier with the added tillium was much stronger than anyone had anticipated. Yesterday morning, when I tried to open my door, it completely exploded and turned to dust, which set off every alarm on the island to my complete embarrassment. Once everyone settled and had a good laugh at my expense, I was finally able to get some rest.

Jericho had woken me up later that day to show me the Woland training facilities and explained to Eva and me the different courses on combat and strategy we would be expected to take. He explained to me how the other Wolands would test us and make us prove our worth, not just because I was the prince, because Eva and I were the Keeper of Dragons. Jericho then passed us on to Jules, who took us up to the Temple of Aprella. Even though Galians were known as the nurturers, she explained that most of our Galian training would take place here. We were to study the Book of Aprella and learn the long history of the dragons.

Luka had met us on the steps of the temple to take us into town. It was our first trip into Ochana. Eva and I were in awe at the sights around us. The energy that surrounded the dragons as they bustled about to complete their tasks was intoxicating. While we watched the dragons, Luka explained that we would not complete the same type of course work as the other Siens due to our role as part of the council. Each Sien was trained to complete a specific job, including production of goods or a service provider. They were assessed when they came of age as to what path they would take. Eva and I would be required to take a crash course in both, shadowing different Siens as they completed their tasks and responsibilities. It was the best way for us to understand the importance of the Siens' work.

Luka then dropped us off in the council room where we met with Allas. She, of course, deemed the coursework we were to complete with her the most important—leadership and etiquette. Only a small number of dragons ever got the chance to work alongside the Leslos, for their numbers were much lower than the other founding groups.

A knock at the door brought me out of my memories from the day before. I walked over to the door and opened it without incident, to my great relief. I had practiced opening and closing my new door at least a hundred times before I went to bed the night before. Sila's smile greeted me from the other side.

"May I come in?" she asked with an even bigger smile.

"Of course." I waved her in.

She sat at the table I had only used so far for eating breakfast. That thought made my stomach growl and I wondered where Mira was.

"She is busy helping the others get ready for today. Do not worry, I will escort you to the hall for breakfast." She gestured for me to have a seat next to her. "How are you feeling today? Did you rest well?"

"I did. I don't even remember falling into bed I was so exhausted. I am, however, a bit nervous for the events today." I watched my hand as my fingers picked at the edge of the table.

"I understand your nerves. Today is a big day, not only for you, but all of Ochana. You are the first ever prince to be introduced at eighteen. Every prince before you was introduced just days after their birth," Sila explained.

"Shouldn't we call it a royal debut then, or a grand ceremony? I mean, coronation to me is so formal. Where I come from, it only happens when a royal is to become a king or a queen, but I will be staying in the same position," I reflected.

Sila placed her hand over mine on the table. "Today, you will officially become the Prince of Ochana, a milestone for all that live here. An official ceremony has been written and rewritten many times just for you, just for this day." She squeezed my hand and let go. "When it is over, you will understand why today is much more than just a debut." She winked at me and stood. "Go get ready, I will wait for you in the hall."

I showered and washed up as quickly as I could and threw on an outfit that had appeared on my bed while I was in the shower. I met Sila in the hallway in record time, and as I closed the door behind me, I could hear her chuckle. It seemed it would take quite a bit of time for anyone to forget about my little incident with the door.

***

The procession started much like a wedding. As soon as the music started, Meka, who held the Book of Aprella high in the air above her head, led the council on a walk down the path that would bring us to the castle steps. Eva and I followed behind them, our hands held tight. Rylan and Sila were behind us, and Zane behind them.

As we reached the steps, Meka trotted to the top with the book still held high. The council stopped at the bottom of the stairs and bowed, then split into two groups as they took their places on the steps below Meka; two to the right and two to the left. Eva and I stopped at the bottom of the steps and bowed as we'd been instructed to do earlier in the day. Rylan, Sila, and Zane stopped behind us to do the same. As I looked up at Meka and the council, I made note of their robes, each represented the four founding dragons. Allas wore a green robe that represented the Leslos, Luka donned the Siens' signature silver, Jules was draped in a blue robe for the Galians, and Jericho wore a red robe that represented the Wolands.

Rylan and Sila walked around us and took their spots in the center, halfway up the steps, while Zane strode up and stood on the other side of Eva.

Rylan lifted his arms. "Welcome, all of Ochana on this momentous day. This day will be marked in our history books as we celebrate the coronation of my son, Prince Colton of Ochana!" Rylan exclaimed as the dragons behind us clapped and cheered.

I took my cue and walked forward to ascend the castle steps, stopping right below Rylan and Sila, head bowed. I prayed no one could see how nervous I was.

"Eighteen years ago, you were born to Queen Sila and myself, giving us great joy." Rylan tilted my chin up so I had no choice but to look him in the eyes. "With joy came sadness as we handed you over to your human parents, Michael and Ella. We will forever be grateful to them for raising you to be the man you are today. The bond that was created between the three of you will live in your heart for the rest of your life. Use the love you have for them as a light during your journey as a protector." Rylan placed a hand on the top of my head, his other held high in the air as he continued. "Today we offer you the gifts of our four founding dragons, gifts that will reinforce your title as Prince of Ochana and guide you on your passage as our next king, if you so do accept." Rylan removed his hand from my head and stepped away from me.

Luka took Rylan's place in front of me. In his hands, he clutched a golden robe fashioned with the insignia of each founding dragon. He held the robe out for me. "I offer you this robe, created by the eyes and stitched by the hands of the Siens, as a gift and a promise to always stand by your side. This robe represents togetherness and friendship. Do you accept, My Prince?" Luka asked.

"I do," I answered as Luka placed the robe over my shoulders and walked back to his spot.

Jules stepped down next and stood in front of me, holding out a scepter; on the end of it were four dragon heads with one of the largest gems I had ever seen held between them. "My Prince, I offer you this scepter to represent power and wealth. The Galians handpicked the diamond from the royal hoard to be placed between the four founding dragons. This scepter represents our everlasting bond and commitment to each other. Do you accept our gift, My Prince?" Jules asked.

"I do," I responded as I took hold of the scepter with my right hand.

Jericho stood in front of me next. He held out a sword enclosed within a scabbard. "My Prince, it is with honor that I offer you this gift representing strength and courage." He pulled the sword out of its scabbard and held it high. "This sword was created with the strongest of graphene and the fire of Wolands. Do you accept this gift?" he asked with his head bowed.

"I do." Jericho placed the scabbard over my head, positioning the sword by my left hip.

Allas joined me next, standing in front of me with a crown held out in front of her. The crown was a single layer of gems. "My Prince, I offer you this crown to represent knowledge and leadership. This crown was crafted with four precious jewels to represent our four founding dragons. The emeralds represent the Leslos, the rubies, the Wolands, the sapphires, the Galians, and the obsidians represent the Siens. These four gems are welded together using dragon fire. Do you accept our gift?"

"I do." She placed the crown over the top of my head. It rested just above my ears.

Rylan returned to his position in front of me. "It is an honor to introduce to all, my son, Prince Colton of Ochana!" Rylan announced as he turned me to face the dragons below.

It was my first real glimpse of all of Ochana. It seemed every dragon was here to witness my coronation. They clapped and cheered as they took me in donning the gifts I just accepted. Rylan's voice brought my attention back to him as he turned me around to face him again.

"Not only today do we acknowledge your birthright as Prince of Ochana, but we acknowledge your right as the Keeper of Dragons," Rylan stated. "I ask that your other half join us as you both take your oath as such."

Eva climbed up the steps and stood to my right. Her beautiful gold dress—custom created by a group of Siens to signify Eva's role as the golden dragon—sparkled as it flowed behind her.

Rylan placed one hand on my head and the other on Eva's. He then tilted his head up toward the sky as he spoke. "The Keeper of Dragons have been gifted to us by our mother, Aprella. We accept her gift with open hearts and fierce protection." The crowd behind us echoed Rylan's last words.

He looked down at us, his eyes glowing bright green. "I offer you my protection as you lead us out of this time of fear." Again, all of Ochana repeated his words.

"Do you, the Keeper of Dragons, accept our gift?" Rylan asked.

Eva's hand found mine as we spoke together, "We do."

Rylan's hands fell from our heads and we turned to face the dragons of Ochana. Everyone clapped and cheered. Music started to play and many dragons began to dance along the grassy grounds that surrounded the castle. I watched as a few shifted and blew their dragonic breathing fire into the air to demonstrate their excitement.

"Wherever you lead them, they will follow," Rylan whispered in my ear as he passed by to lead our procession back through the streets of Ochana. "Our trust lies with the two of you."

My future was full of unknowns and I knew the constant threats would continue to be placed on my shoulders. I didn't know what the future held or how it would turn out. But one thing I knew for sure—as long as I had Eva and my new family by my side, I would fight.

THE ELVEN ALLIANCE
KEEPER OF DRAGONS
BOOK 2

For my lone prince Gabriel.

Chapter One

Bam! My back slammed against the floor for what felt like the hundredth time this morning. My ears rang as I dragged myself back to my feet, glaring at Jericho. My body ached everywhere; we had been at the Woland training facility for the last three hours. It consisted of three separate levels, and when you graduated one, you moved up to the next. Once you reached the third floor or level, you were considered a trainee for the Woland guard. Jericho was determined to make me a Woland warrior, but had so far only succeeded in making me a laughing stock among the other young hopefuls; I had been unable to move off of ground level. Hence the fact that I was still stuck on the ground floor.

When sparring with other Wolands, my uniform consisted of a pair of dark red shorts and a black t-shirt bearing the royal insignia. The insignia illustrated a green dragon wrapped around a silver, red, and blue sword to represent the four founding dragons in all of their colorful beauty. Right now my clothes were in disarray, accurately mirroring how the rest of me felt. I chanced a glance around the room only to be mortified by the laughter in my fellow trainee's eyes as an eruption of whispering dispersed amongst them about my constant failures. It was clear I wasn't a warrior or any kind of fighter. I had no place in the Woland guard, obviously Jericho hadn't received the memo yet because he continued to drag me here each and every day.

"Back of the line, Jameson," Jericho growled.

It took me a minute to regain my wits so I could head to the back of the line. I was still getting used to being called by my last name during training. The one shining light throughout this horror was that they let me keep my adoptive parents' name.

As I stumbled to the back of the line, the other Wolands elbowed me here and there through spiteful snickers. You would think they'd be scared to treat the Prince this way. Then again, each one of them had been successful in taking me down more times than I could count. The average Woland only stayed on the first level a week. I was now on week three, with no end in sight.

From the back of the line I was unable to see over the heads of my fellow recruits. The sounds of the next match drifted back to me at the end of the line as the next sparring session begun, and I exhaled a sigh of relief. For the time being I was glad to catch my breath and regroup before attention was sure to be back on me. At the present moment, all eyes were on the fight ahead. The other dragons cheered and whistled with each sound of skin on skin as I hid in the back. The last three weeks had been horrible. Each morning Jericho would drag me from the safety of my room to train with the other Wolands, who arrived daily as they turned 18. Without a moment's rest, I would be shuffled off to my next session, usually with the Sien's, and then off to the next with the Gailan's. My last session of the day was usually with the Leslo's or one of the councilmembers. As a result of my failures during the incessant training, Eva and I had been separated almost immediately. She had excelled in every area and moved up quickly to the third and final levels. Jericho squashed my moment of solitude with a growl.

"Focus," he snarled.

I turned to give him my attention, which was the wrong move. Jericho grabbed my chin and forcefully shifted my head towards the fight I still couldn't see from my vantage point. He held my head in place until he was satisfied I wouldn't move.

"Stop sulking and pay attention. You will learn nothing if you do not focus," he huffed. "Tell me, what do you see?" He placed his hands on my shoulders from behind.

I hesitated a moment. "I can't see anything from back here," I explained.

"Wrong answer. Look again."

I searched my surrounding area, but all I could see were my fellow dragons as they hooted and hollered at the match ahead. Their camaraderie made me feel even more isolated as they patted each other on the back and pointed at the two Wolands wrestling ahead.

"That is the right answer." Jericho stated after reading my thoughts. With one last squeeze to my shoulders, he strode to the front of the room, out of my sight.

I lowered my head with a slight shake. I wanted to be a part of the group. I wanted to make some friends. But the truth was, I didn't know how, and even if I did, no one wanted me around. As the Prince and the Keeper of Dragons, I had so many things working against me. You'd think my rank would give me an added edge, but in reality it meant I had to prove myself even more. My clumsy, uncoordinated, cowardly self didn't stand a chance. I was no Woland.

"You're dismissed." Jericho's voice reverberated through the air with a solid conclusiveness.

The Wolands collected their things, chatting as they exited the training center together. I stayed behind and waited for my next directive. Each day brought something new, and I never knew exactly what was going to happen day to day, or what would be expected of me. I walked over to the corner of the room to retrieve my belongings I stashed when we first arrived. Quickly, gathering my stuff, I walked towards Jericho. He was deep in intense conversation with two Woland instructors. None paid me any mind as I plodded over to them. Not wanting to seem like I was eavesdropping, I looked around the room for something to do. I noticed the mats were still out and began to walk towards them. That's when Jericho stopped me in my tracks.

"Follow me," Jericho growled, throwing his bag over his shoulder.

I fell in step behind him as he led the way out the doors and into the sunshine. Ochana was a sight to behold. It was midmorning and the day was already in full swing. The market was going strong as dragons shopped and socialized with each other. While we walked, dragons would stop everything they were doing and bow towards me. It always amazed me the respect the older dragons had for me. To my peers, I was a joke, but everyone else showed me complete respect. It was a respect I still felt I hadn't earned. I'd rather fall somewhere in the middle where I could blend in and just belong.

"You will be shadowing Cairo today as he checks the perimeter of Ochana. I realized you have yet to see Ochana for all its glory," Jericho acknowledged, piercing me with his signature red-eyed gaze. "You need to learn the ins and outs of Ochana. That starts with learning the ways to protect it and keep all residing dragons here safe. Trust your dragon and keep your senses sharp. This will be the first time you are off the island since our return."

"What about my other lessons?" I questioned. An excitement I hadn't felt in a while started to buzz around me. I had been dying to see all of Ochana since I arrived, and it seemed this perimeter check would be from the air. A smile crept across my face as I bounced in anticipation

"We have a council meeting later that you are required to attend," Jericho said as he leapt up the steps to the command center. "Your regular lessons will continue tomorrow."

I nodded as we entered the mighty glass building that overlooked the west side of Ochana. Wolands were busy monitoring all of Ochana. I observed the scene as Garrik sat in the back corner tapping on his computer. He was surrounded by glass walls and completely engrossed in his task. I began to walk towards him, but was intercepted by Jericho.

"Cole, my office," Jericho commanded, never breaking stride as he headed towards a group of Wolands.

Jericho had the best office in the command center; it was enclosed around four walls made of complete glass, three of which overlooked the clouds that surrounded and protected Ochana. Plopping down on one of the uncomfortable black chairs in front of his desk, I looked out the nearest window and waited for Jericho to join me. Nervousness zipped through me, I could only imagine what he wanted to speak to me about.

Suddenly, the door slammed shut and Jericho whipped past me to the window. He stood in silence with his back to me. The excitement I just felt vanished. Jericho made me nervous when he ignored me like this. I tried to relax my breathing; the last thing I wanted was for him to know how uneasy I was. For some reason, I wanted him to see me as strong.

"You've been distracted. Have you forgotten who you are? What you are capable of?" Jericho's voice was laced with disappointment.

I knew who I was, but everyone else seemed to have forgotten. I was Cole. Just Cole. Plain, ordinary Cole. Jericho turned to face me, his eyes glowing with fire. I kept my eyes on him as he tracked each one of my nervous fidgets.

"You defeated the farros. Something us dragons have tried and failed many times in our history," he barked, cocking his head in disbelief. "If it takes plain, ordinary Cole to do that, then I will take him." His voice softened a bit.

I had no words. He was right, and wrong at the same time. It was Eva and I who defeated the farros, not just me. I continued to look at Jericho as my mind contemplated a way to explain this to him without causing smoke to billow from his ears.

"You're right." He turned towards the window, his back facing me once again. "You are only one half of the Keeper of Dragons. The two of you need to train together. Keeping you separate is not beneficial to either of you." He huffed out a great breath, causing the condensation on the window to expand and then disappear. He bowed his head. "For now on, the two of you will train together. You're a team. The Keeper of Dragons." He sighed and glared at me over his shoulder. "Go to Garrik, Cairo will be here soon. I need to work." Jericho stated, dismissing me.

I stood and headed towards the door. At least I knew how to open it now. There once was a time I'd be trapped in his office with him until someone else came and opened the door for me. I shook that thought off, placed my hand on the royal insignia, and willed the door to open using my mahier. Once through, I made my way over to Garrik who was still in the same spot, only now he punched at his keyboard with deliberate, angry strokes.

I stood behind him in silence, not wanting to bother Garrik while he worked. He huffed in agitation, pounding harder on his keyboard and grumbling unintelligently under his breath. Abruptly, he stood up and his chair flopped to the ground behind him, nearly hitting my feet. Without so much as an acknowledgment, he stormed towards Jericho's office. The door slammed behind him, effectively barring the two within. Visible through the glass wall, they squared off in a heated discussion. Garrik's arms moved wildly as he explained something to Jericho, who stood with his hands on his hips, nodding his head.

In coordination, both their heads swung my way, eyes glowing in a look I was unable to decipher. I took a step back involuntarily; almost tripping over the chair Garrik had knocked on the floor. I righted myself and picked up the chair, incapable of taking my eyes off them.

What did I do now?

Chapter Two

Garrik and Jericho stared at me through the glass wall, neither making a move towards me. Unable to think of anything I had done that would make them this irate, I wasn't sure what to do now. Even from the distance between us, I could see the flames dancing in their eyes.

Finally, Garrik broke his gaze from me and walked out the crystal door towards me. Jericho kept his glare pointed at me the whole time; I swore smoke was billowing from behind him. I sent a silent prayer to anyone who could be listening that it was only my eyes playing a trick on me. Jericho in full-fledged smoky dragon mode terrified me. Once Garrik reached me he looked over his shoulder at Jericho, and with a shake of his head he gestured for me to follow him.

I broke the connection between Jericho and myself and stumbled behind Garrik out of the command center and into the bright sunshine of Ochana. I took a deep breath to calm my nerves and muster enough courage to ask Garrik what that was all about. I had finally prepared myself to spit out the words when he turned my way and shook his head at me. It was clear I wouldn't get an answer out of him.

"I need you to focus, truly focus." Garrik glared at me as he spoke. "Stay close to Cairo and don't get distracted." He paused "We haven't seen anything out there," he pointed to the clouds. "But having you off the island could attract any number of creatures."

"What do you mean attract any number of creatures?" I stammered. What creatures could be out there?

Garrik sighed. "The farros were attracted to something within you." He flicked my chest with his finger. "Others could be as well." With that last statement he bowed, looked over my shoulder and left.

I shook my head at his odd behavior. What was all that about? Wasn't I supposed to meet Cairo to do a perimeter check? I turned to head back to the castle when I collided with what felt like a brick wall. I fell backward with a solid jolt, hitting what felt like a wall that I realized was actually Cairo. With a puff of smoke, he shook me off, his scales glinting red in the sunlight. Cairo the dragon towered over me.

"Shift." Cairo's voice growled through my head.

I centered myself and willed my dragon to appear. My shifts had become easier the last few weeks. It was the one part of this whole ordeal that I had improved on. I wasn't as fluid as Cairo, but still, I was impressed with my progress. Seconds later, I painlessly shifted into my colorful dragon. My scales breached through my pale human skin and instantaneously gleamed in the sunlight. I stretched my neck high, moving it side to side, waiting for instructions. My upstretched excitement created a sudden buzz of energy. I hadn't been allowed out of an elder's or my parents' sight since the whole farro debacle. I was itching to get into the air and truly see Ochana for the first time.

"We will circle the perimeter of Ochana. Keep your senses sharp because you will sense danger before you see it." As soon as Cairo finished he pushed off the ground with his solid hind legs and leapt into the sky, officially cutting off any response I may have had.

I followed behind as close as I could. Garrik's warning made me nervous. Everything had been quiet since that night at the Grove. Queen Annabelle had contacted Rylan with the arranged punishment for the farros. I had no idea what it was, no one would tell me. But Rylan seemed satisfied.

My head burst through the first sheet of clouds as we proceeded back to Ochana. It was a brilliant sight; I could see the waterfall cascading from the island towards the sea below, the sparkling water disappearing as it made contact with the clouds underneath. Dragons milled around Ochana, stopping to talk with each other and continue on their way. I looked away from the marvelous sight only to find that the fifth realm had surrounded me. I was sandwiched between Cairo and their leader, Jude. The other Wolands circled us restlessly.

I should have known better, especially with that little warning from Garrik. No way would they let me off the island with Cairo as my only guard. Now that I thought of it, I was surprised Cairo was off the island without Eva. He had been her personal guard these last few weeks, never leaving her side.

"You're distracted." Cairo's voice rang through my head. "This is a perimeter check, keep your senses open to everything around you. You just let realm five sneak up on you. They could have been any number of creatures bent on destroying you," Cairo chastised me.

He was right. I steadied my breathing and attempted to open up my senses. Sila and I spent many hours together these last few weeks working on just this. Once I build up enough tolerance and get better control of my mahier, I should be able to keep my senses open constantly. Right now, I'm able to keep them open for a few hours at a time before I become exhausted and need to rest.

Now I was able to feel the six Wolands that surrounded me. I sensed each breath and movement they made, and could even anticipate their next actions. I extended my senses out as far as I could. Thanks to the farro, my mahier was unstable due to the added tilium in my system. Whenever I attempted to exert my mahier, something would blow up or break. The elders believed this was due to the tilium residing in my blood that I had stolen from the farros. Luckily, I could physically feel when I had pushed my mahier to the blowup point. My body would shake and shudder as the energy zipped through me. As soon as I felt this, I would pull my mahier in, rest for a bit, and everything would go back to normal.

I began to tremble. I hadn't pushed my mahier to the breaking point yet; I had barely used any, but that now familiar feeling had befallen me. As quickly as I could, I pulled back my mahier while calling out to Cairo. Something was wrong.

"Relax Cole, reel it in," Cairo called to me, his voice calm and steady.

Energy whizzed through my blood and scales as I nodded to Cairo's words. I pulled almost all my mahier in, leaving just enough out to keep myself shifted. It wasn't enough though, my body continued to shake. My movements became choppy as I slowed and began to lose altitude.

"Release your energy," Cairo shouted. "Release it now!"

I didn't understand what he wanted from me. My mahier was in, and as far as I could tell, so was my tilium.

"No, Cole. Release your fire!" Cairo shouted through my head, clearly reading my thoughts. His voice wavered from fear.

I had no idea how to do that. I had seen the other Wolands eject dragon fire during the battle with the farros, and Jericho when he was angry. But it never crossed my mind that I would also be able to breathe fire. I attempted to focus on myself, feel inside myself. I hoped I could feel the fire and instincts would kick in. But nothing. I felt nothing. My emotions were too unsteady for me to focus.

And suddenly, my wings stopped beating, frozen. My body fell towards Ochana and panic began to take over. Inside my head, realm five debated on how to stop me. The ground was close. Too close.

I tried to scream in fear, but no sound came out. I no longer had control of my vocal cords. Fire exploded from my mouth, almost catching the Woland who had moved close to aid me in my fall. Right before impact, my wings began to flap again and I took off into the clouds. With each breath, more fire burst from out of my throat and viciously poured from my mouth. I should've felt overheated, but the opposite was true. The more fire I exhaled, the cooler I felt. My mind began to clear and I felt more in control of myself than I had in weeks.

During my last fireball blow, silver sparks shot from my claws. In my head echoed the confused chatter from realm five as more Wolands responded to the call for help. Below me, close to fifty Woland looked up at me through the sparkling lights emanating from my talons. Each spark formed a compressed feeling in my throat that I hadn't experienced before, and wasn't aware of its foundation. I closed my eyes, took a deep breath, and as the last spark fell, I exhaled a large veil of smoke from my nose.

Opening my eyes, I met Jericho's red gaze. I could see the fear, but there was another emotion I couldn't decode. Cairo and Garrik flew behind him with puzzled expressions pervading their eyes.

"You good?" Jericho asked.

"Yea, I feel great." I laughed. "Better than I have in weeks." And that was the truth.

Jericho shook his large, red head at me and flew towards Ochana. I flashed a look at Cairo, hoping we would continue with the perimeter check, and that my little spectacle hadn't changed our plans.

"Sorry kid. Orders are to head in," Cairo answered my thoughts. "Your spectacle, as you put it, needs to be discussed," he explained with a chuckle.

Once again, realm five resumed their spots to escort me back to Ochana. For the first time, I landed with ease next to the waterfall. I looked up as a sense of déjà vu overtook me.

There stood three dragons in full regalia. Jericho shifted and joined the others as he pushed his long black hair out of his eyes. They stood backs straight and chins high. Four sets of gem-like eyes bored into me. Jericho's red eyes were the first to look away as he turned, snapping his fingers at the now ceased waterfall, and disappeared down the cave.

The council.

J.A. Culican

Chapter Three

I shifted quickly into my human form and followed the council through the waterfall. It poured around us as we walked through. Realm five followed close behind as my personal escort. Once we broke through the large cast iron doors, I darted to my designated seat and sank down with relief. I needed to figure out exactly what had just happened. Jude, seeing that I was safe and sound, signaled to the rest of realm five, and they turned to leave.

The rest of the council found their seats, all the while eyeing me up and down as if I was on display at the zoo. Choosing to ignore their now familiar glares, I averted my eyes from their scowls, and the large, round polished table stood center stage. Above us, an open ceiling let the natural light shine down. Along all four walls were pictures depicting the roles of the four founding dragons: Leslo, Galian, Sien and Woland.

Rylan sauntered in, followed by Sila, who patted my shoulder as she passed by. I enjoyed being gifted with Sila's small smile. My parents exemplified the perfect specimen of royalty. The King and Queen of Ochana—which made me, the Prince, next in line to be King of Ochana. I prayed nightly that such a day wouldn't happen for, say, 500 years. I finally looked around at the council, noticing Eva hadn't arrived yet. Council meetings seemed to be the only time we saw each other nowadays.

"The Golden Dragon, where is she?" Rylan questioned, scanning the room. His emerald eyes stopped on me as he tilted his head sideways.

"On her way, Sir, she was in the middle of a lesson with the Galian, Meka," Jules informed the king. "Cairo just left to escort her here."

Rylan's eyes left me as he nodded at Jules. "This meeting was called to address an incident involving the farros," Rylan stated.

I squirmed in my seat. The farros? I had hoped to never speak of them again. Especially their so-called Queen Tana. The woman frightened me to the core, her black, soulless eyes, razor-sharp teeth and cackle haunted my dreams. As Queen Annabelle had dragged her bound in fairy ropes from Farro Grove, she had threatened revenge. Since I held her tilium, I could only assume that revenge would be directed at me.

Jericho paced around the table. "Queen Annabelle of the fairies contacted us earlier today." He hesitated a moment. "The farros have disappeared."

"How?"

The question came from behind me. I turned as Eva entered the council room and took her seat beside me. She glared at Jericho, awaiting a response. Unlike everyone else, she never seemed intimidated by him.

"That's a good question," Jericho countered. "The fairies had constant eyes on them. The guards on duty at the time said they disappeared right in front of them." Jericho shook his head disbelievingly.

"That's impossible. Cole has their tilium, I can still feel it," Eva said, sliding her golden eyes my way

"You're right. Cole proved that to us mere minutes ago," Jericho said. "However, farros aren't the only creatures who wield tilium."

Jules huffed. "You can't mean-."

"The eldens," Zane interrupted. "The farros and the eldens have been working together for some time now. It makes sense they would help them. The eldens see the farros as dispensable, the first line of attack." He waved his hands around. "They will use them to destroy as many dragons and other true creatures as possible before they officially enter the war."

"Didn't the fairies have protection spells around their grove?" Eva asked, glaring at each of the council members. "How could the eldens break through without notice and take the farros?"

Jericho sighed, placed his hands on his hips and lowered his head to the ground. "The eldens are very powerful. Much more powerful than the fairies."

I tried to keep up. I was still stuck on the idea of Queen Tana being on the loose. "What are eldens?"

"Elves," Jericho explained, looking back up at me. "Like the farros, the eldens are fallen. Fallen elves."

Wonderful. Not only did I have the fallen fairies after me, I now had to worry about fallen elves or eldens.

"Send the Prince to the swamp," Allas suggested. "He's already proven he can steal tilium. Send him to steal the eldens'." Her jade eyes glanced around at the other council members, hoping they would agree with her proposal.

"No," Jericho answered before anyone else had a chance to agree. "We don't know what more tilium would do to the Prince. As it is, he is unable to control the tilium he has. Not to mention, he doesn't know how he stole it in the first place."

"I agree," Rylan chimed in. "First, we need to know for sure it was the eldens. I'm not interested in starting a war with them if we're wrong."

A chuckle came from beside me. "Hate to break it to you, big brother, but you're already in a war with the eldens. We've been through this." Zane chimed in. "They were there the night Prince Colton took the farros down, which means they know he holds their tilium."

"Why don't we make contact with the twins? They will know if the eldens are on the move," Luka, the councilman for the Sien's suggested as he scanned the table.

"Who are the twins?" Eva asked.

"The rulers of the Elves—Gaber and Clara. They come from a very powerful line." Jericho explained, sitting and turning towards Rylan. "May I give a suggestion?"

"Of course," Rylan tapped his long index finger against his chin.

"Let me contact Prince Gaber and speak with him about the eldens. I'd also like to discuss Prince Cole's training."

That got my attention. Why would the Prince of the elves be interested in training me and what would he train me on?

"Continue." Rylan cocked his head at me, then back to Jericho.

"The tilium within our Prince is unstable and hindering his true abilities. I would like Prince Gaber to work with him on it; no one here has ever experienced the likes of tilium before. Even when Tana gave Zane control of hers, he was unable to wield it."

"How do you propose we convince him to train the Prince?" Allas asked from beside Queen Sila, her green gaze directed at me.

"We have a treaty with them," Jericho stated. "Not to mention if the eldens are involved, the elves will want our help. And our Prince is the perfect weapon to defeat them for good." He explained before he turned his attention back to Rylan.

With a nod, Rylan responded. "Agreed. Contact Prince Gaber. I would like both Keeper of Dragons to be trained by the elves."

"My King," Cairo stood. "I would like to escort both the Prince and the golden dragon. Regardless of who freed the farros, they are out there and will be looking for the two of them." Cairo pointed at Eva and I as he spoke.

"Realm five will also accompany them," Jericho stated. "We have had little dealings with the elves in the past. Even with a treaty, we must be on alert."

"Make the arrangements," Rylan commanded. "As for the farros, find them." Rylan glared firmly at the council. "And find out who freed them." Rylan stood and walked towards the closed iron doors. "Colton, come with me," he spoke over his shoulder as he willed the doors to open.

I scrambled out of my seat at the surprise summon, and followed Rylan out the doors. In a much calmer manner, Sila followed behind me. While she was closing the doors behind us, I ran up to Rylan as he was passing though the waterfall and strolled to the edge of the island.

I stood behind him, afraid of getting too close to the edge. The view was remarkable; the pinnacles of the clouds blew peacefully by. Hard to believe a war was brewing beneath us.

"How do you feel?" Rylan's simple question pierced the quiet that had enveloped us.

"Okay," I answered quietly as I shifted from foot to foot.

Sila chuckled from behind me. "You breathed fire for the first time today. How does that make you feel?"

I thought about the question. I felt more myself than I had since I arrived. It was almost like releasing the fire made me more human.

"That's an interesting take on it," Sila answered my thoughts.

Rylan turned to face me. "You're more dragon now than human. It takes most new dragons many years to breathe fire. It took you mere weeks. Quite remarkable." Rylan had a look of pride on his face. "Then, of course, we have the tilium." His face expressed pure wonder.

"You're the first dragon to carry both maheir and tilium. The two are not meant to be mixed. It is why the tilium is so unstable within you." Sila placed her hand on my shoulder. "The elves will be able to help you control it," she said with a squeeze.

"Are you sure?" I asked with trepidation.

"The elves are the most powerful beings that wield tilium. Prince Gaber and Princess Clara are two of the strongest elves in existence," Rylan stated with confidence.

If they were unable to help me gain control of the tilium, I was in big trouble. Some of the council wanted me to head out to the eldens and take their tilium. Somehow. I sighed and looked up towards my parents, anxiety written on my face.

"It will all work out," Sila stated, removing her hand from my shoulder with one last squeeze.

I hoped she was right.

J.A. Culican

Chapter Four

I had been up and ready for at least two hours. I abandoned any attempt at sleeping after the last nightmare woke me in a cold sweat. As soon as I closed my eyes, visions of Tana and the farros flooded my head. I couldn't keep the dreams straight. One second, Tana and her flock of farros were descending on me, the next second they were gone. All that remained was her malicious laugh echoing through my head. Then there were the ones with the elves, or what I assumed to be the eldens. They were even creepier than Tana.

Looking out the floor-to-ceiling windows in my room, I rubbed my eyes. Ochana was just awakening; dragons trickled down from the mountains to begin their day. The sun had barely breached the mountains when a now-familiar pound on my door had my feet moving rapidly to answer it. As I reached for the royal insignia, the door swooshed open to reveal Jericho, his permanent scowl securely in place.

He stomped into my room and turned to face me. "We leave in twenty minutes. No need to pack, everything you need will be provided for you."

I huffed in exhaustion. What could he possibly have planned for me today? "Where are we going?"

Jericho's red eyes glared at me. For a moment I anticipated him to roll his eyes, but the action surprisingly didn't come. On second thought, it was way too early for that much emotion from him. Who was I kidding? The man never showed that much emotion.

"Prince Gaber has agreed to meet with you. Today." He paused. "Make sure to eat. We won't be making any unnecessary stops."

I looked around my room as if Mira would suddenly appear with breakfast in tow. A sigh to my right was the only sound Jericho made before the door swooshed shut behind him. The man really wasn't a morning person, or any time person.

Mere seconds later, a light knock on my door made me aware of Mira's arrival. In the last few weeks, I've learned to keep my distance as Mira set up breakfast. She darted throughout my room, gathering what she needed and quickly preparing the meal. I mused at her energy; I had never seen her move at a normal pace. "Here you go, my Prince. Is there anything else you may need?" She asked, bouncing on her toes, ready to move on to the next task.

I shook my head, sitting down on one of the chairs she had just set at the table. Jericho must have told her to bring extra food; there was an abundance, much more than I could ever eat.

"Join me?" I asked her politely. I hoped she would validate my thoughts on Jericho.

"No, my Prince. It's all for you. It seems you have a big journey ahead of you today."

I pondered what she said. Just like with the farro, I was going in blind. "Do you know where the elves live?"

"No. Sien's aren't given that type of information. We aren't allowed off the island unless accompanied by the Woland guard. I know very little about the elves." Mira explained, twirling her long black hair around her fingers. "Is there anything else you need, my Prince?"

"No, thanks, Mira," I said as she bounded out the door and on to her next duty.

Looking down at the food covering the table, I grabbed some eggs cooked over medium, exactly how I liked them, and some toast. There was no way I would be able to eat any more than this so early in the morning. I finished my breakfast and grabbed an energy drink off the table as I walked to the door. I had joked to Mira a few weeks back about how she acted like she drank a case of this caffeinated drink each morning. She's brought a can with my breakfast every day since. I had no idea how she acquired them, I doubt they are a part of a typical dragon's diet.

My guards were right behind me as I headed towards the command center. They never spoke to me, just silently stalked me as we walked. Eva and Cairo were waiting by the stairs that led up to the massive glass building. Eva saw me first. She ran towards me and threw her arms around me, enclosing me in the safety of her arms.

"I heard about yesterday. What was it like, breathing fire?" She whispered in my ear while holding me tight.

I laughed uncomfortably as she untangled herself from me. In the last week or so, she always greeted me in the same fashion. It seemed our constant distance from each other had been just as tough on her as it had on me.

Before I could answer, Jericho flew down the stairs, whipping past us as he approached the area designated for take-offs. "Let's go."

I followed behind him, still no idea where we were headed. Eva treaded at my side, and what I guessed would be our entourage for the trip adjacent to us. We maneuvered to the runway where we met my parents and the rest of the council. Sila hugged me tightly. It was a strange move for her; normally I would get a squeeze on the shoulder or a pat on the back. I tentatively hugged her back.

"Stay strong, my son," Sila whispered in my ear as she let go of me. She turned towards Rylan, who had just joined us.

"Prince Gaber is a noble warrior. It's an honor to be trained by him," Rylan nodding as he squeezed my shoulder.

I shook my head, not sure of what to say. A noble warrior? He sounded like Jericho. I wasn't sure I could handle two Jericho's. I turned to Eva, who had already shifted into her impressive golden counterpart. Her gold wings flapped happily in the breeze as she spoke with Sila.

"Shift," Jericho growled, passing by me in mid-shift.

He completed his shift before I had a chance to respond. His Woland stared down at me with piercing impatience enflaming from his eyes. I stood up straight and cracked my neck side to side as I called to my dragon. My transformation happened with ease now, each time a bit quicker. My colorful scales enveloped me as my powerful tail appeared and spikes flew up my back. With a quick exhale my wings exploded from my back, spread wide ready to fly.

The Wolands around me began to shoot into the air, creating a perimeter for Eva and I to fly in. Again, I wondered where we were heading. Where would elves live? The only information I had overheard was that the eldens lived in a swamp. Training in a swamp didn't sound like fun.

"The Congo," Cairo's voice echoed in my head. "Central Africa." With that he pushed off the ground and joined the other Wolands in the sky.

Eva pushed off the ground then too, but did so with an air of grace. I took off and followed behind her. All I knew of the Congo was that it was a rainforest. A rainforest meant all types of bugs and snakes, both of which I hated. You would think growing up in Texas, snakes wouldn't bother me, but on the contrary, they creeped me out.

No one spoke for a long time. They were either lost within their own thoughts, or enjoying the flight. The sky irradiated a clear, bright blue as we made our way south, flying over the Atlantic Ocean towards our destination. I picked up quickly that the dragons preferred to fly over water than land. It was easier to keep themselves hidden, and there were less obstacles to mask themselves from.

"Stay close to me once we land." Jericho's bark interrupted my thoughts. "Do not speak unless I tell you to."

"Okay. How much further do we have?" We had traveled quite far already. Water and clouds completely surrounded us; no land was in sight.

"Not too much longer." He paused in thought. "Prince Gaber will be waiting for us by the shore. He will escort us from there."

I tried to picture what he may look like. All I could imagine when I heard the word elf was Santa's elves- tiny creatures with pointy ears. Something told me these elves would be much different, especially the Prince, considering the warrior status he held with Rylan.

Jericho huffed from beside me; the Wolands around me had begun their decent. In the distance a large area of land, presumably Africa became visible. As the clouds parted, the rocky cliffs spanning along the shore were evident; no beach was in sight, like I had pictured. I saw no one as we approached. Maybe the Prince had changed his mind?

"He's there. I can feel him," Jericho growled through my head.

I attempted to open my senses to get an idea of how many elves waited for us. I steadied my breathing, shot my mahier out, and hoped I would feel something. Nothing. I sensed the dragons that surrounded me and even the sea life below me. But nothing on the shore.

"He's blocking you. Sizing you up," Jericho said. "And he's by himself."

By himself? What if we were here to harm him? I wasn't allowed anywhere by myself because I was the Prince, and yet this Prince was sent alone to welcome a herd of dragons.

The Wolands landed on the shore, quickly shifting back to their humanoid states as they fanned out towards the tree line. I touched ground beside Jericho, who stayed in his dragon form. He stood in a protective stance next to me, his ears back and his snout close to the ground. Cairo and Eva landed to my right, and Cairo took a similar pose as Jericho next to Eva.

I blinked as an image began to form in front of me. In an instant, a man with blonde hair and bright orange eyes stood an arm's length away. His hands were spread open in the air and his head was cocked to the side as he observed me.

Fire formed beside me as Jericho noticed our intruder. The man held his hand high and shielded Jericho's fire before it touched him. With a chuckle, he slapped his hand against the ground and the fire went out.

"My Prince, Keeper of the Dragons." The man bowed his head to me with his hands out to the side. He shifted his eyes to Jericho, smirking. "I am Prince Gaber of the elves. I welcome you."

J.A. Culican

Chapter Five

Prince Gaber's orange, calculating eyes raked up Jericho and then Cairo, finally falling on Eva. His smirk turned into a full-blown grin as he outstretched his hand and lowered his head.

"The Golden Dragon, it's an honor to be in your presence," Gaber shook Eva's hand, grin firmly in place.

"Release her hand," Cairo growled from beside Eva.

"If I wanted to hurt her, she would be hurt already," Prince Gaber remarked, dropping Eva's hand. "We are on the same side." Gaber cocked his head to the side. "Or so I thought." The orange in his eyes glowed, the light spinning around his pupil as he contemplated his next move.

"We are," Eva interrupted their stare down, glaring at Cairo and placing her hand on his chest.

"Prince Gaber," Jericho began, stepping in front of Cairo and Eva in an attempt to take control of the situation.

With a wave of his hand, Gaber spun around and walked towards the tree line. "Keep up." He glanced over his shoulder, his smirk firmly in place. "Prince Colton of Ochana," he sang with a chuckle. "Walk with me, let's chat," he ordered with a jeer, never breaking his pace.

I looked over at Jericho for some kind of direction. Jericho's eyes were on fire as he glared towards Prince

Gaber. With a huff of smoke and a nod, he directed me to catch up with the Prince. Eva began to follow, but Cairo pulled her back with a shake of his head.

As I approached the Prince, my senses prickled. Someone or something was watching us. Gaber walked quickly beside me, leading us deeper into the trees in silence. I scanned the area around us. The further we walked, the harder it was to see. The dense jungle grew thicker, blocking what little sunlight was left of the day, leaving us in a gloomy cocoon of overgrowth and bugs.

A nearby chuckle broke my attention away from the uneasy sensation that lingered behind me. "Relax. Your nervousness is driving me crazy." He shook with laughter as he spoke. "You're the only one who knows of my guards." He tapped my chest. "It's the tilium inside you that draws you to them."

"Your guards?" I asked as I scanned the area again, seeing nothing.

"You don't honestly believe I would be allowed to meet with the dragons alone, do you?" He shook his head. "We haven't had dealings with the dragons in many years. I was quite surprised to hear from them." He paused. "And quite intrigued."

"Intrigued?" I asked.

"A dragon who possesses tilium. I never thought the day would come," Gaber mused.

"You heard how I took possession of it?" I hoped I wouldn't have to tell the story. Queen Tana and the farros still haunted my dreams every night. Just knowing she was free put me on edge.

"The farro." He paused. "Queen Tana is a wicked one."
His laugh was almost appreciative.

"You could say that." A shiver coasted up my back with
the thought of Tana and the farros.

Prince Gaber stopped and turned to me. Only now did
I realize our only source of light was coming from his eyes,
which were now focused on me. With his hands spread
out by his sides, Gaber observed me in silence. I broke eye
contact with him, looking around for Jericho and Cairo.
They were nowhere to be found. We were alone. Well, his
guards were close because I could still feel them. My skin
began to ripple and my breathing became irregular. My
dragon wanted out. Wanted to protect me. From what
exactly, I wasn't sure.

"I won't hurt you," he said as his finger found my chin,
bringing my eyes back to his. "The tilium inside you is very
powerful. It sings to me. Which means it sings to her." He
paused. "And Tana will fight to retrieve what's hers."

With those words, my body began to shift. I had no
control over it. Gaber leapt into a nearby tree, his bright
eyes illuminating through the jungle in an eerie glow. My
shift was erratic, uncoordinated, feeling like the first time,
a regression I hadn't expected. Jericho and Cairo burst
through the nearby underbrush, eyes wide in shock. Eva
was close behind them.

I stood tall in my dragonic form, now eye level with
Prince Gaber, who looked on in awe from his place in the
tree. From behind him emerged his guards with their
arms out in front, knives in hand, ready to attack.

"Stand down," Prince Gaber commanded with a wave of his hand. His guards lowered their weapons, but never took their eyes from me. "Has this happened before?" he asked.

"Never like this," I projected my voice towards Gaber in hopes he could hear me.

He broke his eyes from me, cocking his head towards Eva. "What did he say?"

Eva looked up at me, puzzled. "He said, never like this." She slipped from Cairo's grasp and stepped aggressively towards Gaber, putting herself between the elf and I. "What happened?" She looked around fearfully, an expression I'd never seen before on her face.

A smirk appeared on Prince Gaber's face as he looked down at Eva. "Can you shift back? Night is approaching, we must get you to safety."

I closed my eyes and thought of my human form. The shift came quickly, in the inhale of a breath. When it was over, I was surprised to find myself panting on the jungle floor. What had just happened?

Eva grabbed my arms and pulled me up to a seated position. She rubbed my back, glaring daggers at Prince Gaber. Jericho and Cairo approached me from behind, both emitting smoke.

"Explain. Now," Jericho roared at Gaber.

Gaber and his guards jumped down from the tree with ease, showing off their agility. They marched towards us but a growl to my side stopped their approach.

"The tilium is strong within him. Too strong," Gaber explained.

"What does that mean?" Eva asked.

"It means, we really should keep moving. He will be safer surrounded by my elves." Gaber gestured to his guards to lead the way.

Eva helped me to my feet, keeping her arm looped with mine. Her feet stayed planted to the ground, holding me hostage. Gaber looked back over his shoulder at us with an eyebrow raised.

"You'll keep him safe?" Eva asked, her voice breaking at the end.

Prince Gaber walked towards us with eyes trained on Eva, hand held over his heart. "With my life," Gaber exclaimed, his eyes flashing bright before dying down to their normal orange.

"Why?" I asked. "I'm no one to you."

"No one?" Gaber repeated. "You are the Keeper of Dragons." He punctuated each word. "The one who is destined to save all true beings." He tilted his head as he scanned the both of us. "You are the only known dragon to ever possess tilium. Not just any tilium, but that of over a hundred farro. Very potent, very dark tilium."

"Dark."

Gaber nodded towards me. "Unstable. Unpredictable." His pointy ears twitched. "We must get moving. The night is among us." He turned and walked once again deeper into the jungle.

We followed silently behind Gaber and his guards, senses on full alert. It was clear Gaber didn't care much for the night, and judging by his pace he was in a hurry to get to wherever we were going.

We crested a slight hill and broke through the tree line. Before me, a turquoise lake with small waterfalls flowing from nearby streams rested between what looked like treehouses high in the sky. Each treehouse was connected by rickety walkways swaying in the gentle breeze. Soft yellow glows permeated the air from the tiny windows above us.

"It's beautiful," Eva breathed beside me.

Gaber turned and gave us his full attention. "Welcome to our home." He spread his arms wide and did a little twirl. "The elven swamp." He laughed.

"Swamp." I stammered, taking in the sight before me.

"I never understood it myself. All you creatures," He waved our directions. "You just assume us elves live in a swamp." He shook his head. "The eldens, they live in a swamp. A black hole. Us." He twirled again. "We live in-"

"Paradise," Eva finished.

"You and I are going to be good friends," Gaber announced, pointing towards Eva. "Interesting you would call our home that, for this is Paraiso. Which means just that, paradise in Galician."

"But-"

"A story for another time," Gaber interrupted with a wave. "Let me show you around." He gestured for us to follow, then stopped, laughing. "It seems my elves are very captivated by you already."

I followed his eyes to the bright yellow lights dancing in the sky above us, the only lights shining on this moonless night. "What are those?" I asked, looking up.

"Those," Gaber pointed, "are my elves." He flashed his own orange eyes to shine a spotlight on me.

I squinted in confusion. Another orange glow grabbed my attention as I looked beyond Gaber at a young woman approaching us. She had long brown hair and eyes identical to Gaber's. She was petite, but I had no doubt the girl could defend herself.

Gaber looked over his shoulder towards the girl. "Ah. Let me introduce you to my sister, Princess Clara."

"It's an honor to meet you, Princess Clara." Eva outstretched her hand towards the Princess.

Instead, Clara pulled her into a tight embrace. "No, the honor is all mine, Golden Dragon. And please, call me Clara. Just Clara," she said with a shake of her head and a sigh.

"Clara," a gruff voice came from behind me.

"You," she pointed towards Jericho, "may call me Your Highness. Next time show your due respect." Her strong voice rang of authority.

"Of course, Your Highness," Jericho sighed through gritted teeth.

Jericho's eyes were now firmly on the ground and his jaw was twitching. I had never seen him act so subdued. Clara held her head high; her orange eyes held a fire aimed directly at Jericho. There was definitely some kind of history between the two of them.

Gaber cleared his throat, "This ought to be—"

"Interesting," Cairo provided as he tilted his head to the side, also noting Jericho's odd behavior.

"Come, let me show the two of you your quarters." Clara beckoned with her hand.

I looked back at Jericho once more, meeting his eyes. A somberness was found in the depths of his red gaze, a gaze that normally frightened me. With just a nod, he retreated towards the tree line.

"You're safe here," Cairo reassured as we both tracked Jericho. "Jericho and I will stand watch with the other dragons. Realm five has set a perimeter." His eyes scanned me then Eva. "Stick close to Prince Gaber. He gave an oath. He will give his life for the both of you," he said quietly. "It seems the dragons are now in an elven alliance." He paused. "To the death." He walked towards the trees that Jericho had just disappeared behind.

Death. I hoped it wouldn't come to that.

Chapter Six

Clara leapt onto a low branch sticking out of a massive tree. Climbing quickly towards a wooden walkway about twenty feet off the ground, her feet landed swiftly on the bridge. She crouched low, her orange eyes gazing at Eva and me.

"After you," Gaber insisted from behind us with laughter in his voice.

Eva sprouted her golden red wings, and with a quick push, she bounded upwards to land gracefully next to Clara. She smirked and winked at Gaber. I bet he had expected both of us to flounder. Hate to disappoint, but just I would fail this test.

The branch was two feet above me, taunting me from a distance. I reached my arms above my head, and though my fingertips grazed the bottom of the branch, there was no way I would be able to jump high enough to pull myself up. Not to mention that if by some miracle I did find myself on said branch, I then had to scale the tree another ten to twelve feet.

I sighed in defeat, turning towards Gaber. I prepared myself mentally to show my weakness within minutes of being left alone with the elf. He stood only a few inches shorter than me, a characteristic that bewildered me. I expected the elves to be much smaller, pixyish, like the fairies. Instead, they stood just shy of average. If it wasn't for their pointed ears and iridescent eyes, they'd pass as human.

"The tilium inside you is at war with your mahier," Gaber pointed to my chest. His fingers were longer than the average human, with nails sharpened into cutthroat points. Following my gaze, he lifted his fingers and laughed. "Defense mechanism. They aid in climbing. Trees, rocks, mountains," he said with a shrug.

I looked down at my own hands. Average, short rounded nails. Not made to climb trees. I looked back up to Gaber with a raise of my eyebrow. I hoped he had another way up the tree.

"Nope. If you plan on sleeping tonight or any other night, you will climb this tree," Gaber explained with a serious note in his voice.

A sigh of defeat blew through my lips. I was about to search out a nice pile of leaves to settle on for the night when Gaber grabbed my hand. He placed it on the trunk of the tree, his hand on top of mine.

"You are the Keeper of Dragons. You protect all that is true." He pointed with his other hand. "This tree is true. It will grant you safety"

I looked at my hand entwined with Gaber's, pushed flat on the rough bark. Dragon and elf. It was my job to protect him and all his elves. All true beings. The weight of my destiny fell heavy on my shoulders. I rested my forehead on the tree as I calmed my breathing from what was sure to be an epic anxiety attack.

"Release your energy. This tree will store it for you," Gaber whispered close to my ear.

I relaxed my body. The tree stood strong and immovable in front of me, there for me to rely on. Comforted by my thoughts, I turned my head towards Gaber.

"How?" I asked.

"Trust." He whispered. "You're not alone in this fight."

I couldn't help think he was talking about something much bigger than just climbing this tree. More of a partnership between beings. A support system. A system I knew I would need in the future. A future I feared.

I closed my eyes with my head still tucked against the bark, and placed my other hand on the trunk. I breathed in through my nose, held it and released the air through my mouth. I repeated this action over and over until I no longer feared the climb. In the grand scheme of things, it was just miniscule.

I exhaled out with new resolve. I would climb this tree. I peered over my shoulder to Gaber and found we were no longer on the ground next to the tree. We stood next to Clara and Eva on the uneven wooden planks high in the air.

I turned to meet Gaber's orange gaze, placing his hands over my heart. "It's true. No mistake." His eyes flashed bright, then dimmed. "You are the Keeper of Dragons. And she," he pointed towards Eva, "is the Golden Dragon. The two of you will be burdened with keeping all true beings safe."

Clara's voice drifted to my ears. "The elves of Paraiso pledge their lives to you. We will aid you on your journey in any way you seek." She bowed her head towards me and then Eva.

And right there in the evening breeze under the moonless sky, Clara and Gaber pledged their alliance to Eva and I. The weight that had settled earlier on my shoulders began to lift, it was minor but enough for my breath to return. I nodded my acknowledgement, unable to voice any words.

"Let's continue. We still have a ways to travel before we reach your new home," Clara stated as she led the way.

We filed behind her in a single line down the narrow wooden paths. I held my breath as we walked from treehouse to treehouse in a pattern unknown to me. Orange and yellow lights lit the path as we furthered into the jungle.

"Where are all the elves?" Eva asked. "I mean, I only see their lights."

"Prince Colton holds the tilium of the farro. As bright and strong as it is, it's still tainted with darkness," Gaber explained. "It will take some time for the fear he instills in them to dissipate."

"How come their eyes glow differently to yours?" Eva motioned between Clara and Gaber.

"Genealogy," Gaber stated bluntly.

"You mean like a caste system?" Eva pushed.

A sigh came from behind me. "Kind of. Clara and I are the only known elves who hail from the first."

"The first elf?" I asked.

"No." Gaber paused and tapped his foot on the board beneath him. "The first being."

Eva stopped suddenly in front of me. I stumbled over my feet in hopes I wouldn't fall or crash into her. She peered at Gaber over my shoulder.

"First being," she repeated. "Like God?"

Gaber raised his hands, palms out towards Eva. "I will not debate religion or beliefs with you. You wouldn't understand. You are human, or dramon. You wouldn't understand." He paused, smiling wryly "But you will."

"You seem sure," Eva pressed on.

"Once you see all. All. Once you see evil. True evil. Once you live for centuries. Forever." He shook his head. "You will."

As Gaber spoke, Eva's eyes grew larger. She seemed to be taking in everything he said with great understanding. We knew nothing. We've seen just a glimpse of what this world is.

"We're here," Clara announced as she took the last few steps towards a treehouse. Breaking Eva and I of a truth I'm not sure we were ready to hear.

We stood on a deck that surrounded a circular home made of branches and leaves. The treehouse sat much higher than the rest that surrounded us in a great maze around the lake.

"This was the home of our King and Queen. Our parents," Clara whispered, looking out over the lake.

"This is the safest place for you. You are bordered by our fiercest warriors. And," Gaber pointed to the sky, "the dragons are circling."

"And," Clara's eyes glowed bright as she pointed below, "the trolls are out in numbers." She looked up and over at us. "It seems the forest is alive tonight."

"Trolls?" I stuttered, searching for such creatures.

"Yes. I informed them of your impending arrival so as to not startle them," Gaber added.

"Why all the security?" Eva asked. "I mean the farro are tiliumless and-."

"And. And." Gaber shook his head. "We will start both of your training in the morning." His voice rose. "Do not underestimate Queen Tana, the eldens, carnites and-." He pointed at Eva, his eyes a dark orange. "This is a war. And the two of you tip the scale in our favor." He paused, fisting his hands tight. "Your mere existence proves we're all in great danger. We must keep the two of you safe or darkness," he sighed. "Evil will win."

"No pressure." I muttered under my breath.

I held tightly to the railing enclosing us in our new cell. The more Prince Gaber explained our predicament, the angrier I grew and began to panic. My fingers started turning white the harder I squeezed. My thoughts suddenly flew to Tana and her crazed laugh and the expression in her pitch black eyes as Queen Annabelle dragged her from Farro Grove.

With a harsh exhale, the railing I'd been holding onto for dear life shattered between my fingers. It quickly turned to dust and the energy inside me buzzed into frenzy. I dropped the shards that still stuck to my hands to the ground and fell to my knees on the unforgiving wood beneath me. My eyes searched for the ground in the darkness below me. I was met with bright yellow orbs of light and the sound of thin nails running up the tree trunk towards me. I fell back in an effort to get away from the impending arrival of elves or trolls or whatever was on its way.

"Cole!" Eva yelled as she ran to my side. "What's going on?" Her voice was full of panic as she searched my eyes for answers. "Breathe."

I grabbed at my ears, tucking my head against Eva, the noise of claws loud in the quiet night shook through me.

"It's the elves. You called to them. You asked for help," Gaber said as he knelt down next to me. "You've never been around another being with tilium, have you?"

The night was quiet once again as I looked up towards Gaber and thought of his question. "The fairies," I whispered.

"No. Actual contact?" Gaber pressed.

"No," I grunted, my head pounding.

Gaber stood, rubbing his face with his hands. He walked to the other side of the deck and looked out over the edge. "The tilium within you is tainted with darkness. The tilium within myself and the rest of the elves is light and pure." He turned to face Eva and I as we sat sprawled on the deck. "It's at war within you." He shook his head. "I thought it was just your mahier and the tilium together, but it's much more than that." He squatted next to me. "Your tilium is trying to decide whether it wants to steal ours or run, like the coward the darkness is," he growled, eyes blazing. "Tomorrow, we'll shed some light into the darkness." He stood and moved to the wooded walkway.

"If you need anything, my home is at the end of this path," He disappeared into the night.

From my other side, Clara's voice echoed through the night. "You can find me at the end of this path. Get some sleep, you'll need it." Then, she too disappeared.

I looked over at Eva as we sat in the middle of the dark rainforest. We were surrounded by guards. Guards who were willing to give their lives to keep us safe. Lives I now knew were in grave danger.

Chapter Seven

I woke to the sun shining bright through one of the many windows dotting the walls. I lay on a hammock-style bed attached to a huge tree that sat in the middle of a round hut, spanning to the northern wall. Said hut was suspended hundreds of feet in the air attached to said tree. I could hear Eva as she began to wake. She was also lying on an identical hammock on the opposite side.

The night before came back to me in a rush. Pushing myself up, I staggered out to the deck and fell to my knees. I held my head in my hands, resting my fingers on my temples and squeezing my eyes shut. Darkness lay within me. Dark tilium. It wasn't my mahier mixed with the tilium, it was just the tilium within me that had created such turmoil inside me. Unstable. Unbalanced.

A familiar hand rested on my shoulder. "Actually," Eva caught my attention, "you're the only one of us who is balanced."

I opened my eyes and glanced at her over my shoulder. Her long red hair lay effortlessly down her back, and her standard Woland trainee uniform was pristine. I contemplated her words. Balanced, me? It was clear-.

"Unstable. Yes," Eva finished for me. "But you are the only one who holds both light and dark within them."

"The Golden Dragon is right," a voice rang out from behind us. "You must choose a side." Gaber walked towards us from the path that led from his hut.

"I thought I already did," I croaked, my throat dry.

Gaber crouched down beside us. "Tell that to your tilium." Gaber winked and stood. "Today, we'll see how much control you have over it." He laughed. "Or how little."

Eva and I stood up, too. I broke away from her and rested my hands on the railing of the deck. The sun had just begun to rise above the tops of the trees. From here, the entire compound surrounded us. Paraiso was much larger than I had first anticipated. The tree houses dotted the trees as far as I could see. The turquoise lake broke into slender streams throughout the maze, surrounding the whole compound like a moat.

Gaber placed his hands next to mine as he too looked over Paraiso. "It's quite beautiful, isn't it?"

"Peaceful," I responded as I continued gazing at the sight before me.

"The water intertwines throughout Paraiso." Gaber pointed. "It's enchanted with protection spells. If a being were to wander out this far, they wouldn't see us."

"What would they see?" I asked.

"The jungle," Gaber stated. "If they attempted to walk through here, they would be transported to the other side. None the wiser that they had just walked through an elven camp."

"That's remarkable," Eva said, joining us.

Gaber turned to give her his full attention. "The elves have been here since the beginning. The enchantment living within those waters is ancient. When an elf passes, the tilium they possess is absorbed within the water, keeping all that live here safe."

"I figured you were immortal," Eva stated.

"Immortal, yes." Gaber paused as he turned to look over his home.

"Immortality does not mean death will not find us." Clara spoke from behind us.

Eva and I turned to face her, watching as her eyebrows lie scrunched together forming a v. Her orange eyes glowed in sadness. "Breakfast is ready in the main lodge." She turned and walked down the rickety walkway, out of sight.

"Let's go," Gaber whispered, following his sister.

Eva looked towards me with a shrug of her shoulders. The two of us followed behind in silence. The walk to the main lodge was shorter than it had been the night before. The silence continued as we entered a circular tree house that was at least five times larger than the one I had slept in the night before. Long wooden tables sat in rows with matching benches pushed underneath. In the middle of the room there was a great round table overflowing with bright fruits and vegetables.

"Eat up." Gaber gestured to the table. "I want to test your tilium today," he said, gathering a plate full of mangos and different types of berries.

Eva and Clara dug right in. They each piled a plate full and took a seat at a nearby table. I caught an orange gaze staring at me across the pile of fruit in front of me. With a laugh, Gaber shook his head and wandered over to the table with the girls. I grabbed a banana and joined them.

"You won't find any of that processed, sugary food you humans are used to here. We live off the land." Gaber pointed back at the table. "All of that will be gone within an hour of our leave. The elves will make sure nothing is wasted." With that, Gaber stood with his now empty plate and placed it in a log at the end of the table. "Your peels and cores go there," He explained, pointing to another hollow log at the opposite side of the table.

"Better eat that quick." Clara pointed to my banana as she also stood to clear her plate. "Gaber is itching to try out your tilium."

Eva followed Clara and Gaber out onto the deck. I quickly peeled my banana and dropped the yellow skin in the designated log, meeting them outside. Clara and Eva were discussing the water below us, and Gaber was off to the side, looking up. I followed his eyes to the clear sky, where I noticed three Wolands circling above us. They were too far away to know exactly who they were, but I had an idea.

"They can't see us," Gaber's eyes lowered and met mine. "The enchantment covers the sky as well. I'm sure your guards are going nuts." Gaber laughed. "They know you're here. They can feel the two of you, but all they see is jungle."

"Did they know this when they left us here?" I asked cautiously.

"Yes. It was part of the deal. You are the first dragon to ever step through our wards." He cocked his head to the side. "Don't worry, we will check in with your guards later today." He paused. "Also part of the deal." He shrugged his shoulders and rolled his eyes.

I nodded my head. My bet was Jericho and Cairo had already figured out a way to keep an eye on us through the enchantment. No way would they let us out of their sight, especially Cairo. He kept Eva within arm's length at all times. I'm not sure they had ever been apart this long since the day they met.

Gaber clapped his hands together. "Let's get going. I'm excited to open you up," he said with a grin as he waved his hand towards a ladder.

We descended the ladder to the ground below. Not much sunlight broke through the thick trees, which left us in an unusual light shaded in orange from Clara and Gaber. Gaber strolled to the edge of one of the tiny streams flowing from the larger body of water. He knelt down and sang a short melody in a language I'd never heard before. Just as he finished and began to stand, the water shimmered and created a bright aqua glow that lit the surrounding area.

"This place truly is magical," Eva venerated, twirling wide-eyed in the cerulean glow of the water.

Tiny specs of silver floated in the air. They gleamed like stars on a clear night as the ground around us morphed into a moss-colored rug. The bushes dotting the ground grew, attaching themselves to the trees that surrounded us. The scenery had created a jungle-themed room of privacy.

"Amazing," Eva whispered as she reached her hand out to touch one of the walls.

"As you can see, tilium is very powerful," Gaber said as he turned towards me. "It's one of the reasons your council felt it necessary for you to be trained by me, and to follow our rules."

Clara placed her hand on my chest. "You have an abundance of tilium within you. Enough energy to feed an army of farros. Potent, very dangerous, very dark," she explained.

"Clara and I will train with you daily on controlling the tilium." He paused. "With that you will learn to be one with all that surrounds you. Everything you see will aid you in storing this energy." Gaber stood next to Clara as he pointed to me. "For you are not strong enough." He put his hands in the air. "No one is. Not I, not Clara, and not the Golden Dragon."

"Where do we start?" Eva asked.

"Well," Gaber looked around. "Let's start with releasing the tilium. Think of it as draining a battery. Then, we will see if you can control what's left."

"How do I do that?" I asked.

"I'm told you already have." Gaber looked over at me. "Once. The day you breathed fire-"

"What?" Eva interrupted.

I looked to Eva then back to Gaber. "I don't know how that happened. It was like-"

"You had exceeded your fill point," Gaber finished.

"Yes," I whispered, looking at the ground.

"You're there again. Your uncontrolled shift. Super strength." Gaber ticked off his reasons with his fingers.

"Okay. So, how do I release it?" I asked.

"Easy." Gaber pointed to Eva with a growl. "She. Is. Now. My. Prisoner," he stated.

"Wait. What?" I asked in confusion.

"Look around, Prince. No one is here to save you. Did you think we created a training center for you just now?" Gaber laughed. "No, Prince. This is a cell. Made just for her." Gaber pointed towards Eva with a sneer.

"Clara, chain her up." Chains unexpectedly shot from the wall and dropped to the ground.

"No! Stop!" I screamed as Clara grabbed Eva, who was attempting to shove her away with headstrong thrusts. After a brief moment of pushing and shoving, Eva was out of luck.

"Cole, run!" Eva yelled towards me. "Go get help!"

"Where will you go? Once you leave you won't be able to get back in. Remember?" Gaber jeered.

"Please." My body trembled as my emotions took over. "Let her go." My dragon itched to be set free as small sparks trickled from my fingers.

Gaber pointed to my fingers with a laugh. "Is that all you've got, Keeper of Dragons?"

Streams of silver light flew from my fingers towards Gaber, who hastily threw up an invisible shield to protect himself. The tilium bounced off and made a hole through one of the walls. Energy coursed through me. No way were these elves going to imprison Eva.

I stood tall and flicked my hands towards Gaber once again. Energy zipped through my body as the tilium was released through my fingers, aiming right at Gaber's head.

"Stop!" Eva screamed. "You're breaking through his shield." Eva ran towards me. "Cole. Stop!" She grabbed my hands in an attempt to stop the force of my tilium.

Amazingly, the tilium obeyed her command. Gaber was slumped on the moss-covered ground. Clara was by his side, shaking him in an attempt for revival.

"It was a trick," Eva whispered, tears falling down her face.

"What?" I asked.

"Gaber was helping you release your tilium." Eva hid her face in her hands as the tears began to fall faster.

What have I done?

Chapter Eight

Silence surrounded me. I watched helplessly as Clara shook Gaber incessantly, attempting to resuscitate him. Nothing. He lay crumpled and soundless. Unmoving. Why would they trick me? Especially when they knew how unstable I was. I rubbed my temples roughly with my fingers. I had to help Gaber. This was my fault.

A screech caught my attention. Clara jumped away from Gaber. The water from the nearby stream inched towards him, moving until completely enclosing him. A bright blue glow emitted from the water, making it difficult to see Gaber.

"No," Clara sobbed, falling to her knees. "Don't take him." Her body shook profusely.

I shielded my eyes with my hand, attempting to see through the bright glow. The water silently rose and blanketed over Gaber. I squinted as the iridescent water progressively shined brighter. The once-cerulean water now glowed a bright purple as it shielded Gaber from us. Before I could comprehend my actions, my feet moved towards the water. Tiny specs of gold and silver particles floated in the now dark purple liquid. Right before I reached the water that held Gaber captive, a voice spoke.

"It will be okay, darling Clara," a woman's voice echoed around us.

"M-mom?" Clara stuttered, searching for the source of the voice. "Is that you?"

A woman looking remarkably similar to Clara flickered between the three of us. Long brown hair, orange gaze and pointy ears, a shadow of a woman stood amongst us.

"Darling." She reached towards Clara. "I promise Gaber will be all right." She assured as her hand passed through Clara's.

"What?" Clara looked at her hand.

"The fates are granting us this brief moment while they tend to your brother," she spoke softly.

"You can't stay?"

"It has been an honor protecting you and your brother these past hundred years. Even if I could stay, I wouldn't. It would not be safe for any of you." She gestured towards the three of us.

"What do you mean?" Clara asked as she once again attempted to hold onto her mother's hand.

"The eldens are near. I fear they will attack soon. My tilium will aid in protecting you all." She spread her hands wide. "My role is no longer here on Earth as an elf." She sighed.

"Your tilium? I thought Eldrick stole it?"

"He tried. But as with all true elves, our tilium will always find its way home." She looked behind her as the water began to recede. "I must go. I love you deeply and am always watching." She spoke as she faded to nothing.

"Mom?" Clara whispered, staring at the spot her mother once stood.

On our first night here, I had pieced together that Clara and Gaber's parents were gone. But killed by King Eldrick, the same elden who had freed the farros and Queen Tana. Tana, the fallen fairy was surely searching for me as we spoke. Tana and Eldrick together. Their power seemed endless.

"Gaber?" Clara's voice brought me out of internal panic. "Gaber!" She ran towards him.

Gaber rolled to his side with a groan, pulling his knees to his stomach. Clara fell to the ground by his side and pushed his soaked blonde hair out of his face. Gaber's eyes were squeezed shut and his teeth were clamped tight in pain.

"It's going to be okay," Clara cooed over and over as she rubbed his shoulder.

"We need to get help," Eva stated. She persisted when she was met with no answer. "Clara!"

"Gaber will have to release us. He was the one who created our barrier," Clara whispered as she continued to soothe Gaber.

I knelt down beside them. Gaber was pale, the only sounds coming from him were moans and groans as he held his knees tight against his chest.

"This is my fault," I whispered.

"No. No," Gaber moaned.

"Shh, Gaber," Clara soothed. "It was the only way. Your tilium is controlled by your emotions, fear being the easiest to trigger it."

"But I killed him." I gestured to Gaber.

"Not. Dead," Gaber groaned.

"Not anymore," I responded.

Gaber attempted to sit up, only to fall back down. He released his legs and sprawled out on the moss, staring at the trees that covered us.

"Mom was here?" Gaber quietly asked Clara.

"For a moment." She paused. "Eldrick doesn't have her tilium." She sighed.

"And Dad?"

"I don't know." She whispered.

"Help me up." Gaber reached his hand towards me.

"Maybe you should rest. I mean-."

"Now." Gaber wagged his hand at me.

I wrapped my hand around his long thin fingers and helped him sit. His pain seemed to be dissipating rapidly, considering he was dead just a few moments ago. I shook my head at that thought. This place truly was magical, just like Eva had said earlier.

"This wasn't your fault," Gaber said gruffly. "It was my choice to egg you on. Now, we must get going. I'm sure the elves are in a tizzy since their Prince just died." Gaber snickered and grabbed his side in pain.

"Maybe you should take it slow," I stated.

"Nah. Never felt better." Gaber heaved himself up to a standing position, leaning on me for support. "Let's go." He pushed off me and stumbled towards one of the tree-lined walls.

"Let him walk on his own." Clara grabbed my shoulder as I began to follow Gaber to help. "He's stubborn, refusing to ever show any weakness. The fact that you're stronger than him bruised his ego for sure." She shook her head as she followed after him.

Gaber held his hands on the wall, once again whispering words I couldn't hear. Eva came up next to me as she, too, watched in awe.

"You okay?" Eva asked, looking over to me.

"I don't know," I paused as the wall shimmered but stayed solid. "I mean," I gazed down at my hands, "the tilium. It killed him. If he weren't an elf or-."

"I know." The wall shook a bit as Gaber smacked it angrily with his hand. "The fates saved him." Eva shook her head. "Their parents were killed." She whispered.

"By King Eldrick." I added.

Finally, the wall shimmered and dissipated. Gaber sighed in relief. Yellow lights met us from the other side as what seemed like hundreds of elves swarmed around Gaber. Questions flew from their mouths as they tried to explain what they felt.

Gaber raised his hands and all noise ceased. It seemed even the birds stopped chirping and the toads stopped croaking. "I'm all right. Princess Clara is all right. The Keeper of Dragons are safe." Gaber gestured towards us as his voiced boomed across the jungle.

The elves parted for Clara as she strolled to Gaber's side. She held her head high, her orange gaze penetrating the elves around her. Once they were satisfied she was also unharmed, their golden gazes landed on Eva and I. The elf closest to us snarled, leading the rest to follow suit. Growls echoed through the air. Eva grabbed my arm as she pulled herself closer to me. Creatures not much shorter than me with pointy ears and golden eyes began to creep towards us.

"Enough!" Gaber's voice roared. "You will not harm the Keeper of Dragons."

All eyes turned towards Gaber and Clara as I exhaled in relief. "It is because of them my mother, Queen Clarena, was able to warn us of grave danger," Clara stated.

"The Queen? How is that possible?" A black-haired elf standing as tall as Gaber asked.

"The fates saved your prince and sent your queen to warn us about the eldens. So, as you can see everything has happened for a reason. Do not ever doubt the fates," Clara said with conviction. "And trust in the Keeper of Dragons." She gestured towards us. "For they will save all true beings."

"How do you know this isn't another trick by the eldens?" the same black haired elf asked. "I can feel the darkness within him."

"He is the reason the farros no longer hold any tilium." Gaber pointed towards me. "Trust his strength in protecting you. Trust your prince to protect you."

"Of course, Prince Gaber," the elf replied as the others echoed their agreement.

"Let's go then." Clara waved her hands. "Back to work."

The elves climbed the trees to the huts above, but the black-haired elf stayed behind.

"Keeper of dragons," Gaber grabbed our attention. "I would like for you to meet my second in command. Bran."

I nodded my acknowledgment. The elf reminded me of Jericho. He frightened me instantly.

"Care to explain what you did to our prince?" Bran sneered, his bright gaze dark as he awaited an answer.

"Bran," Gaber said. "That was my doing."

"You chose to die?" Bran questioned. "I felt it all. As did the rest of the tribe."

"His strength exceeds my initial expectations," Gaber countered. "And as Clara already explained, without my death, the warning of the eldens would not have been made. My mother, your queen, gave it to us."

"The eldens are always a threat. We did not need your death to tell us that," Bran disputed.

"Enough," Gaber said. "We will no longer discuss my death." His voice rose. "We need to heighten our security. Make contact with the dragons." Gaber sighed. "And the fairies."

"Sir?" Bran questioned as his eyes left me to settle on Gaber.

"The fates would never have sent my mother if the threat wasn't real. Different than normal," Gaber stated. "We need to be ready."

"Of course, sir," Bran replied.

"Now," Gaber turned towards Eva and I. "Let's go make contact with your dragon guards." He clapped his hands.

"Do you think they felt what happened?" I asked Gaber.

Gaber laughed. "No idea. We have shields up. But each being has its own connection to each other." He shrugged.

"What do you think? Do your guards know you killed me?"

I hung my head. My guess? Yes.

Chapter Nine

"We're leaving," snarled Jericho as we appeared before him back on the coast. The water crashed against the rocks below. It looked like a storm was near.

"It is imperative that we continue his training," Gaber said with an eye roll. Jericho paced in front of us, hands and teeth clenched.

"Imperative?" Jericho bellowed. "There is no saying what damage your games will have on my Prince. How could you put the Keeper of Dragons in danger?"

"Your Prince?" Gaber laughed. "It was me who was damaged."

Jericho snarled. I saw the first signs of smoke escape from behind him as his nose flared in anger. "You placed the Keeper of Dragons in grave danger. You deserved the pain."

"Wait just a minute," Eva said, stepping between Jericho and Gaber. "Cole needs to stay. This incident only proves that further."

"No," Jericho growled. Smoke billowed behind him in waves; his fiery eyes pierced at Gaber over Eva's shoulder.

"I'm staying," I stated; Jericho turned his gaze on me.

"No. I'm in charge of your safety. Anything could have happened and I had no way of getting to you," he roared.

"Why not let Jericho and Cairo through your wards?" Eva asked Gaber, but she glared at Cairo as she spoke.

"That way they can see with their own eyes that we're safe."

"No," Gaber replied. "Absolutely not. You two were the first dragons to ever enter our home, and only because you are the Keeper of Dragons."

"Then we leave," Jericho stated; smoke now surrounding us.

I was pinned between the most stubborn creatures in existence. On my right, Gaber smirked, which only promoted Jericho's scowl to deepen. On my left, Eva and Cairo were glaring angrily at each other. What was going on?

"I thought we were all on the same side," I huffed.

Four sets of eyes turned my way. "Same side?" Jericho shook his head.

"We're on your side, Keeper of Dragons, not theirs." Gaber pointed to Jericho and Cairo.

"That doesn't make sense. I mean, I'm a dragon, and so are they."

"You are special. The Keeper of Dragons exists to protect all true beings. The two of you are a neutral party that represents all true beings," Gaber explained. "The dragons protect all, but ultimately protect themselves."

"That's rich coming from an elf," Cairo growled. "When was the last time you protected anyone but yourself?"

"You know nothing of the elves," Gaber said, stepping closer to Cairo.

"And you know nothing of the dragons," Cairo stated.

"I know your cowards, hiding away in your island in the sky." Gaber's voice rose. "You forgot your oath. The treaty we all agreed upon. You deserted us for hundreds of years."

"Let's all take a breath," Eva said, placing a hand on each of Cairo and Gaber's chests. "Let's focus on now."

Gaber turned his orange gaze on Eva, casting an unnerving glow around her. "And forget all that has happened?"

"That's not-"

"While the dragons were licking their wounds, forgetting all that relied on them, the eldens and the farros raged a war amongst all true beings who still stood against them." Gaber turned to Jericho. "Where was the Woland guard then? It was your responsibility to come to our aid, just as we had come to yours before. But instead, you deserted us."

"We had just lost a great warrior. Our Prince!" Jericho shouted.

"And we lost both our King and Queen to the eldens," Gaber whispered. "You ignored our cries for help. The lives of all elves were forever altered with their deaths, and the dragons were nowhere." Gaber met Jericho's eyes; orange flames danced with hatred. "And yet, you ask for help, and here we are, upholding our oath."

"Is this true?" I asked, searching Jericho and Cairo's eyes for answers.

"Yes," Jericho growled. "For two hundred years we stuck our heads in the sand. The dragons had never felt such a loss."

"Excuses, excuses." Gaber sneered, turning away from our group. "The impact of losing two royal elves was devastating. Only three royals remain. Three beings who hail from the first. Without our tilium, all elves will parish." Gaber hung his head. "And now the Keeper of Dragons are here. Which means the chances of losing another is good." Gaber looked over his shoulder. "Who will care for my elves when their tilium is gone?"

"We won't let that happen." Eva broke away from Cairo and walked towards Gaber. "We will fight to the death for both dragons and elves."

"Your elf has already made that oath," Cairo interrupted. "He promised to protect the two of you to the death."

"Why death? Can't we just stand together, united? Why must everything be to the death?" I asked.

"It's the way of our world," Gaber answered with a shrug.

"Maybe it's time to change that world," Eva stated. "We need to work together or the eldens and the farros will win."

Gaber turned to face us. "We stand with you!" Gaber exclaimed.

"We also stand with them," Jericho stated. We all turned to face him. The smoke that trailed behind him had thinned, and the fire in his eyes had weakened. "Which means we stand with you." Jericho stared at Gaber.

"It doesn't mean we trust you." Gaber rubbed his hands together. "The wellbeing of all elves is in my hands-"

"Our hands," Clara walked from the tree line and stood beside Gaber. "We carry the struggle together."

Gaber nodded his head. "An alliance, then." He looked towards Jericho and Cairo. "Dragons and elves together."

"An alliance," Jericho agreed. "Someone should contact Queen Annabelle."

"Ah, yes, the fairies will want in on this," Gaber stated. "We have already made contact with her; she will arrive tonight."

"Does this mean you are going to open your home to the dragons?" Eva asked.

"It means," Clara paused, glaring at Jericho, "we will open a portion of our home, away from the rest of the elves."

"Thank you, your highness." Jericho bowed his head.

"I'll be watching the two of you closely. One toe out of line and you will never be granted access to our home again," Clara warned. "Understand?"

"Yes, your highness." Jericho and Cairo said in unison.

"Now, for the ground rules." Gaber clapped his hands together, venturing close to the cliff overlooking the ocean.

"Ground rules?" Cairo asked.

"House rules?" Gaber suggested.

"Continue," Jericho demanded, shaking his head at Cairo.

"One, you go nowhere without myself or Clara. If you suddenly find yourself out of our wards, you will not be allowed back in."

Both Jericho and Cairo nodded.

"Two, I am in charge of training the Keeper of Dragons. You are welcome to watch, but do not interfere. Not for any reason."

"Unless he is in danger," Jericho added.

"No. He was in no danger today and he will be in no danger tomorrow," Gaber stated. "And three. If I tell you to do something, you do it. No argument."

"Excuse me?" Jericho asked.

"You heard me. You are here to protect the Keeper of Dragons, nothing else. This is my home. If I tell you to do something, it's for a reason. I will not waste my time arguing with you." Gaber turned fully towards Jericho. "Got it?"

"Yes," Jericho answered through gritted teeth. The smoke that had begun to disappear mere moments ago was now back in full force.

"Good, now go shift. Your dragon breath stinks." Gaber wrinkled his nose.

In a blink Jericho was in the air and out of sight.

"That dragon needs some anger management." He shook his head with amusement.

"I will let the trolls know of our new visitors. I will set them up on the north quadrant closest to their hole," Clara said.

Gaber nodded. "Perfect. Invite Evander to dinner tonight. Dragons, fairies, elves and trolls." Gaber laughed. "Should make for a fun-filled time."

"Hole?" I asked.

"Yes, the trolls live underground. Most of their home is situated underneath our land," Gaber explained.

"They can enter your ward?" Eva asked.

"Yes, elves and trolls have been side by side since the beginning," Clara said.

"Their numbers are much smaller than the elves. They came to our aid the last time the eldens attacked, and many fell in defense of Paraiso. We owe them our lives." Gaber explained.

Jericho landed next to me as he shifted back to his human counterpart. "Are we ready?" He asked hoarsely.

"Yes." Gaber exchanged a look with Clara as she turned, disappearing into the jungle.

"Your quarters are quite far." Gaber held his hand up. "And no we cannot fly there. The only way to travel through our wards is by foot, unless you're the golden dragon. Her wings sprouted easily within our walls," Gaber chuckled as he walked toward the jungle.

"And what need did she have to sprout wings?" Cairo growled.

Gaber shook his head. "Take it down a notch. She was just climbing a tree. Geez."

"You seem to think the safety of the Keeper of Dragons is funny," Cairo examined.

Prince Gaber's feet stopped as he turned to look at Cairo. "By now, you should have figured out just how much the lives of the Keeper of Dragons means to me." Gaber paused. "It is you I find funny."

Cairo huffed in front of me, but we continued to walk deeper into the jungle. The further we ventured, the more the trees blocked the sunlight from reaching us. Gaber stopped a few feet away from one of the many streams that wound around Paraiso. The bright turquoise water gave off just enough light to see the emotions swim within Gaber's eyes.

"You will only be granted access once," Gaber whispered. "Do not make me regret this." He knelt down to the water, bowed his head and whispered words I wasn't able to hear.

A shimmering wall appeared around us. Tiny particles broke away from what looked like a glass wall. Gaber stood and turned to us.

"The ward is down. You may enter," Gaber turned and stepped through the bright glow of the water.

The three of us followed behind Gaber in a single file line. In silence, we strode along one of the larger streams for what felt like miles. We broke through a thick bush and I noticed Clara standing by a large boulder. As we approached, the large gray boulder shuddered. I was about to place my hand on the rock when Jericho pulled me behind him.

The boulder shook and trembled, morphing finally into a creature that stood half the size of Clara. Its solid features resembled that of a god-like statue. Large yellow eyes blinked open. He tilted his head and took in the sight of the four of us.

"The Keeper of Dragons," a gruff voice sang. "I am Evander, ruler of the trolls." He knelt down on one knee and bowed his head.

Eva came to stand beside me. We both stared in shock, absorbing the sight of our first troll.

Dinner should be interesting.

Chapter Ten

Gaber pointed through the branches to a hut high in the air. "That is where you will stay." He then walked towards Evander and shook his hand, clasping his shoulder.

Jericho and Cairo followed Gaber's finger, beginning to search around for a way up. Gaber took notice and laughed.

"And this is when the Golden Dragon sprouted wings," Gaber sang.

"And Cole? How did he fly up?" Jericho asked with a lift of his eyebrow.

"Believe it or not, even I don't have the answers for everything," Gaber responded with a chuckle. "Don't leave your hut." Gaber pointed to Jericho and Cairo. "We will gather you when Queen Annabelle arrives." He turned back towards Evander.

"You allow the fairies through your wards?" Jericho asked.

Gaber turned towards Jericho. "Of course. They have been noble allies since the start."

"Don't you think King Rylan should be here for this assembly of crowns?"

Gaber walked menacingly towards Jericho until mere inches from him. "Don't push your luck dragon," he growled. "The Prince and Keeper of Dragons will sit in his place." Gaber turned and bolted towards the tree line,

Clara and Evander close behind, leaving Eva and I alone with two fired up Wolands.

"Elves," Jericho growled. "One second they're laughing and the next..." He sighed, shaking his head.

"Minus the laugh, sounds like someone I know," Eva countered.

Jericho turned towards me. "Tell me everything that happened."

I hung my head. "I almost killed Gaber with my tilium."

Both Wolands stayed silent. I chanced a look up to see a grin had formed on Cairo's face, and Jericho stood shaking his head.

"It wasn't his fault," Eva chimed in. "It was actually Gaber's idea. He was trying to release Cole's tilium."

Jericho waved his hand in the air, effectively cutting Eva off. "I don't doubt for one second this was Prince Gaber's idea. However, he didn't seem dead." Jericho lifted his eyebrows at me.

Eva and I exchanged a look. Neither of us could explain it. Was it the fates? His mother? The water? All I knew was that something had saved him. I shrugged my shoulders at her.

"I—"

"The fates saved him?" Cairo sounded struck with awe. "That means-"

"The Keeper of Dragons will stay and be trained by the elves," Jericho finished, looking up towards his hut. "And we will be calling this place home until that training is complete."

"If we let you stay that long." Clara's voice rang from behind us. "The Keeper of Dragons will hold an open invitation here. The two of you are on probation." She paused. "Queen Annabelle has arrived." Clara turned towards a nearby stream. "Stay close," she called over her shoulder.

We followed a thin stream that seemed to go around Paraiso. A walkway overhead blocked all light from above. Our only light source was the glow of the indigo water beside us and the auburn glow from Clara in front of us. The walk was quick and silent. I could sense Jericho's aggravation behind me.

Clara stopped in front of an enormous rock barricade. She knelt down on one knee and bowed her head. The rest of us imitated her stance. Clara chanted in a language I didn't know but had heard from Gaber before.

The rock before us shook and groaned as it split in half. Hidden behind the rock was a closed archway with two great wooden gates. Clara stepped up to one of the gates and placed her hand on the lock as silver sparks flew from her palm. A tingle raced up my back as she released her tilium. The gate opened and Clara swung her arms out wide to welcome us in.

While inside, we were met by a round courtyard dotted with old empty planters and a long, rectangular table. I looked around for another door but found none, only ashen concrete bricks fenced the sides.

"Do not worry, Keeper of Dragons. It's all a trick of the eyes," Clara explained as she waved her hands through the air.

"Yes," Jericho said. "Elves and their tricks."

Clara kept her eyes straight ahead. "You can leave at any time, dragon." She strolled to the long table and sat in a bulky chair. A tingle of energy vibrated through the air as she folded her hands in her lap.

The ground shimmered as sparks chased each other around the room. The dirt beneath me turned to marble, and large, vine-covered granite archways sprang from the ground. Bright exotic flowers sprouted from the empty planters, and the once plain table turned to strong, solid stone. The chair Clara sat on turned to gold, gems sparkling as they contacted the lights still bouncing around the room. Gaber, Evander, and Annabelle strolled down a spiral stairwell that seemingly appeared just moments before.

"It still amazes me each time," Gaber stated. "Welcome, Keeper of Dragons, to the Crowne Assembly Hall," he said, gesturing around the room. "Please, please have a seat." He sat at the head of the table in what could only be described as a throne.

Just as the last of us settled at the table, a burst of light shot from the middle. As it blinked out, a generous amount of food was left in its place. Fine china sat in front of me, and a cloth napkin folded in the shape of a dragon was perched on the plate. An elaborate goblet full of water sat behind it. I gazed around the table to see similar set ups in front of everyone. Across from me, Jericho's eyes were closed as he shook his head, clearly unimpressed with the show.

"Dig in!" Gaber exclaimed while filling his dish with a variety of colorful vegetables. Gaber popped a carrot into his mouth, ignoring the rest of us as he dug in to his dinner.

Clara cleared her voice from beside me, which gathered the exact attention she had sought. Once all eyes were perched on her, she gestured around the table, glaring at her brother.

"Ah, yes. Where are my manners?" Gaber rolled his eyes. "Introductions of course." He pointed to each member around the table as he rattled names off. "Now, let's eat!"

"Prince Gaber," Queen Annabelle said. "We're all gathered here for a reason. I feel we really should-"

"After we eat, Annie," Gaber replied without missing a bite.

"The eldens aren't far behind us," Queen Annabelle blurted out, glancing around the table. "We could feel their energy on our travels here." She turned towards Gaber. "Do they know the Keeper of Dragons are here?"

Gaber placed his fork down on his plate and met Queen Annabelle's bright eyes. "I don't know. Knowing Eldrick, yes. It's why we called for you." Gaber picked his fork back up and popped a carrot into his mouth. "The elves are officially in an alliance with the dragons."

"We've always been in an alliance. We all signed the treaty," Jericho interjected.

A clink rang into my ears as Gaber threw his fork back down. "We've been through this, dragon. The dragons forfeited the treaty when they neglected our call for help." Gaber's eyes illuminated the whole table as he stood.

"He's right, Jericho." Queen Annabelle spoke as she too stood. "The dragons are no longer a part of our treaty. Your King knows this. However, all true beings are bound together. An alliance is a good place to start towards a new treaty."

"The trolls will stand with the Keeper of Dragons," Evander's deep voice broke in.

"As will the fairies." Queen Annabelle bowed her head towards us. "You've proven your value to us significantly."

"Great," Gaber stated as he sat back down on his golden chair. "Can we eat now?"

"There is much to discuss," Queen Annabelle said sternly as she too sat back down.

"It seems our elven alliance has grown," Jericho observed. "I will send word to King Rylan."

Laughter floated from the end of the table. "How will you do that, dragon?" Gaber asked. "Rule number one." Gaber wagged his finger at Jericho.

Jericho glared at Gaber. "Then you must inform our King."

"He's not my king." Gaber sighed. "Fine. We will send word in the morning informing King Rylan of the elven alliance. Or whatever this is." He shrugged his shoulders. Gaber pointed to the food on the table. "Hurry and eat. Wait until you see what we have for dessert." Gaber winked.

"Elves," Jericho growled under his breath as he glared at Gaber.

I scooped fresh vegetables onto my plate as I grabbed a roll from a nearby basket. All talk ceased as everyone ate quickly. A clink on a glass broke the silence. Gaber stood and swept his hands out to his sides. The food in front of us disappeared as a large silver fountain popped out of the middle of the table. The smell of rich milk chocolate hit my nose; a chocolaty waterfall began to shoot from the top of the fountain as a variety of fruit appeared on the plate before me for dipping.

Beside me, Eva stuck a strawberry under the chocolate. She glanced my way with a huge smile across her face, one I hadn't seen in some time. A smile I may not see again if the eldens have their way.

J.A. Culican

Chapter Eleven

After dinner I strolled through Paraiso. The others chatted amongst themselves, so I kept pace a few feet behind, lost in my own thoughts. As peaceful as Paraiso was, the words Queen Annabelle spoke at dinner haunted me. The eldens were close, which meant the farros were close, and with them came Queen Tana.

The weight of a large hand on my shoulder brought me out of my thoughts. King Evander stood beside me. He was half my height, with a sturdy frame covered in muscles. His green hair was almost camouflaged by the sights around me as his yellow eyes lit my face as he looked up to me.

"You must not fear the farros." His rough voice rumbled through the night air. "Or the eldens. You have many fierce warriors by your side."

"Yes, warriors who have promised to protect me to the death. I'm not looking for anyone else to die." Memories of Gaber dying just a few short hours ago plagued me. My fear killed him. Yes, I was protecting Eva. But I had no control of my actions. I was unstable.

"It is an honor to protect you, for you protect all that is true. Only you and your counterpart can save us from a time of fear."

"How do you know that?" I questioned.

Evander turned to face me. "I can feel it." He patted his solid chest. "Since the moment of your first shift." He looked up towards the sky.

"Queen Tana said she has always known who Eva and I were. How is that possible?"

Evander met my eyes once again. "The fallen are drawn to the light." He tapped my chest with his rock-hard hand. "The light within you shines blindingly. I'm not surprised they were drawn to you immediately."

"Does that mean they're still drawn to me?"

"I would think yes." Evander looked me over. "Do not fear. You are safe here."

"I do fear my own safety." I looked at the group around me. "But I fear the safety of those around me more."

"And that is what makes you The Keeper of Dragons. You care for all beings. Not just your own." He nodded and walked towards Gaber and Annabelle, who were speaking vivaciously to each other.

We stepped off the walkway and headed towards Jericho and Cairo's hut. The space beneath held nothing but dirt as a small streak of water cut through to light the way.

"Goodnight dragons," Gaber said from the front without missing a step. "Don't let the creepy crawlies bite."

Eva and I paused by the trunk of the large tree. Cairo and Jericho stood close as they searched the surrounding area for a way up. Cairo scratched his head and turned towards us.

"You think you'd be able to fly us up?" Cairo sighed as he asked Eva for help.

"Sorry, no way can I lift the likes of the two of you." Eva laughed. "Goodnight." Eva giggled as she shook her fingers at them and bounced after the rest of our group.

My shoulders shook as I attempted to keep my laughter in, biting my lip and looking to the ground.

"And you?" Cairo pushed my shoulder. "How did you get up?"

I looked up at Cairo and shrugged my shoulders. "Honestly, it just happened. One second, I was on the ground, the next I was in the tree."

"Of course," Jericho grumbled from behind us.

I turned to face him as he lowered himself to the ground. His back set against the trunk as he resigned himself to the idea of spending the night on the ground.

"Keep close to the Golden Dragon. We will see you in the morning," Jericho said, dismissing me. Cairo mirrored Jericho's position on the other side of the trunk.

With a nod, I turned and followed the direction Eva had disappeared to earlier. As I approached a nearby trail, I heard a group of voices chatting with each other. I turned down the narrow trail and hoped it would lead me to Eva and everyone else.

As I peeked around a bend in the trail, a huge bonfire blazed before me in an open field. The red and orange flames licked as high as the surrounding trees. The sound of pops and sizzles filled the air. At the base of the bonfire, at least 50 elves gathered, talking and enjoying the fire.

I remained hidden in the shadows on the edge of the trail, observing the gathering. The men and women wore similar clothes as Gaber and Clara; brown shorts and green tops in various shades and styles to permit them camouflage in the jungle when outside their shields.

I moved a bit closer towards the group in hopes to get a better look. That's when I stumbled over a branch on the ground and fell hard onto my hands and knees. I brushed my hands off and looked up. Every yellow eye glowed my direction.

I sucked in a breath and held it in anticipation of the first move. The elves feared me. I crept up to a standing position, holding my hands out in front of me as a sign of peace. One of the elves took a step towards me and cocked his head to the side. His yellow eyes glowed bright. He was hiding his face from me; all I could see of him were his pointed ears and long silver hair that shone from the fire behind him.

"You are the Keeper of Dragons?" The elf asked hesitantly as his ears twitched.

"Yes. I won't hurt you." I insisted.

"I can feel the darkness," The elf said as he pointed at me. "But I sense something else within you, too. Something..." He paused and cocked his head to the side. "Something true."

I dropped my hands to my side. "So, you're not afraid of me?"

Another elf walked forward, pausing next to the other and whispering to him. He continued towards me until he was only a few feet away and I could make out more of his face. He placed his hand on his chest and with his golden eyes, raked me from head to toe.

"My name is Mal," he said. "Yes, we feared what was in you. But now, we're intrigued." He lowered his hand.

"Intrigued?"

Mal waved his hands towards the other. "Let me introduce you to everyone."

He guided me through the crowd, stopping in front of an extended log placed on its side directly in front of the roaring fire.

"Sit. Kick your feet up." Mal settled himself down on the edge of the bench with a smirk. "Everyone." He cleared his voice. "This is the Keeper of Dragons, Prince Colton of Ochana!" He exclaimed with a slight laugh. "Keeper, this is everyone." The elf broke down in a fit of giggles. "Sorry, sorry. It's just... you're not scary. Like at all."

"Well, thanks," I responded uncertainly.

The elves around me bellowed with laughter. A hand shot out towards my face, making me flinch and almost fall off the log, which only amplified the laughter. I looked up into the amber eyes of a female elf, with long brown hair woven into a tight braid thrown over her shoulder.

"My name is Brynn." She said with a smirk. I lifted my hand to shake hers. "I'm lucky enough to be that jokester's sister," she said, gesturing towards Mal with a roll of her eyes.

Loud clapping brought our attention to the back of the group. I stood as the elves parted to show Gaber. He walked forward with his signature smirk firmly in place.

"I thought we lost you there for a minute," he laughed. "Your dragons are in a tizzy after Clara went back to gather you and found you gone." Gaber placed his hands on his knees as he bent down laughing. He held up a finger and spoke through laughter. "How long. Should we. Make them. Wait?" He stood as his body continued to shake. "Maybe until morning?"

"I'm pretty sure Jericho will burn this place down looking for me." I explained. Clearly Gaber hasn't seen Jericho truly angry.

Gaber waved his hand at my words." His fire won't work here. Let him huff and puff all he wants." He turned towards the fire. "I see you decided to party without me. How rude, considering you're my guest," he jested.

"Actually, I was-"

"And I see you've met everyone and no one seems hurt." He eyed the elves next to him with a clap of his hands.

"I wouldn't hurt them!" I proclaimed.

"Oh I know that." Gaber turned back around towards me. "But they," he gestured around him, "would hurt you." The elves continued to laugh amongst themselves. They didn't seem like they would harm me.

"Don't let their small physique and happy attitude fool you. Elves are great warriors," Gaber said with a grin and his eyes shining bright. "They protect the light."

"Which you don't have," Mal added from beside me with a shrug.

"So why didn't you?"

"They sensed your light. It's there, just hidden behind all the darkness you stole from the farro's," Gaber explained.

"Oh." Was the only response I could muster.

"So, where's the music?" Gaber asked. "I thought this was a party?"

Mal slapped his hand on my leg. "Come on, Keeper, let me show you around."

Mal walked me around the fire. On the other side was a large clearing. The night sky was visible for the first time since I stepped foot under the trees of Paraiso. A trio of elves strung along on harps and banjos from a stage in the middle of the field. The moon hung low, bathing the dancing elves in a white glimmer. They swung each other around as they laughed, enjoying each other's company. The sight brought a smile to my face, the first one in a long while.

Beside me, Mal rocked back and forth to the rhythm of the music, humming. I tapped my foot along with the beat. In just a few short minutes, these elves had accepted me as one of their own. Something my peers back home hadn't, and I feared would never.

Paraiso felt more like home than Ochana.

J.A. Culican

Chapter Twelve

Eva danced with Clara amongst the elves. She smiled bright as the elves circled around her. Word spread like wildfire through Paraiso that the Keeper of Dragons weren't all that scary after all, and just about every elf in residence raced to join the festivities. They accepted Eva without an ounce of hesitation, since the light inside of her was so bright and pure. The elves flocked, each begging to dance with her next. Since Mal stayed by my side, some were comfortable enough to stay and chat, making small talk I felt comfortable with him as though we had been friends for years instead of minutes.

Mal had explained to me that this was how every night in Paraiso was, a massive bonfire, a hodgepodge of food, loud music, and lots of dancing. They celebrated life each and every night as a family. The dragons kept to their own founding dragons. Rarely did I see them mix in social situations. Family wasn't the word I would use when describing dragons. They were loyal to each other but kept their interactions to a minimum outside their roles. The dragon I felt closest to was Jericho. Based on the first impression of that particular Woland and last, that thought shocked me.

The sights and sounds around me made me smile, something I did more here at Paraiso then I ever did in Ochana. The pressures and expectations as Prince and

Keeper of Dragons didn't exist. Sure, I was expected to train and learn to control my tilium, but it seemed more natural. In Ochana, I trained to fit in, but I never would. I wasn't a Woland, a Sien, a Galian or a Leslo. The elves around me accepted that fact. I didn't have to fit in one place. I could just be me.

An elbow to my ribs brought me back to the present. Mal tilted his head towards the makeshift dance floor.

"You plan on dancing or just hanging here tonight?" he asked, his foot still tapping to the beat of the music.

"I'm not much of a dancer," I laughed. "Actually, I've never danced," I admitted soberly and averted my eyes to the ground.

Mal bumped my shoulder with his and cocked his eyebrow at me, contemplating what I had just told him. I was worried, suddenly, that my confession would end our new friendship

"Well, no time like the present to learn." He grabbed my arm, pulling me off the log and towards the field.

Eva and Clara were not far from us as they twirled each other around. The beat of the music was much stronger out here as it thrummed through me. I bounced my head to the music, not sure how else to move. Mal was hooting and hollering as he jumped around, and I wished I could be as comfortable as him out here. Truth was this experience is one I had avoided on purpose throughout my life. I always came up with an excuse not to go to homecoming dances or prom. Eva always begged me, but I never went.

Mal crashed into me and dragged me to Eva and Clara." I allowed him to lead me through the mass of elves as they enjoyed themselves. None paid any attention to us. Eva saw the two of us first, a huge smile spreading from one side of her face to the other.

"How did you get him out here?" she asked Mal, clapping her hands happily. "I have never once seen Cole dance."

Mal laughed as he placed my hand into Eva's. "I didn't give the Keeper a choice. He's all yours now. Get him to loosen up, would you?" Mal danced his way into a group of elves next to us.

I turned to Eva. "I have no idea how to dance."

"It's easy. Come on! Spin me around. It'll be fun." She sang.

I threw my arm up in the air as Eva twirled beneath it, laughing. She grabbed my other arm and pulled us around the field, stopping every once in a while to make me twirl her, then continued to dance and swing to the music. I found myself swaying to the beat without a care to anyone around me. I never thought dancing would be this much fun as we twirled around in laughter.

Gaber shook his arms and kicked his legs in the air, moving closer to us. Eva giggled at the site as she twirled under my arm once again. Gaber smacked my shoulder and gestured around him.

"This is the real Paraiso," he sang. "And now the two of you are a part of it." Gaber turned and looked me in the eyes. "You will always have a home here. The tilium within you gives you that option." He gestured to Eva. "And she goes where you go," he lifted his shoulders and grabbed us both, squeezing us into a big bear hug. "Welcome!" he shouted, flinging his arms up in the air and dancing off.

"Wow," Eva whispered.

"I know. I wish the dragons had welcomed us like this," I muttered.

"What are you talking about? They threw you a royal coronation," she laughed.

"Yes, an official ceremony. But this." I paused, gesturing around us. "This feels like a home. A family."

I hadn't spoken to my adopted parents since we arrived in Paraiso, and I missed them with a sudden pang. I called them a few times a week while we were in Ochana, but I had not been in touch since arriving in Paraiso. As I looked over to Eva, I knew she was thinking about her own grandparents. We would have to talk to Gaber in the morning about calling them, for they were our real home. Our real family.

"Yeah, you're right," Eva said just as Clara came bounding up to us.

"Are you two hungry?" she asked, pointing to a table on the side full of food. "If so, grab food now. Once the music ends, there will be a mad rush to what's left."

Eva and I swayed over to the table. As we approached, Mal and Brynn stood stiffly, staring at the sky. I elbowed Eva and jutted my chin towards them, then followed their sight to the sky. Nothing seemed amiss, and the stars twinkled above us in the clear night sky.

"Something's off," Eva whispered next to me. "Look." She gestured to the other elves.

Most stood staring upwards with puzzled expressions on their faces.

"Mal, what is it?" I asked from across the table.

"Don't know. I sense something though. Something dark, but nothing's there."

I looked back to the sky, opening my own senses. I inhaled through my nose and exhaled through my mouth in an attempt to center myself. I needed to throw my senses out as far as I could. Nothing. I closed my eyes and inhaled again.

"Get down!" Jericho flew over the table and tackled me to the ground.

Cairo was beside me, shielding Eva. Jericho crouched above me, two swords in his hands as he too gazed at the sky.

"Get off!" I pushed at Jericho to no avail.

"Cole," Jericho paused as he breathed deeply. "Someone's here." His eyes were blazing and smoke billowed from his ears.

"I don't sense anything," I stated.

"They're blocking you," Gaber interjected. He too crouched low, holding the same two knives he held the first day I met him.

"Who?" Jericho growled.

"The farro," Gaber answered.

"How?" Eva asked. "Cole still has their tilium."

"They have help." Gaber stood and walked towards a furious Bran.

"I don't understand. Where are they? Do you see them?" I asked as I searched the sky once again.

"No. I sense them." He looked down at me, eyes aglow. "Realm five is out there, but I cannot contact them through the elven wards. We must trust in their strength."

"Evander and Annabelle are in Crowne Hall. I recommend we get the Keeper of Dragons there," Gaber stated as he walked towards us, Bran hot on his heels. "It's the safest place in Paraiso."

Jericho grabbed me by my shirt, pulling me to my feet. "Let's go. Move quickly." He prodded me from behind as Cairo grabbed Eva's hand to pull her with him.

An unfriendly cackle echoed throughout the field. It was a laugh that haunted my dreams. I sucked in a breath as my body went stiff, and Jericho slammed into me from behind.

"What are you doing?" Jericho growled. "Move!"

I pressed my hands against my ears. "Don't you hear that?" I asked, my legs trembling. "Hear what?" Jericho looked around. "I hear nothing."

"Tana," I stuttered. "I hear Tana." My knees buckled as her laugh continued to echo through my head.

Jericho grabbed ahold of me as he exchanged a look with Gaber. Cairo pulled Eva towards Crowne Hall. Eva protested, digging her feet into the soft ground.

"Stop!" She struggled against Cairo's hold. "We can't leave Cole."

"Eva, I need to get you to safety," Cairo pleaded with her. "I cannot protect you out in the open."

I belong next to Cole," she whispered to Cairo. "You know this."

Cairo nodded, releasing her hand. She ran towards me, stopping mere inches from my face. The gold in her eyes swirled a mesmerizing spiral around her pupil.

"Cole, look at me. Fight her. She is only in your head."

"The Golden Dragon is right. She is playing with you." Gaber uttered as he stood next to us in the field.

"Just breathe, Cole. Breathe with me." Eva's voice soothed me, just like Sila's had done in the past.

I copied her breathing as my surroundings gradually came back to me. Bran and other warrior elves escorted the elves out of the field to safety. I turned to where Mal and Brynn had been standing and saw they were gone. I breathed a sigh of relief for them being escorted to safety already.

"Cole," Eva called. "Are you back with me?"

"Yes." I swayed a bit as I pulled away from Eva and Jericho to stand on my own.

"Let's go." Jericho pulled us out of the clearing.

As we jogged towards the hall to join the others, the echoes of Tana's shrill laughter still rang in my head, and I knew that this was far from over.

J.A. Culican

Chapter Thirteen

Jericho slammed the solid iron doors shut. The concrete blocks shook from the vibration. I stood in the middle of Crowne Hall with Eva, Cairo, Jericho, Annabelle, Evander, Clara and Gaber.

"Release my mahier. Now!" Jericho shouted at Gaber. "I am of no use in my human state. I need to protect the Keeper of Dragons."

"Agreed. We don't know what's out there," Cairo added.

I plopped down on one of the bulky chairs that surrounded the table and hung my pounding head. At least Tana's cackle had stopped. Eva rubbed my shoulders as I massaged my temples. What had just happened?

Gaber sighed. "Cole, are you okay?"

"Mmhmm." Was all I could manage as I peeked up at him.

"Fine." Gaber crossed the room towards Jericho and Cairo. "Don't make me regret this, dragon." Gaber pointed a long finger in Jericho's face.

"We're on the same team," Cairo reminded.

"So you all keep saying," Gaber muttered.

"Well?" Jericho shook his arms. "No mahier, still."

"What did you think? I could just snap my fingers and poof, your mahier is back." Gaber shook his head. "It's a bit more complicated than that." He turned towards Evander. "Are the trolls in place?"

"Yes, we have the base of Paraiso secure. A perimeter has been set. No one has seen anything," Evander informed the group.

"Bran is in the trees. Once all the elves are secure, he will set a perimeter outside the ward."

"We have dragons in the sky," Jericho added, "but we have no way to contact them."

Gaber nodded. "Once you have your mahier, will you be able to contact them?"

"Not sure. Your ward is much stronger than I anticipated," Jericho said, a hint of admiration in his tone.

"If not, you can join Bran when he ventures outside the ward." Gaber waved his hand towards a small waterfall in the corner of the hall. "Come, kneel down next to me," he said to Jericho and Cairo. "Let's see what we can do about your mahier."

Gaber placed his hands above the water at the base of the waterfall, and began to chant a now familiar tune, "Eon ti sun, leiro ti seef." The water below his hands began to glow and swirl a bright turquoise. White light rippled out of the water in thin lines towards the open-aired ceiling. Gaber leaned back on his heels and tilted his head to the sky as he continued to chant, "Eon ti sun, leiro ti seef." A bright flash erupted from his hands, and a wave of energy bounced around the room. Two large bolts slammed into Jericho and Cairo, causing them both to tumble hard to the ground.

For just a moment, everything ceased. The air around us froze. My breath stopped. Then everything crashed back into movement. I grabbed my throat, sucking in air and glancing around the room as everyone else did the same. Eva now sat on the ground below my chair as Cairo crawled towards her to make sure she was okay. He crashed on the ground beside her as his body began to shake.

"What's happening?" Eva's voice trembled as she leaned over Cairo.

Jericho lay on the ground in a similar state. Pushing off the table, I staggered to him and collapsed, leaning over his prone body. Clara joined me but could only look on, as helpless as the rest of us.

Breathlessly, Gaber answered. "It will be over soon." He climbed to his feet and wobbled over to the table to sit beside Annabelle and Evander. "Inviting mahier inside our wards is a complicated process."

"But Cole and I hold mahier. Nothing like this happened to us?" Eva questioned.

"We were prepared for the two of you to enter. Plus we never blocked either of your mahier. We blocked theirs." Gaber pointed to Jericho and Cairo as they continued to tremble on the floor.

"The fairies are on their way as well," Annabelle brought us back to the present situation at hand. "We should contact King Rylan."

Gaber sighed. "Yes, I suppose we should." He looked down at Cairo, who now lay still on the floor, his trembling finally subsiding. "Once the dragons are back with us, we will have them contact Ochana."

Jericho grumbled under me. I looked down in time to see his red eyes dart open and smoke billow from beneath him as he attempted to push himself from the ground to a seated position. Come to think of it, his smoky dragoness had shown itself earlier too, before his mahier had returned. How was that possible?

"Stop," Jericho growled. "Your thoughts are screaming at me."

Jericho pushed his hands against the ground and stood. I noticed Cairo as he too stood with Eva's help.

"Can you call the others?" Gaber asked as he rubbed at his temples.

"Yes. They are in the air. They see nothing even though their senses are going haywire. We definitely have company," Jericho informed. "I will call and inform the King."

Gaber nodded his head as Clara took the seat next to him. Eva helped Cairo to a nearby chair and plopped herself down on the one next to his. Jericho paced the room while I stood, frozen. Now what? Everyone looked around at each other, hoping someone would have an answer.

"The farro's," Jericho said, breaking the silence. "You're right Cole. I felt some of my mahier earlier. For just a split second." He shook his head. "They're trying to break through the ward."

"Impossible," Clara muttered.

"Why do you think that?" Gaber asked.

He pointed to me and then tapped his head. "Cole remembered seeing my dragon. Back at the field. It slipped my mind," he said, looking to the ground.

"How would that be possible? Cole has their tilium," Clara said.

"They're getting help." Gaber stood. "We need to get everyone to safety. Now."

"Who would help them?" I asked, already knowing the answer as dread permeated my body.

"There is only one creature strong enough to help them," Gaber whispered as he looked towards Clara. A look of unease passed between them.

"The eldens," Evander answered. "Last time they were here-"

"Let's focus on the now," Gaber demanded.

"The fairies are close," Annabelle piped in. "They feel it too. Something's out there."

"Two realms of the Woland guard were just dispatched. They'll be here by morning," Jericho added.

"I need to check in with Bran and make sure all the elves are accounted for." Gaber walked towards the double doors.

"We should come with you," Eva suggested.

"No. You need to stay here. The two of you need to be kept safe," Cairo said.

"It's our duty to be out there." I pointed to the doors. "It's why we were sent here in the first place."

"No, you came here to train," Cairo persisted.

"We came here to train in order to defeat the eldens." I shrugged my shoulders and shook my head. "And to protect all true beings."

My thoughts immediately went to my new friend, Mal and his sister. I was thankful I met them tonight. It would give me the courage to walk out those doors, and the drive to protect Paraiso in any way I could.

"I agree," Eva said. "We're going with Gaber." She stared at Cairo as she spoke. "It's our duty."

Cairo looked to the ground. It was clear he'd lost the fight. "Let's go then." He pushed past us and headed to the door.

Gaber opened the door and we all filed out into the night. Gaber and Clara lit the way as we passed over the glowing water. Gaber brought us to the same tree as our first night here, and then nodded to the wooded walkway as both he and Clara disappeared from sight only to reappear on the bridge.

"How?" Eva whispered next to me.

"It seems our elf friends have been keeping some secrets," Jericho answered.

Eva released her wings and flew to join them. Beside me, Jericho and Cairo were, disappointingly, still in their human forms.

"Not enough space." Jericho shrugged. "Not to mention the ward is still up. If we fly through it, we won't be able to get back in."

"Right." The trio on the bridge eyed those of us stuck on the ground.

Gaber shook his head at the three of us down below. With a snap of his fingers, we swiftly joined them on the bridge. I looked over at him with raised eyebrows, but he just laughed and began the journey to wherever Bran was stationed. That little trick would have come in handy the first night we were here.

The higher we climbed through the trees, the clearer the night sky became. The bright moon and stars that were out earlier had disappeared. Blackness covered us. Whatever was out there even spooked the moon and stars into hiding. A tingle of fear shot through me. We reached a large hut, much larger than the one Eva and I had stayed in, and entered to find Bran and a handful of other elves rushing around while he barked orders. The elves disappeared only to reappear at a different location in a blink as they prepared themselves for combat.

"What do we know?" Gaber interrupted Bran as he shouted at the elves.

"Not much." He huffed in anger towards an elf that just stumbled in. "We're preparing for the worst."

"It's the farro's and the eldens," Gaber mouthed.

"How do you know that?" Bran stiffened. "Why would the eldens come back here?"

"I just do." Gaber tilted his head towards Eva and I. "We have something they want."

Bran pierced us with his golden stare. "Then give them what they want," he snarled. "No reason to put the rest in danger."

"The elves made an oath," Gaber growled.

"As did the trolls," Evander added.

"And the fairies," Annabelle said.

"We stand by the Keeper of Dragons. To the death," the three said in unison. Great. More promises of death.

"So." Gaber clapped his hands. "Fire up that tilium, Keeper. Looks like we're in for one heck of a battle."

Chapter Fourteen

Jericho jumped off the side of the hut, shifting midair. His powerful dragon stormed through the air to brief realm five. The other realms would arrive shortly. Queen Annabelle directed orders at the fairies that had just landed. They were not the same fairies I remembered from the grove. These fairies were ready for battle; they were covered in camouflaged armor from their wrists and chests down to their ankles. Long swords crisscrossed their backs hidden beneath their wings, and platinum helmets enclosed the tops of their heads. On the back of the helmets, a numbered rank was visible.

The sight of the warrior fairies made me uneasy. The sound of their wings as they buzzed in nervous excitement shot a pain through my temples. Everyone truly was scared of the eldens, not to mention the farros. I wondered what our plan was, especially now that everyone was here. How exactly did Queen Tana think she would get her tilium back from me?

Eva bumped my shoulder with hers. "Don't think like that. Tana isn't getting her tilium from you."

"That's why they're here," I whispered.

"Maybe. Maybe not," she muttered.

I looked over my shoulder at Eva. Her golden eyes were glued to Cairo, who was in deep discussion about battle strategies with Gaber and Evander. It was something about which I knew nothing of. Cairo peeked back at us, a worried look on his face. Cairo and Eva had become close since we arrived in Ochana only a few weeks ago. Something I had neglected to truly see until now. I hadn't seen it earlier, but I saw it now, in the way his red gaze swirled with fear, and in the way he kept raking his hand through his golden brown hair.

Gaber's body stiffened. "The dragons have arrived," he announced. "Your Woland is on his way back now." He pierced me with his amber gaze.

"How do you know that?" I asked.

They didn't have any phones or computers anywhere that I saw. The hut was set up similar to Crowne Hall; a large round wooden table sat in the middle with mismatched chairs haphazardly pushed in around it, stationed beneath a wide-open roof that reminded everyone of the disappearing stars as darkness enclosed us. A few plants dotted the walls, and that was it. Not a single person sat at the table. Clusters of beings took up space in front of the grand windows that surrounded us.

Gaber chuckled and tapped his head. "I know everything that goes on in Paraiso."

"Do you plan on letting him back in?" Cairo asked.

Gaber rolled his eyes. "Unfortunately, yes." He waved his hand at the window. "He's already here."

A large thump hit the rail outside the hut. Jericho stomped inside, shaking his arms at his side and cracking his neck side to side. His black hair covered his eyes, illuminating the scowl on his face.

"Thirty-five dragons have arrived, twenty of which are already patrolling the sky." Jericho pushed his hair out of his face. "The elden and the farro are here. The sky stinks of their stench."

"You didn't see them?" Eva asked.

"No. But they knew I sensed them." He turned to Gaber. "They're playing with us."

"As is the way of the fallen," Annabelle commented.

"So, what's the plan?" Eva asked.

"We wait," Gaber said.

"Agree. They're impatient. We won't have to wait long before they show their hand." Jericho added.

"Bet you never thought you'd agree with an elf," Gaber chuckled.

"Don't push it, elf," Jericho growled and sighed. "Are all of your elves accounted for?"

"Yes, Clara is with them now. We have them bunkered underground with the trolls," Gaber explained.

"Good. We will need to concentrate on the threat at hand, not civilians," Jericho began to pace the room.

"They prefer to be called true," Evander's rough voice piped in. "Yes, this is a war. Just remember who you're fighting for."

Jericho glanced over at Evander and shrugged his shoulders, then looked to the pitch-dark sky with a shake to his head.

"What do they want?" I asked.

"It's more than you." Gaber rested on the sill of one of the windows. "They wanted us all to gather, and we did."

"Now we wait." Jericho looked back over to us. "We will know soon enough."

***

Exhaustion took over, and I leaned against one of the walls to the hut. The sun peeked over the trees to signal the start of a new day. We were at a stalemate, each waiting for the other to show itself.

Eva picked her head up off my shoulder and yawned. "Maybe they left?" She muttered.

"They're still here," Cairo answered from across the room where he sat with his arms resting on his knees.

Jericho continued to pace, stopping at each window he passed. He searched the area and continued to the next. Gaber lay flat on the large round table, arms crossed behind his head. His amber eyes stared through the open ceiling as he too searched for something, anything. Queen Annabelle sat delicately in the seat at the head of the table. Her hands were folded in her lap and her eyes were closed. The only one to leave the hut was Evander, who had left a few hours ago to check on the elves and trolls.

My stomach grumbled in hunger, and Eva's answered with a growl. We looked at each other and broke into a fit of laughter. Jericho paused his pacing and glared at us.

"Something funny?" he asked.

"Leave them alone," Gaber said from his position on the table. "They're hungry and tired."

"And I'm not?" Jericho shot back.

Gaber sighed. "You're what, a thousand years old? They're kids."

288

"I am not a thousand." Jericho pinned Gaber with his fiery gaze. "They are the Keeper of Dragons. Regardless of their age, they have a responsibility-"

"Save it," Gaber interrupted. "You threw those kids into a war without even looking. It was luck they didn't die taking on the farros." Gaber threw his legs over the edge of the table, rubbing his face roughly with his hands. "And now the eldens are hot on their trail. You should have protected them longer. Trained them longer. You literally ripped them from their homes and dropped them in the middle of a war with beings they didn't know existed. It's amazing they're still alive."

"You have no idea the strength dragons possess. They don't need to be coddled," Jericho spit.

"Coddled, no. But they're children." Gaber pushed off the table and stood.

"They're 18. Legal adults."

Gaber shook his head. "They're not human, something they didn't even know or realize until they were 18. You dragons never cease to amaze me."

"Can you guys knock it off?" Eva muttered from beside me. "We are sitting right here. No need to talk about us as if we weren't."

"My apologies, Golden Dragon," Gaber said. "I will find you both some food." Gaber walked past Jericho and headed towards the main door to the hut.

Just as his hand hit the door to push it open, a cold breeze filtered through the hut. The table Gaber had just been laying on froze solid, ice crystallizing across the top and cracking the surface. Water droplets sprung from the streams below, completely surrounding us in an aqua glow. The water continued to rise until it hit the shell of the ward, where it stuck. The droplets attached themselves together as they enclosed us in a cave of water.

No one moved. The only sounds were the noise of our quickened breaths. The water at the shell began to crystalize, and the particles began to freeze as the temperature continued to drop.

"The water of our ancestors," Gaber muttered. "How? We need to stop this." He whispered in disbelief as he walked closer to the center of the room.

"Stop!" Jericho shouted to Gaber, holding his hand up to halt the elf's movements. "Don't move. Something's here."

I searched the hut, but my senses were as frozen as the water, for I felt nothing but coldness. Again, no one moved or said a word. We waited. I sucked in a breath at the same time a sound above us broke the silence. All heads swung to the open-aired roof; we watched in horror as the frozen cave around us began to crack. Tiny pieces of ice fell from the sky and I shielded my eyes with my arm. A shudder pulsed through the hut as the ice exploded outward, shattering into fine flakes of snow falling from the sky, covering all that I could see.

I dusted off my head and arms with my hands. Everyone was doing the same except Gaber, who stood rooted to the ground, eyes closed, unmoving. He sucked in a harsh breath as tears rolled down his face.

"My family," he uttered. "The water. It's gone." He finally opened his eyes.

"It will melt." Eva comforted as she walked towards Gaber.

"Your ward is down," Jericho informed Gaber. "Can you put it back up?"

Gaber shot a glare towards the dragon. "No. The strength of the ward came from within the water, the tilium of my ancestors." Gaber roughly rubbed the tears from his face. "Maybe when it melts."

"We need to get to safety. We're exposed, and I don't sense any dragons in the air," Jericho said as he searched the sky.

"Crowne Hall or the trolls' tunnels. They are the safest," Gaber replied, gesturing to the door.

Suddenly, a loud thud pierced the air as black smoke seeped through the crack in the table, winding into a tight coil and creating the silhouette of a man. The smoke began to dissipate into the air, in its place stood a man with long black hair and pointed ears. His orange gaze was identical to Gaber's as he scanned the room, stopping on me with a smirk marked along his face. His eyes swung to Gaber, who had placed himself in front of Eva.

"Eldrick," Gaber articulated. "You're not welcome here."

A familiar cackle echoed around us. "Coley. You have something of mine," Tana's voice screeched.

Eldrick laughed. "Make me." He threatened as he pierced Gaber with his amber gaze and raised his hands.

Smoke wafted from his fingers as darkness surrounded us. I waved my hands through the smoke, searching for my friends. I walked to where Eva had just stood, but came up empty. Silence enclosed me; blackness met my eyes.

I was alone.

Chapter Fifteen

I fell to my knees and squeezed my eyes shut. Silence. The black smoke burned my throat and made my eyes itch. I rubbed at them in an effort to make the pain go away. It didn't help. I opened my mouth in an attempt to scream. No noise came out. All it did was effectively make me choke and cough.

As I sputtered through the smoke, I sent up a silent prayer for help to anyone who was listening. The oxygen around me began to lessen as I grabbed at my throat. I projected my screams out to anyone who could hear them, but there was only silence. I received no answer. My shoulder hit the ground, and I rolled to my back just as I sucked in the last bit of oxygen.

A sudden bright flash of light exploded through the room. I covered my eyes with my hands. My body trembled as energy zipped through me. I cracked my eyes open just as the smoke vaporized into thin air. I gulped in the fresh air as quickly as I could, attempting to clear my lungs.

"Cole! Cole!" Jericho shouted between pants as he attempted to catch his breath.

He pulled himself off the floor and scrambled over to me. He skidded next to me and dropped to his knees. He pulled my shoulders off the ground and searched me for any injuries. Jericho's eyes held a wild expression between worry and anger. He exhaled in relief when he found that I was indeed okay. The others around us assessed each other for injuries in a hurried mess.

"Where is she?" A panicked voice broke through the chaos. "Eva!" Cairo's voice shook as he searched the hut.

I looked to where she was last standing to find the spot empty. Cairo jumped out a nearby window onto the deck and ran the perimeter. I sat frozen as the thump of his footfalls echoed around me. He entered the room with one last scan, and collapsed onto the ground.

"She's gone," Cairo whispered. "They took her," He looked over to me from where he had fallen. "I failed her."

"Everyone up," Gaber demanded as he found his feet and examined the room. "Is anyone hurt?"

"We weren't the target," Queen Annabelle said. "They came here for the Golden Dragon." She kneeled next to Cairo and rubbed his back.

"We will get her back," Gaber proclaimed, walking to the main entrance of the hut. "I must check in with Evander and Clara. I promise. We will get her back." He sighed and took off through the door.

"We will get her back," Queen Annabelle repeated to Cairo. "We will fight for her until our last breath."

"I failed her." Cairo shook his head. "I froze."

"You didn't freeze. Eldrick froze us. Literally. I couldn't get to Cole either." Jericho pulled me to my feet.

"Why her?" Cairo asked.

"Because he knew we'd fight to get her back, effectively bringing the fight to him. Home team advantage and all," Gaber stated as he walked back in with Evander.

"How?" I shook my head at the sight of the two of them. How did they get back here so quickly? Gaber only just left.

"There is much to your tilium you have yet to figure out. Once we retrieve the Golden Dragon, I will continue your training," Gaber answered.

"One question has been answered," Evander stated. "The eldens did help the farros. We are now in a battle against both."

"My guess is they have more fallen on their side," Gaber said. "Taking the Golden Dragon would, no question, start a fight. They are prepared."

"Battle." Jericho shook his head. "This is a war." He began to pace. "Prince Zane tried to convince me of this fact. My judgment was clouded."

"We've been at war for a hundred years." Gaber looked wryly at Jericho, who didn't notice. "That's old news."

"It seems the dragons have finally joined the war." Evander's eyes followed Jericho's restless movements across the room.

"Yes, but how long will they stay?" Gaber asked, looking between Cairo and Jericho.

Jericho glared at Gaber. "Enough. We stand with you and all true beings."

"As do the fairies," Annabelle added.

"And the trolls," Evander chimed in.

"Dragons, fairies, trolls and elves oh my," Prince Gaber sang. "This ought to be fun."

"Fun?" Cairo shouted.

Gaber held his hands up to ward off Cairo's anger, raising his eyebrows to show off his bright orange eyes. "Let's get the Golden Dragon back, shall we?"

"Where would they take her?" I asked. I prayed they hadn't hurt her; unsure how I'd survive if anything happened to her. She was the one person I had always been able to count on, my closest friend, the only family I truly had in this crazy new life of mine. As it was, we've barely had time to spend with each other. Ever since Eva arrived at Ochana, our lives had been stuck in fast forward.

"The swamp." Gaber rubbed his face. "It will no doubt be a trap."

"The swamp? Where exactly is that?" I was pretty sure I wouldn't like the answer.

"Zulia," Gaber answered, walking to a nearby window. "Venezuela."

"We've never been successful in gaining entrance into the swamp," Jericho stated. "The energy they have protecting them is one we've only seen there."

"Neither have we. Eldrick has found a way to harvest his tilium." Gaber softly touched the snow on the windowsill. "We recycle ours."

"What do you mean?" I walked closer to Gaber as he continued to gaze at the snow, which should have melted by now in the heat.

"When an elf passes on to the next world, their tilium is left behind." Gaber turned to face me. "The streams that crisscross throughout Paraiso contain the tilium of my ancestors, and all past elves." He looked to the ground.

"Used to, anyway. It's what kept our protective wards strong."

"The amount of tilium Eldrick would've needed is incomprehensible," Evander said with a shake of his head.

"Our mahier is strong, and with the tilium of the elves and fairies..." Jericho paused his pacing. "Together. Together we might be able to break through the elden's barrier."

Gaber's amber gaze landed on me. "Did any of you wonder where the smoke disappeared to?"

"It left with Eldrick," Queen Annabelle answered.

"No." Gaber moved closer to me. "The fear inside our Keeper dissipated it." He tapped my chest. "The energy that flows through you is much stronger than the energy that flows through any other being, including Eldrick. Because yours is pure."

"But the farro's tilium is dark," I stammered. "It's not pure."

"No, but you are, and the tilium resides within you." Gaber turned towards Jericho. "Even if Tana is able to pull the tilium out of the Prince, it will be no good to her."

"If what you're saying is true. Eldrick has an abundance of tilium. Wouldn't he have shared the wealth with the farros?" I asked.

"No. I've felt no shift of tilium to any being. Eldrick hasn't and won't share," Gaber answered.

"Why? I mean, I can only imagine the damage they could cause together." A shiver of fear raced through me.

"Power," Gaber whispered.

Power. The last thing we wanted was for either of the eldens or the farros to have any kind of power. Their own hunger for control and selfishness just might be their downfall. I shook my head in an attempt to erase that thought; first we needed to find Eva.

"Why would Tana stay with Eldrick?" I asked. "She must know then that he won't help them."

"Oh, I'm sure she does," Gaber replied. "But I'm sure she has a plan to stab him in the back as well." He shrugged his shoulders. "But Eldrick is smarter. He will see it coming." Gaber turned back towards the window. "Fallen creatures never truly work together. That's what makes them unpredictable."

"And unstable," Jericho added. "Which means we need to make a plan now on how to get the Golden Dragon back."

"Time isn't our friend," Evander added. "That's how Eldrick wanted it."

"He wants us to rush to the swamp." Gaber's ears twitched in thought. "He expects us to be careless." He rubbed his hands roughly across his face.

Jericho stooped down to meet Cairo's eyes. "We need you to get your head on straight. I've never seen you so-"

"Emotional?" Gaber suggested as he cocked his head towards the two.

"There is more to this," Cairo whispered.

"What does that mean?" Jericho asked as he stood to his full height.

"Verum Salit," Gaber stated. "Our ace." He turned towards me. "Two aces."

Smoke steamed around Jericho as Gaber spoke. The flames in his eyes danced from Cairo to Gaber. "What do you mean?"

"The elf is right." Cairo shook his head. "It's how I found her that day."

"That's impossible," Jericho barked. "The Golden Dragon is a dramon. You're a dragon."

Laughter spilled from Gaber. "And that means what exactly? The last set was many years ago. And as you know, they weren't of the same species, either."

Confusion wrapped itself around me. Verum Salit. What did that mean? And why was Jericho going into smoky dragon mode over it? Gaber continued to laugh as he turned towards Evander and Annabelle.

"This is good. Eldrick will never see this coming!" Evander exclaimed.

"And he has no clue how powerful the Prince is," Annabelle said, pointing at me.

Gaber hurried towards the table, as he passed by two chairs that had been tipped over, he stopped and picked them up. He tucked the chairs in around the table and plopped down on the larger of the two chairs sitting at the head of the table. Annabelle took the one to his left and Evander grabbed another to sit next to her. Revitalized energy zipped around the table as the three began to talk strategies.

"Hold on." I waved my hands in the air. "What does all this mean?"

"It means secrets have been held," Jericho stated. "Sit." Jericho pointed to the table. "Tell us everything."

J.A. Culican

Chapter Sixteen

Verum Salit. Those two words bounced in my head as I took a seat at the table next to Cairo. Jericho paced from one end of the hut to the other, stopping every few feet to huff out a growl then continue. The smoke that trailed behind him was light and airy, much different to the smoke Eldrick had dropped on us not too long ago. The snow that still lay on the table served as a reminder of the devastation he had left in his departure.

"Verum Salit," Cairo spoke from beside me. "True mate."

I pondered those two words. True mate. I knew from school that some animals—like wolves—mated for life. Were dragons the same way?

"Mate? You mean like werewolves?" I asked as I closed my eyes for the ludicrousness of that question.

Laughter exploded from the head of the table, reminding me that we weren't alone.

"And what do you know about werewolves?" Gaber asked.

"Just what I've read in books." I shrugged, feeling the heat from my embarrassment cover my neck.

"Books," Jericho echoed from across the room. He turned to face us in a swirl of smoke.

"I mean I know they aren't real. I just-"

"They're real," Gaber cut me off. "Just as every creature you've ever read about in your books is. Where do you think those ideas came from?"

"I'm not a werewolf and neither is Eva," Cairo said. "Verum Salit is a belief we learned from Aprella, but not many beings believe it to be true."

"It's quite rare," Annabelle stated.

"You mean extinct," Jericho growled. "How do you know this is the case?"

"You never questioned how I found Eva that day? The day of her first shift." Cairo shook his head. "I was doing a perimeter check of Ochana, and yet I found her in Texas."

Jericho pointed his red gaze at Cairo. "Now's your chance to explain."

Cairo rubbed his hands across his face and dropped them to his lap. "There was a light in the distance. One I didn't fear. It felt close. Much closer than it was."

"I don't understand," I said.

Cairo's eyes met mine. "The light within her sang to me. I followed without a thought." He tore his eyes from mine and met Jericho's. "I found her in a park near her school. She'd just begun a morning run." He hung his head.

"Four thousand miles." Jericho placed his hands on his hips. "So you're saying, for four thousand miles you flew without a thought? Towards a light in the sky?" He raised his head and stunned both Cairo and me with a dark red glare.

"Verum Salit," Cairo whispered. "I reached the park just as her first shift began. Her strength amazes me. She had no knowledge of what was happening to her. No idea she was a dramon, or even what a dramon was."

"What does it mean to be true mates?" I asked.

"It means their souls are aligned. Just as the stars aligned the day the Golden Dragon moved in next door to you," Queen Annabelle explained. "A much higher being has been preparing this for a long time."

"The Keeper of Dragons would come at a time of great fear." Gaber pushed his white hair out of his face. "The fates knew the two of you would need the fiercest warriors by your sides."

"I was created almost 150 years ago," Cairo stated, "which means they have known this time of fear would come for quite some time."

Cairo looked to be around 25 at most. His golden brown hair fell to his shoulders in a tangled mess. He constantly pulled at his hair in frustration, which he was doing as we spoke.

"Have you explained this to the Golden Dragon?" Queen Annabelle asked.

Cairo cleared his throat. "No. I am her protector. I will always be her protector. I need her to see me as such in order to keep her safe." He looked to me. "And she is one half of the Keeper of Dragons. I must focus on aiding the two of you on your journey."

"So, the two of you are going to get married?" I asked.

Cairo chuckled. "It's a bit more complicated than that."

"Meaning?"

"Meaning they share a soul," Gaber chimed in. "I'm surprised the Golden Dragon has not sensed the connection."

"She has." Cairo shook his head. "It took much persuasion on my part to chalk it up to her being my charge and I may have had to use my mahier a few times to block the connection." He shrugged his shoulders.

"But the connection's there. Which means you can find her." Gaber stood, his chair scraping indents through the snow. "We can use that connection to find her."

"But I thought you knew where she was?" I asked.

"We know where the eldens live. But none of us has ever been able to get through their wards. It's complex. They've managed to harvest more tilium than I've ever seen or has ever existed," Gaber explained as he paced around the table.

"Even if Cairo can locate the Golden Dragon, how do we get through the wards?" Evander shook the snow off his green hair.

"Maybe the Prince will be able to get through. He wields the power of both mahier and tilium," Queen Annabelle suggested.

"That's a big maybe," Gaber said as he scratched his chin. "We need to have a back-up plan. My guess is that even the Keeper won't be able to get through."

"Why do you think that?" I asked even though I completely agreed with Gaber. Chances are I wouldn't have a clue how to even use the tilium and mahier to get through, especially without Eva by my side.

"Somewhere around 1,000 strikes of lightning hits the swamp every hour of every day, almost every day of the year." Gaber shook his head. "I have no idea how Eldrick did it. But that's how he has been so successful in not only hiding from us, but in harvesting their tilium."

"The wards are impossible to get through" Evander mused.

"No one has noticed this?" A constant lightning storm. As cool as it sounded, it also frightened me to death. Lightning in a swamp seemed a bit dangerous.

"Of course they have. Humans have blamed all sorts of different things on the lightning. Weather. Gods. It changes every hundred years or so." Gaber shrugged and plopped back down in his seat.

"The eldens go in and out through the wards unscathed. So, there's a trick to it," Jericho stated as his pacing continued.

"Wait." Annabelle jumped from her seat. "We have someone on the other side of the ward." Her wings began to flap quickly. "No one has ever been on the other side of their wards."

"Do you think we'd be able to project our thoughts to her?" I pondered out loud.

"What do you mean?" Gaber asked. "Project your thoughts?" His yellow gaze lit up the table.

"It seems many secrets will be revealed today." Jericho sighed behind me. "Our mahier gives us the ability to speak to each other" He tapped his head. "In our minds."

"Real words?" Gaber asked. "I thought you could only send out feelings to each other. Like an alert for help or something." He looked between us. "That's so cool!"

"Don't get excited. Your wards were strong enough to block our thoughts. Chances are, so are the elden's."

"Maybe. I mean we knew you could send signals to each other, or so that's what we thought. Essentially, we designed ours in a way to block them. We just added that measure when we invited the Keeper of Dragons here." Gaber rubbed his hands together. "There's a possibility Eldrick hasn't even thought about it."

"What would we tell her? I mean, if we can actually speak with her." I asked.

"Maybe she has seen something, or knows of how they get through the wards. The lightning surrounds the swamp. So even if the wards are down, we still have the lightning to compete with," Gaber answered.

That thought transported me back to the time Eva and I attempted to dig a hole under our cabin to create a secret escape route. A small smile crept along my face at the memory. We spent days using little gardening shovels to dig up a hole big enough for us to fit through. At just 12 years old we thought this was the coolest idea ever. Until we hit the cinder blocks that held the cabin up. Our little shovels didn't stand a chance against the cement blocks. We attempted to dig under them but after about a week, we gave up. As a consolation, we ended up kicking out a piece of rotted wood in the back of the cabin. In its place, we tailored a secret door that was hidden by bushes on the outside. Every time it rained we ended up with a puddle of water in our cabin. That small hole still existed today, even though I'm pretty sure neither of us could fit through it anymore.

I dropped my chin to my chest and sighed. The last few weeks I'd barely been able to spend time with Eva. The time we did spend together was in training or council meetings, and even before that, we had grown apart in our senior year. Eva was so focused on college and graduating, and I had brushed her off when she tried to get me focused on the same. I wished I had done things different. I missed out on my last year of being human, of being a kid with no worries and no responsibilities.

"What's turning in your head?" Gaber asked, breaking me of my thoughts.

I shrugged my shoulders. "Maybe there's a hidden entrance or something?" It seemed such an elementary idea that they had surely looked into already.

Gaber chuckled quietly and turned to Jericho. "Have the dragons looked for a hidden entrance?"

"No," Jericho huffed. "Most of our efforts were focused on seeing through their wards to find a chink or hole. We haven't attempted to get through their wards in many years." His head drooped in what I realized must be shame.

"No surprise there," Gaber shot back. "We always have eyes on the swamp. Unfortunately, we haven't been able to get very close."

"Same here," Queen Annabelle said. "A squad of fairies is always circling the swamp."

Jericho's eyes shot to Gaber and Annabelle. "Have they seen anything? Can you make contact with them?"

"Nothing's changed," Gaber answered. "Bran has made contact. No one has seen an elden come or go from the swamp in years."

"Are you sure they're there? Maybe they moved?" I asked.

"Your hidden door idea is making more sense by the minute," Jericho growled. "No one thought it was strange that the eldens never left the swamp?"

"She's there," Cairo whispered. "And she's scared." His body trembled with each word.

Eva was the bravest person I knew, so if she was scared, I hated to think what that meant for the rest of us.

Chapter Seventeen

The dragons were coming. All of them. Gaber was fit to be tied. The last thing he wanted was the dragons invading Paraiso, but with Eva kidnapped by the eldens, he had agreed on the condition that the dragons would have no contact with the elves or trolls. Most had gone into hiding underground, while the few that ventured out would be housed in Crowne Hall until the wards were back up.

My eyes fell to the snow still covering the ground and trees around me. The snow sparkled from the sun beating down, but the beauty around me came at a steep cost. The price was all the ancient tilium recycled by past elves. I searched for a single melted drop. One drop would give hope back to the elves. Hope for security and hope for the connection they felt to their ancestors. I found none.

I sat on a nearby log and dropped my head to my hands, raking my fingers through my hair, which had grown longer in the past few weeks than I'd ever let it before. My dull brown hair now curled around my ears. I desperately needed a haircut, but Eva had always cut it for me. I didn't remember how it started or why. One day during one of our cabin visits, she told me to sit on an old milk crate, pulled the clippers out and cut my hair, laughing each time I flinched. Every few weeks the clippers reappeared, and that was that.

Eva was gone. Taken by the eldens and farros. King Eldrick and Queen Tana. I prayed they hadn't harmed her. For Eva to be scared, I couldn't imagine what they had done to her or what she had seen. Then there was Cairo. Cairo was Eva's true mate. Verum Salit. The concept confused me. But I knew Cairo would protect and fight for Eva more than any other being and that knowledge gave me a bit of comfort. She would need a true warrior for life by her side. A time of fear was no joke. I pulled my head from my hands and found Cairo's red gaze inches from my own. Startled, I tumbled off the back of the log.

"I'm sorry, my Prince." Cairo held his hand out to help me up.

I took it and he yanked me from the ground. I brushed the snow off and sat again, this time with Cairo beside me. We sat in silence, gazing at the wonderment around us. Cairo sighed. I turned my head in his direction, taking in his pale complexion and stringy hair. He looked horrible.

"Thanks, my Prince." A small smile pulled on the corners of his lips. "It seems my appearance mirrors my emotions."

"Can you still feel her?" I asked. Cairo right now was our only link to Eva.

"Yes. Her fear has spiked a few times in the last hour or so." He closed his eyes. "She is strong. Stronger than any Dramon I have ever met."

"We need to go to her. We need to save her," I mumbled.

"And we will. I can promise you that." Cairo's voice was strong. "They need her alive. It's the only way all will fight. And Eldrick wants us all."

"Why would he want to take on all of us at once? Wouldn't it be easier one at a time?" I wouldn't want to take on the dragons, elves, trolls and fairies all at once.

"I don't know, but he will be prepared. Which means he thinks he can win." Cairo raked his fingers through his hair. "I wanted to talk to you about what was discussed earlier."

"Verum Salit," I whispered.

"Yes." Cairo turned his head to look me in the eyes. "Our souls are aligned. It means her strengths are my weaknesses and her weaknesses are my strengths. One complete soul."

"But you're a Woland. Woland's are brave and strong. Just like Eva," I stated.

"You're right. But she is also smart and cunning. Loyal and trustworthy. Nurturing and peaceful." His eyes glowed. "She is many things I am not."

"And you're sure about this?" I asked.

"Yes." Cairo looked down at the snow. "I will protect you as I protect her. Together, the two of you create an entity we've never experienced before. The strength possessed by the two of you is unfathomable."

"It's hard to believe you all think we are this powerful force." I gazed out over the snow-covered trees.

"Not believe. We know." Cairo tapped my chest. "The proof is within you right now. The proof lies with the tilium. The tilium you so easily stole from the farros."

"It's not who I am. I'm petrified of the eldens and the farros. I'm scared I will let you all down." The truth spilled from my lips without a thought. I didn't fear rejection from Cairo.

"It's who you are now." Cairo's eyes glowed brighter as he spoke each word. "And everyone is scared. Fearful of the unknown. It's new to you. It's not to us. Well them." Cairo tilted his head towards the hut above us. "I was raised a human, like you. Human parents. Human friends." Cairo paused. "When I was sent to my biological parents, I was petrified. I even tried to run away. Coward is not a Woland trait and yet here I sit, red eyes and all."

"You were just a kid." I shook my head. "Of course you were scared."

"And you are also just a kid. 18 yes, but to a dragon, you're a baby," Cairo stated.

"They don't treat me like a baby. Within a few days they dropped me in the Grove-"

"You're a dragon." Cairo looked to the ground. "The dragons around us—the ones who make the rules—they were born and raised on Ochana. They don't truly understand our fears."

"What color were your eyes?" I asked, unsure where the question came from.

"Brown. Much like yours." He pointed to my now light brown eyes. "Before they changed. Don't get stuck on the colors of who or what any of us used to be or who we are now. Who we are in the future, that's what matters."

"Future. Is this how my future will be? Constantly being hunted by the fallen. Constantly hunting the fallen."

I closed my eyes, attempting to erase the vision in my head. "It's not how I thought my life would go. That's for sure."

"It's the hand that was created for you. You have many who trust in you and the fates. You will always have an army behind you. You will never have to fight this life alone." Cairo stood as his gaze reached the tops of the trees. "The Woland guard is here. We better get back up to the hut." He gestured to the elves' command center above us, hidden amongst the trees.

"Yea. Cairo?" I stopped.

"Yes, my Prince?"

"Promise me that no matter what happens, you will protect Eva. Get her to safety." A chill ran up my spine. Something bad was going to happen.

Cairo turned and gave me his full attention, placing a hand over his heart. "I promise I will protect the Golden Dragon with my life." He nodded and walked towards the ladder Jericho had procured. Just as his foot left the ground he turned back to me. "I will protect you with my life as well. She would never forgive me if something were to happen to you," he said before ascending the ladder two rungs at a time.

I absorbed the winter wonderland around me one last time before I followed Cairo up to the command center. Once I reached the deck I could hear the commotion going on within the hut. It seemed the dragons had indeed arrived. Jericho barked orders to the team leaders of each realm, with about twenty new Wolands in attendance. Once Jericho finished with each leader, they would take off out the door to bid whatever order they were given. Jericho would then move on to the next. Gaber and Evander stood on the other side of the hut, well out of the way, speaking to a small group of elves and trolls. Queen Annabelle was nowhere to be found.

"Responsibilities are being divided," Cairo said from beside me. "This isn't just a rescue mission for the Golden Dragon. We must also protect the elves and trolls until the wards can be restored."

"When will that be?" I whispered.

"They've never been down. No being has ever been able to break through." Cairo shrugged his shoulders. "At this point we don't know." Cairo tilted his head towards Gaber and Evander. "That's what they're discussing now."

It never crossed my mind that all the elves and trolls would be left here unprotected as we all stormed the elden's swamp. We couldn't leave them unprotected. We would need to wait until the wards were back up. If something happened to them while we were gone, it would destroy us all.

"Don't worry, my Prince. The elves and trolls will be protected," Cairo assured me.

"Yes, the dragons are wonderful elven protectors. They have always protected us in the past," Clara sneered from behind us. "Excuse me." She glared at Cairo as she walked past us towards Gaber. "Keeper, thank you for your concern."

"I'm sorry, my Prince," Cairo apologized. "Our relationship with other true beings is stressed. We will earn their trust once again. We must."

"I understand. You all lost one of your own. It's not easy to forget or forgive." I answered.

I watched the interaction between Gaber and his sister. Clara's voice rose as she expressed her concerns for whatever the plan was. Her arms swung around as she eyed each person in the group. Her eyes grew brighter with each second that went on until they were nothing more than two orange spotlights glowing right at Gaber.

"A decision has been made," Gaber announced from beneath her unhappy glare. "The tilium of the elves and trolls who reside here will raise the wards. Their tilium should be able to keep the wards up for 48 hours." Gaber turned to Clara. "In my absence, Princess Clara will be left in charge of Paraiso."

"Two realms of Woland's will also stay behind to patrol the sky above Paraiso," Jericho added.

Queen Annabelle entered the hut. "I fear I only have fifteen fairies to leave behind. Eighty-five have already been dispatched to the swamp and the rest were sent back to the grove to protect the rest of the fairies back home."

"We appreciate all that you have done and all that you offer for protection," Gaber said to both Jericho and Annabelle. "We leave for the swamp in the morning. Together we will rescue the Golden Dragon. Together we will defeat the farros." Gaber's voice grew stronger. "Together we will defeat the eldens. Together we will end the time of fear."

J.A. Culican

Chapter Eighteen

The journey to the swamp would only take a few hours. The plan was to make contact with Eva and search for a hidden entrance, but if we were unsuccessful within two days, we would return to Paraiso. As much as the idea to leave Eva there longer killed me, I knew she would never forgive herself or us if something happened to the elves and trolls in our absence.

Once the last of the dragons returned from feeding, we would be on our way. I wondered about the elves and few trolls who planned on crashing the swamp with us. How would they transport themselves there? Would they ride on the backs of the dragons? A slight breeze blew through my hair as I leaned against a lone tree overlooking the ocean. We would depart Africa from the same spot we arrived at, only we wouldn't be heading towards Ochana, but Venezuela. Gaber and Jericho were confident Eva would be there. I prayed they were right, even though we had no idea what would be waiting for us when we got there.

Quiet thuds sounded behind me, the dragons returning from their hunt. I felt them as they approached from almost a mile away. My senses had grown stronger these last few days when they weren't blocked by the eldens.

"My Prince," Jericho called. "It's time to leave."

I pushed off the tree and turned towards him. In front of me, most of the Woland guard took up the space to my right while a large group of elves, with a sprinkling of trolls and fairies stood to my left. The two groups ignored each other. How were we supposed to fight as a team like this? I hung my head. This wouldn't work.

"Together. You promised we'd fight together. Stand together." I picked my head up and leveled my gaze to the beings around me. "Together!" I shouted as my emotions took over.

"My Prince-"

"Divided we will lose," I cut Jericho off. "Eva. The Golden Dragon. The Keeper of Dragons will be lost." I inhaled a large gulp of air and exhaled it in anger. "Without her, a time of fear will destroy you all. The fallen will win. Evil will win." I shook my head. "You have five minutes to fix this." I wagged my hand between the two groups.

Without waiting for a response, I turned and jumped off the side of the cliff. I shifted mid-jump and took off over the water. The fear I held deep within exploded, causing my brief surge of courage. The elves and the dragons needed to work together, just as they promised the night before. My anger drifted away as I soared low over the water. I dropped one of my hind legs and let my claw splash through the cool ocean water. Twisting to the side, I commenced my flight back to the cliff. We didn't have time to waste. I prayed I would at least find that a temporary truce had been reached during my brief absence. If not...I stopped my train of thought before it had the chance to devour me. No matter what, Eva would be saved.

The lone tree came into view as I approached the cliff. The closer I flew, the clearer the Wolands and elves appeared. I could see Jericho smoke-free in his human form while he spoke with Gaber. That was a good sign. Landing with a low thump, I shifted back to my human form, looking between Gaber and Jericho. Gaber sported a small smirk, and Jericho's usual glare was plastered on his face. Another good sign.

"My Prince-"

"Are we ready to go?" I asked, glancing around the group. "We have less than 48 hours."

"Yes, my Prince," Jericho answered. "Each being here holds the same goal."

"Let's go and get the Golden Dragon, shall we?" Gaber clapped his hands. "See ya there." He winked and disappeared.

My mouth fell open as I looked to the spot Gaber had just stood. I waved my hands in the general direction of the other elves. "Where—?"

"Elves," Jericho growled. "More secrets. Get in the air. We must fly fast."

I turned back towards the group of elves and watched as they disappeared one by one. When the last elf was gone, the trolls began their own disappearing act. Queen Annabelle strolled over to me with her wings buzzing from flapping in the breeze.

"Just another perk of the tilium," she said, resting a hand on my shoulder. "You will learn to do the same soon enough." Her feet left the ground as she looked down at me and tilted her head to the ocean. "We better get a move on it. Who knows what Gaber will do in our absence," she smiled softly and took off over the water.

"Tilium. Then why is she not disappearing as well?" I asked Jericho and Cairo.

"We are here to guide you in safety to the Golden Dragon," one of the fairies stated before she took off after Queen Annabelle.

Cairo chuckled beside me. "It seems the fairies plan on keeping our Prince safe." He bumped Jericho's shoulder, shifted, and soared into the air after the fairies.

Jericho shook his head. "Stick close to Cairo and me. We get the Golden Dragon and we get out. Do you understand me? We are not there to defeat the eldens." He paused. "Not today, anyway." Jericho shifted into dragonic mode and glided off the side off the cliff.

I took a large breath, shifted, and followed after Jericho. Cairo swept back and followed behind me. The sun reflected off the water as we sped towards South America. Everyone was on alert. The eldens and the farros were unpredictable. No one knew exactly what we would be faced with once we arrived in Venezuela. I threw my senses out as far as I could, crossing my claws in hopes I wouldn't feel any other beings, except the ones who currently surrounded me. Nothing. I exhaled in relief. We flew in silence, fully aware of the dangers we would face soon enough. When land became visible ahead, the first signs of exhaustion swept over me.

Venezuela's coast came into view. The peaceful sound of the waves lapping over the sandy beaches was a beautiful deception. The dragons and fairies began their descent on what seemed to be a deserted part of the beach. As each dragon landed, they shifted into their human forms. I landed next to Jericho, who had already begun to shout orders.

Gaber and Evander stepped out behind the nearby dunes, their appearance effectively pausing all movement. Gaber shook as Evander guided him towards us. He spoke low under his breath with his eyes closed. I took a step in their direction but was stopped by a heavy hand on my shoulder.

"It's okay," Queen Annabelle said. "Gaber has placed a protective ward around us. It's much like the one at Paraiso. No being can enter without permission."

Evander sat Gaber down on the sand as we all encircled him. "He's almost done. The energy here is strong." Evander stuck his tongue out to taste the air, his rough green hair blowing wildly in the breeze. "It has taken much of his tilium to protect us. He will need to rest."

"How long will he need?" Jericho barked.

Evander shrugged his shoulders. "I don't know. The air is saturated with tilium. I've never felt anything like it."

"Me neither. The tilium has never been this potent before." Queen Annabelle observed. "The eldens have grown much stronger than we had anticipated."

"Where are the rest of the elves and trolls?" Jericho barked, scanning the area.

"Scattered around the edge of the ward." Evander gestured to the barrier that shimmered around us. "I suggest you get some dragons in the air. The ward isn't stable."

I watch as the ward flexed and tightened around us. It was the first time I was able to see the gleam that protected us. In Paraiso, the ward was invisible.

I pointed towards the top of the ward. "Can humans see this?"

Evander looked up. "See what?"

"The ward." I walked towards the side where it met the sand, and placed my hand over the shimmer.

"You can see it?" Evander asked as he squinted towards the sky.

"Of course. Can't you?" I turned to face the troll.

"No." He walked next to me and looked at my hand that still hovered over the wards wall.

"The tilium," Gaber croaked from his spot on the sand. "He holds so much in him. He can see it where we can only feel it." He stumbled to his feet and placed his hands on his knees. "We must move. No doubt they know we've landed."

I turned to Cairo. "Can you feel Eva? Is she here?"

"Yes, she's here," Cairo responded as he walked towards the dunes. "Her energy flutters in and out."

"Gaber, you good?" Evander asked as he walked towards him.

"Yup." He shook out his arms as he stood tall. "Let's go save the Golden Dragon!"

The elves and trolls that remained followed behind Gaber as the Woland guard lifted into the air. Cairo, Jericho and I followed the elves as Queen Annabelle and the fairies surrounded us from behind, walking along the Tablazo Strait. Gaber had explained earlier that the Strait would lead us to Lake Maracaibo, or what the elves affectionately called the swamp. We decided to walk the Strait instead of fly in hopes that Cairo would feel Eva nearby.

My feet ached as I rubbed the back of my neck. No one spoke. My senses worked overtime as I searched for the eldens and farros. We broke free from the Strait as a large body of water became visible. The sight that welcomed us was one of sheer magic.

I stood with my mouth agape; lightning lit the sky in what seemed to be one continuous strike. The air shimmered, full of energy. The tilium encircling me energized my exhausted body, and I breathed deeply to allow my lungs to fill with renewed power. My body trembled as my senses picked up new energy sources.

The eldens and farros were here.

J.A. Culican

Chapter Nineteen

The hairs on my arm prickled. The energy in the air zipped around me as we circled the lake, searching for the swamp. My heart raced and sweat ran down my face, the tilium buzzing in anticipation of release. With each step we traveled, Cairo reassured me we were getting closer and closer to Eva.

A sinking feeling in the pit of my stomach suddenly stopped me in my tracks. I grabbed at my stomach and scanned the lake around us. Duckweed covered the edge of the lake, making it impossible to see through as lightning struck in the distance. The beings around me paused and stared at me.

"Cole. What is it?" Jericho searched the area around us.

"I don't know. I just feel—" I paused, wiping the sweat from my forehead. "Something."

"Your tilium is attracted to the tilium in the air. It's how Eldrick has been able to gather so much of it, by stealing it. I'm struggling to hold on to my own, and you, Keeper, hold much more than I." Gaber pushed his long white hair out of his face and shook his head. "You should go back to Paraiso. I fear Eldrick lured you here to steal the farros' tilium from you."

"No, not until we find Eva," I choked out and turned to Cairo. "How close is she?" I dropped my hands to my knees and sucked in a deep breath.

"It feels like she is standing next to me," Cairo stated. "She has to be close."

"It could be a trick. It's clear the eldens have grown much stronger than we anticipated," Queen Annabelle said as she flew next to me, rubbing my back. "I agree with Gaber. You should go back to Paraiso. We will continue our mission to rescue the Golden Dragon in your absence."

"No." I stood, shaking off Annabelle's touch. "We continue."

"Cole, you look unwell," Jericho said. "I agree with the elf. I will escort you back to Paraiso. Cairo will stay-"

"No." I shouted at him. "I must find Eva. She would do the same for any of us."

"My Prince, if something were to happen to you..." Cairo placed his hand on my shoulder. "She would never forgive herself."

"We're wasting time." My voice echoed through the charged air.

"That you are," a bellowed voice chuckled from behind us.

We all turned to see Eldrick hovering over the water, his dark hair blowing in the breeze. The lightning had picked up speed and more and more bolts crashed to the ground in the distance behind him. I stepped towards him but was effectively blocked by both Gaber and Jericho.

"The Golden Dragon, where is she?" Gaber asked as smoke began to billow behind Jericho.

Eldrick chuckled. "Your dragon won't work here." He waggled his finger at Jericho. "The farros have been good for something. Tana taught us how to block your mahier."

"The Golden Dragon!" Gaber screamed. "Where is she?"

"Oh brother dearest, do not fear. Your precious Golden Dragon is safe." Eldrick laughed.

"You are no longer my brother, Eldrick. You lost that title the night you killed our parents. The night you decimated the trolls. The night you killed your own kind." Gaber shook in fury as his voice rose.

"You're still not over that? It's been two hundred years." Eldrick shook his head as a grin spread across his face.

"And if that wasn't enough. You come back to our home, destroy our link to our ancestors and kidnap the Golden Dragon!" Gaber roared. "Where is she?"

"Right under your nose, safe as can be." He floated closer to us. "I'm not interested in your precious Golden Dragon. She is nothing to me."

"But I'm interested," a familiar voice shrieked from behind us.

I swung my head around to find Tana and the other farros enclosing us. Cairo placed himself in front of me, forcefully blocking me from sight.

"She's all yours." Eldrick snapped his fingers. "As a thank you."

The water under Eldrick began to spin. The longer it spun, the faster it whipped around him until a water funnel appeared below his feet, the center disappearing below the surface, and every inch of water drained from the lake.

Eldrick shrugged his shoulders. "You came to find the swamp," he said, spreading his arms out wide. "Let me show you the way." He chuckled as he lowered himself to the muck that now lay under him.

"We're here for the Golden Dragon, and that's it." Jericho shouted. "Give her to us and we'll leave."

"Scared, dragon? What could you possibly be scared of? Dragons don't do scared. They don't do feelings. Right, brother?" Eldrick looked to Gaber. "I'm quite surprised you teamed up with them, considering they ignored your call for help all those years ago." He laughed. "As if it would've made a difference."

"The Golden Dragon. I repeat, where is she?" Gaber's eyes lit up the space between Eldrick and himself.

"Patience, little brother. She's on her way." He rolled his amber eyes.

"My patience is thin." Gaber glared at Eldrick.

"Tana, could you help our dear Golden Dragon? She seems to be a bit stuck in the mud." Eldrick pointed his thumb over his shoulder.

"Gladly," Tana squealed.

Tana ran through our huddled pack and straight towards a hole that had begun to form in the mud. Just as she reached in, Eva flew out. Tana shrieked and fell backwards, covering herself in mud. Eva hovered a few feet over the hole, her head lolling to the side and her long red hair covering her face. Her arms and legs were crossed as if invisible ropes held her hostage.

"Whoops." Eldrick laughed. "Guess she wasn't that stuck." He raised his eyebrows and smirked. "As you can see, your precious Golden Dragon is right here, safe and sound."

"Eva!" I shouted as I attempted to get past Gaber and Jericho. "Eva! Wake up!" I continued to struggle against them until a strong pair of arms wrapped around me from behind.

"She's okay," Cairo whispered in my ear. "It's a spell. Her life force is strong."

I didn't care what it was. I needed to get to her and remove her from this swamp. Between Eldrick and Tana, I knew something horrible was about to happen. How was Cairo so calm? His Verum Salit was right there, so close.

"Ah, yes. The other half of The Keeper of Dragons. The one who stole the farros' tilium." He gestured to Tana, who stood to wipe the mud from her hands, a scowl on her face. "You and I really should talk. Can you feel it? The power of the tilium I've stolen over the years?"

"This isn't just stolen tilium." Gaber stepped forward. "You're growing it, creating it. An energy that's unnatural."

"You mean I've created an unbalance in the system. For once the fallen are more powerful than the pure. No longer equals." He raised his arms in the air as a bright cloud of smoke shimmered above him. "I control all the tilium that resides here, and soon I will control all that resides in Paraiso." He looked down at us and rose into the sky. "Bet you wish you chose the other side now, little brother." Eldrick shook his head as his dark amber eyes glowed. "It's too late now. Soon you will be left with nothing. Soon there will be nothing left of you."

"That's where you're wrong. I choose the side I belong on. I protect those that are true, those that are pure. I will fight until my dying breath to do just that." Gaber shouted, streams of light flew from his fingertips towards Eldrick.

Eldrick lowered his hands and pushed the light to the ground. It struck inches from where Tana still stood. She jumped back and landed smack dab in the mud, shaking in anger.

"Tsk, tsk, tsk, little brother." Eldrick wagged his finger at Gaber. "Did you really think it'd be that easy? Look around you." He waved his hands around the swamp. "I control everything you see. Even things you don't see." He laughed, throwing the cloud of smoke above him towards Gaber, who rolled out of the way, sprang up and returned a bolt of energy.

Smoke enveloped me as it seeped off the dragons. None were able to shift into their true dragon forms. My mahier was silent as my tilium roared inside me. In front of me, Gaber and Eldrick continued to throw streams of tilium at each other. Through the light, Eva floated behind Eldrick. In the midst of the fight before me, I escaped between Jericho and Cairo and ran towards Eva.

Tana stepped in front of Eva just as I reached for her, effectively pushing her out of my reach. Her black eyes bored into mine, and we stood toe to toe, a sneer lifting her lips. She raised a pointy black fingernail and raked it under my chin, drawing a bit of blood. I stood frozen in fear.

"My tilium for the Golden Dragon, Coley," she jeered.

I stepped back and wiped the blood away from under my chin. Over Tana's shoulder, Eva floated paralyzed, unaware of the fight around her. The other farros encircled the three of us. Behind me, Jericho, Cairo and the other Wolands fought against an invisible barrier that left them immobilized. Fear radiated from them.

"It's just us. Eldrick has taken care of those pesky dragons." Tana wiggled her nose in disgust. "Now, my tilium. Give it to me!" she screeched.

I took another step back and bumped into a group of farros who pushed me forward, sending me to my knees. Looking up, I met Tana's coal black eyes and the anger I detected from her sent a chill through my body.

Tana smirked down at me. "You know what?" She leaned down until we were nose to nose. "I'll just take it from you." She stood and nodded to the farros behind her.

Abruptly and without any time to react, I felt hundreds of hands push and pull me to my back, causing me to sink into the muck below. My body trembled as my fingers sunk in the mud. Over me, Tana stood with a slow smile spreading across her face to expose her shark-like teeth. The energy inside me felt ready to explode.

A time of fear was real.

J.A. Culican

332

Chapter Twenty

Tana sunk her nails into my chest. A sudden screech flew from my mouth and fire raced through my veins. The farros pushed harder, forcing me deeper into the mud in an attempt to keep me still. The pain became unbearable, and I couldn't take much more. I closed my eyes and prayed for the beings around me; that Cairo could get to Eva and the pain would end.

A loud shriek in my vicinity probed my eyes open. I could see light surrounding the farros, weaving around them. Tana continued to push her hands further inside my chest, and my breath finally stopped. A look of triumph crept over her face. With one last gasp, light shot from my body. Tilium enveloped the herd of farros as they inched closer to me. They pushed and shoved each other in order to reach closer to the tilium as it shot through the air from the holes in my chest.

Tana cackled in pure joy while the tilium continued to flow from me. The omnipresent pressure that had encompassed my being since the night in the grove, had suddenly been ridded from my being, every ounce of tilium was suddenly gone. My eyes grew heavy and my body became numb. I no longer felt the pain. The battle between Gaber and Eldrick continued to explode, along with the grunts and growls from the dragons fighting to free themselves echoed in my head. The imbalance

Eldrick had declared was real. The true, the pure, the good, were losing.

Eva. My eyes shot open. Eva dangled in the air behind Tana, powerless. We came here to save her, to bring her home, and we failed her. I failed her. Eva, the one person in my life I knew I could count on. No matter what, she'd had my back since the day we met all those years ago. My one true family.

"Get away from our Keeper," Gaber grunted just as a bolt of tilium flew my direction, flinging Tana away from me.

Tana's hands left my chest and I gulped in a large breath of air. Eldrick heaved a bolt at Gaber just as he turned back to face him. I watched in horror as Gaber took the bolt straight on and flew through the air and out of sight.

Eldrick turned to face me as he shook his head. "Such a letdown. I was itching for a real fight. Not this." He waved his hands towards the dragons and rolled his eyes.

I followed his sight towards the dragons and realized the fairies, elves and trolls were nowhere to be found, and Eldrick was the only elden here. I pulled my head up off the ground and rested on my elbows behind me. Eldrick looked satisfied with the view before him. Me, a crumpled mess in the mud who was barely able to catch my breath; the dragons, tied up with invisible ropes unable to use their mahier; and Eva, paralyzed in the wind. Then there were the farros dancing around the swamp in joy as their tilium returned to their bodies. The farros' wings began to shoot out their backs and flap as an exasperated buzzing bordered me.

In my peripheral, I watched Tana pick herself up off the ground once more and wipe the mud on her now filthy gray shorts. She stomped towards me, her black wings ferociously beating behind her. She spat some dirt from her mouth onto the ground, and her heavy boots squelched in the mud.

"Did you honestly think you could beat us? That we would hand over your precious Golden Dragon just because you asked?" Tana stopped directly above me. "Did you think you could win?"

"I'm sure the noble dragons and elves promised you victory" Eldrick said with a laugh. "Promised you we were no match for the army of the true." Eldrick shook his head as he observed the farros. "Did they tell you we were evil? The fallen?" Eldrick placed his hands on his hips.

"You killed your own parents," I grunted. "That would make you evil."

"I see my baby brother has been telling stories again." Eldrick's feet touched the ground and he began walking towards me. "I didn't want to kill them. I wanted them to join me. I wanted the elves to be the top of the food chain. Dominate over all other beings." He knelt down beside me. "I wanted the elves to rule all. But of course fear overtook them. Fear of losing. Fear of war. Fear of standing up for what was right. Instead of joining me, they banished me. Exiled their own son, heir to the throne." Eldrick moved closer until I could feel his breath on my cheek. "Today, I take back my throne. Today, I take my rightful place as King of all beings. Today, you will bow to me."

"Never. You will never be my King." I fell back in the mud, my strength waning.

"Oh, Coley," Tana jeered. "Look around. Your army has been destroyed. You have no choice but to kneel to King Eldrick."

"And you?" I blew out a breath. "Is he your King? Will you be kneeling to King Eldrick?"

"I am the Queen of the farros. I kneel to nobody," Tana sneered.

I laughed, grabbing my chest in pain. "But King Eldrick is the King of all beings, isn't that right?" I turned my head towards Eldrick, who was smirking down at me.

"You and I both know I have nothing to fear from the farros. But your courage is admirable. It's a shame today will be your last. You're rather growing on me." He stood and faced Tana. "Dispose of the Keepers how you wish. The ward will only be up for the next ten minutes. Do not kill my dear brother. I want him alive. He will soon know what true fear is." Eldrick looked back down at me and winked. "Your time of fear is now." In a blink, he was gone.

"Finally! I will never kneel to that elden." Tana wrinkled her nose. "He will be joining you soon enough, and I will be the Queen of all beings." Tana cackled and rubbed her hands together. "Now, what shall I do with the two Keeper of Dragons? And those pesky dragons?" Tana glared at the group of dragons behind me. "Never mind them. It's you I want Coley. It's you who stole my tilium, who broke my wings." The other farros halted their dancing and joined Tana around me. "Lucky for you the clock is ticking; the last thing we want is for the wards to go down before I'm done with you."

Tana rolled her shoulders back and cracked her knuckles before kneeling next to me, once again. Her obsidian eyes twinkled with revenge, a small smile slowly spreading across her face as tilium sparked from her fingertips. I closed my eyes in anticipation for the end. My body lay numb, powerless, the fight in me vanished. The buzzing and squeals of the farros were to be the last sounds I heard. My thoughts flew to my parents, my real parents, Michael and Ella Jameson. Would they be told of my death? How long would they wait for my call before they figured it out? Would the dragons keep them safe? My last prayer was for them. For them to be safe. For this war to never harm them.

"Goodbye, Keeper of Dragons," Tana whispered next to my ear.

Unexpectedly, tilium slammed into my chest, knocking the air from my lungs. The stream of energy zipped through my veins, setting my body on fire. I quaked from the torture. But then, my breath returned in a rush, and Tana screeched. I cracked my eyes open and saw light shooting through her body from odd angles as she fell to the ground, writhing in agony. The farros around me fell to the ground as the tilium shot out into the sky. The streaks of energy met above me in a great explosion, like a firework, sending sparks in all directions.

Beside me in the mud, Tana's eyes rolled to the back of her head as one last tremble shook her body. In a burst of light, she exploded into sparks. One by one, the farros around me followed their Queen to their demise, rocking the ground beneath me. The tilium that was once the farros swirled above me and around the hovering ball of fire.

My body buzzed with renewed energy as the light fell from the sky and crashed into me. My body lifted in the air as the tilium hurled through me. The last of the light flickered out and I fell back to the ground as darkness filled the ward around us.

"Cole! Cole!" Jericho shouted.

The dragons broke through their barrier and barreled towards me. The ward around us shattered with a loud crack, exposing the bright sun above us. I threw my arm over my eyes to block out the brightness. Water seeped up through the mud as the lake began to fill back up, drenching my clothes. Large hands grabbed ahold of me and rushed me to the bank.

"Eva." I croaked out as exhaustion hit me.

"Cairo has her, she'll be okay," Jericho reassured me. "Where are you hurt?" he asked, sitting me down on the bank.

I assessed my pain and found none. I was exhausted but felt fine otherwise. How was that possible? "Gaber?" I asked as I recalled the last strike he took.

"Is also okay." Jericho glanced behind me. "King Evander and Queen Annabelle are with him now."

"Where were they?" I attempted to sit but failed, falling back onto the muddy bank.

"They were trapped on the other side of the ward. My Prince, please don't move." He placed his hands on my shoulders as he assessed the damage in front of him.

"Tana?" I asked as I looked around the now full lake.

"Gone with the rest of the farros." Jericho shook his head. "I have no idea how you did it. But the farros are no more."

"You mean-"

"You truly are amazing, Keeper of Dragons," Gaber announced from over Jericho's shoulder. "The tilium you stole from the farros turned pure while you housed it. When Tana attempted to take it back and use it for darkness, it rejected her. Her own tilium ended her."

Gaber's platinum hair was a mess and blood soaked through his green jacket. Evander, Annabelle and the other true creatures encircled us. The only ones I could not see from my prone position were Cairo and Eva. We needed to get back to the elves. Eldrick and the eldens were still out there.

I pushed my back off the ground and rested on my elbows. "Paraiso. We should head back now." I pushed up to a sitting position and dropped my arms into my lap. "Where are Eva and Cairo?"

"Keeper." Gaber said. "They are right—" Gaber fell to the ground in a tumbled heap. His body quaked as the orange light in his eyes dimmed. "Paraiso," he muttered right before he passed out.

J.A. Culican

Chapter Twenty-One

Eva rested her head on my shoulder. We sat against a tree by the shore of Lake Maracaibo, or better known as the eldens' swamp. Queen Annabelle and King Evander knelt on both sides of Gaber, who lay unconscious on the ground. Jericho paced as Cairo stood in guard mode alongside us.

"I'm scared," Eva muttered.

I nodded against the top of her head. Her long red hair lay in a disarrayed mess, and her eyes fluttered as if fighting to stay awake. I grabbed her hand and squeezed.

"What'd they do to you?" I whispered, staring at Gaber's unmoving body.

"Nothing. I mean I don't remember anything until just a few minutes ago." She squeezed my hand. "One second, I was standing in the hut in Paraiso, and the next I was laying on the ground here with Cairo begging me to wake up. I—" She shook her head against my shoulder and sighed. "What happened here?"

"The farros are gone." I whispered. "But they were nothing compared to the eldens. I don't know how we're going to defeat them. I don't know if it's possible."

"Together. We'll figure it out together," Eva said. "We need to get back to Paraiso. I have a horrible feeling. Why would Eldrick leave Tana to take care of us?"

Jericho paused his pacing and looked down at us. "He knew." He glanced towards Gaber. "He knew you'd end them. Somehow he knew."

Eva lifted her head from my shoulder and turned her now golden eyes towards me. I missed her sky-blue ones, the ones I grew up laughing with. They were home. I sighed and closed my eyes. This was my new home. A home where war encircled me. A home where my job was to protect all. Protect all that was true. When I opened my eyes, Eva was staring at me, a sad smile on her face; she must have been listening to my inner thoughts.

"How'd you end them?" Eva whispered to me.

"I don't know. She had won. I thought it was over. I didn't do anything." I looked over Eva's shoulder and shook my head.

Gaber's foot twitched as Queen Annabelle slapped her hands against her chest "He's waking up. Thank the fates," she happily announced as her light pink eyes glanced our way quickly, then back down to Gaber, who was struggling against Evander to sit up.

"Gaber, stay down and remain calm," Evander said as he pushed Gaber's shoulders to keep him flat. "You passed out."

"Paraiso. The elves. My elves. We must go," Gaber rambled. "Paraiso. The elves. Now. We must go now!"

Eva crawled towards Gaber and pushed Evander out of the way. "What about the elves?" she asked.

"Eldrick. Clara. We need to save them," Gaber stammered as he tried to sit up.

"Why would we save Eldrick?" Eva asked as she helped Gaber sit up.

"No. He has Clara. Paraiso. He has them." Gaber looked around in a panic. "We need to go now."

"We left an army protecting Paraiso. Not to mention the wards were back up." Jericho stated.

"What?" Eva turned to Jericho. "You mean the wards Eldrick exploded?" The gold in Eva's eyes began to swirl. "Cole, oh god. It was a trap."

"Of course it was a trap. Eldrick thought he would be able to defeat us tonight," Jericho stated.

"No, he doesn't want us," Eva whispered as she looked back down at Gaber.

"The elves." Gaber pushed off the ground to stand. "The elves. I feel their fear. I feel their pain. Paraiso is under attack." Gaber's orange gaze met mine. "Hurry." He disappeared in a flash.

The trolls and fairies that remained vanished before us, following Gaber back to Paraiso. The dragons around me shifted and pushed off the ground without a command. Eva and I mirrored their actions, and were up in the air within minutes.

Visions of a battle between elden and elf haunted me during the dragging trip back to Paraiso. My mind raced with a hundred different possibilities as to what we'd find when we arrived. The sight of land ahead relieved and frightened me at the same time. I landed mid-shift and ran full force towards Paraiso, my feet thumping through the snow the closer I got. I broke through the final set of brush and skidded to a halt at the sight before me.

Gaber knelt in the snow with his head bowed. His shoulders trembled as he slowly raised his dimmed orange eyes to meet mine. The thumping of my blood swooshed in my ears and my breath halted as I took in his hopeless appearance. Evander and Annabelle stepped up behind him, both of their heads lowered. I felt Eva pause behind me as the other dragons cleared the brush. No one spoke. No words were needed. The elves were gone. The trolls were gone. All were gone.

A time of fear was now.

THE MERE TREATY
KEEPER OF DRAGONS
BOOK 3

For Annabella, may you continue to grow-up strong and fearless.

Prologue

Sixty-seven minutes. That's how long it had been since Eldrick won. Not just won, but demolished us. Gaber hadn't moved from the spot we found him in and no one had said a word. Reality of the events hadn't kicked in yet, or maybe I was just in shock.

I finally found my feet and wandered a few yards away to an old tree stump. My whole body ached, and not just physically. My heart was broken. All the Elves and Trolls that we'd left behind were gone, kidnapped by the Elden. My head spun with all the possibilities of their fate. A fate they entrusted to me.

A loud clanking sound met my ears as a large shadow enveloped me. My heart jumped when my eyes met Jericho's.

"You need to stay close, my prince." He growled and tilted his head to the ground beside him.

On the snow-covered dirt lay an old sword enclosed in a brown leather sheath. The thin handle glinted at me even though the sun had stopped shining on our home that once seemed like paradise. The sword beckoned me as I grabbed the hilt and pulled it from its cover. It was lighter than I had expected as I held it out in front of me.

"This is not a toy." Jericho grabbed the sword from my hand. "Weaponry is the last level of training, but given the circumstances, it is imperative that we skip some lessons and start your training immediately."

Was he really discussing training with me right now? We just lost.

"A dragon's sword is a part of him." He leaned down and sheathed the sword. "Always keep it attached to your back. You will learn to use your mahier to keep it close even when shifted into your dragon."

Jericho dropped the sword into my lap and I wrapped my hand around the soft leather. "Why would a dragon need a sword?" I asked. I mean, dragons had fire and could fly. Why would we fight with swords?

"These battles you have fought have been nothing more than a path to war. In a war, it is vital to keep your mahier strong. When you shift, you use your mahier. When you breathe fire, you use your mahier. Your sword uses none. It is always available while keeping your mahier full." The more Jericho spoke, the brighter his eyes shone. "You are the Keeper of Dragons. A time of fear is upon us. The fate of all True beings is in your hands. Keep them strong."

I attached the sword to my back, pulling the leather straps tight around my chest. With each breath I took, I felt the sword shift on my back and the straps dig into my upper body. Jericho was right. For some reason, Eva and I were chosen by the Fates to be the Keeper of Dragons. It has been our destiny since the day we were born.

My eyes scanned the other creatures as they slowly began to come back to reality. Cairo was almost glued to Eva's side. Tears ran down her cheeks, but he had his arm around her shoulder as he whispered words of encouragement in her ear. Evander found his feet and helped Gaber to stand. His body shook as he blew out a harsh breath. His once bright eyes looked dull, as if his internal light had been extinguished. Slowly, Evander, King of the Trolls, escorted Prince Gaber toward one of the walkways.

"Keeper of Dragons." Queen Annabelle of the Fairies' voice made me jump. "Please keep me informed of any developments. The Elven Alliance is still in effect. But I must return home to check on my remaining Fairies. It seems the few that remained have been scared off."

I nodded my agreement, unable to find the words. I was scared, too.

"You defeated the Farro tonight. For that, we will forever be grateful." My eyes met hers as a sad smile formed on her face. "They are alive. I feel it within me. We will find them. And you, Keeper of Dragons, will save us all." With that, she turned her back to me and took off into the evening sky.

Both Jericho and I watched Queen Annabelle and the few remaining Fairies until they were nothing more than spots in the sky. The weight of her words held me in place. The Fairies placed their fate in me even after we lost to King Eldrick.

Jericho put his hand on my shoulder, pulling me from my thoughts. "Meet in the command center in an hour. We must prepare for war." He growled and stomped off toward Cairo and Eva.

War. A war solely on my shoulders.

Chapter One

I stood on the steps of Ochana Castle, Sila and Rylan behind me to either side, and stared out over the sea of dragon faces. They all stared up at me with pleading, adoring eyes, chanting at me to save them. Save their families. Save their homes.

From behind, Sila whispered in my ear, "We have faith in you, Son. You are the Keeper of Dragons. For you, everything is possible. I know you can do it."

They were all wrong. I shook my head and tried to tell them I was just a boy. Okay, so maybe I was eighteen, but that was barely an adult in human terms, and I was almost a baby to the dragons. "I—"

The roar from the audience was so loud that it drowned out even my own voice. How could Sila's whisper have reached me over the crowd? I needed to make everyone understand that I was going to let them all down. I wasn't a warrior, I wasn't brave. I was just scared. I still felt like a kid, sometimes.

I shouted over the noise as loud as I could, hurting my throat, but it worked. I could hear my words over that racket. "You don't understand. You need to run. The Elden are coming for us all. Run! Fly!"

Shouts from the crowd grew louder, echoing off the castle's stone steps. Their cries went from pleading to a rumble of cheering. It was as though I'd just told them I could defeat the Elden all by myself, don't worry about a thing, it'll all be done by lunchtime. What on Earth was wrong with these people?

I looked around, trying to spot the Wolands who should have been protecting me, but I couldn't see anything but the crowd as it surged forward. Some people in the crowd held their kids up at me like they were lion cubs. I knew they would all be gone soon, parents and kids. Their faces burned into my mind, and I saw them wherever I looked, like an afterglow from a bright light.

They wouldn't listen. The Elden were coming, and I couldn't save them. I'd have to—

I felt a tingle in my mind. I grabbed at my head as I sensed the darkness grow around Ochana and press inward. After a few seconds, though, the shell of dark reached the wards that protected the floating island. For the moment, it had stopped creeping tighter around the island. When it hit the wards, the shadow-like substance shuddered like it was straining as hard as it could to break through. As it pressed harder still, the shadow grew even darker, until it blocked out almost all the sun's light, making it look like dusk.

From the corner of my eye, I spotted water droplets from Ochana's crystal-pure waterfall begin to rise up into the air. Once beautiful, the waters looked sinister and putrid as they rose higher and higher, spreading out as they went. In less than a minute, the fouled water had spread to coat the inside of the protective wards, like a bubble.

A glimmer overtook the bubble like a million little, dazzling stars. The sight on any other day would have been beautiful if it wasn't for the danger we were in. My stomach dropped as I realized what was going on. Ochana's waters had coated the magical protection keeping us all alive and now it was freezing. It looked just like Paraiso's spirit water had when it froze—Eldrick's cruel way of stealing almost all the Elven tilium. Was that what was happening here?

I didn't want to think about that right now. I had more urgent things to worry about, like staying alive. I shouted to warn the other dragons, but the crowd's roaring cheer drowned out my voice again. Couldn't they see the danger we were in? I thought it must have been Eldrick using some magical trick. Then I tried to run, but no matter how hard I pumped my legs, I wasn't going anywhere. I was stuck there, forced to watch and be a part of whatever was about to happen.

The thin, frozen shell cracked. I hated to be reminded of the tragic things that happened at Paraiso, but the way this ice was cracking was a terrifying replay of what had happened there, even down to the exact sounds the ice had made. It was like a recording. Every crack and tinkle noise was the same as it had been the first time in the elven homeland.

Suddenly, the ice shattered. Frozen shards rained down on us like broken glass. Dragons in the crowd cried out when the razor-sharp ice shards hit them.

I pushed my mahier senses outward as I tried to find Eldrick, but I felt something missing. For a second, I thought back to the first time I'd gone camping with my parents, and I had woken up in the middle of the night scared for some reason. It had taken me a minute to realize that everything seemed wrong that night because there was no city noise. Something I'd never realized was there had been missing, and I had felt it before figuring out why I felt it.

This was like that. What was missing, though?

The wards! I could *feel* the wards missing. I quickly looked up, expecting to see something terrible happening because the wards were gone. The darkness, which had been straining against the wards, jerked into motion when the resistance vanished, bearing down on Ochana again, along with me and all the dragons, but it was now going even faster. There was a vibration in the air as it snapped forward.

I screamed, but no sound came out. My lungs felt like they were full of water, like the air had turned into gelatin inside me, and it hurt deep inside my chest. I panicked, but still couldn't do anything more than run in place.

The approaching darkness seemed to form a face. A terrible, huge, menacing face. Glowing orange eyes were like spotlights that only lit up one person—me. The Dragon Prince shouldn't have been so terrified that he screamed, but that's what I did. Or I tried to, but failed because I still felt like I had breathed in a lungful of jelly. My mind reeled, and I couldn't think of anything to do but stand there, screaming in silence and trying to warn everyone.

Even with so many of them downed by shards of ice, my people still looked at me with hope shining in their eyes. It was like they couldn't see the icy doom all around them, or Eldrick's laughing, snarling face. Why didn't they move out of the way? My eyes grew teary. I failed them, but could it ever have ended another way? I'd been trying to tell everyone I was going to fail them ever since I'd come to Ochana, and now it had come true.

Just before the darkness reached the crowd, I felt the energy inside me spin, making my vision whirl. Silver sparks came from my fingertips, like sparklers on the Fourth of July. I had felt that before. My tilium was almost at capacity—and there was nothing I could do about it, not with the whole crowd standing in front of me. If I just let it go and overflow, people might be hurt.

Energy rushed through me, filling me up until I felt it pressing on my heart. As the heat inside me went from just warm to an almost painful hot, I started pouring sweat. I fought to hold it in.

My tilium grew stronger than me and burst out, shooting like spotlights from my fingers, my eyes, my mouth, until even my skin glowed and shot beams of light everywhere.

The tilium inside me flashed outward like a shockwave, washing over the crowd and my parents. I'd lost all control over it.

Where the shockwave hit the crowd, people instantly froze like glass and then shattered into thousands of pieces. It wasn't possible! That was nothing like what I had seen before, when my unstable tilium grew too big for me to hold it back.

The powerful wave kept speeding outward until it crashed into the blackness coming for us all. For a moment, I thought it might push King Eldrick's darkness away and bring the light back to Ochana. But as my tilium crashed into the darkness, it rippled and then just...vanished. My heart sank. I thought again of the ripple in a pond after throwing a pebble in, violent at first and then fading away to nothing.

The menacing face in the darkness laughed, so loud that it made my ears ring. What seemed like a black curtain crept forward, coming closer, until it closed in over us all. Eldrick's open, laughing mouth surrounded me. Everything went pitch-black.

* * *

A few moments later, light appeared in front of me. It ran like a slit from left to right and, as it widened even more, I saw huge teeth. They were easily as tall as me. The beginnings of panic stirred inside as I realized I was somehow *inside* the giant King Eldrick's mouth. Or I had shrunk, I couldn't be sure which. Nothing made sense.

I scrambled over the huge teeth, hoping to drop down to the ground below, but when I got over them, I found I was standing on something soft. I looked down to see that I was on Eldrick's bottom lip, hundreds of feet in the air. There was no way Eldrick was that tall, even as huge as he was. I was trapped in the mouth of a giant, flying Elden king.

Far below, the ground sped by, going faster and faster until the smaller details were just a blur. Far ahead, I saw something moving. Small spots dotted the ground like ants. It had to be a trick of my imagination.

A solid line reached across the grass and rocks ahead, green on one side and white on the other. I squinted to get a better look and realized there was a thick, even layer of snow. Everything was covered in ice and frost. Even the trees were white, and some were bent over from the weight of the deep snow piled on them.

The tiny dots grew larger the closer we got. I took a deep breath and willed my senses to expand, reaching out to them. I felt nothing, sensed no one. It was impossible, because I could clearly see them. My jaw dropped and my scalp tingled with shock. Far below, the missing Elves and their Troll companions laid in fear.

Each Elf and Troll was staked out, spread eagle on the ground. Over them stood Elden, some carrying whips and others with some sort of staff. Cries of pain and fear faintly carried to me on the wind. My dizziness grew, and I had to grab onto the teeth to keep from falling. I was helpless to do anything as the Elden hurt my allies, beings who had sworn to defend me with their lives. I reached out toward them, willing my mahier to bring my dragon, but nothing happened.

A deep, booming thunder washed over me, and I realized King Eldrick was laughing. It was a terrifying, evil sound.

How dare he? How could anyone do such a thing? And the Elden and Elves were cousins. My knees shook with fear, and I had to struggle to calm myself, but then I surprised myself by screaming, "You monster! Release them, now." Where had that rage suddenly come from?

The laughter grew louder, and it beat away whatever courage I had. It echoed in my head, seeming to bounce around inside my skull, driving out my thoughts. I was even more terrified.

I contemplated my fate if I jumped. Anything to get away from the terrible king. As I got ready to jump, though, I noticed that all of the Elves and Trolls had blurry faces, like pencil marks smudged with an eraser.

One single face stuck out, his smudged lines wiggling and growing together, becoming clearer until taking on the shape of Prince Gaber. He was in Paraiso. How did he get here? He had blood on his face and his eyes were wide with terror. One of the biggest, most frightening Elden I had ever seen stood over him holding a whip, which he was using with enthusiasm.

Gaber's eyes seemed to find mine and they stretched even wider in surprise. He opened his mouth, and in my mind, I could hear him pleading for me to help his Elves. Not him, but his Elves. Tears fell from my eyes. Here I was, the Keeper of Dragons, but helpless to protect the True beings as everyone said I was fated to do.

Some destiny...

Large birds that looked like buzzards flew over the vast field of Elves and Trolls. They were deep purple in color, and I wondered why I had never seen them before. And where on Earth were there purple snow buzzards? The entire scene confused me.

My attention shifted to the Elden standing over Prince Gaber. I wiped the tears from my eyes so I could see better. Something was different. Then I saw what was wrong. The Elden's massive whip was squirming. It turned and shifted like a snake. When it stopped moving, it became a thick stick, ten feet long, and at the end where the whip popper had been, now there was just one huge blade that gleamed in the bright light reflecting from the thick snow.

He laughed at Gaber, a deep, ominous cackle. The sound made my stomach drop and my eyes grow wide. He raised the new weapon over his head with both hands, ready to bring it down on Gaber. I reached out, desperate to do something, anything, but my mahier escaped me, leaving me immobilized.

My anger rose again. I was the Keeper of Dragons. Even without Eva, the Golden Dragon, I had a duty. Not only was Gaber the prince of the Elves, allies of my dragon people, but he was also my friend. Or, the closest thing I'd had to it, other than Eva.

I felt heat in my belly, growing and growing. The rage started to become painful from the heat. I realized immediately what it was—my tilium was about to overflow, *again*.

I snarled and willed my mahier to rise with my anger. Suddenly, I felt it growing inside me, building alongside the tilium. In a moment, it would be beyond my control, too.

For once the feeling of uncontrolled power didn't scare me. Instead, I focused on him; I imagined my two energies exploding from me together in a single instant, and concentrated on making it shoot down at the Elden below.

We kept streaking through the air, aiming at the huge field with all the Elves and Trolls. A thought flashed through my mind—I shouldn't be able to see Gaber in such detail from so far away. Now wasn't the time for doubt, so I shoved the thought aside.

I shouted a warrior's cry as my tilium and mahier reached the point of overflowing at the same time. I imagined my energy washing over the Elden, tearing him down to just his atoms, and—

—the giant Eldrick spit me out. "Pthooey!"

I shot through the air, spinning out of control, and I saw glimpses of his face floating above me, laughing.

The booming voice inside my skull said, "You tasted better before you cleansed it, little stealer of tilium. It's okay, though, because I have *plenty* of my own."

As I kept spinning and falling, the icy, snowy ground came up to meet me. At my speed and distance, I wouldn't survive. I tried once again to call for my dragon. With desperation giving me strength and focusing my thoughts, I called out for it, but I still didn't sense it. Where was my dragon in all this? Why had it abandoned me now, when I needed it most? The dragon was me, I was the dragon. I still had my mahier. It should have worked.

The ground was fast approaching. The panic in the back of my mind exploded into complete terror, and I screamed in my mind, desperate for my dragon. I willed myself to shift.

My mahier flowed from me, searching and seeking. It had a mind of its own as it looked for my dragon. In another instant, I felt...something. It had grabbed onto the shockwave of my mahier, which was reaching out to find my dragon still. I saw a blinding flash, so bright that I had to shield my face. When I opened my eyes, I realized that I wasn't falling—I was flying!

I looked over and saw my wings stretched out. It was glorious. My heart soared, and my fear fled. No wonder I hadn't been able to call my dragon. I'd been the dragon the entire time. That didn't make any sense at all, though. I remembered being just plain Cole a moment before. Or had I just been too frightened to notice that I'd been the dragon that entire time? It was confusing.

I tilted to my left, and swept toward the Elves and Trolls. The ice-covered fields of snow were still several miles away. The only thing that wasn't pure white was a small mass of black spots, which had to be the Elves and Trolls. As I leveled out to head toward them, I remembered the brilliant flash of light. Had that been when I shifted?

Far above, the sky's usual blue hue suddenly seemed to split apart like sunlight hitting a crystal, and then the raw beauty of what I saw in the skies took my breath away. As far as my dragon eyes could see, in every direction, there was a multitude of colors that seemed to twist and boil across the sky, gleaming and then fading, then shining again, never the same colors twice in a row. I realized they must be the Northern Lights, though I had never seen them before. Nothing else could be so strikingly beautiful.

I shook my head hard to clear my mind of the distraction, and reluctantly turned my eyes to the scene below. I had almost reached Prince Gaber and the Elden, but King Eldrick seemed to be missing. I had the strange idea that the Northern Lights display pushed the evil king away, but with him gone, I wasn't quite as afraid as I had been.

I dove at the Elden who stood laughing over Gaber and opened my mouth, releasing a geyser of purple fire far larger than any fire-breath I'd seen among the Wolands.

Then I realized I wasn't breathing fire, but a deadly frost as cold as space. It only moved like flames. As I dove at my target, mouth still open and breathing the ice-fire, I let out all my fear and anger with one mighty roar that shook the ground...

* * *

I sat bolt upright and threw my blanket off, my scream echoing off the cabin walls before fading away. I was covered in sweat, gasping for air. My entire body felt as sore as if I had been laboring all day. I was so confused. Had the Northern Lights sent me back to Ochana? That strange, beautiful light...

No. As the sleep faded and my senses returned, I realized that I wasn't in Ochana—I was still in Paraiso. It had been a dream. I felt it slipping away, escaping my memory like most dreams do. I struggled to remember as many details as I could, but by the time my nightmare-sweat evaporated, I could only remember a single detail. It was burned into my mind, and I knew I would never forget those beautiful and frightening Northern Lights, pulsing high above a frozen land.

I climbed out of bed and picked my blanket off the floor, tossing it back to where it belonged. Nearby, I found my clothes and newly-issued sword neatly arranged.

The memory of what had happened just a handful of days before came crashing back to me. Eldrick had frozen the sacred waters of Paraiso, and with it, the Elves' tilium, leaving both Elves and Trolls powerless. They couldn't fight back when his Elden had swarmed over them and then vanished, taking the defenseless Elves and Trolls with them as prisoners.

He had also used the Farro like pawns, getting them to kidnap Eva to draw me to his swampy home in Venezuela. It got me out of Paraiso, along with the fearsome dragons and most of the warrior Elves. It let him attack their home while it was defenseless.

I smiled briefly at the memory of destroying the Farros and their ruler, Queen Tana. Their own greed and hunger for power was really what destroyed them. The first time they had attacked the dragons, I tore their dark tilium from them with Eva's help and drew it into myself, but nothing that foul could *stay* evil inside the Keeper of Dragons. Somehow, I had cleansed it and turned it pure. When Queen Tana and her Farros ripped their tilium back from me, they drew it into themselves greedily. Dark souls and purified tilium were a bad combination, and it had cost them all their lives.

I let out a deep breath, sat on the bed, and let the nightmare's tension drain away. I knew what that dream had been about. Basically, my own insecurities. But the land of ice and snow with the Northern Lights, there at the end...it certainly hadn't felt like a dream. Deep inside, I was convinced there was something important about it. But if it was a message, who had sent it?

I didn't know what it all meant, but I had to tell Jericho, no matter what sort of training or missions they had all decided to put on me for the day. Those could wait. This was more important.

Jericho's deep voice boomed in my head, startling me. "Cole, you're sleeping the day away while a war rages. I'm at the command center. Come find me immediately."

Jericho sounded more irritated than usual, but I thought I heard an edge of fear in his voice. Usually he was just angry or grumpy, so it had me a bit worried. I wanted to talk to him about my dream anyway, so I jumped out of bed and headed down from my borrowed treehouse.

Chapter Two

My feet thudded across the twisting sky-bridges of Paraiso. There didn't seem to be any pattern, but I had a sense there was one. I just hadn't been there long enough to see it. I had only recently remembered how to get from my assigned cabin to Gaber's command center. It was lucky I did, because Eva wasn't around. She knew the paths better than I did, so I usually just followed her. I was on my own this day, though.

When I got to a place I thought was near the command center, I let my mahier reach out, trying to sense Jericho. He was down there, and I grinned for a moment, happy to have gotten it right this time. Deciding to jump down, I let my dragon take me on wings to the jungle floor, rather than zapping there or climbing down. I really did need to figure out how I zapped last time. My first night here in Paraiso felt like forever ago.

Once I reached the ground, I called to my human, then walked to the command center. The first person I saw was Jericho, the leader of the Wolands—the red dragon warriors who defended all dragons. His eyes were glowing bright red as he talked to Gaber and Cairo. Few people were brave enough to stand up to Jericho when he was angry, but the Elven Prince Gaber looked as smug as ever, even with the dimness in his eyes. I couldn't imagine the turmoil he must be feeling. Almost all of his Elves and

Troll allies had been kidnapped, his sister included. I shook the thought away as I continued my assessment of the room.

Cairo was standing his ground for once, too. He was another red dragon, and his job was to protect Eva. He thought they were soulmates, *Verum Salit*, though he had yet to inform Eva of this.

King Evander of the Trolls was there, too, but he stood back a bit, talking to an Elf soldier I recognized as Bran. He, too, had lost so much. It was evident by his ragged appearance he was failing at staying strong. Evander's green hair stuck up everywhere and the bags under his eyes did nothing to hide his lack of sleep.

With Cairo there, I looked around the room for Eva. Sure enough, I spotted her sitting alone in a chair off to one side. She was my best friend as a human, and now she was the Golden Dragon, half of the Keeper of Dragons. For some reason, everyone seemed to think that she and I would save the day together. I had doubts about that. I nodded to her and she rewarded me with a sad smile.

Jericho looked almost agitated enough to begin billowing smoke. Cairo finally looked away, even though he was one of Ochana's best warriors. Gaber didn't. I had no idea what had Jericho riled up. Not that he wasn't always wound tight, but today he seemed ready to blow.

I gave Gaber and Evander a slight bow after I stepped through the door. Jericho looked from Cairo to me, and everyone else went silent, too, and turned to watch. I wished I knew what was going on, but Jericho hadn't told me. I gathered up my courage and said, "Morning, I came as quickly as I could."

He rolled his eyes. "What else would you do, sit in your room? We don't have time for idle chatter. We need to talk about what to do for the missing Trolls and Elves. They're our allies, and we let them down once while we hid with our heads in the sand."

Gaber snorted and said, "To your everlasting shame."

Jericho kept his eyes on me, ignoring Gaber. "We will not let them down again," he said, and drove his fist into his palm.

Cairo bowed to me, like most of the dragons did, then said to Jericho, "Eva has the right idea."

Gaber coughed, catching our attention. His smirk was contagious. I guess it amused him that everyone turned to him. I could almost hear him thinking, *made you look!* He said, "I like Eva. For a Dramon, she's pretty nice. But I'm not sure her idea holds water."

Cairo said, "She did make it sound pretty convincing. We travel to the Mermaids and ask for their help. We need to bring them into the Elven Alliance, anyway."

I knew very little about the Mermaids. I knew they had their own form of magic, very similar to tilium, and that they didn't interact with others often. Other than that, they were a mystery to me. Just another creature I thought didn't exist, much like dragons.

Jericho's eyes flared a brighter red. "That's foolish. We need to find the other Fairies in Greece and see if they'll join us. We can get extra help that way, and we owe Queen Annabelle and her Fairies at least that much, don't you think? They fought bravely by our side, and they, too, have lost some of their own. Besides, Fairy tilium is strong, and the Mermaids can't do much for us in this war. If the Elden lived at the bottom of the sea, you'd have a point."

Gaber leaped to his feet. "At least I can believe that from a dragon. Leave it to them to ignore a whole race because it's not useful at the moment. It isn't the first time."

My single strongest memory from the nightmare came back to me, then. Before Jericho could bicker some more with Gaber, I decided to argue the point about the Mermaids. From the corner of my eye, though, I caught Eva shaking her head at me. She raised her eyebrows and her eyes were as wide as she could make them go. She was giving me a warning to stay quiet, thanks to reading my mind again. But why should I be quiet? I was going to have to tell Jericho soon, either way.

Cairo looked angry, but bowed his head in submission. I thought he looked tense and stiff-necked when he did it, though, and I worried that he might be about to take a swing at Jericho, or at Gaber. Probably Jericho. He said, "Compared to the Elden, there are only a few Fairies in Greece. And besides—"

Jericho cut him off with a bark. "Numbers aren't the question, and you know it. No one is more motivated to help Elves and Trolls than Fairies, even if they have to team up with a dragon to do it. And the Fairies also suffered while we dragons were thinking about other things. We owe Fairies just as much as we owe the Elves. If we don't bring the Greek Fairies into this, would Queen

Annabelle ever forgive us? We need her as an ally in spirit, not just a formality."

I could see how irritated Eva was as she snapped, "But what about everything I heard about the mereum? They say it has the ability to—"

Jericho growled, interrupting her. He was good at interrupting people. "No. They never allow outsiders to try it. Only Mermaids have ever traveled that maze, not since the first Elf walked through the reef and created it in the first place. The maze's powers are strong, sure, and its tilium might even be a match for the Elden, but it's all useless to us out there in the ocean."

Gaber rolled his eyes, but I watched Eva, not him. She squinted at Jericho. She was brave and reckless, and she looked ready to say something she would regret.

She had already warned me not to do the same thing, and she'd been right, so I jumped into the conversation before she could reply. "We should listen to Eva, and if not her, then to Cairo. They both think the Mermaids are the best idea. I don't know anything about them, but..." My voice trailed off as I tried to think of what to say next. I knew I'd just lost any chance at convincing Jericho.

He laughed, little smoke rings coming from his nose. "It seems you're right—you don't know what you're talking about. Eva can speak for herself, but why are we even discussing Mermaids? Stick to what you know, Cole, that's lesson number four."

I felt my anger rising. Just because he was the high and mighty Jericho, he didn't have the right to ignore people or talk to them that way, especially when the other people might be right. And *definitely* not if those people were the Keeper of Dragons.

He turned his attention back to Cairo, not even waiting for me to reply. He shouted, "*Your* duty is the protection of the Golden Dragon. *My* duty is the protection of Ochana and all that is True. Do your own job, and let me do mine. We need to go to Greece and rally the other Fairies. It's our only real choice. Fairies have the strongest power in the world, other than dragon mahier, and we can't even get to the Mermaids fast enough to make a difference in this war. You know they move around all the time."

I listened and clenched my jaw. Even Jericho could be wrong.

But my dream kept pressing at me, and I decided it couldn't wait any longer, despite Eva's warning. I raised my voice above the noise and said, "Actually, there's a third option." I hoped I sounded steady and confident.

Everyone turned to me again, but I forced myself to stand tall. I looked each of them right in the eyes. My nightmare clues were important. "I had a nightmare last night, and part of it was more than just a dream. It was a *message.*"

"A message?" Jericho eyed me warily.

"I had a vision of the Elden somewhere in a land of snow and ice. They were torturing the missing Elves and Trolls. There were lights in the sky, beautiful lights. The Aurora Borealis, I think. We need to find our missing friends while we still have time to save them. To do that, we need to look in a place like the one I saw. North, not east to Greece or the Dead Sea."

Jericho let out three odd sounds, hollow and deep, from the back of his throat. I realized he was actually laughing. I wasn't sure I'd ever heard him laugh before. "Colton, I know you think you have some sort of a clue, but it was only a dream. None of your training has been in dream interpretation. But even if you had the training, could you trust it with the way your training has gone so far? The only area you are even close to keeping up with is your sword. What makes you think you know what that dream meant?"

I gritted my teeth in frustration. If I was fated to save the world from the Time of Fear, he should be listening, not barking orders. It had been more than some random nightmare. I *knew* it, deep in my gut. "It wasn't just a dream, it was—"

He cut me off again, saying, "No. We're not going to abandon our duties and go pursue a dream. Not even a dream, but a silly nightmare. After we get to the Greek Fairies, then we can send Realm Two to explore the far north, just to make you feel better, but I won't waste precious resources on it. We're at war, my prince, and half of winning it will be to manage our resources well. The rest of us have to deal with the real world, and you might want to join us there."

"It's not abandoning our duties," I said. I was desperate to make them believe me. Too much depended on this. "I'm telling you, it was a clue or a warning. I don't know which. But I do know it was important, and we should go look."

As Jericho's eyes flared red again, little puffs of smoke came from his nostrils. He wasn't used to anyone challenging him, especially me, and he sure wasn't laughing anymore.

Eva stepped between the two of us, facing me. "We all know dreams are just our subconscious fears getting worked out." She paused for a moment, hands on her hips as she cocked her head to the side. I had the feeling she was sizing me up, and it felt awkward.

She said, "What else was in this dream besides snow, lights in the sky, and our missing allies?"

My mind raced as I tried to figure out how to explain everything. I wished I remembered more of my nightmare. The purple buzzards must have been simple dream stuff, but the rest was *real*. It definitely felt real. Eldrick swallowed Ochana, then whisked me away to somewhere up north. That's where we would find the Elves and Trolls, and Ochana was in danger. I had to get them to understand.

Eva laughed out loud, and I lost my train of thought. When she saw the irritation on my face, she touched my shoulder. "I'm sorry, Cole. I don't mean to laugh. But purple buzzards? A giant King Eldrick flying around? Come on, it's normal nightmare stuff. I get that it bothered you, but that doesn't mean it was important. Dreams just let you know what you're afraid of. Instead of focusing on your fears and a dream, we need to focus on something real, right?"

It didn't usually bug me when she read my thoughts, because it made me feel like we were somehow closer. Together we were the Keeper of Dragons, and best friends. But this time, it felt like she had invaded my privacy. "I know the difference between a regular dream and a warning."

She shook her head, eyes showing sympathy for me. I knew she could feel my conflicted emotions radiating from me. "I'm sorry. I'm not ignoring how you feel, but you might be still feeling the nightmare's effects. You need to let that go, Cole. Dreams can't hurt you, no matter how real they feel."

She turned around to face Jericho, who had been standing there smirking at me. She started in on Jericho again about how we should go to the Mermaids. Her whole argument boiled down to the fact that Earth was mostly water, and that was the domain of Mermaids. They were like hermits, I had heard, so outsiders usually didn't know much about them.

Jericho snapped, "Yes, but Elden aren't water-breathers. The Greek Fairies are the ones who can help us deal with Eldrick up here on dry land, where the Elves and Trolls are. What don't you get about this?"

I turned away from their arguing and wandered over to a chair, sitting with a thump. When they ignored me, it bothered me. More than it should have. I knew my dream sounded weird, and taking a stupid dream so seriously was also weird, but one of them should care how I felt about it.

The dragons pulled me out of their toolbox when they needed something from me, but the rest of the time, they wanted me in that box where I wouldn't be in their way.

There was a sharp noise, and I looked over to see Jericho clapping his hands. He said, "No more of this. I'll discuss it with the Council, but for now, it's time for the Keeper of Dragons' training." He turned to look directly at me and said, "Your first session for today is in the arena. We need to get you more comfortable with your sword. Meet me over in the clearing by the shore in five minutes."

Then he turned away to talk to Cairo again. They had put me in the toolbox yet again. I let out a frustrated sigh and headed toward the lakeshore. More arena training... Well, that was fine with me. I was kind of angry, and I felt ready to let off some steam.

On my first step, my stomach began to churn, and I stopped in my tracks. I felt suddenly hot and started to sweat. I shook my head to clear the feeling and took another step, but then my vision began to spin, faster and faster. When my stomach cramped up, pain shot through me like a lightning bolt. Everything looked like it slid downward—my eyes rolling back?—leaving only darkness.

I felt myself falling over backward. It all went pitch black for a second, but then I saw a blinding light ahead. I squinted, then gasped. Far below me was a flat field, covered in snow and ice.

Chapter Three

I struggled against the darkness and clawed my way back toward the light, then slowly peeled my aching eyes open. Eva and Jericho stood over me, one on either side, looking concerned. The vision I'd seen was still fresh in my memory as my fuzzy mind cleared.

Eva said, "Are you okay? What happened?" She chewed lightly on her bottom lip, her nervous habit.

I nodded and propped myself up on my elbows. "I'm fine. Just a little dizzy. I didn't get a chance to grab breakfast."

That wasn't the entire truth. In my vision, I went back to the land of ice and snow and saw a scene a lot like the last time. King Eldrick wasn't there, but within the crowd of Elves and Trolls tied up, I saw Mel and Clara looking up at me. Somehow, I could see their faces close up, even though the crowd had been far away. They both spoke together, warning me, "Be careful. They have a trap waiting."

I'd only had a glimpse, but it had that same weird, real feeling as the nightmare. I was sure it wasn't just a vision—it was a message. I couldn't have explained how I knew that, but there was no point in bringing it up anyway. They would just push it aside and ignore me again. But I knew the truth.

Jericho rolled his eyes, throwing an apple at me. "If you're fine, and you're done messing around, we have work to do. Into the arena, both of you."

I was a little angry that he didn't give me some time off after my vision hit, but he had a sense of urgency I hadn't heard from him before. It was like he was afraid, which kind of scared me a little. Jericho was never afraid.

Over the next hour, Eva and I trained hard. I showed a little bit of improvement, but my performance was still embarrassing. Every time I connected with a jab or hit my opponent with a leg sweep, they turned around and knocked me into the dirt.

That was frustrating, but I was more concerned about Eva than about how I was doing. Every time I glanced at her, she seemed to be moving in slow motion. Her heart just wasn't in it, like she didn't have any motivation, and she kept getting knocked down.

That was surprising because before that, she had been advancing quickly. Now, even I was doing better than her, and it hadn't gone unnoticed. Every few seconds, Jericho barked at her. Normally, she had a quick reply and a sharp, witty answer, but today she was suffering his insults in silence. She hadn't even been looking him in the eyes, and gave only short replies. I thought she spent a lot of time looking at the ground. That was definitely not how my best friend usually acted. I was a bit worried.

When the shout went out to break up the matches, I made sure I was in line for water next to her. She gave me a faint, forced smile. I really wanted to give her some encouragement, because she looked way down in the dumps.

Once we got our water, she walked to an empty corner in the little arena field, and I followed. When she sat on a stool to rest, I pulled one over and sat with her. After a long drink from my canteen, I said, "Hey. You feeling okay?" I gave her what I hoped was a reassuring smile.

She took a short drink of water and then rested her arms on her knees as she bent forward, looking down at the ground. She didn't answer for a few seconds, but just when I thought she might ignore me completely, she looked up and said, "I'm frustrated, Cole. I don't know why I'm struggling with the training. I was doing so great before, but now I just feel... I don't know. Weak, I guess."

That came as a real shock. She was always confident, and seeing her like this was kind of depressing. I needed to cheer my best friend up. "Yeah, I saw you out there. I thought maybe you were feeling sick, but I'm surprised to hear you talk like this. I mean, you flew through the training floors in Ochana way faster than me. I haven't even really advanced yet, but you went up a floor in the first week, right?"

She just shook her head, and her eyes grew red-rimmed. If she started crying, I had no idea what I would do. Should I put my arm around her? Try to comfort her, somehow? I just didn't know. This was Eva, after all, and she was always stronger than me.

She said, "You're wrong, Cole. All these things we're doing to save Ochana... It's not *me* finding a way through them, it's *you*. It doesn't matter how my training was going, because it's not going well right now. That's just like when we were dealing with the Farro and the Elden. All I did was get lost and get knocked out. You had to rescue me, and it almost cost us everything. I'm totally doubting my whole right to be the Golden Dragon."

I was stunned, but I knew she was wrong. She was sharing the same thoughts I'd had since coming to Ochana, and it hurt to see that. I said, "I haven't really done anything. It might've happened *through* me, but I was just along for the ride."

"I just feel useless. I miss home and all my friends. I came here because it seemed like the right thing to do, and because I didn't want to put my parents in danger. And you needed me, and we're friends, you know? But I have to wonder if I did the right thing. Maybe you're better off without me."

I took a chance and put my arm around her shoulder, and we just sat in silence for a minute. She was always there for me when I felt down, so being there for her was the least I could do. Besides, she deserved it, and she was being too hard on herself. "I can't really believe you feel this way. I mean, whatever I did to the Farro, I couldn't have done it without you. Together, we're a team. We're the Keeper of Dragons. I know it's rough right now, but in the end, it's not going to be me who saves us all. It's going to be you and me together. There are lots of people counting on us, good people who deserve help. Even if we fail, we have to try, right? When I get doubts, I ask myself, 'What would Eva do?' So you can't be like this or I'm going to be really confused next time."

She didn't laugh. She just kept silent. I didn't know what else to say, so I squeezed her tighter for a second. Maybe a little gesture could help her see how strong she was. Definitely stronger than me, not to mention braver. She had a confidence I never did, and sometimes that was the only thing keeping me going. I couldn't afford to lose that now, so I just sat with her until the shout went out to train again.

I stood and held my hand out toward her, offering to help her up, but she batted my hand aside and popped up to her feet. She looked me in the eyes for a couple seconds, and there was a fierce look in them. Was she back to normal, or did I upset her?

She walked away with her head down and her fists closed, but she didn't head back to the field. She was walking into the jungle. Where was she going? I looked for Jericho but didn't see him. I saw Cairo, though, already jogging after her. He was only a dozen steps behind her when she reached the tree line.

I shook my head. Nothing I said seemed to help. I let out a frustrated sigh and went back to my training.

Half an hour later, Jericho shouted for the day's training to end, and not a minute too soon. I was totally exhausted. My whole body ached from the training. I would be surprised if I didn't have a dozen huge bruises tomorrow morning. My legs felt weak and rubbery from all the effort.

Cairo and Eva still weren't back, so I returned to my treetop room. Inside, I looked around for any clue that someone had been in there, but didn't see anything. I checked the places someone could have hidden—Jericho's advice to always be alert and never trust anyone made sense with everything that had happened recently. We were in a warzone, and it made sense to be careful.

I glanced at my bed as if it had called out to me: "Sleep! Come and sleep on me." That sounded like a great idea. I could get a nap and maybe feel a little better before my next training. It would probably be training with Gaber, so I needed to get control of my tilium. I took off my boots and my jacket, got into bed, and stared up at the ceiling. In moments, I felt myself drifting off into a warm, fuzzy, and very welcome sleep.

The shrill and sudden sound of someone screaming made me bolt upright in bed. Only half-awake, I listened carefully. Were we being attacked, or had I been dreaming?

Another scream echoed around me, and I recognized the voice. It was Eva. A chill ran up my spine as I leaped out of bed, grabbed my sword and ran for the door.

Chapter Four

When I was halfway across the first tree bridge, I used my tilium and blinked down to the jungle floor. I didn't have time to wander around up there because from the sound of Eva's voice, she was on the ground somewhere. I didn't know the paths well enough yet to find my way.

Once on the ground, I wondered where my guardians were, but I had no time to go look for them. I put my head down as I sprinted toward where I thought her scream came from. As I ran, she screamed again. This time, she sounded closer, like she was directly in front of me, but so was the maze of jungle. I had wandered the jungle enough since I got here to know how to find my way through. I was learning what to look for to find the clearer paths.

Seconds later, I emerged into a large clearing and skidded to a halt. My eyes bugged wide as I took in the scene. Eva was sprinting toward me from the other side, and right on her heels were four huge Carnites. They were practically giants; I'd seen them rip up trees by their roots. Well, I had heard them do it and seen the damage later.

Without hesitating, by reflex, I reached out with my mahier and summoned my dragon. The transformation happened almost instantly, and I barreled toward her.

Far away, other creatures began to scream. The Carnites must have invaded the entire area, but I was here and so was Eva. I couldn't help them, but I could help her.

Together, I thought we might be strong enough to survive this.

In moments, I had reached the first Carnite. At the last second, I tipped my wings and streaked upward with my claws in front of me, raking the monster. My claws dug into its thick hide, and it crashed to the ground. I wished I had control of my fire, for this would be the perfect time to use it. Jericho would tell me to conserve my mahier and fire would definitely diminish it, but I had a feeling it would help us with this fight. I spun around and flew back. When I swooped past Eva, running the other direction, I landed by her and turned back into my human.

Her eyes were wide, full of fear, but she stopped when I landed by her. We both drew swords; the other three Carnites would be on us in seconds, and the one I'd knocked over was scrambling to its feet. It wasn't bleeding, though, and I realized my claws had only torn up bits of its thick hide without really hurting it.

How on Earth could we defeat these monsters? The whole area could be full of Carnites by now, for all I knew. "There's nowhere to run, Eva. We take out the one in front first." That's all I had time to say before the Carnite reached us. It carried a huge club, an uprooted tree, and it swung down at us. We charged to meet it.

Running at top speed, with my full momentum behind me, I dove through the air and somersaulted when I landed, so I ended up back on my feet and running. Eva did the same. A moment later, I leaped into the air as I passed the monster, swinging my sword at its belly as I flew by. Thank goodness we had been training with our swords daily since the Elves and Trolls were kidnapped. It still felt awkward at times in my hand, but at this very moment, I felt invincible.

Eva spun and swung her sword at its ankle as she passed, and finished her spin so that she ended up facing the same direction she had been traveling. We both kept running, leaving the Carnite behind us. I didn't know if we'd hurt it, though.

With two Carnites knocked over behind us and two on their feet up ahead, I knew we were in trouble. We had let them surround us. I felt panic rising up, and I struggled to keep it under control. I had to be able to think clearly.

"On the left," I cried out as we ran. Then we would only have to deal with one Carnite between us and escape. Still, that one could do a lot of damage.

As we approached the one on the left, it swept its tree trunk club at us over the ground, left to right, instead of swinging it overhead like the last one. As the club came at me, I jumped and used my mahier to carry me over the deadly weapon. I had no idea how I did it, but it worked. I passed right over the club as my mahier turned my jump into a leap. When I hit the ground, though, my ankle turned. Not enough to injure me, but I fell in a heap.

I glanced around for Eva, but couldn't see her. She must have run into the jungle. I jumped to my feet, but had gotten up too late. One Carnite was swinging its club right at me, and I grit my teeth, bracing for a hit that would probably kill me. It came at me faster than I thought possible as it moved in an arc over me and then came streaking down. My last thought was to hope that Eva had escaped.

When it was just a couple feet from my head, though, it froze in midair. Confused, I stared at the club that hung above me. Two lines of bright light were wrapped around the club on one end, and stretched behind me.

I risked a glance back and saw two Wolands a few feet away, standing with their hands outstretched. They must have used their mahier to bind the club, I realized. I scrambled away from the Carnite in a panic.

The creature roared. It shifted its weight and swung its club to the side, and the two guards flew through the air, mahier still bound to it. One landed in the dirt and rolled, but the other struck a tree. I heard a loud snap and hoped it was just a branch breaking. He bounced off and hit the ground, then lay still.

The other scrambled to his feet in an instant, but he wasn't fast enough. Another Carnite leaped through the air, swinging its club over its head. When it hit the guardian, it buried itself halfway into the soft jungle floor.

With a shout, I jumped at the Carnite in front of me, landing at its feet. It was raising its club, so I used my momentum to somersault between its legs, swinging my sword with all my might as I rolled by. I came up on my feet with our backs facing each other, and I heard a pain-filled roar behind me. I grinned.

Then, to my left, Eva ran out of the jungle. "We have to fall back, Cole." Her eyes were wide, and if the fearless Eva looked scared, I definitely took her word for it. I turned to run back into the jungle with her.

I suddenly found myself flying through the air end over end, spinning fast enough that the sky and the ground flickered into view, one after the other. I felt pain throughout my body, and I caught a glimpse of Eva beside me, looking like a limp rag doll as she spun. I spotted the Carnite I had just cut, one foot in the air in front of it, and realized it had punted us like footballs. We landed in the soft dirt together, tumbling and flopping as we came to a stop.

I tried to get up, but my body wasn't responding. All the fight had been knocked out of me. The Carnite wasted no time, running toward us with its club held over its head in both hands. As that club came down toward me for a second time, all I could do was roll and scramble away from it on my hands and knees, trying to get to my feet but stumbling.

It walked into striking distance again and roared like an animal in rage and pain, and I understood how it felt. I was sure I'd have internal injuries from being kicked, and there was no way I would survive a hit from that club. As if in slow motion, the club began its decent toward me.

I saw a red streak, a blur of smoke and fire that flew through the air and smashed into the club, knocking it flying from the Carnite's hands. The huge red dragon that had struck it bounced off and landed in a heap. I recognized Jericho. He had saved my life.

Two more Woland guards arrived with him, shifting into their human forms and pulling their swords as they landed next to me. One reached down and grabbed me, yanking me to my feet; the other did the same to Eva.

Neither of them looked at Jericho, and it occurred to me they didn't know he was here.

I pointed, and they nodded. Then they sprinted straight at the Carnite. One climbed up its back and the other swung his blade into its belly. I couldn't stab it without risk of hitting the guards, so I ran to Jericho. I reached out with my mahier as I ran, trying to see if he was injured as I opened up my senses. To Eva, running next to me, I said, "He's alive."

Jericho was stirring when we got to him, and we bent down to help him up. Smoke puffed from his nostrils as he shifted to human form. He looked bad, with most of his face already swelling, the black and blue beginning to show. I assumed the rest of his body was just as bad, maybe worse. He shouted, "We have to fall back. The Keepers must be kept safe!"

I didn't feel like arguing. We ran, Jericho staggering between us.

Chapter Five

Eva and I made a break for it, half-carrying and half-dragging Jericho. With every step, he groaned in pain, but there was nothing we could do about it out here in the jungle. Behind us, the Realm Five dragons were blocking any Carnite chasing us. I felt bad about leaving them behind, but we had to get Jericho out of there.

Eva read my mind again, I guess, because she grunted and said, "I feel bad, too, but that's their job. We defend the True, and they defend us. Now focus. We have to get out of here."

I had begun to sweat and had to pause to shift my grip on Jericho. He groaned, but then his eyes flicked open and he looked at me. "We...have to retreat...away from Paraiso."

He was right, but if an army of Carnites wandered into Paraiso with its wards down and its tilium gone, the few free Trolls and Elves that remained would be lost.

"Eva," I said between gasps for air, "we need to head away from Paraiso. Maybe we can lure the Carnites away."

She didn't answer, but we turned east to move away from the Elves' home. I looked back once, wishing we could go there. Paraiso had been a paradise that felt like home more than Ochana did, but now it was powerless and almost abandoned.

We staggered through the jungle as fast as we could. At one spot, the canopy above us opened up and I caught a glimpse of the sun. It told me we'd been running for at least an hour.

I could still hear the Carnites crashing through the jungle behind us, but we had gained some distance. "We have to stop for a minute. We need to check on Jericho. You feel him sweating? That can't be good," I said, gasping.

"He's in shock," Eva said, and I could hear concern in her voice. "Lay him down gently."

We stopped and lowered him to the jungle floor. I pulled out my water skin and knelt beside him. "Can you hear me? You need some water. No, not too much... There we go, just sip at it."

I stood and stretched my back, looking around to check out our situation. None of the landmarks looked familiar. Then again, I didn't grow up in the jungle. I had no idea how far from Paraiso we were.

"I hoped he would come around while we ran," I said, "but he's hurt worse than I thought. We need to get him to Ochana, or I think he might die."

Jericho's eyes seemed to focus again. Faint and weak, he said, "We're about five miles from Paraiso." Then he coughed, and his whole body shook. I saw a trickle of blood from the corner of his mouth, and he grew pale. His eyes rolled up and he passed out again. I hoped he'd wake up a little before we had to continue running for our lives.

Eva put her fists on her hips and let out a sharp breath, then said, "You're right. I wanted to get farther away before we made any decisions, but I don't think Jericho can wait. We're just going to have to hope we're far enough away. What do you think?"

"I think they were just a wandering band who stumbled into Paraiso's territory, now that the wards are down. Either way, if they knew where Paraiso was, I don't think we could have drawn them away like this."

Eva gave me a curt nod. "Then it's decided. We get Jericho out of here and hope we don't accidentally draw attention to Paraiso. But there's one more problem."

I frowned. "Another problem?"

"He's too weak to hold on, much less fly. One of us is going to have to hold him."

I hadn't thought of that. She was right, it was a problem. "I don't think you're big enough to carry us both so far. I'll have to do it."

She nodded, but said, "Do you think you can? We're already tired from carrying him through this jungle."

I rolled my shoulders in circles, stretching my muscles a bit. I would need those to fly. I didn't feel any strains or other injuries, though, despite being kicked for a field goal by a Carnite earlier, and an hour-long scramble through the jungle. "I think I can at least make it to Ellesmere Island. From there, we can call in for help from Ochana."

She pursed her lips and nodded. I didn't blame her for being unhappy about the situation. If I cramped up over the Atlantic...

She motioned for me to get going and it looked like it was time for me to step up. The idea of me saving Jericho seemed somehow wrong. I didn't even have full control of my mahier, and I was a terrible warrior. But I was the only one who might be able to help him.

I swore to myself that I would never bring this up to him again, if he lived. Then I walked a few feet away and called to my dragon. Claws shot out through my fingertips and my many-colored scales rose up through my skin. My wings burst out as I stretched them wide over some of the smaller trees.

The transition was the smoothest one yet, even though I was exhausted. Quickly, I found my bearings and focused on the task at hand. I concentrated on sending my thoughts to Eva. "Can you get him on my back?"

She bent over and struggled to pick up the half-conscious Jericho. The water bottle fell from his hands, but we left it there. I had another. It took her a few minutes of grunting and sweating to get him in place, then a couple more minutes for her to get him situated and secure between her arms as she sat behind him. She said, "All right, let's see what you got, Cole."

I took a couple of steps and jumped. I beat down with my wings and rose a few feet into the air. But I didn't have enough speed and landed hard. Eva and Jericho almost fell from my back.

I felt Eva patting my side. She said, "It's okay, Cole. You can do this. Try again, but reach out with your mahier, too. Let it flow through you and help push you off the ground."

I launched myself into the air again, beating my wings hard. Summoning my power, I reached out with it just like I would if I was expanding my senses, but instead of seeing or feeling, I willed it to push me away from the ground. Energy flew through me, pushing, and I suddenly felt lighter. It worked. I had the little bit of speed I needed to have more lift. Excited, I flapped hard and we slowly rose up.

I still had my energy pushing down on the ground, and so I sensed it when the Carnites rushed into the clearing. One jumped as high as it could and swung its club, but it missed by at least ten feet. It was sort of scary to realize that if we had waited another minute, they would have caught us.

I thought of Realm Five, who had stayed behind to buy us time to escape, but I couldn't feel them. Hopefully, they were simply too far away to sense, but I worried about them. They may have given themselves up to let us escape.

The thought was too sad. I pushed it from my mind and focused on flying. Faster and faster, higher and higher over the jungle. I only hoped I could keep that up. It would take hours to get to Ellesmere Island.

* * *

With all that weight on my back, it took me half an hour to get up to a good altitude. When I got to the right height, though, flying got a lot easier. Something about wind drag and air pressure, from what little I remembered in my studies. Most of my concentration went into using my mahier to keep Eva and Jericho from being tossed off by the winds. I left it to her to keep any humans on the ground from seeing us.

About a half an hour after that, I saw the glittering, beautiful Atlantic Ocean ahead of us. We were nearing Africa's west coast. I focused on Eva and thought at her: "I'm getting tired. I need to land, stretch a bit, and rest my wings. Plus, I could literally eat a horse."

I heard her shouting, "I'm sure you're starving by now."

"Maybe hungrier than I've ever been!"

"Going back and forth between human and dragon eats up your mahier. And don't forget you've been keeping us safe back here. You need to refuel. You know what that means, right?"

To the north, farms stretched along the shore. I angled down, and we gained speed as I lost altitude, heading for the shoreline.

Eva said, "You have to land away from the farms, call your human and drop us off, and go find some horses. Or better yet, a cow."

I felt a little guilty at the thought of eating someone else's cattle, or whatever a group of horses was called, but Jericho's life and the war against the Elden were far more important. If they won the war, the humans would be in for a lot more trouble than just a missing horse or cow. I decided I'd have to do it, even if I felt bad about it.

When we got close to the ground, I put my wings back to slow us and then drifted down, landing on my hind legs. For once, I didn't do a faceplant when my front legs hit the dirt. Eva dragged Jericho off my back, trying to be gentle on him. As a dragon, I couldn't do much to help, so she grunted and struggled on her own. When he finally came free, she fell over backward and he landed on top of her. At least she broke his fall.

"Oh yeah, at least I broke his fall. Thanks, Cole." She flashed a smile, so I knew she wasn't really upset. I did wish she would stop randomly hearing my thoughts, though.

I called my human, and the transformation was quick. I rolled my shoulders and stretched my arms out, feeling a little sore from the flight. I wished I knew how to use my mahier to fix the aches and pains, but I was not doing well in my studies—and not just in warrior training. "I'm going to go find some food."

She settled Jericho onto the ground and got up, dusting herself off. "Don't worry about us. He hasn't spent any mahier since he was hurt, so you don't need to bring any meat back. Just eat it all yourself, okay? You need as much of a recharge as you can get."

I nodded, then headed north, moving slower than I would have liked because of the thick jungle. Vines covered everything and there were stumps and fallen logs all over the place. I was determined, and I eventually made it out of the jungle and into a clearing.

There were two farms side-by-side. One was small, with a single ox. They probably used it to help plow their fields. The farm next to it was larger, though, and they had a pen with a bunch of animals. As I got closer, I saw some looked like cows, but they were different from any cows I'd ever seen. They were smaller, with long fur. The ox next door would be a lot tastier, but that farm didn't look like they could afford to spare it.

Once I got close to the big animal pen, I called my dragon. The shift happened almost immediately, my multi-colored scales popping up through my skin in an instant. The cows were suddenly nervous, and started to make some noise. I didn't really want any attention, so I grabbed one between my two front legs and jumped into the air, flying back to Eva and Jericho with the thing. I ate the whole funny-looking cow all by myself in less than fifteen minutes. I had never been so hungry.

Once I picked the bones clean, it was time to get back to work. "Eva, are you ready? You're going to have to get him up on my back again."

She said she was, but it turned out she wasn't as ready as she thought. It took her ten minutes to get Jericho up, and another five to get him propped up the right way. It wasn't easy, and I hoped she hadn't hurt him even more.

Once she told me they were set, I leaped into the air again. This time, I felt stronger. Probably because I had just devoured a whole cow. I got up to the best cruising altitude fast, and from there on, the flying was easier. Up above the clouds, gliding through the thin air, it was a lot easier to keep the winds from blowing Eva and Jericho away.

We flew north like that for hours before I spotted Ellesmere Island ahead. Before I could say anything, I heard Eva shouting to let me know we were almost there. I was too tired to use my mahier for anything but the wind barrier, so Eva had to let Ochana know where we were and our situation. We made it the rest of the way by simply gliding to the island because that was about all the strength I had left. I sure couldn't have lasted another hour.

Once we landed, she dragged Jericho off my back faster than she had the first time, and she didn't fall down. I could see it took all her strength, but she laid him down as gently as she could. I staggered, my exhaustion taking over. I just didn't have any strength left. My mahier was tapped out. With so little left, I couldn't maintain my dragon and started transforming back into my human form. As soon as that was done, I fell to my knees.

Next to me, holding Jericho's head in her lap, Eva said, "A Realm of dragons is on its way. I've been using my energy to try to help Jericho, and I don't know if it did any good, but I used up most of my power, too."

I could only nod, too tired to answer her. Jericho looked even worse than I felt. His breathing had gone from steady, deep breaths to a rapid, shallow wheezing. He had a trickle of blood coming from the corner of his mouth. I tried to sense his injuries, but I didn't have enough power left in me; all I could feel was his heartbeat. That was enough to scare me, though, since it was beating as fast as a hummingbird's.

His whole body suddenly shook, and his breath rattled around in his chest, wet and bubbly. I was no doctor, but my first thought was that he had a punctured lung. I couldn't lose him now, not when help was so close. I grabbed Eva's hand and focused on pushing my energy into him, willing it to flow through him. I only needed to hold him together for a little while longer. I didn't know if it would work, but it was worth a try.

Suddenly, I felt a warm tingling in my hand where I touched Eva's. I could feel her mahier flowing into me and through me. There was only a trickle of it, but that was more than I could give him. I cleared my mind and focused on him, using both our power to try to keep him alive.

A hand grasped my shoulder gently, startling me. I looked up and saw a human with a Woland's red eyes. He said, "You did well, Keeper. We'll take it from here."

My eyes drifted around to find four other dragons. One shifted out of his human, and two others lifted Jericho onto the dragon's back. One of them followed him up onto the dragon's back and held him steady. Two more summoned their dragons, and the fifth one, the one who had put his hand on my shoulder, said, "One of you ride each of them. I can feel how empty your mahier is, Prince, but we don't have time to feed."

As Eva and I climbed aboard, Jericho's dragon mount took to the air and disappeared, along with another dragon. We were left alone on the island with our mounts. A moment later, they were in the air as well, and I could feel my dragon's muscles heaving beneath me. They were flying as fast as they could, I figured.

And then, pop. We were descending on Ochana, and I'd never been so happy to see it before. Jericho was below me, being lifted from his dragon mount. As we slowed down and banked in to land, they were putting Jericho on a stretcher, and he was whisked away. I wondered where they were taking him.

Once we landed, a blue dragon came up and bowed slightly. "Prince Colton. We are all happy to see you and the Golden Dragon safe and well."

I looked away, trying to see where they were taking Jericho.

The blue dragon nodded and said, "You're right to worry. His eyes were rolling up and he was breathing his last breath when they landed. Several of us had to use our mahier together just to keep him from passing. You saved his life, you know. The healers will do all they can, of course, and Ochana has the best in all the world. If there is any place on Earth where he could live, this is it. You did well to bring him home."

I was too exhausted to care about anything except Jericho, so all I really heard from her speech was that he almost died and they were trying to keep him alive. That was enough to understand, for now. It was far more than I could have given him on my best day, and with this being one of the worst, I couldn't ask for much more.

J.A. Culican

Chapter Six

Eva and I waited outside Jericho's room, pacing. It felt like I'd been there for hours, and maybe I had. Some of the healers told me to get some rest. I'm sure I looked terrible after wearing myself out on that long flight to Ellesmere Island, but there was no way I'd leave Jericho until he woke up. If he even did.

My parents—Rylan and Sila, not the humans I grew up with—had come by once for about twenty minutes, and it had taken me awhile to stop being angry at them for leaving. I knew they had a kingdom to run and a war to get ready for, but part of me still felt they should be there for him, or maybe I was angry they left Eva and me here alone.

Eva must have seen my expression, because after they left, she said, "They *are* being there for him. By defending Ochana, they'll make sure he still has a kingdom to protect when he wakes up."

I gave her a nod. She was right and I knew it, so I tried to set aside my feelings. It didn't help anyone for me to stay angry about things I knew were outside anyone's control. I still kept pacing, though. It irritated Eva, but she didn't say anything. She knew I needed to keep moving so I didn't lose my mind.

An hour later, the lead healer came out of Jericho's room. She had a sour look on her face until she spotted us and put on her "doctor face"—calm and clinical. I went over to her right away, eager to hear any news. She held up her hand to stop me. "Before you hit me with a thousand questions, let me tell you what you really want to know. Councilor Jericho has several broken bones, his lungs were punctured in two places, and he had a lot of internal bleeding. We can make mahier do wondrous things to heal, but it has its limits."

"Is he dying?" I blurted, unable to stop myself before the words came out.

She shook her head. "I can't say for sure. It depends on how strong he is, and how much he wants to live. But this is Jericho we're talking about."

"If anyone can survive those injuries, he can." It was true, too, not just me trying to convince myself.

"We'll have healers working on him for as long as their mahier remains, but they have to stop and eat; they need to recharge sometimes. There's also a limit to how much we can do at once without straining his body. That would do more harm than good."

I looked down at my feet and took a deep breath. I had experienced draining all my mahier before, so I knew what she was talking about. I just didn't like it. "When will we be able to go see him?"

She gave me a faint smile and put her hand on my shoulder. Looking me in the eye, she said, "I believe we might be able to let him wake up after his current treatment is done. We have two healers in the room, working on his lungs. Once they use up all their energy, Jericho should wake up by himself shortly after. We can't be sure what condition he'll be in mentally, but like you said, if anyone can survive those injuries, he can."

The exhausted-looking healer walked away, leaving the hallway empty except for Eva and me. I knew the treatments lasted about a half an hour, having watched the healers coming and going for a while by that time. I let out a deep sigh, then went to go sit by Eva to wait it out.

She grabbed my hand. I didn't know if she was trying to comfort me, or if she needed comforting, or both. Either way, I appreciated it.

* * *

The last healer came out of Jericho's room and stopped long enough to tell us he should be awake soon, and that we should be there when he did. That was the whole reason Eva and I had been sitting there for hours, but I thanked her. Then Eva and I waited inside the bare room. Jericho lay on his bed, eyes closed, hands folded across his stomach. In one corner, his assistant was reading a book. She looked a lot like Mira, my own assistant.

She glanced up, saw that it was me, and bolted to her feet to bow.

"No," I said, "no need for that. We're all just here for Jericho. Have a seat, read your book. Pay us no mind."

There were two wooden stools next to the bed and I plopped down on one. Eva joined me on the other. It didn't take long for Jericho to stir. I had been sort of absentmindedly sensing him with my mahier to keep distracted, tracking his breathing and his heartbeat. The first thing I noticed was his pulse speeding up a little bit, and his breathing wasn't as even.

His eyelids fluttered open, and he tried to say something, but coughed instead. Eva handed him a glass of water and helped him take a few sips. The effort seemed to drain him, and he lay back and closed his eyes for a moment.

After he caught his breath, he opened his eyes again and gave Eva a quick nod. That was as much thanks as she was likely to get from him. He tried to talk again, but this time his voice was less cracked. "Pleased you're...OK, both of you... The Keepers need to be kept safe."

I smiled at him. "I'm OK, but only because of what you did. I think I owe you my life."

He shook his head faintly. "My duty. My honor...don't owe..."

Eva reached out and rested her hand on his arm. "So how does it feel to be a golf ball?"

I grinned. He really had taken quite a whack, but I wasn't sure he would get the humor. Did Wolands play golf?

"I feel like I've been run over by a steamroller," he said, some of his strength coming back to him. "But something is wrong, deep inside, something with my mahier, I can't be sure. All I know is, I have no strength."

I could tell that just by looking at him. "When will you be better? We need you. I don't think I can do this without you. I'm not ready to save the world all alone." It was awkward telling him my fears, because Jericho had no room for fear in his world, but I wasn't going to lie to him. We did need help.

He actually gave me a faint smile, which surprised me. He said, "You aren't alone. You're only one half of the Keeper of Dragons, and the other half is your true friend. You have Cairo, who would go to the ends of the Earth to protect Eva. You have your parents, who love you even though they only just met you. You have every Dragon in Ochana and every free Elf and Fairy, plus the Trolls that remain."

I forced a smile onto my face and said, "You shouldn't talk so much. You're weak and need to save your strength." He was right, though. I had three kingdoms supporting me, and my best friend. Meanwhile, Jericho was bedridden and somehow sick, and I was feeling sorry for myself. I straighten my back, sitting taller on the stool. "Of course. You're right. Now the question is, what do we do next?"

Eva blurted, "We go see the Mermaids. A fourth kingdom to help us."

I waited for him to argue with her. Instead, he closed his eyes for a moment. With my mahier sensing him, I felt his exhaustion. "I know there's no stopping the Golden Dragon, no matter what I say, as long as I'm here in bed. She'll convince you to go to the Mermaids, and you'll follow her. Too tired to fight, so I'm just going to go with it. Maybe she's right. I doubt it, but I hope I'm wrong."

Eva grinned and gave him a wink, even though his eyes were still closed. She said, "Well, you're right about that. So, where do we find them?"

He coughed, a wet and raspy sound. It didn't seem as bad as it had before, but I could hear the fluid in his lungs.

When his coughing eased, he said, "You'll find them in the Dead Sea. Trust the Fates. If you're meant to find them, you will. We haven't spoken to them in a long time, and I have no idea how you'll be received. Their leader is Queen Desla. Find her, tell her what's at stake."

Eva nodded, enthusiastic. "Thank you. I just have this feeling that we're meant to go there. I couldn't tell you why."

He didn't reply, and I thought maybe he had passed out again. Then he opened his eyes and looked right at me. "One more thing. In their kingdom grows a certain plant. Whatever this is that I feel deep within me, it might help me. If you can, get a handful of that. Queen Desla will know of the plant. I might be able to do without it, but I just feel so weak. Not sure I have the strength, even with the help of the healers. I only wish we'd known of this plant for your Uncle Jago." Jericho's voice trailed off.

I clenched my fist and nodded. "I'll get that weed, no matter what. I'll make them give it to me." I glanced at Eva, who looked at me oddly. Maybe she didn't understand my determination. The Farros had killed my uncle and now the Carnites might kill Jericho. All because of Eldrick.

Jericho's heart slowed down a bit and his breathing became slow and steady.

"He's gone back to sleep."

Eva patted his arm and said, "Let him sleep. He needs all the rest he can get. Come on, let's go. We need to get ready for a long trip, then you need to say goodbye to your parents."

* * *

After we left Jericho, Eva went to her room to bathe and change while I went to go find my parents. In the middle of all this, I didn't know if I would see the king and queen again. Maybe I hadn't grown up with them, but they were still my parents. I knew they loved me anyway. In a way, I loved them too, even though I didn't know them. There was a sort of bond in being related by blood.

I found Rylan in the throne room at the head of a line of assistants with papers for him to read and sign. Being the king didn't look like a lot of fun.

As I entered, his eyes locked on mine and he smiled. "Colton, my son. It is so good to see you. Come sit next to me, let's talk."

I walked up the steps to the platform and sat on the smaller throne to Rylan's right. The king waved the assistants away. They made their way to the back of the throne room, giving us our privacy.

"How is Jericho?" Rylan asked. "I haven't had time to go visit him in hours."

I squirmed a little in the uncomfortable throne. No matter how I shifted, I couldn't quite get settled in. My whole life was kind of like that now.

"He's still badly wounded, and he seems to have some sort sickness; he thinks it's his mahier. The healers' mahier isn't curing it, something about how he's reached the limits of how much the healers can help him. If they keep pouring mahier into him, it will do more harm than good."

Rylan looked up at the ceiling for a moment, and he looked troubled. "I see. So then, whether he recovers depends mostly on how strong he is. It's a good thing that if anyone is strong enough, our friend Jericho is."

My father didn't sound convinced. Maybe the news I brought would help him deal with it better. Or maybe he'd refuse to let Eva and me go. I decided I would go anyway, if that's where Eva went, but I had to tell him our plans.

I took a deep breath, then said, "Eva and I are going to the Dead Sea to bring the Mermaids into the Elven Alliance. The good news is that some sort of special plant grows in the Mermaid kingdom, and Jericho says it could heal him. I just need to grab a handful while we're there, and then the healers can do the rest."

Rylan nodded and gave me a faint smile. "Yes, I think I know the one you mean. It's the one that has more yellow than green, and grows on a stalk like kelp, but I forget the name." Rylan closed his eyes and sighed. "I am told if we had known of such plant, it may have saved my brother." Rylan's eyes flashed open and studied me. "Going to the Mermaids would not have been my first choice, but if the Keeper of Dragons have both decided that's the best course, then I'll leave it to fate. You're destined to drive back the Time of Fear. Whatever you two do together, things will happen the way they're meant to. Who am I to get in the way of that?"

That was surprising. I had figured he'd demand we go to Greece, or maybe some other plan I hadn't thought of. The trust he put in me made me think of my nightmare, where everyone cheered at me and believed I would succeed, even while the darkness was coming for them.

I shoved that thought away. If I dwelled on it too much, I might freeze up and do nothing at all. Whether going to see the Mermaids was the best plan or not, it was still better than just sitting in Ochana, waiting for the end to come. I said, "Eva and I are leaving right away. We'll head back to Paraiso first, pick up Cairo and Realm Five, then go east to meet the Mermaids."

He let out a long breath, like all the fight had left him. I suppose he was afraid of losing me, yet the whole world depended on him letting me go. In a way, I was glad my real parents—the ones I grew up with—didn't have to know about what I was doing. I missed them so much, and I know they would have feared for me greatly.

He said, "Then I suppose you had better get going, my son. Your mother's heart and mine go with you. I'm afraid for you, but I know this is what you were born to do, you and Eva both. I just wish this hadn't happened in your lifetime. Sila is sad she hasn't had time to get to know you better since you came back to us."

Then he stood and faced me, so I got up, too. I was kind of surprised when he leaned forward and gave me a quick hug instead of putting his hand on my shoulder or shaking my hand, like he usually did. He must have been really afraid for me, and Jericho getting hurt couldn't have helped him feel better about it. When I came back with those leaves for Jericho, and he got better, maybe Rylan would feel better, too. I smiled at the thought, and he smiled back at me. Then it was time to go.

* * *

After stopping at another farm along the African coast to eat, Eva and I landed back in Paraiso to gather up Cairo and Realm Five before heading east. Now that the decision had been made to go see the Mermaids, I was kind of excited. It wasn't very long ago that I thought Mermaids didn't exist. Neither did dragons, or Elves.

We both shifted back into our humans as we landed. I was getting much better at it, and could usually do it in the blink of an eye, now.

"Let's go find Cairo," Eva said.

I grinned. I had no idea why Cairo didn't want to tell her he thought they were soulmates, because to me, it was pretty obvious she felt the same way, even without knowing about the weird, magic soul-bonding thing Cairo thought it was.

She said, "What? Don't smile at me like that. You know he and I have just gotten close since I got here. I mean, we work together every day. It's only natural."

I shrugged and smirked. "I didn't say a word."

Eva rolled her eyes and I fought the urge to laugh.

A new voice to my right shouted, "Eva, Prince Colton. I'm so glad you two made it back. How is Jericho?"

I looked down at the ground. It was good to see Cairo again, but I really didn't want to have to tell him about Jericho.

Thankfully, Eva answered before it got awkward. "The healers brought him through the worst of his danger, at least for the moment. He says he feels some sort of sickness, with his mahier. He also gave us his blessing to try to recruit the Mermaids. I know it wasn't his first choice, but with him bedridden, he knew he couldn't stop us. Plus, there's a plant that grows there he asked us to gather for him."

I added, "Get the dragons ready to fly out. We'll head east again just as soon as Eva and I get something to eat. We only ate enough along the way for us to get here safely."

Cairo nodded, then waved over a Woland and told her to make sure we got all the food we needed. He said, "Food is on the way. Now, then... I thought the plan was to head to Greece where the rest of the Fairies are. Just because Jericho can't get out of bed doesn't mean he was wrong."

Eva glared at him and said, "Oh, so you don't believe he gave us his blessing? I would have thought you out of everyone here would trust me. Well, Mister Thinks-He-Knows-Everything, I guess you didn't get the memo. Jericho said we should go after the Mermaids, which you would know if you had been at your friend's side when he woke up. Like we were."

Cairo stood his ground. He looked her in the eye and said, "Someone as badly hurt as Jericho might say just about anything in that condition. And you're being unfair—you know perfectly well that I was here doing my job. I'm always doing my job. I sided with you earlier about going to the Mermaids. You had a good point, but Jericho was right. We can't waste our resources chasing the Mermaids."

Both Eva and Cairo stood tall, backs straight and fists clenched. It was clear neither was going to back down. Emotions were running high with everything that had happened recently and it seemed both were ready to take their frustration out on the other. Hoping to stop the standoff, I said, "Actually, Jericho did say that. It was something along the lines of, since he couldn't stop us from going, then he wished us luck and put his support behind us. Behind Eva, actually, because I still think we need to head north. I'm telling you, my dream—"

Eva clenched her fists tighter and yelled in frustration, glaring back and forth between Cairo and me.

Not backing down, Cairo said, "I know you're mad, but listen to reason. We need to go after the Carnites. They're going to be the easiest ones to find out of all our enemies, and they might lead us to a clue on King Eldrick's location, or even where the Elves and Trolls are being held."

I snarled, "You can't cut me off and then ignore what I said. I'm telling you, as the Keeper of Dragons, we need to head north. I don't see why we're even arguing about this. That's where the Elves and Trolls are." And since when were we planning on chasing the Carnites?

Eva gave us each a final glare and then turned on her heels to walk away.

Cairo and I both looked after her in disbelief.

Over her shoulder, she said, "When you two are done arguing with each other and ignoring what I have the say, then we'll talk, but I'm not going to let you treat me like this. I'm going to get something to eat, and you two can beat the snot out of each other for all I care."

She let out a shout of frustration and stormed back toward the dragon encampment in Paraiso. Cairo and I watched her leave, and I realized my jaw had dropped. I snapped my mouth shut and looked at Cairo.

He looked back at me and shrugged helplessly. "I can't believe she was so mad at us. I mean, it's just one little disagreement, right? We'd have figured it out eventually."

I could only shake my head at him. He didn't know Eva the way I did. She never just walked away from any fight, unless she was really angry and had enough. "Actually, I think you're on thin ice with her. Trust me on this. Eva is way angrier than you think, and she can hold a grudge when she wants to."

I let out a deep sigh, letting my frustration flow away. She was my best friend, but she was making a mistake, and Cairo was letting her. I added, "If you honestly believe that stuff you said about being her *Vera Salit*, I think you need to go and apologize, whether you think you did anything wrong or not. Seriously, this is the time to tell her you believe that you two are soulmates. If you don't, things might really get away from you. I wouldn't leave it to chance like that."

Cairo's eyes flared, flashing red. His whole body stiffened and he stood straighter, it was clear I had stepped over some invisible line in the sand. He said, "I'm not ready for that. This isn't the right time. You think you're the only one who knows her? I don't think you give her enough credit, Cole. Anyway, it's between me and her whether we're soulmates. It has nothing to do with you. With all due respect, you need to back off and leave me alone right now. If you want to stay here and follow me around arguing, whatever happens will be on your hands."

I couldn't believe what I just heard. I didn't think he would really hurt me, but he was definitely ready to take a swing. I had no idea what would happen to him if he did, considering that I'm the Prince of Ochana and the Keeper of Dragons. I didn't want to find out. No matter how mad I was at him at the moment, he was a good dragon and loyal to Ochana, and I didn't want anything to happen to him.

So, I turned around and walked away, fuming. I swore that later, after we had both cooled off a bit, Cairo and I were going to have a long talk and straighten things out between us, one way or another.

Chapter Seven

I looked down on the small room almost as though I floated above it. King Eldrick stood over someone sitting in a chair, but I couldn't see who it was. Eldrick blocked my view.

"I promise you, the pain will end when you tell me what I want to know." Eldrick's voice sounded like he had a sneer on his face.

"I'll tell you nothing. Not because of who he is, but because of who you are." The voice sounded familiar, and it only took a moment to realize it was the Elven Princess Clara, Gaber's sister.

Eldrick stepped around behind her, and I could finally see both of their faces. He said, "I don't see why you protect him. After all these years, you don't owe him anything. He's certainly not out there looking for you, Clara. He's back in Ochana, doing nothing."

She shook her head and glared. "Someone is looking for me. I sense it, and when they find me, your time will be done, traitor."

He laughed and said, "That's a good one. You call me a traitor? The king and queen were traitors to their race. I tried to make us strong, the strongest of them all, and for my efforts..."

"They exiled you, even though your crime deserved death. You were only spared because you're part of our family, or you were until you came back and killed our parents. Tell me, Eldrick, how does killing two of the five originals make my race stronger?"

Eldrick's grip on the chair back tightened, his knuckles turning white from the force, but his voice sounded calm as he said, "Our race, not yours. And that's water under the bridge. I can't change the past, nor can you. But we can still look to the future."

She snarled, "There is no future in dishonor."

He ignored her. "Being crushed by a Carnite should have done it, yet he lives. Tell me how to kill him and I'll let you free to go rejoin your brother. I'll keep all of our cousins here as collateral, but the pain will stop. Think about it, Clara, you can choose right now to go free and end their suffering, or you can keep protecting a dragon, not even one of us. You two were over a long time ago. I promise you'll be OK. You don't owe him anything."

Clara snarled back at him, "You want me turn to the darkness just like you and your followers did. Never! Elves are strongest when we embrace our nature, our Truth. I'll never help you, no matter what it costs us."

Eldrick laughed and reached out to a table that I couldn't see well. When he drew his hand back, he carried a small, wicked knife. "I would say this isn't going to hurt, but that would be a lie. Are you ready?"

I sat bolt upright in bed, Clara's screams echoing in my ears. I was covered in sweat and shivered in the cold night air. Why did I keep having these dreams? I didn't know what they all meant, and had a feeling I was missing some part of a bigger picture. I didn't think they were really dreams at all. They felt real.

I decided to go for an early morning walk to calm myself down a bit, and threw on my clothes before walking outside. I blinked down to the jungle floor, then strolled toward the Elves' mystical lake with my head down, lost in thought about the dreams.

Before I ever made it to the lakeshore, I heard a loud bang. I stopped and listened, trying not to even breathe so I could hear well. There were some rustling noises, and I walked toward them. In a small clearing at the jungle's edge, just outside of Paraiso, Cairo was stuffing supplies into a backpack. Was he leaving? What could make a dragon like him abandon his duty? He was supposed to be here protecting Eva.

"Tell me you aren't just running away, Cairo. I'd be mighty disappointed, and I think Eva would, too." I clenched my jaw and stared at him, angry and ready to take a swing. "Tell me why you're running away now, when we all need you most."

He looked up, startled. It seemed he hadn't heard me approaching. "I'm not running away. I'm a bit offended you would think that. The truth is, Eva left in the middle of the night to go find the Mermaids without us. I guess she got tired of waiting. I'm going to go find her—she's not safe out there alone, and we can't risk losing the Golden Dragon."

My jaw dropped. How could she do that? She knew how dangerous it was out there. Then again, she always was the braver of us. Well, I couldn't let Cairo go alone, not when he was determined to go out and find Eva himself. And something told me he wouldn't wait for me to gather a team to help track Eva.

I took a deep breath, shoved my anger aside, and said, "We have to find her. We should work together. We'll be safer together than apart."

He nodded and said, "Ten minutes." Then he began stuffing things back into his backpack.

I blinked back up to my room and grabbed my own pack. I had never unpacked it, so I just slung it over my shoulder. A couple minutes later, I was back with Cairo.

He gave me a nod, then turned and began walking east. "My senses tell me she was walking. I don't know why she didn't fly, but we can't just turn into our dragons. I'd lose track of her from the air."

I frowned. That meant it would take longer to find her, if we could even catch up to her. "Are you sure you'll be able to find her? How?"

Cairo said, "I told you, we are soulmates. *Vera Salit* can use our mahier to reach out and sense our soulmate's direction. When we get close to her, I'll be able to feel it more clearly. But like I said, if we fly, we'll be moving too quickly and I'll lose her path."

Together, we moved away from Paraiso and deeper into the jungle. We walked for the rest of that morning, stopped for a quick lunch of berries and plants we'd gathered along the way, then continued on. The hours ticked by. From the occasional glimpses of the sun overhead through the jungle canopy, I guessed it to be about four o'clock.

As we reached the top of a small hill and began walking down, headed ever eastward, I sensed something. I had my mahier pushed outward, hoping I could sense any danger or humans we came across before we were seen. I said, "Stop. There's something dark nearby, and it's heading our way. No, wait, there's more than one. Five, seven... Ten. I count ten of them."

Cairo's head whipped around as he looked for any danger. "How far away are they, and what are they?"

Suddenly, my senses reeled. Whatever was out there, they were powerful. And familiar.

J.A. Culican

Chapter Eight

"Elden. Ten of them, a few hundred yards away and coming on fast. They're almost on us," I muttered as I concentrated on the Elden.

He said in a half-whisper, "Elden? We have to hide. There's no way we can win against ten of them."

I didn't need to be told twice. The Elden must have known where we were somehow, because the odds of them coming straight at us were just too small. I felt fear rising up in my belly.

I looked around, desperate to find a place to hide from the approaching Elden, but there was nowhere that looked good enough. But if they knew where we were, there was no use in hiding anyway. Not here.

To our east, something moved. A quick glance told me it was the Elden reaching the top of a small hill. One of them pointed at us.

I looked at Cairo. "Too late, they found us."

His eyes widened, just for a split second, and he said, "Run."

Once again, we found ourselves running for our lives. There was no way we could beat so many of them, and in the back of my mind, I wondered where they had come from. I wish I knew how they'd found us.

We ran as fast as we could, our mahier helping give us energy. I really wanted to ask why we didn't just turn into dragons and fly away, but Cairo was an experienced Woland. If he didn't shift, it must've been for a good reason. I shoved that thought aside and focused on running.

We bolted down a little path between two low, rolling hills. I realized we were trying to stay out of sight as much as possible while we ran. Then, up ahead about fifty feet, a pair of Elden came into view. Their black, beady eyes and razor-sharp teeth zeroed in on us and they charged.

Cairo slowed and pulled his sword, so I did the same, but we didn't stop. Side-by-side, we crashed into the two scouts. There was a quick flash of blades as Cairo defeated one and I held off the other. Then he dealt with the one attacking me.

"Come on, we have to get out of here," he half-shouted before putting his sword away and sprinting north again.

I was hot on his heels. We kept moving long past the point I should've been exhausted. I found it easier to use my tilium to keep the fatigue away, but Cairo wasn't having any problem keeping up using mahier. It was an odd thing to think about at that moment.

An arrow streaked past my face and I almost missed a step. Cairo shouted to keep going, so I did. I put my head down and ran as fast as I could.

We rounded another hill and up ahead, a forest stretched into the distance. My heart leaped for joy. All we had to do was get to the tree line and we might be able to lose our pursuers. Cairo saw it, too, because he changed direction to head directly at it. The minutes passed as the forest came closer and closer, but there were no more arrows flying by. I didn't look back to check, but I figured the Elden decided they could run faster without trying to shoot us. Once they closed the distance or chased us into exhaustion, they'd have plenty of time to shoot us. It was not a pleasant thought.

One instant, we were running through open rolling plains, probably visible for miles, and then we burst through the tree line. Hah! Let them try to shoot us running through that thick jungle.

My tilium was slowly draining. I knew it wouldn't last forever, and I figured the Elden had more of it than I did. When I ran out, I would be able to switch to my mahier, but Cairo would just be out of power. I couldn't leave him behind, so I'd have to stop, and we'd have to fight the Elden alone whether he had any mahier left or not.

That seemed like a bad idea so I said, "We have to hide. They'll outrun us eventually."

"You're right. Follow me."

There wasn't time to ask questions, so I just followed him through the forest, jumping over logs and dodging branches as best we could. The twigs and branches still left scratches and cuts on my face and arms. I noticed he was running us right at a large clump of fallen trees that formed a huge bramble. I really hoped he was going to go around it, but no such luck.

He shouted, "Hide in there." Then he jumped, and when he landed, he slid into that big cluster like he was sliding into home plate. I did the same. "Give me your hand," he said.

Before I could reach out, he snatched my hand in his and closed his eyes. I could feel his power surging, just like I could feel mine being drained. Whatever he was doing, I hoped it would work.

Not far behind us, I could hear the Elden scrambling and shouting as they crashed through the woods. They were coming through the trees like hunters, spread out to find us. All of a sudden, one stopped and shouted. The others stopped, too, gathering around him.

A second later, he pointed west, to the right of where I lay hidden in the brambles. The whole troop ran off in that direction. They seemed to think they were hot on our trail from the way they were carrying on. Then their voices faded with distance.

When I decided they would be out of earshot, I looked at Cairo and raised one eyebrow. I didn't know what he had done, but I was sure curious. He had his eyes closed, and I waited like that minute after minute. I started counting my heartbeats, just to have something to focus on and take away the fear. About four minutes later, he opened his eyes and grinned at me.

"What did you do?" I asked.

"I made every tree in the forest look like us," he said. "It sure confused them, but when I started letting go of the disguise in different parts of the forest, it made it look like we were running west. Then when our little hiding spot was going to be the only place around here that still showed 'us' to their powers, I used your energy to make us seem like trees. They could've seen right through it if they were close enough, but they were tracking us with their tilium, not their eyes. I don't know how they were following us."

That was incredible. "So you mean to say, we look like trees to them right now?"

He smirked and seemed awfully full of himself over the whole thing. Although I had to admit it was pretty clever. I grinned back at him.

He said, "They're running west, so we should head east."

"Yeah, that was the way we were going, right? I don't think that's changed. So I guess it's a good thing you sent them west."

He chuckled, and we climbed out from under the brambles. For the next few miles, as we walked fast to the east, he still kept hold of my hand. It slowed us down, but I could feel him still using my energy. He was probably still luring those Elden away from us, so I didn't mind.

After a few miles, he let go of my hand; I suddenly felt how low my mahier was. I sensed his power had been mostly drained, too. We walked in silence, trying to slowly absorb more mahier and recharge a bit. I was sure we would need it again, probably sooner than I wanted. Only a big meal of meat would let us recharge quickly, though.

We finally came to the end of that stretch of jungle and stepped back out into the bright light of day. This time, there were no gentle hills, only flatlands. It was kind of scary looking, or depressing. Maybe both. We kept walking.

A few hours after that, we dove back into another jungle. This one wasn't as thick as the last one had been, and it didn't look like it was quite as large, but the sun was ready to go down soon. "Maybe we should make camp here," I said. "The trees will give us some cover, and if anymore Elden come along, it will give us something for you to disguise us with."

He nodded. "Good idea. After you, my prince." He held his hand out toward the forest. Once we were fairly deep inside the woods, we made camp. Cairo used his dragon breath to start a fire, I couldn't wait to have control of mine. It burned low and slow, and I hoped it wouldn't give away our position, but the forest was damp. I figured it would get pretty cold at night. Getting hypothermia wouldn't help our mission, so it was worth Cairo spending that little bit of energy. Besides, as we slept, our power would recharge.

As the daylight went away and darkness fell, we cooked a couple of rabbits Cairo had caught. We set them up on spits to cook over low flames, slowly turning them by hand while we chatted about Eva, Jericho, and so many other things. I didn't know why we both felt the need to fill the silence. Maybe we were both just scared and trying to distract ourselves, but we ended up talking more in that couple of hours than we ever had before.

After one of the inevitable lulls in conversation, he looked at me intently.

"What? Do I have some rabbit on my face?"

After a pause, he said, "How do they keep following us? That's what I want to know. I didn't mention it to you, but when we were going through the jungle earlier, there were a couple of times where I had to use my power to hide us from different patrols. They all seem to be heading in whatever direction I made the jungle illusion look like we went. I keep expecting Elden or Carnites to pop up right in front of us. You can bet I'm going to sleep with one eye open. Whether I'm watching for Elden, or watching you, I haven't decided yet."

I cocked my head. "I don't think you really need to watch me. What makes you think I have something to do with that?"

"Simple. It didn't happen until you and I were alone together. Maybe you brought the Carnites that almost killed Jericho, for all I know."

"You know I would never do that. Why would I? I've been fighting them every step of the way, and you know it." I was starting to get angry at him. It definitely hurt my feelings, and my natural reaction to that was to get mad. I didn't think I could get to the Mermaids and Eva by myself, though, so I bit my tongue. It was hard not to say everything else that was on my mind, especially after the friendliest chat we'd ever had before.

"The only thing I do know is that they're following us. Not just one group, but several. That means they're coming from farther out than I can push my senses. And that means..."

"That means that either they planted something on one of us that they can track from a long way away, or one of us is reaching out to tell them where we're at. Is that what you're going to say?"

Cairo let out a deep breath and seemed suddenly very interested in his hands. He stared at them as he said, "Yes that pretty much sums it up. The thing is, I don't really think you're a traitor. You're the Keeper of Dragons, after all. If you're a traitor, then the whole world is doomed. I don't want to believe that."

There was no point answering him. If he thought I was a traitor, he wouldn't trust me anyway, and if he didn't think so, then I didn't know any more than he did. I looked up through the trees and into the sky, taking a deep breath. The forest smelled wonderful. If the Elden won, then simple pleasures like this would probably be gone soon. That was depressing, so I decided to think of other things. Like how we were going to get through the night without being tracked.

"Cairo, will you show me how to do your trick where you disguised us as trees back there in the jungle? That way we can sleep in shifts, and you won't be completely drained by morning."

It didn't take long for him to show me how to do it. It seemed simple enough, and like everything with mahier, it involved simple willpower more than anything else.

I decided to take first watch and let him get some sleep. He needed it more than me. It was really boring, but that was a good thing. Boredom meant our hunters weren't trying to kill us at that moment. I was also relieved. The fact that Cairo let me take first watch meant that deep down, he knew he could trust me.

Halfway through the night, I woke Cairo. When I was sure he was fully awake, I lay down on the soft forest floor, using my elbow as a pillow, and dozed off into an uneasy sleep.

* * *

The next morning, Cairo greeted me with a couple of eggs cooking on a hot rock and some sort of a flat, dry biscuit he made with some cornmeal from his little backpack. I was practically starving. It wasn't much food, but at least he shared. I couldn't ask for more than that. It wasn't like there was a convenience store anywhere out here in an African jungle, after all.

We gathered up our things and headed east again. We were making good time toward the Dead Sea. I figured Eva had probably already arrived and was talking to the Mermaids without me. I was a little sad at the thought. The idea of meeting real Mermaids was kind of exciting.

During our walk, we had to hide twice, but it was easy to avoid being spotted. Since Cairo had taught me the trick of looking like trees to their tilium senses, it got easier each time I tried to do it. Now, I barely used any power.

After that, there was more walking. Anyone who said walking wasn't great exercise had never done it like we did that day. It wasn't like walking on a road, where everything was flat and level. Walking cross-country was totally different, and every step meant we had to climb, duck, sidestep, or push through something. Every step was tiring. Thankfully, I had my mahier and tilium to keep me energized and alert.

We finally reached low, rolling hills again, and the walking became a little harder, but it became a lot easier to hide us. That's what Cairo said, anyway. He kept busy camouflaging us while I pushed my senses outward, trying to sense any threats coming in our direction.

I stopped suddenly, by reflex, and planted my hand on Cairo's chest. My body had reacted before my mind registered the threat, but it only took half a second for me to realize what it was. Something bad was in the valley on the far side of the hill we were climbing—something big and evil. "Carnites," I whispered hoarsely.

Cairo grabbed me by the front of my shirt and hit the ground, dragging me down with him. He nodded toward the top of the hill, then turned and began to slither on his belly. I followed. It took maybe twenty minutes to get to the top, but when we did, my jaw dropped. Down in the valley between three different low hills was a group of huge Carnites sitting around, talking.

And in the center, I saw a familiar face. Eva! She had been captured.

Next to me, I heard Cairo whisper, "Oh no."

My thought exactly.

Chapter Nine

I could practically feel Cairo tensing up. He said, "No! This can't be happening. We have to rescue her." He started to scramble to his feet.

I realized he was about to rush in to try to save Eva from the Carnites. We'd never save her once they knew we were there. As he rose, I wrapped my arms around his waist and locked my hands together, then used my whole weight to drag him back down to the ground.

"Be smart!" I hissed. When he struggled again, I squeezed even harder, hoping to knock the wind out of him. "Yes, we have to rescue her. You won't do it by rushing in and trying to fight three Carnites by yourself. You'll only get her killed, and you with her. I won't let you do it." I was gasping from the effort of trying to hold him down.

After a couple of seconds of struggling, he said, "Cole, let me go. You're going to give away our position." His face was turning red as he tried to get out of my grasp.

"Then stop fighting me. We have to talk about this. The Carnites don't know we're here. We can surprise them, but only if you don't rush off and do something stupid."

A couple of seconds later, he relaxed. Hesitantly, I released him, but I didn't unlock my grip.

No longer resisting, Cairo said, "Okay. Thanks. I know you're right, but I will not just leave her in there. I—"

"Shhh," I hissed. I wanted to hear what the Carnites were saying, but I couldn't make it out over him talking.

He snapped his mouth shut, then turned his head to try to listen with me.

"... are you going? Who are you, little human?" one Carnite said.

"Who cares who she is? Meat on bones, meat in mouth. We should eat the tasty morsel."

The first Carnite smacked the second one across the back of its head. "You are too stupider. How she see us? She not a morsel, no, she maybe a dragon?"

Eva looked at it right in the eyes, and even from where Cairo and I were hiding, I could see that her helpless, scared expression was faked. That was Eva, always keeping her head on straight and looking for the opportunities. She said, "What's a dragon? There's no such thing as dragons, everyone knows that."

The Carnite looked doubtful. He said, "If you not a dragon, why you in the jungle? Where you village? Why you see us?"

Eva shrugged. Her crisp, clear voice carried to our ears easily. "You ask a lot of questions. I'm just a helpless human, walking in the jungle for the same reason you are, I bet. I was gathering Lilacost; they're perfect for the flower arrangements we make back in my village. It's just north of here."

The second Carnite scratched its head, then after a second, said, "What's a Lilacost?"

Eva kept her face perfectly straight, from what I saw from my hiding spot, and said, "About twenty bucks, if it's arranged well."

I groaned inside. She was caught by Carnites and surrounded, and she was making jokes? Part of me envied her courage, and the other part of me wanted her to be quiet before she got herself killed. I whispered, "I don't think we have much time. Got any ideas?"

Cairo got back up to his hands and knees and looked at Eva. He was very quiet for a few moments, then said, "Actually, I do. If we're going to save her, we need two things. First, a distraction. Then, a way to slow the Carnites down after we grab her."

That made sense. Better yet, it was pretty simple. Now the only question was how to do the two things. I remembered how he had lured away the Elden in the jungle, and thought that might work again. Especially since the Carnites weren't the brightest creatures on Earth. "Okay. You can do that trick where you make every tree look and smell like us, right? So if you handle that, and I handle the distraction, we might be able to do this."

Cairo nodded. It was about as good of a plan as we could get, at least in the time we had available. He was about to say something but I held up my hand to shush him. the Carnites were talking again.

"The morsel lies. I never see no Lilacosts here. No bucks, too. How we get truth from it?"

The other Carnite, the one who'd been smacked, shrugged its giant shoulders. "They could be real. Maybe new name for old thing. I bet King Eldrick would know."

Then it chuckled, and the sound sent a shiver down my spine. "And he use his strong powers, gets the truth for us."

Eva let out a little chirp of shock. She blurted, "You work for King Eldrick? You know you can't trust him, right? Whatever he promised you, it's a lie."

The first Carnite shook its head. "No. King Eldrick make promise. We work for him, we work for promise."

Eva shook her head. "You're making a mistake, I promise you. What did he say he'd give you? It can't be worth being his slave."

The two Carnites began to argue amongst themselves, and I couldn't tell what they were saying anymore. Their accent was just too thick when they were angry. They were shoving each other back and forth. I hoped they would get in a fight, giving us the distraction we were looking for, but I didn't count on it. I kept trying to think of other options.

In a couple of seconds, however, they settled down. Then the second one told Eva, "Eldrick promise Carnites their own home. A Carnite king. Carnites get all of the Congo, new Carnite homeland. We get a home, just like stupid Elves, stupid Trolls. All we have to do is help him get rid of dragons."

I filed that away, hoping it might be useful later. At least now we knew what the Carnites were doing and that their attacks were directed, not random. We suspected it before, but now we could be sure.

Cairo whispered, "Now they have a plan—taking Eva to King Eldrick. We can't let that happen. We can't let them split up the Keeper of Dragons, Cole."

He was right, but we still needed that distraction. I had an idea, though. I remembered the brilliant light that came from the mahier ropes the dragons had used when they rescued me and Eva from the Carnites the last time. I wondered if we could use it to tie their ankles together. Big Carnites would probably fall hard, right? At least, that was my idea. I told Cairo, and he didn't look enthusiastic, but he hadn't come up with any ideas of his own yet.

I heard Eva say, "Where are the Elves and Trolls? You helped get rid of them, right? If you didn't, he wouldn't give you the Congo, so I bet you did help. Where did he take them? Or didn't he tell you."

The first Carnite sat up straighter, lifting his chin in the air as he said, "King Eldrick tell us. We took Elves there. Took Trolls there." Then it leaned forward until his face was only a foot from Eva's and said loudly, "But we not tell you, little morsel. Fake village girl. You think we stupid, but we not."

Eva said, "I don't think you're stupid. I think you're very smart to want your own homeland. People must underestimate you all the time, right? King Eldrick did. He got you to help him, even with no guarantee he would give you the Congo. He must think you're really dumb." She shook her head slowly, looking sympathetic.

Cairo whispered to me, "That idea could work, but do you know how to do it? Binding things with your mahier takes a lot of energy."

At least this concern, I had an answer to. "No, I don't how to do it with my mahier. Fortunately for us, though, I'm a lot better at controlling my tilium. I bet I can do something like it with the Farro energy I took."

"I'm not a betting dragon, but it looks like we don't have much of a choice. You think you can do it, so I guess we'll have to try. It's just too bad you're betting on Eva's life at the same time."

He was right. I was betting I could do it with my tilium, and if I failed, she'd be gone or dead. Still, I felt reasonably confident that I could make it happen, and what other choice did I have? I couldn't think of any.

One Carnite said, "Enough. Tasty morsel think she can fool Carnites. Everyone think Carnites stupid."

Oh great, now they were repeating themselves.

It continued, "We smart enough to take dragon girl to King Eldrick. We smart enough to know, you not village girl."

It had practically shouted that last sentence, and as it sat on its knees, it began to bounce up and down, smashing its tree club into the dirt next to it and crying out a deep, animal grunting, like what I imagined gorillas would do when they were excited.

"Cairo, we've got to do something right now. As soon as I manifest the bindings, you create the illusion. Can you make it sound like someone is crashing through the bushes just south of us?"

He raised one eyebrow and nodded, and I guessed he hadn't thought of it himself. The Carnites would chase that noise, hopefully, leading them away from Eva. It was worth a shot.

I closed my eyes and focused on bringing out my tilium. I willed it to stretch from my hands and fingers out toward the Carnites. As it went farther and farther, it got thinner and thinner, going from a cone to a tight focus, looking like a rope. I made it slither across the jungle floor and, when it reached them, I had it wind in and out between their ankles. I tied it in knots as it went. The Carnites would be in for a rude surprise when they started chasing the distraction.

Then, using my mahier, I pushed outward with my mind until it enveloped all three Carnites. I focused on putting thoughts into their heads. I wanted it to sound like a scream coming from behind them when I alerted them that we were here.

I felt my mahier sliding into their heads fairly easily. I didn't think I could've controlled them, or done anything super exciting while I was inside their heads; I had a feeling that their stupidity somehow protected them from the worst of what a dragon could do, not that I knew how to do the worst.

I took a deep breath and then mentally screamed the words into their heads, "Elves, Trolls, they're coming to take the girl, they want the reward for themselves!"

In an instant, all three Carnites were standing, looking around. Then they heard the phantom sounds of people crashing around in the bushes to the south. The first two, who had been arguing, moved faster than I thought possible as they tried to run after the noise. I would sure hate to try to outrun those things without a good head start.

Halfway through their steps, my tilium rope went tight and they crashed to the ground. I could feel the ground shake, even from that distance, and the noise was terrible.

Only one problem—the third Carnite hadn't left with the others. It had stayed with Eva.

I said, "Go get her." Then I focused on stretching out my tilium again, going back over their ankles and weaving the two threads together to make them stronger. Then I yanked my hands back, drawing the tilium ropes tight.

Cairo sprinted toward the third Carnite, and although it saw the movement coming out of the jungle, it didn't seem to be able to make sense of what it was seeing. It stared at Cairo dumbly until almost the last second. When Cairo was five feet away, he leaped into the air and swung his sword over his head with both hands, bringing it down on the Carnite's skull. Eva jumped to her feet and ran back the way Cairo had come, heading toward me.

I threw my hand out, shooting a tilium rope at the third one's tree trunk club. It wrapped around it, and the club slowed, but it didn't stop. It snapped my tilium rope in half, but slowing it down had been enough; Cairo dove out of the way.

I drew my sword and rushed out into the open area between my hiding spot and where they had been questioning Eva. I ran right at that third Carnite, passing Eva going the other way. I didn't have time to worry about what she was doing. The Carnite tried to raise its club again, but it was too slow. I ran by and swung my sword as hard as I could one-handed, and felt it bite deep into the creature's gut.

I turned and saw that Cairo hadn't slowed down when he dodged the club. He kept running, and then jumped onto the two bound Carnites. From the dirt, the two simply stared, apparently not believing their own eyes. In moments, Cairo had ended their threat permanently.

Eva came walking back into the clearing, looking around and nodding as though impressed. I wanted to yell at her, shout at her for leaving in the middle of the night without telling anyone, but we didn't have time. The Carnite I had cut was badly wounded, and if we wanted to get any information from it, we had to ask quickly.

We didn't ask fast enough, though. It didn't get the chance to say anything before it died, joining its two friends wherever Carnites went when they died.

I looked at Cairo and said, "That wasn't quite the plan, but it worked. I'm sorry we couldn't get this one to talk before it died."

He shrugged and said, "I'm sorry, too, but that's the way of war."

J.A. Culican

Chapter Ten

Cairo leaned on his sword, catching his breath. He glanced up at Eva, and his face turned even redder than usual. I understood just how he felt, too. She almost got herself killed, and us. None of the Carnites were still alive, so most of our questions were still unanswered.

Eva looked at him for a couple of seconds, then exploded. "What are you looking at?"

I couldn't tell if it was a challenge or a real question, but it made him stand bolt upright. He waved his hand to show the jungle around us and shouted, "You shouldn't have run off like that. How could you just get up and leave without telling anyone? Don't you know—"

She cut him off, shouting back at him, "And why do you even care? Come on, tell me. And don't say it's because you're my guardian. I'm not an idiot, and I felt something from you. Right?" She put her fists on her hips and faced him directly. Her voice had sounded as much like she was asking as she was telling him.

He got a little twitch by his left eye as he turned away. He bent down to begin cleaning his sword as best he could with a bit of grass. He had his back to Eva, and I glanced over to see what she would do.

Instead of yelling at him some more, as I thought she would, she walked over to me and stood shoulder to shoulder. She said, "You know, I thought he actually liked me. Not just because he was forced to be around me. He should have been glad when I left, so he didn't have to be responsible for me anymore." She said it just loud enough to make sure Cairo heard her.

I took a deep breath and let it out slowly, feeling the frustration build. Instead of answering her, I changed the subject. "So, you think these Carnites were working for Eldrick, or did they just wander into the area?"

She looked at me like I was an idiot. "Oh, come on. I know you heard them say they were going to turn me in to King Eldrick and he was giving them the Congo. Now you're just stalling. You're as bad as he is." She stomped away and sat down, leaning against a tree at the edge of the clearing.

Over by the Carnites, Cairo stood slowly, stretched his back, and then started walking east. Over his shoulder he said, "Come on. We shouldn't stay here and we have a long way to go, thanks to her." He didn't even look back.

I glanced over at Eva and shrugged. When I started following him, Eva fell in line a few feet behind me. It would've been a lot easier to just call out my dragon, but I was far too exhausted to fly. I was sure they were, too, since no one mentioned the idea. Not only was my mahier about drained, but I was physically exhausted.

We walked through the jungle in a straight line, spaced out a little bit, alone with our own thoughts. One of us occasionally stopped and grabbed something edible. With our mahier drained so much, I was sure they were starving just as much as I was. We were in kind of a desperate situation, but there was nothing we could do but keep walking. So we did.

After a few more hours, Eva finally caught up to me. Her hands were in her pockets and her eyes were on the ground, watching where she put her feet so she didn't fall. I also thought it might be her way of not having to look at anyone. I mean, even as clumsy as I was, I still managed to glance up every once in a while. That's how I knew Eva had caught up.

Quietly, I said, "How are you doing? I know you've got to be exhausted."

She nodded. "Yeah, I'm tired. And half the reason I'm so exhausted is that I'm starving."

I simply nodded. It was all true, so what could I say? We walked on in silence for a few minutes, but I noticed she kept up with me, always beside me. Maybe she had something on her mind, but I wasn't going to push.

Eventually, she said, "Actually, I do have something on my mind. I mean, besides just how hungry I am. It's Cairo. Don't you think he's been acting a little weird lately? Like, every time I come around, he stops laughing or talking. I keep catching him looking at me out of the corner of my eye."

I began to feel a little uncomfortable. I never really liked to get caught up in the middle of Eva and other people. She could be unpredictable and wild, and sometimes her frustration got pointed at me. It was the last thing I wanted to deal with, as tired as I was. She kept looking at me like she expected a response, though.

"Maybe he's just keeping an eye on you, since that's his job."

"Maybe. But I think it's more than that. I thought we were getting along really well, you know? And then all of this. Now I think he was just trying to get along because it made his job easier. I don't think he really liked me at all."

I felt my heat rise and I began to sweat. Part of me wanted to tell her the truth, just to get it out in the open, and because it would make her feel better. She clearly cared what Cairo thought of her.

But before I opened my mouth, I decided it wasn't my place to say anything. I knew how he felt, but only because he told me. It was up to him to tell Eva when he wanted to. So I tried to dodge it. "What's not to like about you? Sure, you're headstrong and stubborn. And you do reckless things, mostly because you're way braver than I am. But you're also a really good person, that's why you decided to be my friend, right? You were the only person at school who took a chance to get to know me." Then I forced myself to laugh a little and said, "Then again, look how that worked out for you."

She let out a deep sigh, but we walked on in silence for quite a while. I didn't know how much later it was, but eventually, she said, "Cole, do you think I did the right thing going after the Mermaids?" She hesitated a bit and I could hear the worry in her voice. "Right now, it seems like it might have been kind of foolish."

Of course she was worried. She'd made a decision that should have been all of ours, one that could spell victory or doom for the dragons, all the other mythical creatures, and even humankind itself. "Of course you did the right thing. I mean, running off like that was stupid, but sometimes you do stupid stuff."

I turned my head to look at her and grinned. When I got a faint smile back, I continued, "But seriously. I don't think we really had any other choice, so yes, I think you did the right thing. Most of the Elves are already captured, and the rest have limited tilium until their wards are restored. We don't know where the loyalties lie for most of the other magical creatures, so going to Greece wasn't a great option."

Her face showed a bit of relief. She ran her fingers through her sweat-damp hair, pushing it back out of her face. "We don't know where the loyalties of the Mermaids are, either, though."

"All the things we've heard about them tell me they aren't rushing to join up with Eldrick. They may only be minor players up here on land with us dragons, but water covers most of the Earth. Why would they want to sign up to be Eldrick's slaves, when they're the masters of most of the planet?"

She put her hand on my back as we sat down side by side. "Thanks, Cole. I knew I could count on you for the truth, even if I didn't want to hear it. You're a good guy, you know? That's the biggest reason I decided to be your friend, way back in the day. But doesn't that seem like a whole different lifetime ago?"

I chuckled. "Yeah, it does. I think—"

Out in the jungle, off to my right, I heard a sudden loud *crack!* It rolled over us and echoed off the trees and hills like thunder, deep and rumbling. I fought down the sudden urge to run. Then I heard another crack, another rumble. This time, though, it came from somewhere to our left. Eva and I looked at each other, eyes wide with shock and fear.

Chapter Eleven

As the sounds grew louder, we took off running at the same time. Whatever was coming at us, I sure didn't want to meet it. We jumped over fallen logs, went around trees, and once, I grabbed a vine without slowing down to swing over a coiled snake. I didn't know what kind it was, and I was pretty sure my mahier would be able to handle a snake bite just fine, but it would slow me down. I felt the sweat building on the back of my neck and on my forehead, and after half a mile, I was panting.

The whole time we ran, whatever was crashing through the jungle was getting closer. We had been running a few miles when I heard the deep, frightening noise right behind me. I risked a glance over my shoulder, but what I saw surprised me. It wasn't some strange beast, and it wasn't a Carnite. It was an Elden. I saw it reach out and somehow zap a tree with its tilium. The tree was only damaged, though, not even destroyed. That was what had been making the noise.

I saw the Elden were stretched out in a row, half a dozen that I could see. They were randomly zapping trees as they ran toward us. There was no way I wanted to get hit with that, though I was curious why they were shooting trees, so I ran even faster. We had to put some distance between us and them because even if the ones I saw were all of them, we were outnumbered. I was pretty sure there were more I hadn't seen.

As I caught up to Cairo, I said, "Run faster, it's the Elden! Shooting trees... At least six of them..."

Eva and Cairo sped up. Another mile went by, and I could hear the Elden finally falling farther behind. We were getting away! I was exhausted, but I had my tilium to draw from. I knew we were all low on mahier, yet they kept up. Cairo and Eva were just in better shape than me, I guessed.

The jungle kept going on and on, but there was no way to tell how much farther it stretched. I hoped it didn't run out before we could escape and hide again, though I wasn't sure where to hide if they were zapping all the trees. I sure didn't want to get mistaken for a tree. Cairo's trick where he made their tilium senses see all the trees looking like us wouldn't work now that they were just blasting away. I wondered how they had enough tilium to keep that going.

I was in the middle of that thought when Cairo let out a yelp. I turned to look, and saw him streaking up into the air. I skidded to a stop and turned back, then realized he had stumbled into a simple, old-fashioned net trap. In the distance, the rumbling sound of the Elden's blasting continued.

Without hesitating, Eva jumped up and grabbed onto a lower branch, then scrambled up the tree like a monkey. In moments, I'd lost sight of her, but shortly after, Cairo came crashing to the ground, wrapped in the net. I helped him get out of the net, then we looked up into the tree.

From above, I heard Eva shouting, "Get up here. Hurry."

I didn't know what she had in mind, but we didn't have time to argue. Cairo and I scrambled up the trunk and found ourselves in the dense foliage. It took a while, but two scratches on my face and one small cut on my hand later, we reached Eva.

Panting, I asked, "Why are we up here?"

Eva held up her hand to be quiet. I saw that she had her eyes closed. The seconds ticked by, then she said, "Instead of making all the trees look like us, I'm making us blend in with this tree."

"When they blast this tree, is that going to matter?" Cairo asked.

She said, almost in a whisper, "They won't shoot us up this high. When they had almost caught up to us, one of them did that thing to a tree just ahead of me, and it hit about chest-high. They're only checking to see if we've disguised ourselves as trees."

I nodded, then heard the sounds of movement below. I looked, but I couldn't see anything through the leaves. We sat silently, waiting. Cairo had his eyes closed, and his lips were moving but I couldn't hear what he was saying. And I heard the sounds of Elden everywhere below us, stretching out to either direction, way more than six of them.

After they had passed, I realized I had been holding my breath and let it out.

Cairo said, "That was way too close. Something is definitely wrong here."

"Why do you say that?" Eva asked. "I mean, we got away, right?"

"How are they following us?" He turned to look at me.

I shrugged. "I don't think they're following us. They must just know the area and they're looking as hard as they can, but they're not following us. I think."

Cairo let out a long, frustrated breath. "No way. This is twice now that they've come right at us. Once, I could see. Twice? That's deliberate. Elden are evil, but they've never followed us like this. I wish I knew what was going on."

I didn't know, either, so I didn't answer.

After enough time had passed for the Elden to be long gone, we carefully climbed down and made camp for the night.

***

Back in the land of ice and snow and the beautiful lights in the sky, I hovered over the field. Again, it felt more like a vision than a dream. Midway through it, I realized I really was dreaming, but I couldn't wake up so I just watched.

When I awoke, it wasn't the panic-filled jolt that made me sit bolt upright, the way the others had. I just opened my eyes, and knew I had to tell Eva and Cairo. They were still asleep, so I settled back into the leaves I used for bedding and slept restlessly until morning.

Once everybody was fully awake, I said, "So. I had another dream."

Cairo rolled his eyes, but Eva frowned and asked, "What was it about this time?"

"Eldrick is there in the north with the missing Elves. He's giving them each a choice—either join him and become dark Elves, or lose their tilium. Most of them are taking the deal, from what I saw. He's turning them one by one. It seemed to take a long time to turn each one into a dark Elf, but Eldrick has time."

"Thanks for calling them dark Elves," Cairo said. "Those are not Elden, whatever deal they're making. They're still my friends, Gaber's family."

I nodded. No surprise he had caught that, but it just didn't feel right calling them Elden. They weren't really Elden, they were just Elves who had gone dark. "I think the Elden are like that forever. I hope they get the chance to come back to the light, someday."

Eva put her hand on Cairo's shoulder sympathetically. "I think the longer they're dark, the harder it will be. We have to hurry. If we don't rescue them soon, Eldrick will have a new army of dark Elves behind him."

At last, Cairo blew out a harsh breath and said, "It is what it is. We need to get to the Mermaids quickly and I just hope that, when they join us, they have what we need to go rescue our friends."

I hoped so, too.

J.A. Culican

Chapter Twelve

As we soared through the clouds, I could see the shores of the Dead Sea far ahead. Thankfully, once our mahier had recharged a bit, we had all been able to summon our dragons. We kept our speed slow so we didn't need to spend mahier on keeping the air around us still, and after a bit, I had more energy.

I felt a little tingling in my mind and realized Eva was trying to talk, so I opened up my perceptions and let her in. We had spent most of the journey in silence, so I was curious. "Is everything okay?"

"Yes, I'm fine. I've just been thinking about these visions or whatever they are. You say they feel different from a normal dream, right?"

"Yes." I was interested to see where this was going. "I have lots of dreams, and nightmares even, about Eldrick, but sometimes they just feel different. I know in my gut they aren't dreams."

"I didn't really believe you before, but you keep having them. And you've never been the kind of guy to make things up. Heck, it took you longer to believe in all this dragon stuff than me."

Finally. Someone was paying attention. I'd figured if anyone would believe me, it'd be Eva, and it had hurt when she'd dismissed me. Excited, I asked, "So I take it you've been thinking about this? Got any ideas?"

"No, but I think it's important for us to figure out where these dreams are coming from. The more I think about them, the more they scare me."

That was surprising. "Even if they're visions, not just dreams, I don't see why they would scare you. They scare me, but I'm the one with the nightmares."

"But we don't know why you're having them, and I have to wonder if Eldrick is somehow using them against you. Your visions are just as likely to be coming from him as from anywhere else, right? Maybe more likely. And if he's sending them, it's not to help you. What trick does he have up his sleeve? If he's sending them, he has a sneaky plan."

That was definitely something to think about. I hadn't considered that before. But I didn't really have time to think about it at the moment—Cairo banked down and to the left, heading toward the Dead Sea shoreline. We were finally there, where the Mermaids were supposed to live.

I heard Cairo's voice in my head saying, "Look alive, Keepers. We're here, and we don't know what kind of reception we'll get."

We swept downward, flying low above the scattered trees, and landed about twenty feet from the water. I managed to land without doing a face-plant, so it was a good landing as far as I was concerned. Then we called our humans and shifted.

We wandered around the beach, slowly making our way toward the water. I wasn't really sure what to look for, but I figured if there were Mermaids around, I'd see something unusual. We searched an area about 100 feet long between the scattered tree line and the water, but none of us found anything worth mentioning.

Cairo whistled, and we all gathered together by the water. "I don't really understand. The last time I was here was maybe a century ago, but they had lines of shells and trees planted in different formations, showing us where to find them. I didn't see any of that from the air, and I'm not seeing it here on the ground. I wonder where they went."

He scratched his head, and I looked past him, out over the water, trying to imagine what a Mermaid city would look like down there. Then I noticed ripples in the water, and my eyes went wide.

Cairo spun around to see what I was looking at, then froze. At least a dozen people were rising up out of the water. I knew right away they were Mermaids, from the watery plants woven into their braided hair to the slightly blue skin. I thought I saw flaps behind the ears of one who turned to look at the others, but I couldn't be sure. I also didn't know how they would get out of the water, but then they just walked right out, legs and all. Each of them carried a short spear or trident. They were a couple inches shorter than most people, and I could see webbed fingers wrapped around their weapons. I was a little disappointed they didn't have fish tails.

The twelve of them kept their weapons pointed toward us and moved into a circle, with us in the middle. I found myself turning my back to Cairo, and saw Eva do the same, so the three of us were facing outward at the Mermaids.

One who was a deeper shade of blue than the others said, "Hold. Put down your weapons now. I warn you to do as I say." His voice had a sort of wet, bubbly sound, and came out raspy. Along with his sharp, pointy teeth and big, fin-like ears, the water plants woven into his green hair, green glowing eyes...he looked kind of creepy.

I slowly drew my sword, then tossed it into the sand a few feet away.

Cairo hissed, "What are you doing, Keeper?" I could hear the concern in his voice. He might even have been afraid.

I said, "We're here to see the Mermaids, aren't we? Well, they're not going to talk to us while we're armed. There's too many of them for us to fight off, anyway. Just do what they say, and trust in Fate."

I heard two more swords land in the sand. Thank goodness, because I hadn't been sure Cairo would do it.

The Mermaid nodded. "That was smart of you. I will ask you this once: what do dragons want with Mermaids? You wanted nothing to do with us when we needed your help, but now you come here alone. We hear things about what is going on out there, so you're either here to ask for help or to demand it. In either case, you have wasted your trip. Leave, or die."

Cairo held up both hands and took one step toward the leader. "I don't think you understand the situation. This is the Time of Fear, and these two with me are the Keeper of Dragons—the Golden Dragon and the Prince. Your queen will want to hear of this."

The dark blue Mermaid lowered his trident a little. His gaze clicked over to me and Eva, then back to Cairo. "You lie. They are too young."

Cairo shook his head. "No. They grew up within a mile of each other among the humans. You think that's a coincidence?"

"Then they grew in strength so close to each other... But that's impossible."

Cairo shrugged. "It's very possible. And it's the truth. All signs point to the Time of Fear. We've come to ask the help of the Mermaids, and I know we failed in our duty to you, once, but if the Elves and Trolls can forgive us for our foolish century, maybe Queen Desla can, too."

The Mermaid turned to the others and said something that sounded like trying to sing while gargling water. The soldiers kept their spears and tridents pointed at us and inched closer.

Their leader said, "Come. I will take you to our queen, not as guests, but as prisoners. She will decide what to do with you."

From his tone of voice, I got the impression he hoped they would just kill us and be done with it. It seemed Ochana had a lot of making up to do for whatever they had done in the past to all these different peoples. We were prodded toward the water, and I wondered if they were just going to drown us. Cairo didn't seem concerned, so I hesitantly followed him.

J.A. Culican

Chapter Thirteen

I found myself holding my breath, which made sense because I was underwater. Half a minute later, I panicked. I turned and tried to run back to shore, but it was really more like thrashing. As soon as my head broke the surface, I took deep gasps. I hadn't even worried about the Mermaids with spears.

When I turned back around, I found the Mermaids standing half out of the water, staring at me. Cairo and Eva looked amused, while our captors looked irritated. I looked at Cairo and said, "What?"

Eva rolled her eyes. "Didn't you pay attention during our training?" Eva paused and shook her head at me. "It's just like when we fly and use our mahier to keep the wind from tearing us apart. Use it to lock a bubble of air around your head, and just draw fresh oxygen from the water."

Cairo shook his head and let out a frustrated sigh, like he was dealing with toddlers. "You both need to pay more attention during training. Anytime someone with power—mahier or tilium—goes into the water with Mermaids around, you can just breathe the water. It doesn't even get into your lungs. I mean, as long as they aren't trying to kill you."

I felt my face flush. Of course my mahier would work underwater. Of course there was more to it than just Mermaids driving us to our doom. Otherwise, Cairo wouldn't have calmly walked into the Dead Sea. "Okay. I'm sorry. I've never tried to breathe underwater before, so it didn't occur to me that I could."

Cairo turned back around and walked away from shore. "Of course it didn't. Stop fooling around, and let's go."

We headed back into the water, and although I paused just before my head went under, I took a deep breath and felt my mahier around me. I trusted that way more than I trusted the Mermaids to keep me alive down there.

My wet clothes stuck to me as we walked for what seemed like a mile, and at first it was really slow going. Then Cairo was in my head, telling me to just use my mahier to open the way, just as we did with the air when we were flying fast. After that, it got a lot easier. I was kind of tired of feeling dumb, and all of that would have been good to know before I embarrassed myself in front of the Mermaids.

All around us were Mermaids swimming faster than I could run on dry land. Only our captors seemed to bother walking, and I got the impression they were only doing it for us. The Mermaid town had no walls, just like all the other fantastical creatures' homes I had been to. They must have had wards, though I didn't feel any of it. Cairo explained that their tilium was different from the Elves'.

Once we got to the town proper, my eyes bulged. It was one of the most beautiful things I had ever seen. Every dwelling, every building, had been made to look like seashells or choral, or had been woven out of the many plants that grew all over. I hadn't seen any such plants before we got to the town, so they were probably hidden from outsiders.

The light was murky down here, but there were hundreds or even thousands of small, floating globes tethered in place, shining brightly. They gave off enough light to see by. I had noticed our guards' eyes were a lot larger than a human's or Elf's, and then I knew why. It was so they could see better in the dim light at the bottom of the Dead Sea.

There were no streets, so we did end up having to swim. After a little bit of practice, Cairo taught me how to use my mahier not just to keep myself breathing, but to sort of push myself through the water, almost like swimming. No, more like flying. That would've been a lot more exciting before I had flown halfway around the world as a dragon, but it was still kind of cool.

We got to what I assumed was the palace. It was the biggest building in the Mermaid town, and the only one that didn't blend perfectly with the nature all around. It was obviously constructed, a large dome with towers all over it.

We were led into the castle through a huge arch that spanned twenty feet or more. Inside, it was even more beautiful. There were marble tiles on the floor, marble walls, marble pillars holding the dome up. I wondered whether the pillars were decorative, though, because I thought domes didn't need support.

It didn't seem like the right time to ask about the architecture, though, so the three of us meekly followed our guards across the gorgeous foyer, then down a long hall lined with guards standing at attention. We reached a huge set of double doors, and the guards posted there opened them for us.

I looked inside and saw what must have been the biggest room in the castle. A dome inside a dome, it was a couple hundred feet across, and I couldn't really tell how high the ceiling was at its peak. There were so many of the glowing balls embedded into the walls that it was almost as bright as daylight. It was a softer glow, though, and didn't hurt my eyes. With the Mermaids' huge eyes, I was surprised it didn't hurt theirs, but they didn't seem to flinch.

We were marched up to a lone woman sitting on a raised throne. She stared ahead, looking bored, ignoring the dozens of Mermaids wandering around the throne room below her, talking in little groups.

When we got closer, a dozen more armed Mermaids appeared out of person-sized archways to either side of the platform and formed a semi-circle around their queen.

I almost didn't notice her because I was so busy looking at the crowd of Mermaids. Down in their own homeland, they didn't bother with legs. Just like the old drawings, they had tails, but no scales. More like a dolphin's tail.

When we got to the platform, one of our captors said, "Kneel before Queen Desla and pay your respects. Pray she is merciful, all hail the queen."

I didn't need to be told twice. I knelt right away, as did Cairo. Eva was slower, but followed us down. The room grew quiet, all the hushed conversations stopping at once, and all eyes turned to us. It was pretty intimidating, but there was no backing out.

She said, "What is the meaning of this. Why do dragons invade my realm? Answer true, or die."

That wasn't the warm welcome I had hoped for. Cairo glanced at me and tilted his head toward the queen. He wanted me to talk? I supposed it was up to me as the Keeper of Dragons.

"Hail, Queen Desla of the Mermaids. I'm Cole, the Keeper, and this is Eva, the Golden Dragon. We beg an audience with the queen." I held my breath and prayed what I said was right.

Her eyes shifted to Cairo, who only nodded very slightly, and then her eyes were back on me. "I asked a question, dragon."

My mind raced. What question? Then I remembered. "I'm sorry, but we haven't come to invade. We've come in peace, and to warn you."

Several of the guards took an angry step toward me, lowering their pitchforks and spears at me, but the queen said quietly, "Hold."

The guards stepped back into place, but eyed me angrily.

Hastily, I said, "Not to warn you about us! I mean to let you know of danger. As friends."

Desla tilted her head back and laughed. It was a sweet, musical sound. Her eyes showed no joy, though. "I have no need of protection from you, or from any dragon. Why are you here, and what is your warning? Speak quickly."

I spent the next twenty minutes telling her my story, even the parts I wasn't really proud of. She had to know the whole story to know I was telling the truth about the Time of Fear arriving. I ended by telling her that the Keeper of Dragons was fated to end the Time of Fear, but that it was time for the Mermaids to play their part, a very important part.

She was quiet for a long moment. She stared at me, unblinking—actually, I had not seen any of them blink—and found myself holding my breath. I had to consciously make myself take even breaths, and my heart was racing.

At last, she said, "Colton, Prince of Ochana, I have heard your story, and I am unmoved. We are safe here in the water, as we always have been. A few hundred years ago, I might have joined you, but we do not forget that the dragons turned a blind eye to the fighting and suffering of the Elves, Trolls, and others of our kind. We took in many refugees during that time, and lent our soldiers to the Elves. Meanwhile, you hid in your clouds and did nothing."

This wasn't going according to plan. I felt the opportunity slipping away. I had to say something! "My Queen, I don't think you—"

"Silence!" Her shout echoed across the room, and I saw even a couple of soldiers flinch. She must not raise her voice very often, but then again, why would a queen need to? I lowered my eyes so I wasn't looking at her directly and shut my mouth.

"I have no wish to harm dragons. Our friendship goes back almost to the beginning, and you've done us no wrong, personally. If the Elves and Trolls and Fairies can forgive you, who am I to hold that grudge for them? So, go in peace, Keeper of Dragons. I wish you well, but you will have no Mere help. Maybe if you had come sooner, we could have helped, but the damage is done. The Elves and Trolls are gone, the Fairies divided. The dragons fight alone, now. Be gone from my kingdom."

I stood there with my mouth open, stunned. We had come all this way, faced all those dangers, risked our lives... And now the Mermaids would do nothing? We had come here for nothing, when we could have been searching the north to look for the imprisoned Elves and Trolls. Like a light switch, my shock and disbelief turned to anger, burning the common sense right out of my head.

I glowered at their queen. "How dare you call the Elves your friends? You don't care about the Trolls, the Fairies. You sit here safe in your lake while your so-called friends suffer."

"How dare you—"

"They're dying out there! And the Elves probably wish they were dying. Do you know what King Eldrick is doing to them? He's forcing the Elves to choose between losing their magic or becoming dark Elves. Slaves. You want to talk about the dragons sitting by and doing nothing? At least we're out there fighting, and don't think for one minute that when Eldrick is done with the dragons he won't turn on you, too. You sit here safe and sound until the end, and then there won't be anyone left to help you when it's your turn!"

I think the only reason I was able to say all that before one of their guards knocked me to the ground was that it was such a surprise. They didn't expect it. But then one did slam me down and stood over me with his trident, ready to plunge it right into my heart. I only survived because the queen shouted, "Hold! Do not harm the young dragon."

Every eye in the throne room flicked from me to the queen. They all looked surprised, probably because she had let me talk to her like that without killing me on the spot. I wondered if she had even worse in store for me than just death, but I didn't care. I sat straight up, my fists clenched, staring her in the eyes, daring her to tell me I was wrong.

For the first time, she rose from her throne. She glided to me and stopped ten feet away, then floated there, looking me in the eyes. The way my heart was beating, every second seemed like a minute. I waited for my fate, too angry at her to care what she did next. If she didn't help, we were all dead, anyway.

She lowered her eyes and bent at the waist in a half-bow, then said, "Keeper, your words ring true, and they shame me. They shame us all. It is hard to imagine that a dragon so young spoke more truth than the Mermaids."

I climbed back to my feet and looked at her suspiciously. I didn't know where it was going, but at least she hadn't yet ordered them to do something horrible to me or my friends. "My apologies for my outburst, Queen Desla. As a guest here, I shouldn't talk to you like that, but what you said made me so mad I just didn't know what to do with myself."

She nodded slowly, considering. Then she said, "The war is coming here sooner or later. If it comes sooner, we have allies, allies who won't be there if it comes later. The only hope for all the Elves, Trolls, Fairies and eventually the dragons, is for the Mermaids to stand up now and do what is right."

"Yes! Stand up for the Truth, while you still can. I'm begging you, help us save them all. And yourselves." I glanced over at Cairo and Eva and saw them staring at me incredulously. I'd surprised them just as much as I had the Queen.

Desla said, "I accept your apology, Colton, Keeper of Dragons. I feel the truth in your words and the goodness in your heart. Your anger wasn't misplaced."

My heart leaped and my anger vanished. Excited, I blurted, "So you'll help us? You'll march with us against the Elden?"

The Queen smiled, but I thought it looked sad, not happy. "This still isn't our war. We always kept to ourselves, only helping the Elves and the others during the last war because you dragons neglected your duties. As I said, if the Elves can forgive you, surely I can."

She let out a long breath, her bubbles rising up and out of sight toward the ceiling. "Alas, the Mermaids will not march with you. However, I feel obligated to help our other brethren."

I wasn't sure what to think of that. "What help will you give, then? We're grateful for any help."

"Instead of sending soldiers, I will send you wisdom and knowledge. I will help you by training you and your two friends here, showing you how to defeat Eldrick and this new threat. With the knowledge we will give you, I'm confident you will win in the end. If you truly are the Keeper of Dragons, then Fate will make sure that truth wins. Eldrick and his lies will fall. This is the best we can do."

I was disappointed. "The best you *will* do, you mean."

For the first time, I saw Queen Desla's genuine smile, and it lit up her face. I didn't know what I had said that was so amusing. "That's right. It's the most that we *will* do. If the legends are wrong and the Fates do not intend for you to win in the end, then we must look after ourselves as we always have. I feel you were brought here for a reason, and I think that reason is to seek the wisdom and knowledge to stand up to Eldrick yourselves, as the legends say you must."

From what little I heard of the legends, she had a point. I was still disappointed about the troops, though. But at least we weren't thrown out or worse. Something told me the Mermaids didn't allow outsiders in often, if at all.

I guessed I would take what I could.

Chapter Fourteen

I was pretty sure that if we hadn't been in the middle of the Dead Sea, I would have been sweating a whole lot after the workout they gave us. The Mermaid who put us through our paces said they only meant to get a feel for our physical condition. I guess that swimming everywhere his whole life gave him the kind of endurance and strength matched only by athletes.

All I knew was that I was dog-tired after only an hour of swimming hard. I looked at him and said, "How did we do?"

Cairo and Eva turned their heads to our conversation, probably trying to hear his answer.

"You are Ochana's warriors, yet your stamina is like a Mere child's. Humans and dragons must not train the way we do." He smirked, but I sensed that he was just giving us a good-natured ribbing.

After the session, we were led back to the quarters they'd given us. It was a fairly large dome with entrances on both sides which angled down into the Dead Sea floor before coming back up again. The water had been pumped out, replaced with air, and it was actually pretty dry once we got inside. I glanced at my hands; I'd never seen them so wrinkly. I wondered if they might start rotting off with enough time in the water.

We sat at the one table in the place, which had four chairs around it. I propped my elbows on the table and rested my face in my hands.

Cairo said, "Tired, are you? I can't blame you. All I want to do is sleep."

"Me, too," Eva chimed in. She sounded as tired as I felt.

Cairo sat and rested his chin on one fist and drummed his fingers loudly on the table.

"Something on your mind?" I asked. "You look like something is bugging you."

He stared at the table, and I could almost see the gears turning in his mind. "I'm just uneasy. We're here among the Mermaids like Eva wanted, but they don't want to help us. We're basically at their mercy, right? I mean, we're underwater. Their environment. Their homeland. What if they decide to take the easy way out and try to buy Eldrick's goodwill by turning us over? I don't know that we can trust these Mermaids. Their reaction when we showed up was definitely not what I expected."

Eva let out a long breath and rolled her eyes. "I understand how you feel, but really, if we're fated to win the war and push back the Time of Fear, then everything will turn out okay. We're stuck here for now and we need them. So, I suggest we do what they say and just go off the assumption they won't backstab us. What choice do we have but to trust them?"

Cairo shook his head, looking unconvinced. "Yes, but if they betray us, we're in the middle of the Dead Sea.

There's literally nowhere to go. We could never make it to the surface before they caught up to us."

I thought Cairo was being dangerously paranoid, so I interrupted him before he got on a roll and convinced himself to do something stupid. "The Mermaids haven't given us any reason to mistrust them. They've made it clear they don't want to help us, but here they are, helping us anyway. And you're right, there's nothing we could do if they decided to betray us. So, no offense, but I think that as long as we're stuck here, it might be best not to make your fears be a self-fulfilling prophecy."

Eva nodded. "Cole's right. The more you treat people like enemies, the more they will be, right? That's how it worked in high school, and it seems to be how it works out here in the so-called real world, too."

He grinned. "So-called? What do you mean by that?"

"I'm still not convinced this isn't just all a bad dream." She reached out and knocked his elbow out from under him, and his head almost hit the table as she laughed.

I left them talking and play-fighting and went to bed. I could barely keep my eyes open after the day's workouts.

***

The next morning, we woke, dressed, and ate the meager breakfast someone had left on the table for us. As I returned the dishes to the counter, a splashing noise drew our attention to the entrance.

A Mermaid with a spear walked up the ramp from the air hatch. Once he could see all three of us, he said, "Your presence is requested at the training grounds. Today's training will be different, so I hope you all got rest." I wanted to ask questions, but he turned around and left without another word.

I turned to Eva and Cairo. "Yesterday's training was terrible, but I already feel stronger. No wonder the Mermaids are supposed to be the strongest of us all."

Eva said, "Yeah, they spend all day swimming, every day of their lives. It's like wearing weights around your wrists and ankles all the time. I guess we should get going."

We walked to the murky water at the bottom of the air tunnel, then swam through the town to reach the training grounds. At the field's far end, a small cluster of Mermaids gathered, but I couldn't make out any faces. I figured those were our trainers for the day, so I veered a little to the right, aiming toward them. When we were about twenty feet away, I let myself drift to the bottom, then continued on foot. The small crowd of half a dozen stepped aside, revealing Queen Desla herself. She didn't smile, but she did nod in greeting, so I did the same.

"Keeper of Dragons, I hear your training yesterday went well," she said. "Today, I will be your instructor. While I work with each Keeper individually to show you the ways of our mereum magic, the other two will work with my hand-picked team of instructors to master our style of war. History has shown that not even the dragons can defeat us, unless we were greatly outnumbered. Ours is a defensive style that focuses on allowing our opponents to tire themselves while we wait for the opportunity to strike. That is when the fight usually ends."

I was in total awe. "Mermaids have fought dragons before?"

She grinned and held her chin up as she said, "No, of course not. We're all on the side of truth. But there have been... What do you call them on the surface? 'Joint training maneuvers.' That's it. Long ago, we all used to train together—dragons, Elves, Trolls, and many of the other good-hearted creatures of the world."

I hadn't been told that, but it made sense since the current war was supposed to be the closest the True beings had come to being defeated. And the fact that we all had stopped training together also made sense after the dragons had our time of being completely self-absorbed. In a way, I was kind of honored to be the first dragon to train with Mermaids in a long time, and I gave Desla a polite bow.

She said, "Cole, will you please follow me? We will get out of everyone's way to practice our water magic. I will instruct you personally. Cairo, Eva, will you please go with my instructors? *Your* training begins today, as well."

Cairo bowed. Grinning back at her, he said, "I thought yesterday was when our training started."

"If only that were true," she said, eyes twinkling, "but that was only the warm-up."

The other Mermaids dragged my friends away and I followed Desla onto the sidelines. I thought the training arena looked a lot like a football stadium. When she took my hands in hers, I could feel a kind of energy flowing through everything around us. I hadn't noticed it the day before. I sensed an energy flowing between our touching hands, too. It wasn't mahier, but it also wasn't tilium.

Maybe she read my mind or maybe it was a lucky guess, but she said, "That's right, the Mermaids have a kind of power all our own. It comes from the waters all around us. Even when we walk among you air-breathers on dry land, water is still all around us in every plant, every animal, even in the air itself."

I was impressed. "You draw power even from humidity in the air!"

She shrugged. "More like the water is a channel that lets us use and manipulate our mereum. But that power also gives us control of water itself, the element of Life. We can gather it or scatter it, move it and make it do as we wish. Down here, where everything is water, we are at our most powerful. It is also the hardest to see our power in action down here for the same reason. Just as you can't see the wind within the air, you cannot see mereum at work when you are surrounded by water."

I was astounded. She definitely had my attention. "Even the water in the air we breathe? What can you make it do?"

"Anything you can imagine, once you have practiced a particular spell. For example, I can create tendrils made of water that obey my commands. I could use them to bind you, or I could have them strangle you. I can make the water gather inside someone's lungs, or I can move water out of their brain. Those kinds of deadly attacks require months of training, even years. Not even every Mermaid reaches that level of mastery. But I will teach you what little you can learn in the short time we have together. It will be one more weapon in your arsenal."

I bowed again. I was surprised that Queen Desla, who hadn't even wanted us here, was willing to try to teach me to use the power of the Mermaids. The only explanation I could think of was that she at last believed I was the Keeper of Dragons, and that the Time of Fear really was at hand.

For the next hour, she taught me the Mere water magic, mereum. The thing we practiced the longest was simply how to reach out with my senses and feel the water through my power. She said I couldn't begin to control the water until I could sense it with my mereum. I wasn't sure I had any, but I went along with it.

At one point, I glanced toward Eva and Cairo where they were desperately trying to learn how to fight with the Mere spears and weird, small shields. Their opponents continually got around their shields, delivering what would be killing blows had they been really fighting.

Desla frowned. "Pay attention, young prince. Only once you can recognize the energy that flows through the water will you begin to control it."

I eventually got to the point where I could sense the water, but only barely. After an hour, I was still a long way from learning to control it, and I was getting frustrated. When the bell rang to mark the end of the session, I was relieved. I needed to do something less frustrating for a bit.

Another hour went by with Cairo and me training with the fighting instructors, and Eva with Desla. It only took a minute or two to realize how difficult their combat style was. I did a little better than Cairo for some reason, but not by much, and my instructor seemed to take a lot of pleasure in making fun of how I was doing. He also told me that in only twenty minutes, Eva had done better than I was doing after an hour. I glanced over to where she was training with the queen. She stood with her arms stretched wide, gliding her hands back and forth through the water. I figured she was feeling the energy Desla had told me about, which was a little frustrating. That meant she was already doing better than me with mereum, too.

After we took a short break, Desla asked me to work with her again. It took a couple more hours before I was able to feel the water all around me like Eva had done hours ago. Frustrated, I wondered why I was even along for the ride.

At last, when I stretched out my hands, I felt tingling all up and down my arms, my legs, my whole body. I realized with a shock that I was finally gathering mereum. Desla said that the more I practiced, the faster I could draw it in. I'd be able to soak up mereum just from the dew on blades of grass, or even from the humidity in the air. The drier the air was, the longer it would take to pull in enough energy to use, but no air on Earth was completely dry—I could always gather mereum no matter where I was.

The drawback to mereum was that I couldn't actually hold on to that energy for long. I had to draw it in as I used it, unlike mahier. Recharging mahier quickly only happened if I ate a cow. There wouldn't always be a lucky cow around to scarf up, as I had already learned.

The next task she had me working on was to separate the water to form a ball of emptiness. It was hard because the water pressure kept smashing through my ball. At first I could only make one as big as a marble.

During a quick break while I gathered more mereum, I asked, "Can this do anything besides control the shape of water? With mahier, we can use it to push our senses outward, sometimes a great distance. There are other things we can do with it, too."

"Yes, of course. We can push our senses out, too. There is water vapor in the air, and every moving thing disturbs that vapor. Living things also are mostly made of water, and because you can sense it, no illusion can fool you if you are looking hard enough."

I grinned at her. "That would have been handy a few times already, you know."

She nodded and said, "You will also be able to cause rain, move it away from you so you stay dry, or even keep it from raining. I told you earlier that you can use mereum to flood an enemy's lungs, or dry out their organs."

I thought about how I could use this new power, so different from mahier and tilium. "So yes, I'll be able to do a lot more than just feel the water. I'm impressed, again."

"It has been a millennium since we taught anyone but our own kind how to use mereum." She grinned and added, "Your slow progress reminds me why."

I could tell it was only friendly teasing, but I still had to remind myself not to get too proud. I smiled back and focused on my training.

With more practice, my control grew better, and she began to push me harder, taking me through a series of exhausting mental exercises. Controlling mahier was all about willpower, but mereum was more about a way of thinking, of concentrating hard. I was exhausted mentally, but she said time was of the essence and I had to learn fast. That was true—we didn't have years to train like the Mermaids did. We had to leave soon. So, with her hammering away at me, I pushed myself harder and harder.

Evening was beginning to settle in when I began to tremble. My hands shook and my left eye twitched. Still, I pushed myself even harder. I was beyond exhausted and the shaking grew worse, but I didn't say anything to the queen. I pushed on and pushed harder.

Maybe an hour later, I realized I should have said something to Desla about my shaking, but it was suddenly too late. A giant tremor started at my toes and shot up my legs, along the length of my spine, and when it got to my head, my eyes rolled back and everything went black. I knew what would come next.

Chapter Fifteen

... Confusing visions ... Trolls staked out under the sun, under night skies ... in snow, in jungle, in desert, in farmlands ... I stand over them, one after the other and all at once ... I hold a knife I've never seen before ... I say words I don't understand ... the knife plunges into a Troll's heart ... the snow melts, the desert scrubland turns sandy, the jungle withers, the crops die ...

... I rise up above the scene of another Troll ... I see King Eldrick, laughing, holding the knife ... the Troll dies, the land dies ...

My eyes flew open as I sat bolt upright. I was confused about where I was, then realized I was still underwater, still in the Mermaid city, still in the training yard. Only now, a crowd of Mermaids had joined my companions to stand around me as Eva and Cairo knelt beside me. Eva had my head in her lap, and she looked worried. But the Mermaids didn't look worried for me. Their faces were painted with shock as they all stared at me. Many had mouths open, jaws dropped. Queen Desla looked pale and her eyes were wide and fearful.

What had I done to shock everyone during my vision?

As I tried to figure out how to tell the queen what I'd seen, someone in the crowd shouted, "Banish him!" I could hear the fear in his voice. A woman repeated it, and then more Mermaids took up the call. In seconds, the crowd was chanting it, their tone getting louder and angrier each time they said it.

Queen Desla stared at me. Her face was set in stone, her lips pursed tightly. I wished I could tell what she was thinking, but it sure didn't look good for me.

Eva helped me sit and had to shout in my ear for me to hear her say, "It was different this time. It was like a seizure. Your whole body shook, and we couldn't get it to stop, even with the queen's magic helping."

Desla turned to face the crowd and raised her hands into the air, fingers spread apart, and the riot of shouts died down to an angry murmur. In a strong, clear voice, she said, "The dragon is not possessed, and you are safe from harm. We will not exile them, but they will not be here much longer. Now go! Return to your homes and leave me to do my duty."

The murmuring started again, but the Mermaids did as she commanded. In a minute, we were alone and I breathed a sigh of relief. If that mob had attacked us, there was no way we could have stopped it.

She said, "Come with me, Keeper. I have something to discuss with you, but not here."

I got to my feet, a little shaky still. Cairo and Eva tried to follow me as I stepped after the queen, but I told them not to worry about me. They didn't look happy about it, but for once, they didn't argue.

I followed Desla out of the training area, through a bit of the town, and then down a narrow, winding path through a field of plants that looked like kelp. They grew about twice my height, and it felt a bit confining.

After a few minutes, the path opened up into a small clearing about twenty feet across. A large, flat rock in the middle was big enough for us both to sit on, so we did, side-by-side. My curiosity was killing me. "Thanks again for breaking up the crowd. I know they were just scared. I am, too, if I'm honest."

As she looked at me, she took a deep breath and let it out slowly, air bubbles rising up and out of sight toward the surface. I felt like she was examining me. Maybe she was less sure about me being safe to be near than she told the crowd. Still, I didn't think she'd be here with me otherwise.

"What are you looking at?" I asked, grinning awkwardly.

She didn't grin back. "Cole, I'm afraid I have bad news. I had hoped this beautiful place might take some of the sting out of what I have to tell you."

My heart beat faster when she said that. "It is pretty here," I said, though I didn't really think so. I was just being polite. "So, what did you want to tell me?"

She said, "I will be blunt, since you seem to prefer that. The truth is, your visions aren't just dreams or hallucinations. I think you knew that already, in your heart. What you don't know is that you're having these visions because Eldrick is sending them to you. Each time the visions touch you, he can sense exactly where you are. That's why the Carnites and Elden kept finding you—it wasn't just a coincidence."

"That does explain a lot. How do I get rid of that? We can't finish our mission with him chasing after us all the time."

She looked away, out into the fields of seaweed she thought were so pretty, and then said, "The reason you see him and what he is doing is because when he touches your mind, you also touch his. You're seeing his memories."

"So that's why I saw him turning the Elves dark, and killing the Trolls."

Her head whipped back to me. "He's killing the Trolls? Where?"

I frowned. It was disturbing, sure, but she looked almost panicked. "All over, from what I could see. And when he killed the Trolls, he was saying something I couldn't understand. Then the—"

She cut me off, saying, "The ground around him changed, too. Dying. Right?"

I nodded. If the visions were *real*, and the Trolls really were being killed all over the world, we were in trouble.

Almost as though she read my mind, she said, "He's poisoning the earth with a ritual, but it is one he shouldn't even know. One of his new dark Elves must have told him about it. He can only be trying to make a new Earth, one more to his benefit. That's bad for us all."

"That's an understatement. We have to stop them," I said, wishing I could make her understand the urgency I had felt since seeing the vision.

She pursed her lips and looked away. Softly, she said, "Yes, he must be stopped. There is a problem, however. These visions you are having drain your magic. But they also harm you. That's why the side effects keep getting worse, and if you have another vision... I am so sorry to tell you, it will probably kill you. I've seen this spell before, long ago."

I sat dumbfounded, staring at her. I think my jaw dropped, I was in such shock.

She paused, then added, "There is one thing that might save you, though."

She had my attention! "What? You have to tell me," I blurted.

"If you can learn to block the visions, they can't harm you anymore. We Mermaids can teach you how. It's difficult, but if you give it everything you've got, and you can dedicate your whole self to it, I can teach you to block it. The question is, can you learn it? Not many people can dedicate their entire self. Heart, mind, and spirit must be in line."

My heart sank. If I didn't master it, I would die, but my track record so far hadn't been very good. I struggled to learn the basics, so how could I learn something so powerful, so complex? In my heart, I felt like I was dead already. It was just a matter of time.

Chapter Sixteen

My two companions and I plopped down at the queen's long table in the great hall. The only other person there was the queen herself. I sat with my face in my hands, elbows on the table. I was still in shock.

Next to me, Eva had her hand on my shoulder. "It's not the end, Cole. The queen can teach you. You just have to try, with everything you've got. Please don't give up. If you do, then we all might as well give up right now."

I knew better than anyone how hard it was for me to learn even basic spells like summoning my dragon. What kind of a dragon can't summon himself? Well, I hadn't been able to, not at first. "I'm willing to try," I said, but even I could hear the defeat in my voice.

The queen slammed her hand on the table. The sharp crack echoed through the room and made me jump. She half-shouted, "Keeper of Dragons, you disappoint me. I don't care if you give up on yourself, but how can you give up on Eva? How can you give up on the dragons? What about your allies, the Elves, Trolls, Fairies... And now, the Mermaids?"

I looked up, surprised. After the way her people reacted to my latest vision, I thought she'd be kicking us out sooner rather than later. "You'll agree to a Mere Treaty?"

"Yes," she said as she sank back into her chair. "Listen. Now that Eldrick knows you're here with us, you're going to have to leave soon. I'm sorry to have to dump more bad news on you right now, but it's just the truth. But before you go, I will teach you how to resist your visions. Without you, everything is lost."

"I don't think I can do it, though. I'm going to let you down. I'll let everyone down." I'm not sure I had ever felt this helpless before.

Desla nodded slowly, taking in my words, and then she seemed to come to some sort of decision. "I am convinced you can learn this. I know you don't have much faith in yourself, but the truth is that you should have been dead after the first vision. The fact that it has taken you this long to be in real danger tells me that you have strength in you greater than almost any I have ever seen. And that makes sense, because you're the Keeper of Dragons. Fate wouldn't have put this in your hands if you couldn't handle it. Will you at least try? Let me rephrase that—you *will* try."

That was interesting news. I had never really thought of myself as being that strong, but if the queen had faith I could learn the Mere magic and protect myself, she would know better than anyone on Earth. I nodded, still not enthusiastic about our chances, but at least I had begun to feel a glimmer of hope. Maybe sometimes hope was all it took.

"Yes, I'll do it." As I looked around the room, everyone smiled with relief. They were relying on me. I decided right then and there that I wouldn't let them down.

Desla said, "Then we begin immediately, because we don't know how much time we have."

I had a sinking feeling that our time would run out before I did what needed doing.

***

For the hundredth time, I felt the Mere water energy building within me as I gathered it like she'd taught me. But yet again, when I tried to create a shield that would keep Eldrick out, it all just fizzled and the power drained away.

I had to start all over again, drawing the energy out of the water as I got ready to try the shield another time. And failed. Each time I tried, I got a little closer, but I knew I had a long way to go. Since I had no way of knowing when Eldrick would try again, the only way I would survive was to master that shield well enough to keep it up all the time, even when I was asleep. I tried to have confidence that I could do it. I told myself Fate wouldn't let me die in such a stupid way. I wasn't sure I'd win, but I just didn't want to believe I'd lose just like that.

As the energy flowed into me, I could feel it gathering in a ball in my chest. It was like a little pressure that wanted to get out. It wanted me to use it. I didn't know how I knew that, but I could tell. Or maybe it was in my imagination. Once the energy was large enough, I imagined invisible hands molding it like clay, stretching it out into a thinner and thinner layer, like rolling out bread dough.

Desla hissed in my ear, blowing my concentration. I felt the energy flow right out of me, back into the water. She said, "We're out of time. The Elden are at the Dead Sea borders. They've come for you. We can hold them off, but not forever. You have to leave now, while you still have time."

I stared at her, confused. "But I'm not ready yet. I haven't figured out the shield."

Desla had a sad look in her eyes. "It doesn't matter if you're ready yet. If you're here when the Elden arrive, they'll kill you as surely as another vision would."

After that, everything was a mad blur, like watching a movie in fast-forward. Everyone ran around, doing whatever it was Mermaids did when they were invaded. Cairo and Eva were just as frantic, gathering all their gear. I got mine ready, too, but I was just going through the motions. I felt like I was already dead, just waiting for my body to figure that out.

And then it was time to go, time to run. Yet again. I was tired of running, but it was better than dying, I supposed. I double-checked to make sure Jericho's sword was strapped tightly to my back, then we walked out together and closed another chapter of our lives.

Almost. Before we could leave, Queen Desla found us and waved us over. We met in the middle, and when she got close, she gave us some good news. "Dragons, you've done well here, and you've shown us things are as they used to be. Prince Colton here has convinced me that the dragons are again noble. When you find Eldrick and the Elves, summon us and the Mermaids will join you on the battlefield. First, though, you have to find his hiding place."

Before I could say anything, she began waving her hands in front of her in an odd pattern I hadn't seen before, more like a dance than a pattern. Her fingertips began to glow, and then it spread to her hands, then her arms. The light left a trail that didn't fade, and the more she waved her arms, the more intricate the light pattern grew.

It went out all at once, and Desla smiled at us. "I have now formally announced the Mere Treaty is in place. Prince Colton bears witness to this."

I nodded, though I didn't think it was very likely that I would live long enough to summon them. At least the dragons wouldn't die alone, though.

Desla had one more surprise for me. She grabbed my arm and dragged me to the side. I looked at her with one eyebrow raised, curious.

"I have one more thing for you before you leave. I see the sword you carry, and I recognize it as Jericho's. It is a fine sword, made by the very best weapon smiths. And yet, it's only a sword. I imagine you didn't have time to finish your training before all this began, either, and that's why you carry such a weapon. It is not good enough for the Prince of Ochana."

She had my attention. "What do you mean?"

She pinched her fingertips together on both hands, put them together, then slowly drew them apart and extended her arms. A soft, sparkling glow formed between her fingertips. It was beautiful. It looked like a million stars inside a million more, and I was mesmerized.

When she opened her fingertips, the glow stayed hovering in the water between us. She reached out and grabbed one end. The glow faded, revealing the most beautiful sword I'd ever seen. If I looked at it hard enough, I could almost see the millions and millions of stars inside it, or maybe they were just sparkles of magic. I couldn't tell, but I knew that was no normal sword.

Desla said, "Cole, this is a sword worthy of a prince or a king. It is the Mere Blade, and it has been in my family since the very first days. I would be honored if you would agree to carry this on your journey. It will be proof of the Mermaids' dedication to your cause. It's no normal sword, as I think you can tell."

I nodded, dumbstruck.

She continued, "The sword is the spirit of my people. With it, you can do amazing things. It has a mind of its own, but when the time is right—if you're ready and your heart is pure—it will know what to do. Until then, I have yet to find anything this blade won't cut through, and you can use it to channel your mahier, your tilium, and even your mereum once you learn to control it."

She held the sword out to me, and I bowed before I took it. As soon as I picked it up, I felt some sort of connection between us. It was as though her sword had bonded to me, and I knew it was deciding whether I was worthy to hold it.

After staring at the sword for a couple seconds, Desla nodded and smiled. "I knew it. Very well. Now it is time for you leave. The Elden and dark Elves are only a few miles from here. Take the sword and your companions, and run hard. Don't let them catch you, and do not rest until you master the shield I taught you."

Eva and Cairo came up beside us, and he let out a low whistle when he saw the blade. "I recognize this sword," he said with awe.

"Thank you, Queen Desla," I said. "All the members of the Mere Treaty will remember the help you gave me. If I survive, I'll bring it back to you."

"Oh, Cole, you don't need to worry about that. When it is time for the blade to come back, it will. But I do hope to see you again after you deliver us all from the Time of Fear. I wish you well. One more thing." She pulled a small, velvet bag out of her pocket and handed it to me. "I do believe you will need this as well. Just a pinch, and your guardian Jericho shall regain his strength." Without another word, she spun around and swam away, streaking through the water like a bullet. She had her own preparations to make.

I turned to Cairo and Eva and said, "It's time for us to leave. Cairo, I'd be honored if you would carry Jericho's sword for me."

I drew Jericho's sword from its sheath and gave it to him. He took it from me with a nod and slid it through his back straps. It was good to see him armed again. Then I slid the Mere Blade into my own sheath, and we left the Mermaids. I hoped it wasn't the last time I would see them.

J.A. Culican

Chapter Seventeen

A couple hours later, we had gone pretty far from the Mermaid city. I said, "We're going to Alaska. We've done what you all wanted and it turned out to be a good idea. Now it's time to do what I say. King Eldrick is somewhere in the north, halfway around the world. I don't know about you, but I'm tired of running. With or without you, I'm done putting it off. I'm going north."

Eva slid her arm through mine, and it was all she needed to say. Cairo, on the other hand, didn't say anything. He just followed us. I had expected a little more argument from him, but I guess he didn't know what else to do.

As we walked, I kept trying the Mere magic. I felt like I got better at the shield little by little, but I was still a long way from mastering it. I doubted I could do it before King Eldrick ended up killing me, which was a depressing thought.

When I was sure we were far enough away that the Elden wouldn't spot us, we summoned our dragons. We flew up through the water, using our mahier to let us move just as we did through air, until we burst out into the sky.

After a couple of hours, we were flying over some huge desert. I wasn't sure which one, since I wasn't very good at geography, but I knew Alaska was east. It was easy enough to fly east, after all, so we weren't lost.

When we were hungry, we landed and raided livestock around different oases. The houses looked different in that region, with lots of bright colors. They were built differently than anything I'd seen before, too. The cows were small and thin, which I supposed made it easier to keep them alive in that desert scrubland, but it meant we each scarfed two cows. I felt bad taking it from the farmer without asking, but he'd lose all his cows anyway if Eldrick won the war.

Then we were flying high above the earth again at blinding speeds.

I felt a tickle in my mind just before Eva's voice reached out to me. She said, "You seem quiet. What's on your mind?"

I didn't feel like lying, so I just told her the truth. "Dying. I haven't mastered the shield, and the next time Eldrick connects to find us, I imagine that'll be the end of it."

"You don't give yourself enough credit, Cole. I've seen you do amazing things. Things you thought you couldn't do. Fate has it all planned out. You just need to follow your gut and your heart, and it'll all turn out all right in the end. We'll beat the Time of Fear and push it back, and you're going to save the world. You just need to have faith in yourself. I do."

I was pretty sure she was wrong, but I didn't feel like arguing. I didn't want my last time alive to be spent bickering with my best friend, so I simply grunted.

"Cole, don't give me that. I know you. You need to listen to me, okay? Everything's going to be fine in the end. You can make the shield. Maybe not right now, but you will when it matters. Trust me."

Why wouldn't she just leave things alone? "I think you're wrong. I don't think I can do it, and that means I'm going to let you all down. Eldrick is going to kill me the next time he wants to see where we are. Then I'll be dead. I won't be there to fight by your side. He's going to kill you, too, then. And there's nothing we can do to stop it." I hadn't meant to snap at her, but I just wanted her to leave me alone. Like I said, I didn't want to spend my last hours fighting with her.

Then I heard Cairo echoing in Eva's mind, because she was still connected to me. He said, "Leave him alone. If he wants to sulk, let him, but at least he's flying east. He hasn't given up, so just let him be. Sometimes, people just want to be left alone for a bit."

Her voice in my head was like a roar when she snapped back. "Don't talk about him like that, and don't you dare tell me not to try to comfort my best friend."

"It isn't like that," Cairo said. "I swear I'm not insulting him. Cole is stronger than he knows, but right now, he's not stable. You don't know what he'll do the next time we have to fight or run. I'm worried he's going to do something stupid or dangerous. When he does, I don't want you around him. I don't want you to get hurt."

She snarled. "Why do you care so much? Cole knows me, but you don't. I'm tired of your overprotective attitude, always saying I can't take care of myself. Seems like you don't know me very well, so maybe you should just let me worry about myself."

"Please," he pleaded. It was a new tone, one I hadn't heard from him before. "I just need you to be safe. And you're wrong, I know you better than you think I do. Don't be mad just because people care about you."

Eva didn't respond, but I felt her break contact just before she streaked ahead, sprinting away from me and Cairo.

He started to pull ahead to go after her, but I focused my thoughts at him and said, "Leave her. She just needs some time, trust me. She'll get over it."

Although he didn't shoot ahead, he didn't reply. The whole aura around his mind was full of irritation and...something else. Fear, I thought.

I said, "You don't want to talk, fine. Maybe you can listen, though. You need to tell Eva the truth before it's too late. You know how dangerous things are for us all, but you want to wait, and wait, and wait some more. She deserves to know the truth. You don't even know if we're going to have tomorrow, so I just don't get why you won't tell her today how you feel."

Instead of answering, he cut me off entirely and sped ahead, flying halfway between me and Eva. We spent the next few days spread out like that, each of us lost in our own thoughts. We didn't even speak when we landed to eat and recharge our mahier.

Eventually, we crossed the Bering Strait into Alaska. The sun was just coming up. I spotted a herd of elk and dove after them. Eva and Cairo were right behind me. It was nice to be able to fill up and recharge off just one animal. And it was delicious.

I was the first one to say anything to the others. "So. Here we are in Alaska. Now what?"

"This is your idea" Cairo muttered. "I thought you knew where you were going."

Eva shot him a dirty look. She took in a deep breath, and I could tell she was about to yell at him, when I spotted movement half a mile away in the tree line.

"Be quiet," I said, cutting off her reply.

They both looked at me, irritated.

I continued, "Look there, northeast. In the tree line. Do you see that?"

Cairo blurted, "Carnites. What are they doing here?"

"I count three of them," Eva said. "I wonder where they're going."

I finally had an idea of what to do. I grinned and said, "There's only one thing to do, right? Let's follow them. After you, O brave Eva."

For the first time in days, she smiled. She adjusted her backpack and headed out after them, jogging toward the tree line some distance behind the Carnites.

I shrugged and grinned, then followed her. At last, something to do. I finally felt a hope of finding Eldrick and our missing allies before I died. As I ran behind her, I kept practicing my mereum shield spell. I really hoped I wouldn't need it any time soon, because it still wasn't working.

J.A. Culican

Chapter Eighteen

We followed the Carnites through the frozen northern forest. With their long legs and huge size, they moved a lot faster than us, but instead of knocking every tree over, they made their way between them. That slowed them down enough for us to keep up, though just barely. After a half an hour, they reached the top of a hill, then continued down the far side.

When we got to the crest, however, they were nowhere to be seen.

Cairo said, "Stop. Let me see if I can find them." He closed his eyes for about ten seconds, and I could feel the air tingle with his mahier as it spread out, searching for the Carnites. At last, he said, "Down and to your right. They're moving through a ravine."

We ran again, as quickly as we could. After a few minutes, I could hear the Carnites. We followed along atop the ravine rather than trying to climb down into it. If they had any traps, they would be in the ravine, and if they saw us, we would have nowhere to run down there.

A few minutes later, a Carnite's enormous block head appeared through the leaves, then its body, and the next Carnite's head. They were climbing up the other side. They turned eastward, moving away from the ravine and deeper into the forest.

I spat a curse. We were going to have to cross over. I looked at my friends and said, "Dragon?"

They nodded, and we all shifted. It was a little nerve wracking to fly so close to the ground, but if we got up too high, anyone could see us from miles around. Not humans, of course, since we always hid ourselves while flying, but the Carnites and any Elden could see through our illusion if they looked right at us.

Once we got to the other side, we shifted back into our humans and took off after the Carnites. I figured we had been chasing them for about an hour when we heard a crash up ahead.

Cairo called a halt, and we stopped to rest. Maybe they had led us to King Eldrick's camp, but we couldn't be sure. After a few minutes, when we had caught our breath and checked our energy levels, Cairo felt we were ready to creep forward and see whatever we would find.

We crawled forward on our bellies and found a clearing in the forest ahead. There were four Carnites sitting around a bonfire, talking quietly. But no Eldrick and no Elves or Trolls. My heart sank.

Cairo's thoughts came into my mind. "I've been checking my senses, and I don't feel anyone else around. Just these four Carnites. Let's head back a bit so we can talk."

We crept away from the clearing until we were sure they wouldn't see us, then walked a couple minutes more.

I sat on a rock, breathing heavily. "Any ideas? I don't feel Eldrick, whether the Carnites work for him or not. We still need to find him and our friends."

Eva knelt on the forest floor, sitting on her heels, and she just shook her head. No help there. Cairo leaned against a tree and shrugged. It looked like we were out of ideas, for the moment.

Hesitantly, I said, "I suppose we just need to keep following them. I don't think they live in that clearing, so they're going somewhere eventually."

I was startled by an ear-piercing roar from behind us and whipped around to look. A Carnite charged through the forest from the ravine's direction, holding a tree in his right hand like a club. It headed right for Cairo.

I saw shock on Cairo's face, and then he spun to face the noise. The Carnite swung its tree like a golf club, and Cairo stretched out his hand toward it. A crackle of energy zipped through the air as he used his mahier to shield himself from the blow he couldn't dodge. The club smacked him and his barrier crackled. The hit sent him flying through the air toward a tree. Just before he struck it, he held out his other arm to make another barrier. When he hit, the tree snapped in half, but his shield held. Instead of being splattered against the tree, he only tumbled to the ground and came up on his feet. Thankfully, he didn't look injured.

More roars echoed behind us, and I almost panicked when I realized the other Carnites had heard the scream and were charging us from the other direction.

Eva drew her simple, well-crafted sword—Cairo gave his to her when I gave him Jericho's sword—and somersaulted at the first Carnite. She slashed its hip as she went by.

It spun around, swinging its club, but she was already out of range.

Its back was to me, so I sprinted at it, drawing the amazing Mere Blade and thrusting it at the creature's spine. Unlike Jericho's sword, this one slid right through the Carnite's thick hide like butter. It screamed in pain and fell.

We turned toward the other Carnites. Four of them were smashing through the trees, sprinting right at us. Then I heard two more mighty roars from my right and glanced over, only to see another batch of monstrous Carnites. There were only three of us and at least six of them. There was no way we could win this fight. The trees were too dense for us to fly away, and it seemed like we might die before we ever found Eldrick.

The six Carnites stopped when they got close enough to see us, maybe fifty feet away at most, and then spread out. They were trying to cut off any chance of escape, and they could move through that forest faster than any of us if one of us got away. I really didn't want to die in the frozen northern forest, but at least I would be fighting alongside my friends when it happened.

Cairo shouted, "Back-to-back, Keepers."

What else was there to do? Nothing. We formed a circle, facing outward. "It's been an honor, Cairo," I said. "Sorry I got you into this, Eva."

She didn't say anything but grabbed my shoulder and gave me one quick nod. Her simple gesture told me more than words could have, and I felt a lot better about whatever was going to happen next with her at my side. And Cairo's, of course.

The Carnites began stomping their feet and slamming their fists into their chests as they bared their yellow, jagged teeth at us. They towered over us. Suddenly, one Carnite stood up straight and its face went slack. It toppled like a tree, smashing face-first into the ground.

A figure wearing loose clothes and a hood over its face stood on the fallen Carnite's back, its sword in the Carnite's head. It pulled the sword out before sprinting at the next one, sword held overhead with the tip pointed forward.

The other Carnites stopped and looked at their fallen comrade, and if Carnites could look confused, these sure did. I didn't waste any time, though. I charged one of the Carnites, screaming at the top of my lungs.

The next few seconds were a blur. I jumped, I dodged. I somersaulted, I swung my sword. Somewhere along the way, I got hit, but I was so pumped up that I didn't feel it. At least, not at the time. Everything sped by faster than I could keep track of it. It was complete chaos, and at the end, I could hardly tell my friends from my enemies. It was like my mind had just switched off, leaving me to run on instinct. I had a vague impression of doing all sorts of things I didn't know I could, pulling off moves I didn't know I could make.

I pulled my sword from another Carnite and spun, swinging it at something behind me—and only barely managed to stop myself from slashing into Cairo at the last second. We stared at each other for a second, swords held ready to hit each other, and then looked around. I was in a daze, but as I slowly came out of the fog, I saw that all the Carnites were down and Eva and Cairo were still up.

So was the mysterious stranger who had saved us. I walked toward them with a grin, laughing for no reason I could figure out. Maybe I was just happy to be alive, or maybe I was still some kind of battle-crazy.

When I reached the hooded figure, I said, "Thank you so much, friend. You came along just in time. I'm Cole, and these two are Eva and Cairo, my friends. Who are you, what are you doing out here? Not that I'm complaining."

The figure collapsed to the ground, and I rushed to their side. But I froze when the hood slid off, revealing their face.

From behind me, Cairo muttered a curse. There in my arms, lying on the ground with blood trickling from her mouth, was Clara, and she was badly injured.

Chapter Nineteen

As we stood around Clara, Cairo examined her. She had more wounds than I could count, most small but vicious, and two larger wounds. One was a deep gash on her left hip, and the other was the ugliest bruise I had ever seen over her right side. It was clear she had multiple broken ribs.

Cairo said, "Form a circle and grab each other's hands and mine."

We did what he said, and then I felt him drawing power from us. Somehow, the circle seemed to amplify our mahier. I'd experienced that once before, and made a note to ask how it was done. It might come in handy someday.

A faint glow spread over Clara, and as the minutes ticked by, most of her smaller wounds closed before my eyes. The bruise over her side faded, and I actually saw her ribs shift back into place. The largest wound, the gash to her side, closed most of the way, but when the glow faded, it hadn't healed completely, though it wasn't as bad as before.

Cairo answered my question before I asked it. "She took all the healing she can handle, just like Jericho. Any more would hurt her more than help. I think she'll make it now, but she'll be weak for a while."

Her eyelids fluttered open and her eyes darted around. She looked frightened, but when she saw it was us standing over her, her whole body relaxed. I hadn't even realized she was tensed up, ready to strike. She was an impressive warrior.

"Relax, Clara," I said. "You're here with friends. I can't believe how great you were, and you were already really hurt! What happened?"

She closed her eyes and took a couple deep breaths before responding. "Our brother, Eldrick, happened. He's been torturing us all, trying to get us to turn to the darkness. When I refused, the torture just kept going. On and on, and it got worse the more I resisted him."

Cairo's lips turned up into a snarl. He said, "I'm so glad you got away. How did you escape?"

"The whole time, I had been working through the ropes he tied me up with."

She pulled up one sleeve, and despite Cairo's healing, she had scars and ugly, open wounds on her wrist. I could only imagine the ropes sawing their way almost down to her bones.

"At last, he told one of his Elden to just finish me off, then left," she continued. "Me, his sister. I wasn't even important enough to him to watch me die. But I'd worked through one rope just in time, and when the Elden came at me with a knife..."

Cairo nodded, understanding. "You finished him off and used his knife to escape. Thanks to all our ancestors that you're safe, Clara."

She shook her head violently. "No! You don't understand. I'm not safe. You aren't. Ochana isn't safe. He has an army of dark Elves, along with his Elden and half the world's Carnites. And he knows I'm gone. He's going to hunt for me with everything he's got, so I can't warn Ochana."

"Warn us?" I blurted. "About what?" I glanced at Eva, and she met my eyes with the same worry etched on her face.

"About his army. They're on the move against the last group standing in his way."

Cairo growled and then said, "Let him come! Ochana is in his way, and he'd be a fool to attack us now, when we're ready for him."

"That's just it, Cairo. You aren't ready for him. He found a way to get by all your alarms and wards, remember? He'll come in by surprise, and Ochana won't have any warning. It'll be a slaughter if we don't get back there and warn them."

An idea struck me. I hoped it was a good one. "What if we get back and warn Ochana, and instead of waiting for him to hit us, we turn the tables? He doesn't know we know. If we can get our army at him before he leaves Alaska, we can fight them here instead of where it will hurt us. With surprise, maybe we can bring him down once and for all."

Clara nodded and then looked at Cairo. "We should leave right away. But before we go, tell me. What happened to Jericho? Did he make it?"

Cairo's mouth turned up into a faint smile. "Yes, he's alive, but poisoned. We received some weeds from the Mermaids that will heal him. So, relax."

The look that passed between them caught my attention. There was a lot that they weren't saying, I could tell. Elves and dragons hadn't been friends in a long time by my counting, so I was curious. "Why are you asking about Jericho?"

Eva snickered and said, "Maybe they were an item."

Ha. Elves and dragons...as if that could happen. I said, "Don't be silly. That's rude." I couldn't help but smile at her joke, though.

"Actually," Clara said, "you're closer to the truth than you know."

Chapter Twenty

I couldn't believe my ears. Jericho and Clara? How could a dragon and an Elf even tolerate each other for long, much less have those kinds of feelings for each other? I thought our kind and theirs just didn't mix, except against a common enemy. But apparently, I had been wrong.

"Can you say that again?" I asked. "It sounded like you said that you and Jericho used to have different kind of feelings for each other."

She sat up and looked at Cairo, but he looked away. "It's true," she said with a sigh. "I started to have feelings for him during the last dragon king's rule, when Ochana took care of dragons and no one else. Jericho had pressed hard for decades to get the dragon king to honor our alliance and come to our help. I respected him for that."

Eva reached out and touched her shoulder. "Let me guess. Respect turned into something more, right?" She rubbed Clara's arm lightly, and I was glad she was there to try to comfort our elven ally.

Clara nodded, and wiped at one eye. "Yes. When I told him how I was confused about my feelings, he told me he felt the same way. He wasn't sure whether it had started before or after he began to press the old dragon king to honor the alliance, though, and that bothered him."

Cairo let out a low whistle. "You mean, he wasn't sure if he wanted Ochana to aid the other races because it was the right thing to do or because of how he felt about you?"

"Yes. For a man like Jericho, you can imagine such a question meant a lot to him. In the end, though, he decided it didn't matter why he had pressed the king to do the right thing, only that he had pressed for honor and duty. We were going to be together, and we'd figure out the problems later."

I was surprised to hear she had feelings for him, but even more surprised to hear he had the same for her—and I was stunned that he had any kind of self-doubt at all. He wasn't just a robot, at least not when it came to Clara. "So, what happened? Why aren't you two living happily ever after?"

She didn't answer right away, looking at the ground like she was trying to figure out what to say, or how to say it. I think we sat like that, all looking at Clara, for half a minute before she finally said, "It was when Jago died. Rylan became the king, and he made Jericho the lead Woland for all Ochana, all in one day. Jericho had new duties, and he became obsessed with finding out what happened to his best and only true friend. And then, there were my own people..."

Cairo interjected immediately. "When the dragons tried to rejoin the world, the Elves again thought of us. And they were angry. Suddenly, they would have noticed if you were spending time with a dragon. They would have been enraged. Does that sum it up?"

Clara nodded and wiped at her eyes again. "Yes. We both decided to go our separate ways for the good of our people. But it was stupid. We never should have walked away. How often do you get to really love someone? Why should it matter that he's a dragon and I'm an Elf? I love him anyway, and as close as I just came to death, I see things differently now. I want to be with him, no matter what it costs me. Even for our kind, life is too short to sacrifice something as important as your heart. I'll find a way to be with him again, I swear I will."

We comforted her, and she fell asleep a little later. We prepared to make the run to Ochana. As we packed our things, Cairo hovered near Eva, and I wondered what he was going to do. He took a deep breath, and then he walked right up to her.

"Eva, listen. Hearing Clara's tale has put my mind right. I need to tell you something."

"Cairo, this isn't really the best—"

He cut her off, saying, "No, it can't wait. I...I have feelings for you. No, it's more than that, I love you. I'm in love with you. Among our kind, we call it *Vera Salit*, and it means soulmates. Destined by Fate to be together. I wish I'd told you sooner, and Cole tried to make me, but I was too afraid. I said it was because the timing wasn't right, but the truth wasn't so noble."

"Stop! Just stop talking, Cairo." Eva's face turned angry.

I was stunned. I couldn't look away—it was like a train wreck.

"How dare you tell me this now, when Clara almost died and Ochana is in danger? Get your head in the game, Cairo."

His expression fell. I thought he might get upset, but he wasn't done trying yet. "You're wrong. There's no better time than now. I couldn't live with myself if something happened to you before I had a chance to tell you."

"I said stop it, Cairo. There's no such thing as soulmates. People meet, they love, they stop loving, they move on. It's the way the world runs."

"No, you're wrong. What about when you were kidnapped? We never should have found you, but we did. That was Fate guiding us. Or what about when you first turned into the Golden Dragon? Think back. You know I'm right. Maybe it's so rare that no one really believes it, but you and me, we feel it. *Vera Salit*. Destiny. Tell me I'm wrong, Eva! If you're honest with yourself, you can't say it."

I saw the anger drain from her face when he mentioned finding her when she'd been kidnapped. When he mentioned the Golden Dragon transformation, she finally looked up at him and met his gaze. Slowly, she began to nod. She said, "I don't know. Yes, I feel...something. And when you said *Vera Salit*, I felt a jolt shoot up my spine, like the word had some power."

Cairo let out a relieved sigh. He smiled briefly, and put his hand on her shoulder. "That's your mahier recognizing the truth when it hears it. I'm right. *Now* we can do what needs doing, and if anything happens to me, I won't die having never told you."

Eva was actually blushing a little, which I didn't often see. It was hard to fluster her. She said, "I feel it, too, even though I didn't want to hear it. But now what?"

She took a step toward him, and I figured they were going to kiss, so I looked at Clara. She was watching the two with a smile.

Then Cairo said, "Now, I have to go warn Ochana about the attack, before it's too late."

Eva blurted out, "Wait. What? You can't go now. You just told me some cosmic reality about true love being real, and you want to leave? Let me come with you, at least!"

"I'm sorry, Eva, but with the dark Elf army running around somewhere out there, it's too dangerous. You're the Keeper of Dragons, too, and if something happens to you, all is lost. Stay with Cole—you're safer together. If I'm lucky, I'll get the dragons to come here to stop Eldrick's attack before it starts. And it's time to tell the Mermaids. They promised warriors, and we're going to need them. I swear I'll be back as fast as I can." He summoned his dragon as he jumped into the air, transitioning in a blink, and flew up and away.

Eva stood with her jaw dropped. Tears welled up in her eyes.

I couldn't leave her like that; she was my best friend. "Eva, he's right. Clara is still too weak to travel, and we can't abandon her here with Eldrick searching for her. He'll be back as fast as any dragon ever could be, I promise. He's been talking about this soulmate stuff for a while, now. I think he'd move the sky and the moon to get back to you."

She didn't say anything, just wrapped her arms around me and buried her face in my shoulder. She was usually the strong, brave one. I think she was feeling something she hadn't ever felt before and didn't know how to handle it. I let her cry softly until she was done, then we rejoined Clara. It made me wish I had a soulmate of my own, but how often could that *Vera Salit* thing happen, if it was practically a myth?

Chapter Twenty-One

We let Clara get a good night's sleep, and in the morning, she felt much better. She still had to hobble a little, but given how urgent it was to find the Elves and Trolls being held prisoner, she insisted she was well enough to travel. Eva and I didn't argue.

Besides, if we hung out there until Clara healed up more, Eldrick would find us. There was no doubt he had minions searching for her, so at first light, we headed out across the frozen Alaska forest.

"It was pretty close. I wasn't able to run very far with the wounds he gave me. In fact, I was about to collapse when I heard your fight with the Carnites."

Eva replied, "I don't think it was a coincidence you found us. Fate led you to us. I'm glad you came along, too, because I don't think we would have made it without you."

Clara shrugged and smiled. "I know I wouldn't have made it without you, so we're even."

As we trudged through the snowy forest, I found myself walking between them. We all ended up chatting and joking. I thought it was the first time I had seen Clara really open up. I figured saving each other's lives made it easier to let our guards down, despite the bad blood between Elves and dragons. I hoped it would make the Elven Alliance even stronger.

After a couple hours, we reached the forest's outer edge. The snow was deeper, but we no longer had to go around trees, climb over logs, or untangle backpacks from creeper vines and snagging bushes. We ended up moving even faster, despite the heavier snow.

"Hey," I said, "does anyone else notice the snow isn't blinding you? I thought it was supposed to be a thing. 'Snow blind.' But it just seems like normal daylight."

Clara laughed at me, and I blushed. She said, "Don't be embarrassed. You haven't been in touch with your dragon for long. Once you reached your teens, your eyes adjust to light like a dragon's. Bright light doesn't blind you unless it's sudden, like a flare. Cool, huh?"

I agreed, it was pretty cool. I wondered what else I didn't have to worry about. Maybe I couldn't freeze to death, either. I hoped not—it was bitterly cold out here, especially when the breeze picked up.

Clara pointed ahead and a bit to the right. "There it is."

I turned to look where she pointed, and my eyes grew wide as saucers. There was a huge castle, right in the middle of Alaska. "Wow. Is that really what I think it is?"

She grinned and nodded. "It's an old Elven family holding. We haven't been there in years, so we had no idea the Elden had taken it over. It's huge, though."

"A castle is awesome and all, but how are we supposed to get in?" Eva asked. "Do they leave the drawbridge down or something?"

I was so distracted by the castle that I didn't notice when Clara stopped walking, and I almost ran into her. "Why did we stop?" I asked.

"Eva asks a good question."

"What do you mean?" Eva set her backpack down and stretched her back and shoulders.

Clara let her pack slide off, too. "The thing is impossible to get inside. The fortifications are impregnable. Also, it's in the middle of a huge lake."

That wasn't what I wanted to hear. "Wait a minute. If it's impossible to get into, how did you escape? If there's a way out, there has to be a way in."

Eva said, "Unless they blocked off the way she got out. That's what I'd do if I were Eldrick."

That did make sense. "So, what now?"

Clara smirked, looking like the cat that ate the canary. "I escaped through a door hidden in a wall, and I'm sure they've blocked that off by now. But I know something Eldrick doesn't. There's an entire system of tunnels running under both the castle and lake. I don't know it all, but I know how to get in and how to get to the castle. I can lead us through it."

Eva snapped her fingers, looking suddenly excited. "That's perfect! Once we get the Elves and Trolls loose, we have to get them out, right? We can just lead them back through the tunnels. With any luck, the Elden won't even know they're gone until it's too late."

I said, "I think they'll notice so many people moving around. They have to have guards watching the prisoners."

"Not if we can give them some sort of a distraction," Eva said. "If we can do something big enough, they won't be looking at the prisoners. That would be the perfect time to try to sneak them out."

That wasn't such a bad idea, actually. "I wonder if showing up at their gate would be enough of a distraction."

She shook her head. "I had something bigger in mind. This castle may have walls no one could get through, surrounded by a lake no one can get across, but that won't stop a dragon. I think when Cairo gets back with the dragon Realms, we can all give them the biggest distraction anyone ever saw. They could attack the castle itself from above while we rescue the Elves and Trolls."

I felt a little embarrassed. "Of course. I don't know why I didn't think of that. I'm just not used to thinking of things from a dragon's point of view, I guess."

"That won't work," Clara said. "Who knows how many decades or centuries Eldrick has had to build up the magical defenses around the castle? They were pretty strong to begin with, and he's had nothing but time to make them even stronger."

Eva grinned, wide enough to show her teeth. "Yeah, but you're forgetting about the Mere Treaty. The Mermaids can swim in the lake, maybe even help the Elves and Trolls to escape, but we can have them focus on breaking down the magical defenses so the troops can attack it."

Clara looked surprised. "You recruited the Mermaids? I can't believe it. The Mermaids stick to themselves even more than the dragons used to. That's fantastic news. I doubt Eldrick is making plans to deal with Mere magic."

I replied, "Yes, it was tough, but we got them to agree to join the alliance."

She looked relieved. "That might make all the difference. Mermaid magic is strong, and mereum isn't the same as mahier and tilium. It could even be the strongest magic there is, but it's also the slowest. That's perfect for bringing down the castle's defenses."

I rubbed my chin, thinking. "If Eldrick didn't think the Mermaids were joining us, then he hasn't had time to put in new magic against them, right?"

She nodded. "That sums it up."

I slid my backpack off and sat on a rock. "Now all we have to do is wait for Cairo and the dragon army. Then we can launch our surprise attack. The Mermaid queen taught me how to get in touch with her, and she said they would be ready for our call. As soon as we update Cairo, we can get the rescue started."

We only had to wait for about an hour before dark specks appeared in the sky on the horizon. I tried to count the specks, but there were too many. It was the dragons! More of them than I had ever seen before. I jumped to my feet and cheered their arrival. I cheered even louder when Jericho was the first to land. The plant must have worked.

Happy to see Jericho once again, I took a step to go greet him, but just then, my head reeled. I staggered as I felt another vision coming on, then toppled over.

Queen Desla's words flashed through my mind when I hit the ground: "...*If you have another vision, you'll die...*"

J.A. Culican

Chapter Twenty-Two

I fell to my hands and knees, snarling in frustration. If Eldrick found us, our cover would be blown and the element of surprise would be lost, just like the battle. And I definitely didn't want to die out here in the snow.

I pushed back against the vision, using all of my strength with both my mahier and tilium. No matter how hard I pressed, though, Eldrick's strength was greater. I could feel him pushing toward my mind, crushing my magic shell as he came closer and closer. His piercing thoughts drove like a nail straight toward my brain, pushing all my power aside. I grew desperate and frantically shoved back at him. He budged, but only slightly, and it wasn't enough. I couldn't keep this up for long, I knew.

My vision was black, but as though from a great distance, a light came toward me. I realized it must be Eldrick's latest vision, coming for me. My tilium was gone, my mahier was almost gone. When that flickered, the vision suddenly sprinted toward me even faster.

At the last second, I threw up all my remaining mahier. I had stopped the vision, but I was sweating with the effort. My strength was about to give out; there wasn't any way I could stop him. I was doomed.

Then, through the deep blackness I was floating in, I heard a voice, Eva's voice, and her soft and welcome whisper echoed all around me. It seemed to be coming from everywhere at once, and nowhere.

"Cole, fight it. You can do it, I have faith in you. You're not alone, I'm here with you. Cairo is here, and Jericho. Clara is here, and Desla. We are all around you right now, so fight!"

In her voice, I heard the love and friendship we shared. I felt warmth and strength flowing through me because of the love and trust they had for me. All of my friends standing around me felt a little different.

Memories shot through my mind like movie screens, whizzing by. Each one was a scene from my life. The day Eva and I met. The first time she stood up for me at school. Rylan and Sila telling me they loved me and had faith in me. Jericho spending long, frustrating hours training me. Desla, teaching me how to use and gather mereum to protect myself from Eldrick's magic.

And then, last of all, one flickering movie screen stopped for a just a heartbeat, right in front of me—my adopted parents on the day I left them, wrapping their arms around me and crying. *"We love you, Cole. No matter where you go, this is your home. You'll always be in our hearts, son."*

Eva was right. They were all right. I could do this. I was the Keeper of Dragons. The Fates picked me for this moment, right? It was my destiny to beat him, even when all seemed lost. To save the dragons, my parents, and my friends. To save the world from the Time of Fear.

I felt the water in the air around me, in the vast lake nearby, in the trees and plants that grew from that water.

Power was everywhere, surrounding me, more than I could ever need. I drew it into myself, feeling its essence.

My flickering mahier flared into life, shining bright in the darkness. It pushed away the vision Eldrick was trying to hammer me with. First an inch, then a foot, I pushed him away from me, away from my friends, away from my people. There was a loud *crack*, like a thunderbolt, and I knew it was his rage. I shoved him from my mind like he was just a leaf blowing in a typhoon.

The darkness faded. When my sight came back, everyone stood around me, supporting me. I looked up and grinned. I had done it.

***

Jericho beamed down at me as I climbed to my feet. He was usually angry like fire or just withdrawn, but now he didn't hesitate to wrap his arms around me in a warm embrace. "Thank Aprella you're all right," he said. "I never would have forgiven myself if anything happened to you while I was ill. Those leaves you brought back...the three of you saved my life. Thank you."

"I'm just glad you made it. I didn't have any faith that a bunch of leaves could fix you up, but here you are. I'm glad I listened to you."

He grinned at me. "Yes, for once. Hopefully, it becomes a habit."

Then Eva barreled into me, wrapping her arms around me. I looked into her eyes and couldn't help but smile. "Hello, there."

She wiped one eye and said, "Don't you ever scare me like that again. I thought we were gonna lose you."

***

After my magic battle with Eldrick, I was starving. They led me back to our makeshift camp, where they stacked tray after tray in front of me, loaded down with food. Once, I would've thought it was too much, but I knew better now. I dug in like I was really starving to death.

As I nibbled the last bits of meat off a rib, I looked around at the camp. It was fairly impressive, but half of it was empty. Maybe that was for the Mermaids when they arrived.

Cairo stood at the tree line with Eva. They faced one another, their bodies stiff and their arms straight at their sides. I smiled to myself, recognizing the nervousness they felt.

Cairo reached out and took Eva's hands in both of his and pulled her to him. He wrapped his arms around her. They stood like that for a minute, then he kissed her on her forehead and walked into the forest, pulling a smiling Eva after him. I was sure they had plenty to talk about before the battle, and I hoped they both made it through it. I didn't know what would happen to a *Vera Salit* if their soulmate died.

But then, Jericho walked up to me on my left, and Clara came up on my right. It wasn't until they got pretty close that they both stopped mid-step to stare at each other, looking surprised. That was interesting; taking a few steps back, I watched them.

Just out of earshot, Jericho talked softly to her. They both looked nervous. He kept scratching the back of his neck, and she grabbed her left elbow with her other hand.

I shook my head a little, not really sure what to do about it. If those two cared about each other so much, they should be together, even if they were from different people. Just because he was a dragon and she was an Elf didn't mean they couldn't be together, right? It seemed simple to me. Then again, I hadn't grown up in their cultures, with the bad feelings that simmered between Elves and dragons. I only hoped they'd figure it out before it was too late.

I grew bored of watching them whisper to each other, so I got busy finishing my food. A couple hours later, I felt like my old self again. I wandered off and found Cairo.

He grabbed me by the arm and pulled me to the side.

I looked around the field and saw two great armies, dragons on one side and Mermaids on the other. They must have arrived while I was eating everything in sight. I couldn't imagine Eldrick fighting off so many of us, but then again, he had beaten the Elves and Trolls together, stolen their tilium, taken down Paraiso, and done half a dozen other impossible things. Plus, we had no idea how many of Earth's dark races he had gathered as allies. Maybe we were outnumbered, for all I knew.

Cairo said, "You have to talk to the commanders. Desla, Jericho and Jude, and Clara, who's leading what's left of the Elves and Trolls. Plus the Fairy queen, since she managed to gather all the scattered Fairies together."

I grinned at him and he raised an eyebrow, looking confused. I said, "It's like the Battle of Five Armies. Our four and Eldrick's. Hopefully it ends with us winning, just like in the book."

He grinned. "I trust our Book of Aprella more than the book you mean. Ours says you're going to win."

"Good point." I chuckled.

I waited until Eva let me know the commanders were all together, then I walked into the tent with Eva at my side. I was nervous talking to so many commanders and members of royalty at once, but they all looked at me with bright, hopeful eyes when I came in. It turned out that, since it was she and I destined to drive back the Time of Fear, we'd be the ones in charge, too. I knew I couldn't let them down.

I told them our plan to use the tunnels to rescue the Elves and Trolls, and what we needed them each to do. Together, we worked out the details. Maybe we could have planned it better, but we didn't have time to get fancy with it. The Mermaids would take over the lake and hammer away at the castle's magic defenses, the dragons of Realm Five would swoop in with a surprise attack from above, and then the last part. Clara would bring Eva, Jericho, and me through the underground tunnel system. I hated the idea of being underground in those tunnels, but it was the best we could come up with.

Just as the sun went down, we broke up so the commanders could go instruct their armies, and Clara led us to the tunnel entrance. It looked just like a mouth, too, ready to swallow us up. I took a deep breath and followed Clara inside just as the battle above began.

J.A. Culican

Chapter Twenty-Three

I looked around at my little group, burning their faces into my memory in case any of us died on our mission. Clara and Jericho stood arm-in-arm, while Eva and Cairo stood so close together that their arms touched.

"Clara, I think we're ready. We'll follow you through the tunnels until we reach the middle of the castle. If you haven't found the prisoners by then, we'll come up underneath and see what we can do to help in the battle up there, while you keep searching." Jericho instructed.

"Follow me." She led us a short distance away, stopping at a large boulder. Then she stretched her arms wide to both sides and muttered under her breath. I couldn't understand what she said, but the words sounded beautiful, like a bird singing.

As she spoke, the rock's flat face began to glow, and a pattern started to shine. It started as a Celtic knot, and little tendrils of light twisted and turned, racing along as more and more of the knot work could be seen. At the end, the entire knot formed a beautiful, huge, door-shaped glyph. It suddenly flared bright enough to hurt my eyes, pulsated, and then in one last, bright flash, the entire glyph vanished. It left behind an archway with stairs going down. A cool, wet breeze blew out from the tunnel, smelling of rock and dust.

"Stay close to each other," she said. "These tunnels go on forever. It's one huge maze. If you get separated, I may not be able to find you. We don't have time to stop and look for anyone, either."

Cairo said, "So, what you're saying is, don't get lost?"

She smiled and nodded, then turned and headed down the stone stairs into the darkness below.

Once we were in the dark tunnel, I noticed small symbols all along the walls, and whenever anyone got within a few feet of one, it lit up. The tunnel branches all looked the same to me, which made me nervous. I was even more nervous when we left the main tunnel we had come in on. Instead, Clara led us to the left, then the right. We skipped a few doorways and then turned left again. Right, right again, and another two left turns. If anything happened to our guide, I'd be hopelessly lost.

I think we had been walking for almost an hour when the narrow tunnel opened up into a huge chamber. The floor here had been chiseled smooth, and the ceiling was smooth and high, maybe thirty feet above us. Scattered all through the chamber, stretching away into the darkness, stone pillars held up the ceiling. From what I could see, the room had been carved *around* the pillars, and they were all one stone with the ceiling and floor.

Clara stepped out onto that floor and all around her, the outline of a complicated symbol lit up, just like in the tunnels, but it stretched away and faded into the darkness. She stepped aside for the rest of us to come out of the tunnel, and wherever anyone stepped on the chamber floor, the outlines in the symbol lit up.

"So much for sneaking up on anyone," Jericho grumbled.

"Yes, that's going to be hard," Clara said. "We need to get through this chamber, though. There's another tunnel on the opposite side, just like the one we left, which takes us up into the castle."

I said, "Let's get moving, then. The war isn't waiting for us." I smiled at her and she grinned back, then she headed out across the chamber.

It was nerve-wracking the way the chamber stretched off into darkness in every direction, like I could easily get lost in a big, dark, featureless sea of stone. I was glad Clara seemed to know the way.

We had been making our away slowly across the floor, staying between one row of pillars. I couldn't keep my eyes off them, because every time we passed one, different symbols lit up in a pale blue light, and I could almost make sense of them. It was like each glyph showed one thing, but together, they told a story. I really wished I could understand the writing.

Ahead, I heard someone screech. I recognized Clara's voice. I scrambled forward, and saw everyone standing together, staring ahead. I followed their gaze to see what they were looking at.

My jaw dropped. Up ahead were rows after rows of iron cages, and in each one sat an Elf or a Troll. None of the cages were tall enough for them to stand up, and I could only imagine the pain of sitting on those iron bars this entire time without being able to stretch out, even.

Jericho muttered, "By Aprella…"

I was awestruck. I hadn't realized Eldrick had taken so many people. Then I realized these weren't even all of them, just the ones who hadn't turned dark yet. The army Eldrick must have gathered from them was stunning.

"Let's get them out of there before Eldrick realizes we're here," I said.

Clara and Jericho wasted no time. They stormed up to the cages and held their hands to the locks, one after the other. Each time they did, there was a flash of light and then the door creaked open. If only the Elves and Trolls still had their tilium, they could have easily released themselves. It made me angry and sad just looking at them, locked up like that.

I hurried after the others and got busy undoing locks. It turned out to be easy with mahier—just will it to open, and it did.

The prisoners started to climb out, but they moved slowly because their legs and backs were cramped from sitting so long. Before they could get out, though, all the doors slammed shut at once. It made a deafening *clang*. I looked around in surprise.

A terrible cackle echoed through the chamber. The noise bounced off the walls and pillars, making it impossible to tell where it came from. Then a deep voice in the darkness said, "You didn't think I knew where Clara was? I may not have been able to follow the Keeper, but once she escaped, I knew she'd be back. I knew she'd come through these tunnels."

Clara shouted back, "That's why you didn't send anyone after me?"

"You fool. You've walked into my trap, and even better, you brought the Keepers with you. Soon this will all be over, and the Earth will be mine."

Across the darkness in every direction, we saw lights coming. Dozens and dozens, all streaming toward us. Elden, and they'd be on top of us in moments.

Jericho shouted, "To arms! Stand back to back!"

Clara's high-pitched, beautiful voice rang out and said, "No! Run, back the way we came. We can come back later. There are too many of them."

In a panic, we all ran, but we only got a few steps before dozens more lights flared up, coming toward us from the direction of the escape tunnel.

"Is there another tunnel?" I asked. "Better lost than dead."

Clara nodded and ran off into the darkness in the only direction we saw no enemy lights. After a minute, we reached the chamber's wall, but it was smooth and unbroken.

I said, "Where are the tunnels?"

She shook her head. "They should be here! He must have closed them."

Jericho drew his sword. "Then get your backs to the wall. They're almost on us, and we're going to have to fight our way out."

That was wishful thinking. Eldrick's soldiers were close enough now that I could make out some of their faces. Some were Elden, others were dark Elves, but there were way too many of them. I drew the Mere Blade, the sword Desla had given me. It glowed brightly. At least I would take as many of them with us as I could.

I said, "Eva, I'm sorry I got you into this."

She grunted, then said, "There's no one I'd rather be fighting next to. We tried to save the world, but win or lose, what mattered is that we tried."

Eldrick's voice rang out again, laughing. "No, what matters is that you died. Soon, friends, I'll dance on your bodies."

The huge crowd of Elden and dark Elves had surrounded us, but a bunch of them in the middle stepped aside to let Eldrick come through. He stopped just outside of striking distance and grinned.

I readied myself to try to charge at him. This was my chance. Maybe I could take him with us.

Chapter Twenty-Four

Eldrick and his forces barreled toward us. He had a sneer on his face, his lips curled up to bare his teeth. As his soldiers rushed us, he threw his head back and laughed, and the menacing sound echoing through the chamber sent a shiver down my spine.

He held his hand up when they were just about to smash into us, and they stopped and backed up. He looked at us for a long moment without saying anything, but then he said, "I could just kill you all at once, but that seems so much less satisfying than killing you one at a time. Just watching the looks on your faces as one friend after another dies on my blade sounds entertaining. You all irritate me, after all, and where would be the justice in killing you all at once?"

I knew he meant it, too. In my mind, I ran through one plan after another, but had to toss each aside. They wouldn't work.

Maybe I couldn't save us all, but I thought I might be able to save some of my friends. I raised my chin at him and shouted, "I don't honestly think you want to kill your sister, and the rest of these people simply did what I told them. I'm the Keeper of Dragons, after all. Why don't you let them go and just take me? When they see what you do to me, all your enemies will know they've been beaten. Kill their spirits, their hope, and let them live with that. That's the ultimate punishment."

"Cole, no, don't do it!" Eva cried.

Eldrick locked eyes with me. He brought one hand up and stroked his chin, making a big show of considering my offer. That's when I knew he was going to say no. It had been a long shot anyway, though.

He said, "Or—and I'm just throwing ideas out, here— why don't I just kill all of them one by one *and then* torment you? I think it's a better ending than letting them go, don't you think?"

He was right, it would be a worse thing than just torturing me and letting them go. I didn't have an answer for him, but nothing I said would have changed his mind anyway.

I fixed my grip on the Mere Blade and got ready for the fighting to start.

"Elden, wait!" Eldrick shouted. "I think I'll kill Jericho first. Attack the rest, but don't kill them, yet. I want them to see them die."

He got a gleam in his eye and strolled toward Jericho while the Elden swarmed toward the rest of us, and the fight was on.

My sword cut through the Elden weapons as easily as it cut through them. I didn't know how many I killed, three or four at least, but even so, they managed to cut us off from Jericho. He had to fight Eldrick alone.

The Elden stopped pressing their attack. They stood between us and Jericho, and there was nothing we could do to help him. We could only watch in horror as he fought Eldrick one-on-one.

Eldrick thrust, but Jericho blocked it and then lunged. He batted Jericho's sword aside and, in one smooth movement, came around with a backhanded slash. His sword left a deep cut on the dragon's left arm, above the elbow.

Jericho roared in pain and lunged again, but Eldrick blocked the attack and his blade missed by an inch. Eldrick swept his blade downward, and left another cut on Jericho's right thigh. This time, Jericho cried out in pain and staggered back. He was wounded, and I could see he was slowing down. I thought the fight would be over soon and fought the urge to try to cut my way through all those Elden to go help my friend. I knew that would have been suicide, though.

Eldrick laughed. He had started to toy with Jericho, adding more cuts but not really trying to kill the dragon. My blood boiled. He said, "And so falls the mighty Jericho, so-called guardian of Ochana. How pathetic."

He lunged forward and there was a quick flash of blades coming together—but then Jericho was disarmed, his blade skittering a few feet away on the smooth rock floor. Eldrick raised his blade above his head and, cackling like a madman, rushed at Jericho to deliver a killing blow.

Clara cried out wordlessly, the most anguished and painful sound I think I'd ever heard, like her soul was being torn apart. She held her hand out at Eldrick and Jericho as if that would somehow stop him, and I closed my eyes. I didn't want to see any of it, not Jericho dying, and not her dying inside. But I peeked anyway—I couldn't help it.

And yet, it did stop him. His blade came sweeping down in a deadly arc toward Jericho's head, but inches away, the blade stopped like it had hit a rock. There was a flare, blindingly bright, and at first, I thought Clara had put some sort of a shield up over Jericho. I think all of our jaws must have dropped when we saw that. But I gasped in shock when I realized the bright light covered not Jericho, but Eldrick and all of his soldiers, too.

Clara screamed, rage and fear in her voice. "No! I'll kill you, brother. Today, you die here." Light streamed from her hand toward Eldrick and his soldiers. It got brighter and brighter, and then began to push them back as she swept her hand to one side—moving him away from Jericho. I had no idea what she was doing and had never heard of anything like it. From Jericho's shocked expression, I could see he'd never seen it, either.

Eldrick and the Elden wasted no time. They began to hack furiously at the light that surrounded them. Then one of the soldier's blades shattered when it struck the barrier. Eldrick snarled and screamed in rage.

I felt a tug at my sleeve and looked over. It was Eva. She whispered, "Come on, now's your chance. Let's free the Elves and Trolls."

We took off, working our way around the blinding light that held the Elden away. I got to the first cage and put my hand over the lock, willing it to open. There was a brief, faint glow and a click, and the door open. One after the other, Eva and I let the prisoners escape.

Nearby, there was an area that looked like it was for guards, with weapons racks and shelves full of supplies. One of the Elves bashed open the locks, then began throwing every sort of weapon to the other Elves and Trolls as they escaped. Soon, we had a dozen or more armed new friends. Some joined Clara and Cairo, but the others kept passing out swords and spears while Eva and I released more of our captured allies.

I realized then that, when Clara's shield failed or she ran out of tilium, it wouldn't matter—the enemy was outnumbered. The only way out for them was to go back the way they had come, up into the castle.

Eldrick must have realized that, too, because he stopped trying to slash through the shield and shouted for the Elden to retreat. They fled away from us and headed toward the stairwell that would lead them up into the castle.

Cairo shouted, "They're getting away. Clara, bring down the shield."

"I can't! I don't know how I did it in the first place or how to bring it down."

Unfortunately, her barrier blocked us from pursuing Eldrick. We could only stand and watch as he ran. It only took a couple minutes for Clara's tilium to be drained, but by then our enemy was long gone.

Jericho shouted, and then there was a commotion. I turned to look just as Clara collapsed. He caught her before she hit the ground and gently lowered her, resting her head in his lap.

I made my way through the freed Elves to join Cairo watching them. Clara looked terrible. Her cheeks were sunken and her eyes were dark with huge bags under them. She tried to talk, but nothing came out.

Jericho said, "Hush, save your strength. Please, just lay still."

The corners of Clara's mouth turned up into a weak smile. She took a deep breath and then, with great effort, said in a feeble voice, "I've always known how you felt about me, Jericho."

"That doesn't matter now," he said. "You need to save your strength. What can we do to help?"

She reached up with one trembling hand and placed her fingertips on his cheek. "It does matter, more than anything. You've loved me, and I have always loved you even before you told me how you felt. Nothing has changed over the years. I wish I had been brave enough to tell you."

He leaned down, and she wrapped her arms around his neck as he planted his lips on hers.

Feeling awkward, I looked away. They deserved privacy. Those two had loved each other for decades, or maybe centuries, and they had been too stubborn to say it, too afraid to take a chance on their love for one another. They both had to almost die to make them realize that none of us have forever, and we might not even have tomorrow. I was happy to let them show each other how they felt after all that time.

A few seconds later, I heard Jericho standing, so I looked back over. He was helping Clara stand, and Cairo rushed forward to grab her other arm. Together, they got her to her feet. She was still weak, but she could finally stand.

I looked around the room and saw all the Elves and Trolls were armed, and there were so many of them that we had a small army of our own. We could throw them into the battle going on in the castle above us, and maybe even make a difference.

"Jericho, Eldrick is getting away," I said. "There's a battle going on right over our heads. Lead us up into the castle. I think a new army hitting the defenders by surprise ought to make quite a difference, don't you?"

He turned and barked some orders, and quickly got the Elves and Trolls divided into smaller units. He put two of the smaller squads under each of us—Eva, Cairo, Clara, himself, and me—and we rushed toward the stairwell, out of the dungeon, and up into the castle.

What I saw when I came up into the light of day was a total surprise. There was still fighting going on, but it was clustered into little knots. There were enough bodies to account for the rest, and it was clear we'd almost taken the castle. Whatever Elden and dark Elves still lived must have fled with Eldrick.

Eva turned and wrapped her arms around me, burying her face in my shoulder. She muttered, "It's over. We saved the Elves and Trolls, and now it's over. We can go back to our lives."

I wasn't so sure about that. Eldrick was still alive after all, but I let her have her moment.

All around us, Elves, Trolls, and everyone else roared, cheering their great victory.

Chapter Twenty-Five

Once the battle was over and the last few Elden had been swept away by swords and flames, our army celebrated. I was happy to join them. At long last, the threat was over, Eldrick was defeated, and we could all get on with our lives.

Somewhere during all that celebrating, dozens more dragons showed up carrying a feast of food, and the lakeshore camp turned into one big victory party. It had been a close battle, and only Eldrick running away in the middle had guaranteed our win. Everyone there had fought and they'd earned a celebration as far as I was concerned.

After I'd had plenty to eat and regained my spent mahier, Cairo and Eva found me while I was listening to a Mere soldier talking about the battle.

"C'mon," Cairo said. "I guess there's going to be a meeting inside and they want you and Eva there, too."

I shook hands with the soldier and followed Cairo into the castle. Once out in the courtyard, I was greeted by Prince Gaber and Queen Annabelle. King Evander of the Trolls, Queen Desla, and Jericho were also there waiting for us.

Gaber said, "Now that the Keepers are here, let's all take a seat. We have much to discuss."

There were a dozen chairs nearby, so I grabbed one. We arranged ourselves in a little circle, which I thought was appropriate. Without a table, no one could be at the head. It was just another sign that the alliance was getting stronger. That was a good thing, because I was sure that although the Elden had been chased off, there were still plenty of enemies in the world.

Annabelle cleared her throat and then said, "Fighting together, we've taken a great victory here today, yet there is still much work to be done. Most of the Elves still don't have their tilium. Eldrick is on the loose, still working with the Carnites. He has two armies under him, the Elden and the dark Elves. So many of them escaped, they could still cause problems."

"I think we have little to fear from him," Jericho said. "The Elven Alliance stands as strong as it ever did, and the dragons will keep working to restore the trust we once had. We went down the wrong path under our old king, but Rylan has always valued our alliances."

Desla stood to speak, shaking her head. "There is still a lot of bad blood between the other races and dragons. Today went a long way toward healing old wounds, but don't make the mistake of thinking that trust is regained because you joined us for one battle. And Eldrick is a master of taking advantage of hidden resentments no one else may even see. He has always seemed able to find the weak points—as any Elf can tell you."

I wasn't sure why everyone seemed so pessimistic. Well, not Jericho, but probably all the others. It was a little frustrating. I said, "I agree. The alliance is stronger than it has been a long time, and it does still have problems. But I promise you, the dragons won't rest until they fix the damage they did. Anyway, why do we need to talk about these problems right now? We beat Eldrick and he's on the run. All of us will hunt him around the globe, right?"

Jericho said, "It's only a matter of time until we find him and finish what we started here."

"Definitely. And for the first time since I found out I was a dragon, I don't have this ball of worry in my gut saying everything is hopeless. Now, I see the hope. I think lots of people will agree."

Eva smiled at me, and I could tell she agreed.

I continued, "I know we need to strengthen the alliance, because there's always going to be another threat down the road. But the Time of Fear is over, right? For now, I think we should all just take one great big sigh of relief. Just let our people party together like they used to. The more we do that, the less damage Eldrick can do before we finally hunt him down once and for all." I slammed my fist into my other palm as I said that.

Jericho nodded at me, and I could see approval in his expression. I think that look was the best part of my day, besides helping to free the prisoners. "And that day—"

I thought I heard a strange noise and stopped talking. I cocked my head, trying to listen. Then I realized what it was—there was a growing roar coming from our army's camp. At first, I worried it was some new threat, but then I heard a clear victory cheer.

"What's going on out there, do you think?" Gaber asked.

Jericho shook his head. "There's only one way to find out. I say we take a break and go see."

We got up and headed toward the drawbridge. Once we stepped out onto those old, thick timbers, I saw the mob of soldiers in the field, making a path for... What? I squinted, trying to see well, and caught sight of people coming out of the woods bordering the camp.

Gaber shouted with excitement, his voice rising into something like a cheer. I looked at him, confused. He met my eyes and said, "I can't believe it. It's the ancestors! They've returned! That can only mean our tilium will be coming back soon, too. They wouldn't have come out if our victory hadn't been total."

Jericho grinned, baring his teeth like a predator and said, "Proof that Eldrick is finished. He just doesn't know it yet."

That's when the party really got going. It lasted long into the night.

***

We were flying back to Ochana and all the dragons were in high spirits. Eva and I flew side-by-side, talking excitedly about the battle and everything that had happened. When the dragon flying in front of me stopped, I almost crashed right into her, but I stopped short at the last second. I saw Jericho hovering, long neck hanging down as he looked at something below us.

I tried to see what he was looking at. There was a black spot way below, on the ground. It had to be really big for us to see it from so high up. I flew over to him and asked, "Is that normal? I haven't seen anything like that before."

He looked up. "No, Cole, that is definitely not normal. I don't know what it is."

I had an itch at the back of my mind that I couldn't scratch. Something about the scene below looked familiar, but I didn't think it was the blackened area.

We kept going after Jericho said we'd send Realm Two out to scout it later.

Two-hundred miles farther on, we saw another spot. This one was bigger than the last. Jericho exchanged a worried glance with Cairo, but called for us to continue onward.

When we had gone maybe another five-hundred miles, we spotted a third blackened area, even bigger.

At each spot, I had that weird itch at the back of my mind. I told Jericho we should check it out. We flew lower, but when we got close, I saw a weird rock formation nearby. It looked like three big boulders stacked together. That's when it hit me, what had been bugging me—I recognized this place. I realized I had seen the other places, too.

"Oh my gosh," I blurted, "I know what these are. I know these places."

"Where do you know these from?" Jericho's voice sounded tight with worry, and with good reason.

I told him, "These are some of the places where Eldrick sacrificed Trolls. I saw them in my visions. They were all over the earth. Farms, jungles, snow... Everywhere."

In his eyes, I didn't see the reassurance I had hoped for. Instead, his eyes grew wide and he said exactly what I had hoped he wouldn't. "The land is already dying. I didn't think he had killed enough to start it, but apparently he did."

My heart sank. I hadn't wanted to believe it, but when Jericho said it out loud, I knew it was true. "The Trolls he killed..."

He nodded. "They were enough to cause the environment to start deteriorating. If you don't find a way to reverse this, the Earth itself is going to be nothing more than a wasteland."

Cairo, sounding terrified, said, "By Aprella, this is the end of everything. Maybe we won the battle, but Eldrick is going to destroy everything anyway. The world will be his, if we can't find out how to stop this."

Without looking, I reached out with one wingtip and grabbed Eva's. The day before had been just one small win in the bigger picture. We rushed back to Ochana as fast as we could go. I didn't know how much time we had to figure things out, but I knew we would all work as hard as we could to save the world—again.

THE CROWNS' ACCORD

KEEPER OF DRAGONS

BOOK 4

For my eldest daughter, Julianna and her wish to share bedtime stories of dragons and adventures with all.

Chapter One

I dove into the lake, slicing through the calm water. The coolness was refreshing, and I swallowed a few big mouthfuls because my throat was dry and raw from all the shouting during combat training.

Coming up for air, I looked across the field to make sure the Mere Blade was still leaning against a nearby rock in its scabbard. The wondrous sword the mermaids had let me use would cut through almost anything just like butter. That included the training swords, so for training, I had to use a normal training blade. We weren't trying to kill anyone, after all.

As I slogged out of the lake, water streaming off of me and dripping from my clothes, I used my hands to wipe as much water as I could out of my hair. My mop had started out shaggy and was now actually getting long. I had decided to let it grow out so I could eventually put it in a ponytail. Eva told me she thought it would look good on me, and I trusted my best friend's judgment.

Dirt and sand clung to my feet as I slid them into my sandals, but they'd dry out soon and be easy to clean. Eva stood on the lakeshore, watching me. She had an amused smirk on her face. "Sometimes I think you're turning into a mermaid. If you spent as much time training as you did swimming, maybe you wouldn't be so clumsy with your sword."

I stuck my tongue out at her. "Haha. Just because you'll only go swimming when Cairo is in the water doesn't mean you enjoy it any less than me. Speaking of Cairo, where is your *Vera Salit?* I saw he and Jericho left halfway through the morning session, but I didn't see them come back."

Eva looked around as if only noticing for the first time that Cairo was gone. I didn't buy her act. With those eagle eyes of hers, she knew where Cairo was all the time. She replied, "Probably helping the Elves rebuild Paraiso. I'm so glad the Elves are back, and they've been treating us a lot better since we rescued them from Eldrick."

I shuddered, and it wasn't from the cool breeze blowing across my wet skin. I wondered if his name would ever stop having that effect on me. "Thankfully, there hasn't been any sign of him these past few weeks, ever since the battle at the castle in Alaska. I hope we never see him again."

"I hope so, too," she said, handing me a towel. "But none of the scouts have seen Eldrick, or the Dark Elves and Elden, or even the Carnites he recruited. Not even the Realm Two scouts have seen them, and I think that if they were anywhere to be found, Realm Two dragons would be the ones to find them."

I looked up at the sun. There was a large gap in the Congo's jungle canopy around the lake. I looked back at Eva and said, "Maybe our break is about to end. Let's go find Jericho and see what he wants us to do. I know we were supposed to help out with some of the rebuilding today, but you know. And like you said, maybe Cairo is with him."

Eva smiled. Of course, she knew where he was, but I played along and smiled back. "Yes, they change our routine every day, usually so we can do more training. I don't know about you, but I would rather rebuild than beat each other up some more. Those sticks hurt."

I was totally on board with that. I was covered in bruises which I hadn't bothered to use my mahier to heal yet. I headed across the training field and grabbed the Mere Blade on my way. Eva followed. I slung the sword over my shoulder and then Eva and I walked together into Paraiso. The Elven capital had been the most beautiful place I had ever seen, and it would be again, someday.

We went to the treehouse everyone had just sort of agreed would be the headquarters for all the building projects. It wouldn't take long for the Elves to regrow their city, but it wouldn't happen overnight, not when it had been torn up so badly by Eldrick's troops. At least the Elves' magic wards were back up, so we didn't have to worry about any wandering humans anymore, or even about enemies finding the place. Okay, that wasn't really true—I still worried about it, but at least we were in less danger of it now that the wards were up again.

When we got to the HQ, I spotted Jericho and Cairo talking with Gaber, Prince of the Elves. Those two had pretty much hated each other since long before I was born, partly because the dragons had abandoned them once and partly because of the thing between Jericho and Clara.

The war had brought them together, and gone a long way toward healing old wounds. Yay for them. I had new wounds to make up for them.

Eva bolted ahead of me and skidded to a stop near Jericho. She stood by quietly, grinning and waiting for him to finish talking. That gave me a chance to catch up—the last thing I wanted to do was more exercise after that last training session.

As I stepped up next to Eva, I heard Jericho say, "You're absolutely right. He should have made a move by now."

Gaber replied, "I know Eldrick better than anyone, though I hate the fact that he's my brother. If he hasn't made a move by now, and he's laying low so well that even dragons can't find his trail, it means he's planning something big."

Jericho's red eyes flared a little brighter, and puffs of smoke left his nose. I could always tell when he was mad, and so could everyone else.

Eva took advantage of the short pause in their conversation. "Is there anything we can do to help right now?"

I cringed a little because when he was puffing smoke like that, it was best to let him talk to you first. His head whipped toward Eva and he snarled. Eva didn't cringe like I had, but then again, she never looked afraid of anything.

"In Aprella's name, what are you two doing standing around?" Jericho snapped. "We don't have time for this laziness. If you had fought the war as slow as you are moving today, we would all be saluting our new king, Eldrick."

I didn't think he was being fair to her, and before I could stop myself, I blurted, "She's not the one you're mad at." When he looked at me, eyes flaring again, I added, "We aren't lazy, we came to find out what we should be doing. It's time to help rebuild Paraiso, right?"

Jericho's eyes flared brighter for an instant, but I didn't back down. That was new for me because before the war, I was afraid when he was talking to me, much less mad at me. He could still be dangerous, but not to me, I had learned. He wouldn't do anything to harm the Keeper of Dragons.

He interrupted my thoughts, yelling, "Why don't you exercise something other than your mouth, for once? Besides, you trying to help around here does more harm than good, clumsy. Let's see how your stamina training has been doing, instead. Both of you, take a five-mile run through the jungle. Hit the obstacle course!"

My jaw dropped. He was obviously more upset than I had thought. I tried to apologize, but as soon as I open my mouth, he barked, "Do it now!"

Okay, maybe things hadn't changed as much as I had thought because before I had a chance to even think about it, I found myself running through Paraiso toward the jungle. My heart was pounding with something suspiciously like fear.

Eva was only a couple steps behind me as we made our way through the trees lined with their once-gorgeous treehouses, and headed toward the thicker, wild jungle outside of the Elves' capital. Once we burst through the tree line, we had to slow a little bit because the going got harder. It didn't take long to feel hot again, and I soon had little beads of sweat building on my forehead.

We got to the beginning of the obstacle course a few minutes later that marked the start of our five-mile run. The O-Course was a marked path through the jungle that took us across all sorts of terrain. We'd have to jump, duck, vault over things, swim across a big stream, go up and down rocky hills that were more like giant boulders than hills, all while trying not to twist my ankle by catching it in a root or running over the uneven ground. Every time a tree fell, it tore the root ball up and left a hole, and the torn-up root ball slowly broke down and gathered dirt to become a little mound. The jungle was full of these pits and mounds, and if we weren't careful, it was easy to twist an ankle. The day before, I miraculously avoided twisting my ankle, but Eva had to limp back to Paraiso and get healed. It all added up to make the O-course run my least favorite training exercise of all time.

Breathing heavily, I asked Eva, "Why don't we just summon our dragons and fly over all this? We shouldn't even waste our time with the course. We'll never use this training, not when we can fly."

Panting, Eva said, "You remember the time we had to fly all the way to Ochana, right? Remember how wiped out we were after that trip? Stop complaining and start running faster, Cole!" She took off, pulling ahead.

I didn't speed up, though. It wasn't worth limping back to Paraiso.

After a few minutes, even though I was jumping and climbing over obstacles, my mind wandered and I fell into kind of a trance just listening to my own steady breathing like Jericho had taught us. He said it made it easier to run farther, but I still felt just as tired.

I almost ran into Eva as I came around a bend. She stood in the middle of the trail. I stopped and put my hands on my knees while I sucked in as much air as I could. "What... What's up?" I gasped.

She didn't reply, and I noticed she was staring at something with her mouth open.

I turned to see what she was looking at, and then I froze, too. Far ahead of us, the dimly-lit jungle grew darker, but it wasn't the light that did it. The Congo had become black in patches. The farther back I looked, the thicker the patches became. Even the trees were blackened. Around the spot's edges, bright green leaves weren't as bright, like someone had mixed gray into their colors. I stared for half a minute, and even as I watched, I could see the green-gray plants turning grayer.

In a whisper, Eva said, "It's like they've been burned. They're getting burned without any fire, Cole." I could hear a rising uneasiness in her voice.

I understood the feeling. A shiver ran down my spine, and every instinct told me to run away. It broke my heart to see the beautiful jungle blackening right in front of my eyes. The Congo was starting to die all around us. It was happening even faster than we had thought.

I spit into the dirt and cursed Eldrick's name. "Come on, we have to go warn the others."

Chapter Two

Without a word, Eva and I both leaped into the air together, shifting into our dragons. We flew back to Paraiso as fast as we could. I scanned as far as I could feel with my mahier. In every black area, I couldn't feel anything with my senses. Actually, it wasn't that I didn't feel anything; it was more like I could actually feel the nothing, as if it was something all by itself—something dark and evil. I sensed the jungle's black splotches getting thicker and thicker the farther away I checked, until they grew together into one giant, growing black mass miles away.

When we reached the Elven homeland, Paraiso, we dove. Elves scattered at our sudden appearance. Right before hitting the ground, we shifted into our human forms and landed. As soon as we got our footing, we bolted toward the reconstruction HQ. I figured Jericho would be there since he was putting so much time into helping the Elves. Eva was hot on my tail. When we got close enough to recognize the people standing around the dozens of boards they used to pin up plans and diagrams I didn't understand, I spotted him.

He saw me running toward him and cocked his head, confused. I skidded to a halt right in front of him, panting and ignoring the cloud of dust I kicked up at him.

Jericho put his hand on his sword hilt and looked all around. "What's wrong? Did you see a Carnite?" I could hear the tension in his voice and wondered if there had been sightings, but that wasn't why we were there.

Eva came to a stop next to me, panting as hard as I was. She shook her head. "No. Worse. The black spots we saw on the way to Ochana after the battle for the Alaskan castle. The spots are here. They're in the Congo!"

Jericho's eyes went wide. I wasn't used to seeing fear on his face. He turned to another dragon and shouted, "Go find Prince Gaber and tell him to set up an emergency meeting. Tell them to bring the Troll king, too. Why are you standing there staring at me? Run!"

He turned to face Eva and me. "Come with me. This is urgent."

No kidding. That's why Eva and I had rushed back so fast. I didn't argue, though, and we followed him as he stormed across the field. He went so fast, I almost had to run to keep up as he left the training area, heading to the Elven meeting hall. His long legs were a blur. I ended up jogging to keep up, and we quickly arrived at the meeting hall.

Prince Gaber was also just arriving, and I noticed he had his weapons on him. He brushed his hands together to knock off the dirt caked on them from reconstruction, then wiped his hands on his trousers. I couldn't tell whether he looked irritated or concerned. I figured both were good reactions, though. "What's going on?" he asked. "Your soldier told me to rush, as though I answer to a mere dragon soldier's summons. I sent a messenger to alert King Evander, just like you asked. He should be here soon."

Jericho put his hands on my shoulder and replied, "Cole and Eva saw something. We'll get into it when Evander arrives. I wasn't trying to summon you, fool, I meant to warn you."

Gaber said, "It isn't healthy to warn me about anything, not here in my own homeland." He scrambled up the tree toward the meeting hall, and Eva and I followed him.

Inside, Gaber took his seat at the head of the table and stared at Jericho as he came in. I took a seat on one side, and Eva sat across from me, but Jericho didn't sit. He paced back and forth, talking to himself and moving his hands like he was having a conversation. I wasn't sure if he really was just talking to himself or if he was letting Ochana know what was going on. I didn't interrupt him since he seemed a little crazy.

The door burst open again and King Evander stormed inside. He looked as dirty as Gaber, and I decided they must have both been working on repairs. He yanked back the chair at the foot of the table, hard enough that it almost flew across the room. He slammed it down on the ground after snatching it in mid-flight, then sat and yelled, "What is the meaning of this? What's the emergency that you feel fit to *summon* me to discuss?"

Well, I thought to myself, at least he was taking it seriously.

Jericho sat between me and Gaber, but he didn't stop fidgeting and shifting in his seat. He said, "The Keeper of

Dragons were out training on an endurance run through the obstacle course—"

Evander cut him off, saying, "That's not why you called me here. Tell me what's going on!"

Gently, Gaber said, "Evander, my friend. How many Trolls did you lose to Eldrick?"

Evander looked around the table, then back at Gaber. "A lot. Unless you found a way to make more Trolls today, I'm guessing that's not why I'm here."

I almost rolled my eyes at his outburst, but I caught myself in time. I said, "No, not a lot—*too many*. That's the right answer. We know there are spots dying all over the world because of what Eldrick did to your Trolls, and I'm sorry for that, and not just because there's not enough Trolls left to keep the land healthy."

Eva stood and planted her hands on the table with a loud bang, then shouted, "That's a problem, but we have a bigger problem right here and now. *The Congo is dying.* Whatever those black lands are, it's grown all the way to the Congo, and it's almost here."

Evander's jaw dropped and his nostrils flared. "I couldn't have imagined it had extended this far so quickly."

Gaber nodded. None of us had thought it would, not yet. He said, "Dragon and Elven scouts all say the same thing—the land is mutating. It's like some sort of disease, and it's spreading through the Earth. We've examined some of it, and it isn't just dead. It looks and feels as though it has been burned, but there is no heat. We dug

560

down and saw that the blackened areas go all the way down into the roots."

"It goes deeper than that," Jericho said. "We dug down, too, following the roots to see where it would end. It didn't end. The roots ended, but reports say that it looks like thin, black tendrils keep going, shooting from the root tips. They tried to follow them to see how far they go, and gave up after twenty or so yards."

It was my turn for my eyes to go as wide as saucers. I had no idea it was so bad. "We have to find a way to stop it before it destroys everything! Maybe we can use tilium, if all the Elves and Trolls got together and—"

Jericho cut me off. "The issue is that there aren't enough Trolls left to heal the land, much less sustain it. Tilium won't do it, so to save the Earth, we have to find another way to bring the land back to life. We must do it before it perishes permanently."

"Are we sure it will even die permanently?" Gaber asked. "Do we know that it won't heal itself or learn to fight off the disease?"

Jericho frowned. "It looks dead to me. Dead, but not dead."

I liked Gaber's idea, but we couldn't count on ideas. "This isn't some normal disease. It isn't because of magic. It's because of a *lack* of magic, so I don't think waiting around is how we fix it. I didn't know the Earth could die permanently, though. Do we know how long it takes for that to happen, once it turns black?"

Everyone shook their heads and my heart sank. I had hoped that Gaber, at least, would've been around long enough to know. I could only guess it had never happened before.

"Why don't we reach out to Ochana for help?" I suggested. "Tilium may not be the answer, but mahier could be."

Gaber glowered at me, catching me by surprise. He said, "Dragons aren't the answer. Besides, I don't trust them. The Elden were Elves, once, and this is an Elf problem. We'll work it out amongst ourselves. As the new saying goes, only a fool trusts a dragon to help when it matters."

After everything we'd been through together, I couldn't believe what I was hearing. What would it take for dragons to regain their trust? The Elves were as stubborn as dragons. My heart beat faster and I had to stop myself from doing something stupid. Instead, I shouted, "The whole world is at risk, and the Elves want to hide it and try to deal with it yourselves? If you could have fixed this, you already would have. This isn't the time for stupid grudges."

Gaber's eyes were almost glowing with anger. He clapped his hands twice, and two Elven soldiers grabbed me by either arm. I tried to argue with Gaber but he ignored me as the two dragged me away.

Chapter Three

When I hit the ground, I staggered and fell. I got to my feet and pressed the leaves and dirt off. I might have even spit on the ground, I was so angry. I didn't know what to do, so I decided to head toward the training ground and let off some steam beating up training dummies with wooden swords. I would've liked to cut them into little pieces with the Mere Blade, but even as mad as I was, I knew that might cause some problems. On my way there, I passed a couple of Elves who smiled and waved, but I only glared at them and kept walking. They gave me a wide berth.

When I got to the training area, I picked up a dull wooden sword and sprinted at the nearest training dummy. I aimed at its neck as I went by, and amazingly, I hit right where I was aiming. The *thwack* was satisfying. One step beyond the dummy, I used my momentum to spin around and from behind, I smacked the sword against the side of its head. *Thwack*. I must've hit it twenty more times—*thwack, thwack, thwack*—before I settled down.

If I was being honest, the truth was that it wasn't as satisfying as I'd thought it would be. Once I realized that, the anger came back like a tidal wave. I screamed, my face turning red, and threw the sword as hard as I could. It flew through the air, end over end, in a graceful arc. The metal bands around the wooden hilt glinted in the sunlight right before it splashed into the lake some twenty feet from shore.

I let out another roar. I'd have to go get it. Nothing was going my way. I kind of felt like the sword had it out for me. The Elves had made it, and I felt a little like they had it out for me, too. They were in it together, the Elves and the stupid wooden sword.

I knew that wasn't rational, but as angry as I was, I couldn't help feeling that way.

I wasn't ready yet to go fish the sword out of the lake. Somehow, leaving it in there for a little while felt good, like I was standing up for myself somehow. I clenched my fists as tightly as I could by my sides and stood looking at the ground as I fought to get my anger under control. I knew I wasn't helping anyone, as mad as I was, and they hadn't really done anything to deserve it. I was just overloaded. Yelling at the Elves might have been satisfying, but it wouldn't get me what I wanted, which was for them to take this seriously and take the help Ochana offered, and work with dragons to try to help save the world. Their stupid pride was in the way.

I really wanted to just punch Gaber in his smug face, but that *really* wouldn't have helped anything. Besides, when I wasn't steaming mad, I liked him a lot and thought the feeling was mutual. He flew off the handle because he's mad, scared even.

Maybe what made me the maddest was just feeling so helpless. I couldn't get the Elves and dragons to work together, I couldn't save the world from black spots I didn't understand and couldn't prevent, and I didn't have any control over my life because I was supposedly this mythical Keeper of Dragons. As if I had asked for that. My whole life, all the way down to that stupid sword landing in the lake, was just out of my control.

With so much anger and nothing to do with it, I actually started to feel like crying. I didn't think I'd ever cried from being angry before, but I could feel my eyes welling up.

I heard the sound of rocks scuffing behind me. Whoever it was, I didn't want to talk to them. I stood still, fists at my side, staring at the ground and hoping they would go away.

Then came a light touch on my arm, and a soft voice behind me said, "Cole, are you okay?"

I recognized Eva's voice. As upset as I was, I knew Eva had nothing to do with it. I took a deep breath and tried not to take it out on her. "No, I don't think I am."

She walked around to stand in front of me, and I could see how concerned she looked. In fact, she looked kind of scared. I hadn't meant to scare her, and it made me feel bad.

I closed my eyes for a couple of seconds, then opened them to look her in the eyes. I said, "I'm sorry, and this isn't your fault. I'm far from okay, but I'm not mad at you."

She clasped her hands behind her back and bit her lower lip, looking at me hesitantly. "You know, whatever is on your mind, you can trust me just like you always have. You're my best friend, and I'd like to think you can talk to me about anything."

I felt some of the anger draining away. It was hard to stay mad with her standing there looking at me. I let out a huff through my nose. "Well, for starters, they threw me out of the meeting."

She looked down and said, "I know. You lost your temper in there. You know most of the Elves don't have a lot of love for the dragons, and you're a dragon. You did talk to him kind of sideways in front of everyone important. Just chalk it up to his pride, and imagine how you would have felt if someone called you an idiot in front of the Ochana council and your parents."

She had a point. I tried not to let that irritate me even more. "That's only part of it. Sure, I got a little hot under the collar, and I shouldn't have. But getting kicked out of the meeting isn't what really got me burning."

She gave me a slight smile and said, "That's what you just said it was."

I clenched my jaw. Clearly, she wasn't going to let me get away with anything, although she was being pretty nice about it. But she only had half the story. "Eva, the only way we're going to win this war is if we all work together. Elves, Mermaids, Trolls, Fairies... And dragons. We're trying, but it's like beating our heads against a brick wall. Everyone seems like they don't trust anyone else, especially not dragons."

She pinched the bridge of her nose, then spread her thumb and index finger out across her closed eyelids. "It's not like the dragons didn't earn it. Maybe you and I didn't have anything to do with it, but we're still dragons. They know that if push came to shove, we would back Ochana.

I know your dad has the right idea, and he always pushed the old king to do what was right, but the fact is that the dragons didn't do the right thing. All these other races suffered because of it. How many decades, or even centuries, do you think they had to fight against the Elden and the other evil races with no help from the dragons? Dragons who, I might add, had a sworn treaty to defend them."

I realized what she was doing and gave her a faint smile. "Now you're just playing devil's advocate. You can't really believe there's any reason for them not to trust us now. It's all just about their pride. I'm scared that it's going to get us all killed."

Eva grabbed my hand and gently pulled me toward the shoreline. When we reached a couple of midsize rocks, she sat on one and motioned to the other. I lowered myself down beside her, and she turned to face the water. For a while, we both just sat there together, staring out over the lake. It really was one of the most beautiful places I'd ever seen. I felt more at home than I ever had in Ochana, taking in that breathtaking view. Despite all the Elves.

After a while, she said, "How far do you think the black spots go?"

I thought about it, but I didn't really have an answer. How many Trolls had been killed? Were the black spots growing from every one of those or only some? There were too many questions, still. "I can't give you a solid answer. I can't even really guess. I only know there were a lot of those black dots, maybe one for every Troll Eldrick killed."

She turned her head to look at me as she reached out and put her hand on my forearm. I appreciated the friendly touch.

"Maybe some sightseeing would do you some good. Just fly around and burn off some steam. I know we aren't supposed to be the ones out there scouting, but if we just-so-happened to accidentally fly over the Congo, and accidentally looked at the black area, and then accidentally figured out where it begins..."

At last, I smiled. That was just like Eva. For a moment, my thoughts turned away from our problems as I imagined being up in the sky, flying, free from all this garbage down here. "Well," I said, "I have always been accident-prone. Accidents happen."

She actually giggled at that, which lifted my spirits quite a lot. I smiled back and added, "Besides, wasn't it Jericho who said it's better to ask for forgiveness than permission, sometimes?"

Eva laughed so hard she actually snorted. "Does that sound like Jericho? He didn't say that, and you darn well know it. But it's still good advice. And maybe we'll find a clue on how to fight the blackness while we're out there. Right now, we don't have any ideas."

"Now is a good time to go, while they're up there arguing with each other. If we're lucky, they won't even notice we're gone."

"Who is going and where?" A voice boomed out, and I recognized it as Cairo's.

Startled, I whipped my head toward the sound. I quickly schooled my features, but it was too late. Cairo had heard just enough to be suspicious, I was sure, and my guilty reaction would confirm it for him.

He burst out with a deep laugh, all the way from his belly. That was not the reaction I expected.

Eva and I both spoke at once, tripping over each other. I said we were going to fly over the Congo to let off steam, and she said we were going to go hunt cows in Western Africa. She and I looked at each other, and then we both spoke at once again, this time switching stories. All the while, Cairo kept laughing at us.

"Now, why would you two want to go fly over the Congo?" he asked. "Let me guess. You're hoping to find some clue about the black spots. Am I right?" His eyes still shone with laughter.

Eva was the first to reply. "Fine, you caught us. Yes, that's what we're going to do. Everyone else is too busy insulting each other up there, and nothing is getting done. Cole thinks we need to do something, anything at all, and I agree with him. So, we're going."

Cairo cocked his head. "Oh, so you two are going, no matter what I say?"

I nodded. "You can't really stop us. Maybe you could stop one of us, but then the other would get away and you'd just be sending one of us off alone. That's worse, and I'm sure Jericho wouldn't like it."

Rather than get angry like I expected him to, he grinned again. "Fine, you got me. I was going to try to stop you. But I guess if you're both determined, I can't let you go off alone. That would be totally irresponsible, wouldn't it? I'll just have to come along to make sure you two don't do anything stupid. Again."

I stepped up next to him and put my hand on his shoulder. Suddenly, I felt much better. He was a good man, and I was starting to be grateful he was my best friend's *Vera Salit*. I wasn't sure I believed in it, but I was happy they were getting closer. I knew he'd protect her, no matter what happened. "Thanks, Cairo. Really." I wasn't sure what else to say, but I hoped he understood how deeply I meant it.

He gave me one curt nod, and a look passed between us. I thought, right in that moment, we gained some sort of understanding or connection. I wasn't sure what it was, but I was pretty sure it was important.

He said, "Well, what are you two doing standing around here like a couple of humans? Shouldn't you be up there, accidentally getting into trouble?"

He turned around without another word and jumped, transforming into a dragon in an instant. With two powerful beats of his wings, he was up and away, streaking skyward.

Eva and I quickly joined him.

Chapter Four

We swept over the treetops, flying low and slow. I soon found the others following me instead of following Cairo. It was kind of weird, being in the lead. When had Cairo switched to viewing me as a leader, instead of a kid who needed babysitting? As I looked down at the black lands below, thoughts about Cairo and that change bubbled in the back of my mind. I wasn't sure how I felt about it.

Everywhere I looked, the jungle had that same burned look to it. From up in the sky, it wasn't as shocking as it had been on foot, looking at the trees directly, but it might've been more horrifying; from up in the air, as far as I could see, the black jungle stretched out to the horizon. Some areas were pitch black, while others were dark shades of gray, giving the Congo jungle a mottled appearance.

Then, about a mile away, I sensed a spot. Since I couldn't sense the black areas at all, I was curious. I looked over and pushed my mahier out to that spot. There was no black there!

In my head, Eva said, "Good catch. Let's go check that out."

Aargh. Again, with the mind-reading. I made a note to ask Jericho how to close my thoughts to casual eavesdropping.

Eva whispered in my head, "Ha, but you'll never block me out. I know you too well. I could probably tell what you're thinking even without you shouting your thoughts all over the place."

I laughed, and a thick trail of black smoke streamed from my mouth. It hit Eva right in the face, which made me laugh even harder. I banked eastward, toward the healthy spot.

We were there in seconds, summoning our humans as we landed. I said, "Look around carefully. Maybe there's something around here keeping the black stuff out. If there is, maybe we can figure out why and make some more of it."

Cairo nodded and began wandering around.

Eva said, "There's nothing here."

I looked around, seeing the whole area for the first time. I had been so focused on finding something interesting that I hadn't really taken in my surroundings. We were in a clearing, and the ground was rocky. Nothing grew on the rocks that covered the spot.

Cairo called out, "Come look at this."

I walked over to where he stood and he pointed at a small clump of grass growing between two rocks. It was black, though.

I spun around and kicked a rock, angry. It went flying into the black jungle surrounding us. "There's nothing here keeping the blackness away. It's just that there was nothing growing here, so we didn't see it. I bet those threads they were talking about are all through the dirt under all these rocks. It's almost like a gravel pit. I wonder what caused it."

Eva put her hand on my arm, reassuringly. "Cole, you didn't think it would be that easy, did you? Trust in yourself. We're going to find something eventually. We just got our hopes up too soon. Let's get back up there and keep looking."

I didn't say anything but simply jumped into the air, summoning my dragon. With a few beats of my wings, I was rising above the tops of the trees. Higher and higher I went, and then I slowly turned back the same way we had been going.

We flew like that for hours, being slow and careful. Everywhere I looked, though, there was the same inky blackness. The farther we went, the darker it got, actually. The dead jungle just went on and on, mile after mile. I figured we had gone far enough to have passed what was on the horizon when we first started the trip, and yet the burned jungle still stretched as far as I could see.

I was getting more and more frustrated, and Eva must have sensed it, because I heard her in my head again. "Cole, there's no possible hope we could ever find the source of this blackness without having to leave the Congo. It just goes too far. If all the other spots have gotten this big, too, we're in trouble."

Yeah, I had figured that out already. I huffed angry smoke from my nostrils and slowly turned back toward Paraiso, hours away to our north. I sent my thoughts out to Eva and Cairo. "Let's get back. Whatever problems I was having, they're nothing compared to what's going on out here. Thank you both for coming with me. This trip put some things into perspective."

I could feel Eva projecting warm, comforting feelings my way. Cairo replied, "It was my pleasure, Cole. My duty is to keep Eva safe, but the Keeper of Dragons is both of you. We need you in top shape, too. Besides, I thought maybe a dragon's version of taking a long walk might clear your head a bit."

It had. They kept me company, flying on either side as we slowly made our way back north. I still kept my eyes open, just in case we might find something useful, but in my heart, I knew it had been a wasted trip. Not entirely wasted, because I did feel a lot better, I hadn't been lying about that. But we hadn't learned anything useful about the black patches. So, instead of feeling mad enough to punch an Elven prince, I just felt sad and overwhelmed.

Something bright and shiny streaked past my face, interrupting my thoughts and making me pull up short, startled. I hovered, looking around, ignoring Cairo and Eva's questions. Then I saw another bright streak. It shot up from the jungle below, nowhere near us. It arced up and over us, then continued back down to the ground on the other side. There was another, and another. Cairo and Eva saw them, then.

I shouted, "Run!" We beat our wings and streaked away, but I hadn't gotten very far when I felt like I had flown into a web of rubber bands. Hundreds of those bright lights were streaking all around us, then. That's when I noticed they left a thin trail, like a spider web.

Where I had flown into the web, they sparkled, becoming visible.

I struggled as hard as I could, fighting to break through, but dozens of the bright flashes were suddenly flying all around me, draping threads over me. They got caught up in my wings. I kept struggling, but I was falling from the sky. Thankfully, we weren't that high. All three of us landed, tangled up, with a painful thump. At least I hadn't broken anything when I landed. I looked at my friends, but they looked okay, too.

I tried to tear away the webbing but couldn't. I snarled, then called for my human. As soon as I transformed, all those threads fell away, hitting the ground and turning invisible again. When I looked up, I could see a sort of shimmer that showed we were basically in a bubble made by thousands of tiny streaking lights. There was no way we could get out of that in our dragon form.

"Run for it!" Cairo shouted.

I didn't have to be told twice. I dug my toes in and took off, running hot on Cairo's heels, Eva right behind me. When we got to the shimmering web shell, Cairo drew his sword and started hacking at it. I couldn't see the threads very well, but it didn't look like he was making any progress. Then I remembered the Mere Blade—I figured it could cut through almost anything, even weird shining webs.

As I reached for my sword, Eva said, "Reach out with your senses. The trap, it's dark tilium." She drew her sword at the same time I did. Dark tilium meant Dark Elves.

I got ready to take a whack at the web shell with the Mere Blade. "As soon as I hit this thing, it's going to cut right through it. Get ready to run."

They nodded and I shifted my grip on the sword hilt. I raised the blade over my head and took a step forward, but then I froze. Just outside the shell, which I could only barely see, there were a dozen Dark Elves charging toward us from the jungle. "Get ready, the Dark Elves are here!"

There was shouting behind me, and I looked over my shoulder. Another dozen Dark Elves were coming at us from the other direction, but they were inside the bubble with us. They must have somehow passed through it. Well, they made it with their tilium, after all. It figured they could get through it. We were surrounded.

Cairo said, "Get back to back. If this has to end here, I'm glad it was with you two. Sorry you had to be here with me, though." He grinned.

I didn't feel like grinning. I felt scared. But I forced a grin on my face anyway. "Me too, friend. If we're going to die, let's take a bunch of them with us."

Eva snarled, "They're going to regret tangling with us before this is over."

I admired her enthusiasm. Just like Eva, always brave, always confident. I wished I could be as brave as she was. Did she even feel fear and was covering it up, or was she just not afraid at all? It didn't really matter, though, because either way, this was a fight we couldn't win. There were just too many of them.

The Dark Elves, twelve in front and twelve behind, stretched out into a circle and then approached more slowly. They had circled us, and the circle was growing tighter.

When they were about 20 feet away, I shouted, "What are you waiting for? Let's get this over with. I promise you're going to regret finding us today." I sounded a lot more confident than I felt.

One of the Dark Elves began to laugh, surprising me. The others joined him. "It was no accident, finding you here!" he shouted back. "But, you silly boy, we aren't here to kill you."

My jaw dropped, and then another Dark Elf said, "But I think by the time Eldrick is done with you, you'll wish we had."

Again, the Dark Elves laughed. It was hard to believe that, just a few months before, those had been Elves. Gaber's people, and probably some I knew. Not anymore.

I reached up with my other hand so I had both hands on the sword's hilt, and adjusted my grip to get ready for them. "I didn't say finding us was an accident, traitor. I just said that it was a mistake. Why don't you come closer, and I'll show you what I mean?"

I spat into the dirt toward them.

The Dark Elves all had swords and shields, and they began to bang their sword blades on the rims of the shields, keeping time. It was spooky, the way the noise echoed through the jungle like an evil heartbeat. And then, altogether as if on cue, they came toward us again. The circle shrank, drawing tighter like a noose around us.

J.A. Culican

Chapter Five

As the Dark Elf circle drew closer, I thought about summoning my dragon, but there wasn't enough room in the magical web-cage they'd put over us. I wouldn't be able to maneuver, and a dragon stuck on the ground was just a big target. Plus, we had used up some of our mahier flying there, and I hadn't refilled. I wasn't sure I had enough energy left to transform *and* fight, *then* escape. I had to toss the idea.

I heard Cairo shout, "Here they come! Get ready." That snapped me out of my thoughts and back to the situation.

The Dark Elf circle shrank as they got closer to us, and now they stood only a few feet from each other. They stopped banging their weapons on their shields and the rhythmic drumbeat stopped immediately. The effect was kind of scary.

I braced myself, knowing what would come next. For some reason, I really wanted them to just get on with it and attack us, just to get it over with. We couldn't attack them or we'd break up our circle and our backs would be left open. When the Dark Elves stopped just out of our weapons' reach and stood still, staring at us, the whole scene felt creepy.

The one Dark Elf who had spoken before said, "Last chance. You can come quietly. We're supposed to bring you back alive. But, you know, things happen in battle. What's it going to be?"

Eva snarled. "Come and get it, traitors! Fate is on our side. Leave now, and I'll let you live."

I nodded. She had said exactly what I felt.

There was laughter among the Dark Elves. Then he said, "Very well. You had your chance. For Eldrick!" Then the circle surged toward us, all the Elves moving at once to attack us. As they got closer, I saw there were too many of them to get at us all at once. Only about half could fit and still have room to swing their weapons. The other half had to stand back, ready and waiting to fill in any gaps.

The ones in front were inching forward. The instant they got in range, I lunged with my left foot, raised my left arm with an energy field I crafted from my tilium, and thrust with the Mere Blade. Two Dark Elves swung at me, but their blades bounced off my tilium shield. The one I lunged at tried to block with his shield, but my blade point slid through it like it was made of paper.

When I stepped back into a defensive position, I saw blood on my sword and the Dark Elf staggered back, clutching his chest before falling over. He landed on his back and lay still. In a second, one of the Dark Elves from the back row had taken his place, and I was kept busy trying to block their blows. I couldn't find an opening to attack again.

All around me, I heard the *clang, clang* of the battle—weapons hitting shields, swords blocking swords. Twice, I heard someone shout in pain, but neither shout sounded like my friends. I couldn't take time to look, though.

Two of my Dark Elves attacked at the same time, one swinging his sword overhead and the other crouching to swing at my legs. I jumped and drew my knees up, and his blade swept harmlessly beneath me. At the same time, I blocked the overhead blow with my tilium shield, sweeping his weapon aside, and thrust my sword tip downward from above in an arc that caught him in the small area right above where his collar bones came together and kept going. He screamed and fell to one side, tripping up the nearest Dark Elf attacking Eva. That one, too, screamed as she caught him with a wicked diagonal slash of her own. Both our targets hit the ground and didn't move.

My heart leaped for joy when I saw that the three dead Dark Elves were getting in the way of the ones who came to fill the gaps they'd left. That made it hard to reach us, and their attacks were clumsy.

A fourth Dark Elf body joined them, but then Eva shrieked. I had just a second to glance over, and I saw she was bleeding from her left arm. There was another scream from somewhere behind me, one of the Dark Elves attacking Cairo.

The Dark Elves' leader shouted, "Fall back!" The rest stepped away, walking backward until they were out of striking distance.

I took a moment to look around and saw six Dark Elves lying on the ground, and only one of them was moving. He crawled toward his fellow Dark Elves. Cairo let him go, which made me glad. It wasn't that long ago that the Dark

Elves had been regular Elves living normal lives, but then Eldrick came along. The fewer we had to kill, the better.

Their leader called out, "You're only delaying this, Keeper. You really think taking out a handful of us is going to save you? There's more where we came from."

I didn't answer, but I didn't like where the conversation was going.

He nodded to another Dark Elf. That one walked away from us about ten paces, then began waving his hands around and talking. I couldn't hear what he was saying, but I felt a strange tickling in the back of my mind. He was casting a spell! I wished I had a bow on me.

As the other Dark Elf kept waving his hands around, the feeling grew stronger. I saw some sort of dark haze rise out of the ground. I tried to look at it with my mahier but still felt that weird sense that the nothing was actually something, all by itself. It was just like with the blackened jungle.

My eyes went wide when I realized the haze was a huge mass of the dark threads we had seen coming off the plant roots. It rose up to form a circle. Then it grew darker and darker. In just a few seconds, it started to look solid, not like mist. The outside edge swirled, like water going down the drain in a whirlpool.

Then the center started to shine. It was a weird, black-and-purple glow, almost like fire embers that cast shadow instead of light. The glowing dot in the center got bigger and kept on growing. When it took up almost the whole once-black circle, leaving just outside edges still spinning, the shadow-glow grew brighter. It looked angry, almost like it was alive.

Suddenly, the whole glowing area disappeared, leaving only the black, spinning outer rim. I could see all the way through the center to the other side. What was on the other side wasn't as it should be, though. When I looked through the hole in the shadow disc, there weren't any trees on the other side, like there should have been. Instead, there was only snow.

Cairo gasped, "What is that thing?"

Then a face appeared in the disk, coming into view from the left just like someone peeking around a corner. Another face appeared on the right. Then, I saw their whole bodies. Dark Elves! First there were only two, but more showed up until I could count at least twenty of them. They lined up in a single-file row, facing me from the other side of the magic disc, wherever that was.

"By Aprella's name, it's a portal," Cairo said.

Eva sounded angry as she said, "Look at all of them. There's got to be two dozen, or even more. I don't think they're standing there just to look at us."

I didn't think so either. They would be coming, and soon. When they got to our side of the portal, I was pretty sure they'd overrun us in a few minutes if not faster, no matter how many we could take out.

From the other side of the portal, someone shouted, "Forward, march!"

Walking in the lock-step, the two rows of Dark Elves started marching forward. They poured through the portal, turning left or right after they came through to make room for the ones behind them. I could see even more Dark Elves getting into line. Dozens more! They kept marching until they had gone all the way around the Dark Elves who were already circling us. They had just drawn the net tight around us, and there was nothing my friends or I could do to stop them.

The Dark Elf leader laughed. "Now what do you think?" he called. "And if you get through them, there's more where they came from. There's always more, Keepers. I'd rather not have to hurt you too much before I hand you over to the king. Just give up, it's hopeless."

Well, it certainly felt hopeless.

Eva shouted, "We've seen what your so-called 'king' does to prisoners. I'll pass. You'll just have to come and get me."

"Very well," the Dark Elf leader said. Then he turned to his army. "I want them alive!" The Dark Elves surged forward, blades and shields ready as they sprinted toward us, leaping over their fallen comrades' bodies to crash into our shields.

After that, the whole scene was just a blur. I dodged, whirled, stabbed, and swung. More Dark Elves fell at my feet, but there were too many. They were going to wear us out just with numbers. Once they realized we were beginning to tire, they got smart, too. They backed off and started toying with us, sending a few at a time to take a swing or two at us before backing out of range, only to be replaced by others. They were wearing us out, while most of them were resting.

Worse, I felt my tillium fading. Every time I blocked some Dark Elf's sword with my shield, it drained me a tiny bit. There were so many attacks coming in, I could feel my battery draining fast. Soon, I'd have to use my tilium, but Eva and Cairo didn't have that. Plus, tilium wasn't as strong as mahier, so I'd lose that even faster than I was losing mahier.

Basically, we were going to lose this fight, no matter how many Dark Elves fell. A glance at the portal showed there were still others lined up on the other side, waiting for their turn to come through.

Eva cried out again and I looked over. She was bleeding from her left leg, just above the knee. She could heal that with her mahier like she had with her arm, but she had to be getting low on power. I could see the pain and desperation on her face, and started to feel something like a black hole in my heart. I was almost ready to just give up and hope they didn't kill us. Or, maybe I hoped they would kill us because I had a pretty good idea of what life was going to be like as Eldrick's prisoner. But if we kept fighting, Eva and Cairo would probably die trying to protect me even after they ran out of mahier. I couldn't let them do it.

I was about to surrender when I heard what sounded like a trumpet off to my right. I couldn't look, though, because I was blocking three Dark Elves as they rushed at me again.

"They're here!" Cairo shouted. "Jericho!"

The Dark Elves didn't pause. If anything, they attacked even harder. I did manage to take one glance over Cairo's head and saw Jericho and Clara standing just outside the dark-magic web shell. My spirits soared until I realized they couldn't get in. They hacked at the shell with swords, and Jericho breathed fire at it, but it rebuilt itself faster than they could tear it up.

I wasn't sure whether to laugh or cry. With help so close, we were still going to lose. It wasn't fair! Nothing about this was fair. Not me being ripped from my family, not getting plunged into a war I didn't even know on my birthday, and not getting treated like an outcast by many of the other fantastical races just because I was a dragon. I couldn't help what I was.

The black hole inside me, the desperation that made me want to give up, turned warm. Then it got hot. It was filling with fire. Not real fire, but anger. Anger at how unfair it all was. I was enraged—and I was a dragon! Everything around me seemed to fade away as I focused on getting at the Elves attacking us. I became a whirlwind! They were falling in front of me as fast as they could get to me over the growing mound of fallen Dark Elves at my feet.

I saw the looks of fear on their faces as they came toward me, and it made my heart sing. The leader shouted something I couldn't understand, and the Dark Elf circle backed away from my friends and me. They stopped just outside of that deadly ground in front of me, enough to let us catch our breaths.

Their leader wasn't afraid, though. He looked over to where Jericho and the others were trying to tear down the shell and laughed. "The mighty Jericho! And Clara, it's so good to see you again. You'll never get through the web, fools. You get to watch as we drag your precious Keepers off to your brother, Eldrick. Long live the King!"

"He's no king!" Clara shouted. "He's a traitor, and so are you. Don't lay a hand on them, or—"

"Or what? Your threats are empty. Soon, Paraiso will be empty, too. No Ancestors, no mahier... Only Dark Elves and the one true king."

The funny thing was, the more he talked, the angrier I became. Instead of feeling defeated, I decided that if I was going to get caught or killed, that traitor Elf wouldn't live to see it happen. I summoned all the mahier I still had in me, and my tilium, too. I drew it all into me, into my chest, a growing ball of power. I didn't know what I was going to do with it, but *it* seemed to know. I felt like I just had to draw it in, and then I could unleash it all at once at the leader and anyone around him. The power knew what to do, even if I didn't.

Suddenly, I felt light-headed. Had I taken in too much power? That was my last thought before I felt everything start to spin. Was I spinning, or everything else? I couldn't tell. My eyes rolled back into my head. A fire-hot wave washed over me, burning me, but I was too dazed to even cry out.

My feet left the ground—I was floating up into the air. There were gasps all around, but I ignored them. Yes... Yes! My power was at the breaking point. I couldn't hold any more of it in, but I still kept drawing it inside me. It was coming to me from Eva and Cairo, too, and then from all the Dark Elves around me.

Their dark tilium and my pure tilium mixed, and it was like adding vinegar to baking soda. It was explosive! A wave of power shot out from me, and then I felt fire and light streaming from fingers and toes, from my mouth and eyes. The streams of light were a part of me, just another arm or leg.

Then the streams split in half, and then half again. Again and again, they split. Each time, the streams became thinner. Soon, they had split so many times that they'd become thin as spider silk. I could feel every thread, just like they were each a natural part of me.

The threads shot outward from me, racing in every direction. They reached the shell around us, and wherever my threads touched it, the web burned away. In seconds, it looked like Swiss cheese with all the holes burned into it. The burns spread faster and faster, growing. Only a few seconds later, the whole shell exploded into glowing, hot ashes and rained down on us all. The Dark Elves shrieked and fell to the ground, crying out as the falling embers burned them.

"Kill them!" their leader screamed. "Kill the Keepers, now!"

Dark Elves struggled to their feet and staggered toward us. They'd been burned in big splotches over every part of their faces and hands, but they came at us again anyway. It was too bad for them, though, because Jericho and Clara didn't waste any time. They sprinted toward us even before the ashes finished falling, and they were followed by the dragons and Elves they had come with.

Jericho roared as they sprinted at our attackers. When our cavalry arrived, crashing into the mob of Dark Elves, their leader shot me a last wicked glare like he was wishing I'd just die already, and then leaped through the portal. It closed behind him in a blinding, purple flash.

It didn't take long for Jericho and the others to finish off the Dark Elves who were left behind. A few fought, but most scattered, running in every direction with my rescuers hot on their heels.

Then, I felt like a tub with the stopper pulled out, suddenly empty and my power gone. I crashed to the ground in a heap as I passed out.

***

When I opened my eyes, a dragon in his human form also knelt at my side, watching me. "Welcome back, Keeper," he said. He looked relieved to see me awake.

"Thanks. How long was I out?"

"Maybe ten minutes. We checked you out with my mahier."

I sat up and nodded. A blue dragon, probably. "Thanks." I tried to smile, but it took too much energy, so instead, I looked up into the sky.

The jungle's blackened tree line was like an ugly picture frame for a painting of the most beautiful blue sky I'd ever seen. I wanted to look at that scene forever, but I knew I couldn't. I shook my head to clear it, then looked around. The dragons were piling Dark Elf corpses for the

Elves to return to Paraiso for some sort of ceremony. That was their business, though.

Then I noticed Eva, Cairo, Jericho, and Clara huddled together, talking. At least, Jericho was talking, and he was waving his hands around as he let out little puffs of smoke from his nostrils. Just great. I was sure I was about to get chewed out.

I climbed to my feet, and Jericho spotted me. He waved me over, so I braced myself for some yelling and made my feet go in that direction. Instead of flinching, though, I tried to keep my head high. When I joined the circle, Eva and Cairo smiled. Jericho didn't.

"What in Aprella's name were you thinking, Cole?" More smoke came from his nostrils.

I was almost as afraid of Jericho's legendary temper as I had been of the Dark Elves. I knew it wasn't rational, but Jericho could be really scary when he was mad. "I was thinking that we could learn something about the problem and get one step closer to saving the world. You know, my job."

I saw his fists clench for a second. He said, "Your *job* is to stay alive, both of you, so that you can end the Time of Fear. You aren't the only one who could scout the black spots, but you *are* the only one who isn't expendable."

"Whoa, wait a minute," Eva interrupted. "This was my idea, not Cole's. He came with me because he couldn't stop me, and Cairo came to keep us both safe. Yell at me, not them."

Jericho puffed a smoke ring from his nose, and his eyes flared for a second. "There is plenty of yelling to go around. You were stupid and reckless, Eva, and it almost cost us everything."

He rounded on me again and leaned forward so his face was only a foot from mine. "You want to be a leader? You want to live up to the Keeper of Dragons' role? If you're going to lead us in this war, you need to stop taking stupid risks with your life. A true Keeper needs to make wise decisions. If we can't trust you to be smart with your own life, how is anyone supposed to trust you with theirs? You have to know how to follow before you can lead, boy." He practically spat the last word.

I couldn't meet his gaze anymore. I had to look away. His words stung with the truth.

He stared at me for long seconds before he finally straightened and took a step back. "This isn't over, not for any of you. I can't even deal with whatever you did to take the web shell down. We'll talk about that later. Right now, I can't stand to look at you."

He turned to Cairo and his eyes flared up again. "If you think you can handle doing your job for once, do you think you can get these two back to camp? Try not to let them do anything even stupider on the way home."

With that, he leaped into the air and shifted into his dragon. He was gone in a blink, streaking back to Paraiso. Clara quickly followed him. I was left standing with Cairo and Eva, and they looked as frustrated as I felt.

Eva stepped toward me and raised her hand to put it on my arm, but she must have seen the look on my face because she put her arm down. They stood there, looking at me, at the ground, at each other. It was amazingly awkward for all of us.

Without a word, I jumped up and summoned my dragon, then headed back toward Paraiso The others quickly caught up and flew with me. I didn't say anything, and Eva and Cairo didn't try to make me. They just flew beside me, quietly. I wasn't going very fast, either, since I wasn't looking forward to getting back to camp. They simply just kept pace with me the whole way. I really did appreciate their silent support. I'd have to tell them later, when I felt better.

Along the way, my thoughts were a jumble. Had I really messed up that badly? Considering how close we came to getting captured, we would need to be more careful in the future, but how was I to know the Dark Elves could use the black spots for tilium? Or that they were hunting the Keepers? And I sure couldn't have known about the portal. I'd have to keep that in mind from then on because it meant they could attack us whenever and wherever they wanted.

Or could they only do it when we were in the black spots? Maybe that was the key. We didn't know anything about how it worked or what it was, except that Eldrick caused it by killing off trolls.

But in the end, Jericho's words ran through my mind more than anything else, calling me stupid. The words hurt, but he wasn't wrong. I had led friends far from home and into danger, and we got nothing out of it. All risk, no reward. The more I thought about it, the more I realized the trip really had been stupid, just like Jericho said. He also said a leader couldn't do those things. He was probably right about that, too.

Like a brick hitting me in the head, I realized he was right. I was a terrible leader. I had just figured being the Keeper of Dragons meant that whatever I did, it would come out okay because Fate was on my side. But maybe even Fate couldn't win over bad leadership. And if I couldn't fly over a blackened jungle, how was I supposed to end the war? No, I decided, I was a failure as Keeper of Dragons and a failure as a leader. I'd almost gotten my friends captured or killed, and me along with them.

Ahead, Paraiso came into view. Eva and Cairo both mentioned it telepathically, but I just couldn't bear to reply. I'd let them down so badly, but they wanted to act like everything was okay, like it had just been one bad decision. It wasn't, though. It had been a string of bad decisions, and maybe only Fate kept us alive this long. Luck would run out eventually, though.

Instead of answering them, I banked left to head straight in. I streaked down toward the catwalk outside the room the Elves had given me. Just before landing, I switched into my human, and then I stormed into the room and slammed the door shut behind me. I just couldn't deal with anyone at the moment, and I couldn't bring myself to face any of the people who mattered to me. I threw a lock on the door with my mahier, climbed into bed, and pulled the covers over my face.

In the darkness under the blanket, I finally felt a little better. I lay there for hours, and I could tell when the sun went down because it got even darker under the blanket.

Not even Eva tried to visit, which I was thankful for. She knew when to leave me alone.

I didn't know when I fell asleep, but I woke up to a strange sound outside the window. Everything else was silent, and it must have been the middle of the night. As my mind cleared from its sleep fog, I realized the sound was beautiful. If anyone had been with me to hear it, they would probably have said it was *hauntingly* beautiful. To me, it sounded like singing, the prettiest voice I'd ever heard.

I climbed out of bed to look out the window. I had to see what was making such beautiful noise! On the jungle floor was a spot of faint light. It pulsed in time with the singing, getting brighter when the voice rose, fading when it went low and soft. I felt the urge to go meet whoever was down there.

With a flip of my wrist, I made my mahier lock fade away. I didn't bother to fly down, I just "blinked" down the way I'd learned from Gaber when I first got to Paraiso.

When I took a few steps toward the light, it moved away from me. Then it paused. I took another step, and it moved away again. It felt like the singing light wanted me to follow it. Some part of my brain told me I should let someone know where I was going, but it was almost like a trance. I just couldn't bring myself to move away from that beautiful, singing light.

Instead of telling someone, I gave in and followed it. Every step I took, it moved away and then paused. After that, I didn't stop again but sped up. I wanted to catch it. No, I *needed* to catch it.

All thoughts of Paraiso left me, and I began to run.

J.A. Culican

Chapter Six

Running through Paraiso, I lost sight of the glow, but I could still hear the singing. Every once in a while, through a row of alley-cropping or between two bigger trees, I'd catch a glimpse of the beautiful glowing thing. It didn't seem to be getting any farther ahead, but I wasn't closing the distance.

I almost ran into an Elf on night watch and shouted an apology over my shoulder as I sprinted onward, leaving him and his surprised expression behind.

Then I bolted down an alleyway between two parallel hedgerows and passed between the two treehouses at the alley's end. I heard the steady, happy murmur of voices talking up above, but I kept running.

Soon, I had settled into a steady pace I could keep up for miles, the same one I used on the obstacle course since no one could sprint forever. Although it slowed me down, the voice didn't sound like it was getting any farther away. Whatever it was, maybe it had slowed down, too, luring me onward. It had been so beautiful; I simply had to see it again, up close.

I didn't know how long I had been running when I reached Paraiso's edge. The beautiful song ahead of me kept going, so I did as well. I plunged into the jungle, running through its pitch-black undergrowth. I used my mahier senses in a way I never had before—to tell me where the trees were, where I had to jump over a log or duck under a branch. In my head, I was counting my steps with one half of my mind while the other half only thought of the glowing light and its mesmerizing song. I wondered if my heart would feel full if I ever managed to catch it.

Then I heard another voice joining it, a deep sound that seemed to rumble in my chest, and then another voice midway between the deep rumble and the bird-like singing. More voices joined; they blended together and wove a harmony I'd never heard before. It was the most beautiful sound I'd ever heard, or ever would hear again in this lifetime. I forgot all about my steady pace and sprinted forward. I narrowly missed a branch but didn't slow down. I scraped my knee jumping over a log but only put my head down so I could run faster.

The voices grew louder. I was catching up! My beautiful song-light!

Suddenly, I burst through the tree line and found myself in an open field, the stars shining down from above. Here, the moon seemed to bathe everything in a faint glow, like the whole scene had been painted with the most beautiful sparkling paints. Even the rocks had a glowing aura, half mist and half moonlight.

On the far side of that beautiful field, as I became aware of my surroundings again, I saw people. Half a dozen, standing in a semi-circle. One in the middle was motioning me to come toward them. Not only did they each glow softly, but a pillar of cobalt-blue light streaked from each one, shooting into the sky like a spotlight. There were sparkling flecks in that light, like the glitter of a snow globe drifting all through the light and around each person.

I skidded to a halt only a few feet from those strange, glowing people. Somehow, I couldn't sense them with my mahier, like they weren't actually there even though I saw them clearly.

And yet, I knew they weren't there; they were Ancestors. My Ancestors. One was Prince Jago—I had seen him before in a portrait, but the painting didn't do him justice. He was tall and noble, his jaw square and strong, and his eyes glinted with joy as he smiled at me.

When they all stopped singing at once, I felt like something priceless had been ripped out of my heart. I desperately wanted them to sing again but knew they wouldn't because their song had already done its job.

"I don't know how I know it, but you are my Ancestors. And you," I said, looking at Jago, "are my father's brother, who should have been king. But how can you be here?"

The woman next to Jago spoke, and I recognized hers as the first voice I'd heard, the one that had lured me out of Paraiso. My heart leaped with joy at the sound. "We are here to help the Keeper of Dragons. I think you knew that already, Prince. We have watched you as we sit at Aprella's side. We've seen your struggles, and watched you with pride."

My heart sank. I felt a deep embarrassment, even though I didn't know any of those people. They were spirits, all passed away long before my time, but I desperately wanted their approval. Even so, I had to tell them the truth, though it would be embarrassing and painful, and I worried that they'd turn away from me. But I wouldn't lie.

"We're losing this war. I'm not the leader you need me to be, and I can't drive back the Time of Fear. Eldrick is stronger than me, and the Earth is dying because of it."

Jago said, "You are wrong, Colton. You are the Keeper, and only you can win this war against the evil one. If you fail, the entire Earth will fall. Our strength is in you, though you don't believe it."

The woman next to him added, "If you fail, there will be no hope for dragon kind, for Elves, or for any who follow Truth. You *must* carry on, for yourself and for them."

I felt the weight of their confidence like a ton of gravel poured over me, choking me. I couldn't breathe, I felt trapped. "I can't do it. I told you, I'm not the right one. Why am I the Keeper? Your mistake is going to cost the whole world," I said, my voice cracking.

Jago tilted his head back and laughed into the night, as though what I had said was the funniest thing he'd ever heard. My cheeks flushed with anger, but he held up one hand toward me. "Don't be angry, Prince. If you could know the things I know, you wouldn't feel hopeless. I see strength in you, even if you don't. How else do you think you stole the Farro tilium? How else could you carry the Mere Blade, forged for the Mermaids alone? How did you breathe fire in a day, when other dragons take years? Your questions and mine have the same answer—you were made the Keeper for a reason. Trust in this."

That was a pretty speech, but it didn't convince me. I shook my head without realizing it. In my heart, I knew he was wrong. Making me the Keeper was a mistake, no matter what he said.

As though he could read my thoughts, another man said, "Put your heart at ease. Maybe you haven't been able to stop the growing blackness from arriving, but you have stopped so many things that no one else could have. If you needed a sign, you only have to look at what you've done so far. What you will do in the future is just as grand, so the Fates have spoken. I know you're afraid, but you must fight on. Win or lose, that's all any of us can do, even the Keeper."

I was going to tell him he was wrong again, but then Jago stepped forward. He left the line of my Ancestors, and they watched him with sparkling eyes. I felt like they had hidden smiles behind the glow as they watched him. He stepped up and looked down into my eyes. I could feel his strength radiating.

They should have made him the Keeper.

Jago said, "No, Cole. It wasn't my time, so I must have lacked the strength. I died so the prophecy of the Fates could be fulfilled. So they could find *you*." He reached into the breast pocket of the gorgeous uniform he wore. It was the uniform of Ochana. When he pulled his hand out, he had something bright shining in it. He turned his hand over and slowly opened his fingers. In his palm was the most beautiful ring I'd ever seen. It was forged in the shape of a dragon, and I thought that if I looked closely enough, I might be able to see every individual scale. I got the impression that it glittered with many colors, even though I could clearly see that it was silver. Two small rubies were set as its eyes, glowing faintly.

Jago said, "This ring is priceless, Nephew. It was forged by the first Dragon Kings and took three generations of dragons to finish. When the time is right, and when your need is most desperate, then you'll see what this ring is for. You alone have the strength and will to use it to summon the ancients to come to your aid."

He held it out, and I let him drop it into my palm. As soon as it touched me, I felt a flood of warmth fill me, and its eyes glowed brightly for a second before slowly fading again.

Without another word, Jago turned around and walked back to the line. They all stood looking at me, smiling as they slowly faded away. When they were gone, the pillars of light were gone, too, and the field didn't glow anymore. It was just an ordinary, star-lit clearing in the jungle at night, and I was alone.

I dropped the ring into my shirt pocket. Then I heard a rustling sound behind me. An enemy must've followed the lights! I spun around and crouched as I drew the Mere Blade, a snarl on my face, ready to fight whatever Dark Elves or Carnites had found me.

Instead of an enemy, though, I saw Eva stepping out from the bushes, her eyes as wide as saucers.

Chapter Seven

I think my eyes went as wide as Eva's when I spotted her hiding in the bushes. "What are you doing there? And— "

"—and how long have I been here?" she asked, finishing my sentence for me. "When I saw you running through Paraiso, I decided to follow you. Just to make sure you were okay."

"How much did you see?"

She looked down at the ground as she bit her lower lip, avoiding my eyes suddenly. Her silence spoke volumes.

I said, "Okay. You saw everything, then. Are you going to tell anyone?" I wasn't sure why I didn't want her to say anything, but I had the urge to tell her to keep it to herself.

"You mean, am I going to tell Jericho that his best friend and the Ancestors had a concert in the jungle and gave you door prizes? No, I don't think so. For some reason, it feels like it should be private."

I nodded. I felt sort of the same way about it, actually. "I don't know why I followed the singing, but it was almost like it put me in a trance and I had to follow. I was as surprised as anyone to find myself talking to ghosts. How do you think they were able to give me something? You know, something physical?"

"I don't know. Jericho might know if you told him. The glow-peeps were right about you, you know. You're a lot stronger than you think you are. I've always seen it in you, even if you didn't."

It was my turn to look away. "The last thing I want is more people telling me how great I am. I'm here and fighting, but let's just leave it at that."

She was quiet for a minute and stared at me, looking me in the eyes like she was thinking about challenging me again. Instead, she said, "Can I see the ring? I didn't get a good look at it, before."

I hesitated. I wasn't sure why. Or maybe I just didn't want to find a ring in my pocket, proving the whole thing had been real. At last, though, I handed it to her.

"Thanks," she said as she examined the ring in the moonlight. "You see how it sort of shimmers? It's like it's glowing, like the moonlight makes it stronger. Or maybe we can only see its power in the moonlight."

"How do you know? Maybe it glows in the daytime, too."

She shrugged. "Maybe. Either way, I think you should wear it. Whatever this thing is, it has to be special for your Ancestors to come and give it to you personally, and if you're wearing it, you can't lose it. You need to take good care of this, Cole. I have a feeling it's going to be important."

I took the ring back from her and held it in my palm. As I moved it around, examining it, I again saw the echo of different colors in it, and no matter how I turned it, I felt like its two little ruby eyes followed me. I was trying to build up the courage to put it on because she was right—

it would be safer if I wore it. I couldn't lose it if it were on me.

At last, I took a deep breath and slid the ring on my right ring finger. It felt warm and comforting for a moment, but then there was a flash of light that dazzled me, and the ring disappeared. I gasped and looked closely at my fingers. That's when I saw that it hadn't disappeared. Not quite. I could see a shape on my finger, under the skin, that looked kind of like the dragon from the ring.

She gasped. "It's like it merged with you. It's a part of you now."

"I hope that's a good thing," I said. It still felt warm, even under my skin. Whatever fears I had about the ring faded away.

She stepped up beside me and slid her arm around mine, joined at our elbows. She looked up at me and smiled. "Let's get back to bed. Maybe we can catch a couple hours of sleep before Jericho starts in on us again bright and early."

I was suddenly exhausted, and sleep sounded like a great idea. "Okay. I don't know about you, but I'm wiped out."

We walked back to Paraiso arm in arm, neither one saying anything, just being there together. It was enough for the moment since neither of us knew if we'd get to do that again in this lifetime. I was glad to have a good friend like her, for however long I kept us alive.

***

"And... Stop," Jericho called out.

Dripping sweat, I climbed to my feet from the side-straddle-hops we had been doing for the last few minutes. It was just the latest torture he inflicted on us. The other trainees and I waited for the next command. While we waited, we rolled our shoulders or stretched our necks.

Suddenly, Jericho was right in front of me. I jumped a little, startled. He shouted right in my face, "Did I tell you to move around? No. I said stop. That means you get in the position of attention. Now drop and give me fifty push-ups."

I glanced at Eva and the others, who definitely weren't at the "position of attention" either.

Eva shrugged and looked confused.

Jericho, still inches from my face, shouted, "Did I tell you to eyeball them? Is that part of the position of attention? No. That's ten more push-ups. Get on your face! Do it now!"

That was totally unfair. The others were still moving around, not at the "POA," but they weren't getting extra pushups. Come to think of it, all the training that morning had been me getting the short end of the stick from Jericho's unwelcome attentions. I dropped down and started pumping out push-ups. When I got to sixty, I climbed to my feet. After that, though, I made sure to stand at attention. I was the only one doing it, but so what.

Jericho marched back and forth in front of our lineup, his hands behind his back, and glared at us one at a time. I thought we'd get in more trouble, but he didn't say anything about how some of the others were slouching.

My irritation started turning into something a bit stronger.

He shouted to us, "Partner up for sit-ups. You'll do it until you knock out eighty of them, then switch. *Prince Colton*, since you feel like eyeballing me, you'll do one-hundred sit-ups. Ready, begin."

The others dropped to the ground, but I didn't move. Forget this guy. I'd had more than enough. Why was he picking on me? I glared at him, trying not to say what I really wanted to say. It wouldn't have been polite, that was for sure.

Of course, in a flash, Jericho was right in front of me again, yelling in my face, his eyes glowing red, but he was so mad that he wasn't making sense. His words came out all jumbled. Whatever side of the bed he woke up on that morning, he didn't have to take it out on me. As he shouted, an image went through my mind of a chicken with red eyes, head bobbing as it clucked angrily.

The image made me laugh, and Jericho's expression at that made me laugh even harder. The jerk was a chicken, clucking at the dog like it was in charge! I couldn't help it. I tried to stop laughing but I couldn't.

Jericho froze mid-shout. He stepped up to me, so close that his face was only a breath from mine.

I tried not to laugh again, but a burst of air came out from between my tightly pressed lips, and his nose-smoke blew away. "Lose your bearing, *Prince*? Are you just stupid, or don't you care if everyone around you is stronger and faster than you are? Maybe you don't care how many people have to die saving you because you're too precious to do a sit-up. I'm sure they won't mind carrying your load, too. Need a rest-break, do we?"

I knew he was just trying to make me mad, but it worked. I clenched my fists and almost took a swing at him, but stopped myself at the last moment. He looked like he was expecting me to.

His lip curled. "You feel like taking a swing at your commanding officer, do you? But you expect these people to follow you someday? Fine, I'll give you the chance to take your best shot. Go ahead—swing at me."

I didn't move. Was he serious? I couldn't tell for sure. I really wanted to take him up on that, though.

He turned to the others, who were on the ground doing sit-ups or just sitting there staring at Jericho and me, and he said, "On your feet, trainees. Pair off for quarterstaff training."

He turned back to me and leaned in so that his mouth was inches from my ear. "If you think you're ready to take a swing at me, do it out there. Let's see what you really got, *kid*."

I thought if I stepped into the square with him, one of us would get hurt. I truly wanted to beat the smug look off his face with a big stick. I didn't know why he was picking on me, and I didn't care. But I knew better than to take him up on his offer. "No. Go fight yourself, Jericho." I put the emphasis on the last word like it was an insult.

He froze, eyes locked with mine. I think he was stunned silent for once. Good. I was tired of the sound of his stupid voice.

I said, "I'm done getting your special treatment. Get out of my face, or I'm going to do something only one of us is going to feel bad about later."

He took a step back, mouth gaping open. After a second, his mouth snapped shut with a click. He said, "This training is going to save your life, Cole. Now get over there and—"

"No," I shouted, loud enough for everyone else to hear. "What's the point of all this training? I won't win anyway."

"You're the Keeper of Dragons. Of course, you'll win. I expect your best efforts—"

"Everyone expects things from me. You just don't get it!"

I felt my eyes burning and my throat got tight. I said, "I'm going to let everyone down. And the cherry on top is, I get to have you bully me in front of everyone. Maybe you just like tearing down what you'll never be, though. A *prince*." I glared at him, practically daring him to say something.

I felt a hand on my shoulder. It was Eva. Very quietly, she said, "The Ancestors. Tell him, Cole, and—"

Jericho interrupted and hissed at her, "What about the Ancestors? Speak more sense than this half-wit."

I couldn't take it anymore. I just kept getting angrier, and none of it was fair. What did they want from me? Save the world. Yeah, right. I was just eighteen, a baby in dragon years. Snapping, I knocked Eva's hand off my shoulder and spun to yell at her, too. But when I saw the hurt, scared look on her face, that was the last straw. She was disappointed in me, too.

I had to get out of there. I turned on my heels and ran. I poured all my anger into running, and it felt good. I kept running, faster and faster, and my rage kept growing. How dare they! I wanted to break things, destroy things, smash Jericho's smug face into the ground.

Behind me, Eva and Jericho both yelled for me to stop, and with my mahier senses, I felt them chasing me, but I also felt their concern and worry wash over me.

Suddenly, I didn't feel angry anymore. It drained away, and all I felt was embarrassed. I had thrown a tantrum, but they still came after me and worried. I couldn't face them, so I ran harder.

I dodged through bushes and over logs, jumped across a creek without slowing down, and soon found myself deep in the jungle. My senses told me they were getting farther behind, and when they came to the creek, they slowed down just enough for me to get a really good lead on them.

In a couple more seconds, they were too far away for me to sense them anymore. Still I kept running. It felt good. Everything I was angry or scared of came pouring out, fueling my legs to go faster and faster, ignoring the burn. I started to feel better than I had in a long time, actually. I came to a decision then, and it was like a huge weight lifting off my shoulders.

I must have run at least a couple more miles like that at a dead sprint, my mahier fueling my muscles, when I came to the gray edge of blackness deep in the jungle. The gray outside edge was closer to Paraiso than it had been the last time I saw it. Jericho didn't want me anywhere near the Congo's black areas, but I smirked and decided that was all the more reason to keep going. Yeah! I'd go in and find a way to fix the jam we were all in, whether he wanted me to or not.

In a moment, I'd passed through the gray and was into the black. I stopped running and looked around. All that blackness made me feel sad. The Congo had been so beautiful and green, not long ago. Before it got painted black.

My senses told me the entire region had no tilium in it. I didn't feel even a trace of mahier, either. Surely, if any animals and insects were still in there, I'd have felt something, even just a twinkle?

But I felt nothing. Out of curiosity, I tried to draw in mereum, the power of the mermaids. The Queen had told me that even air had mereum in it, riding in the humidity. Anything with a trace of water had mereum, even people and animals.

I still sensed nothing! I had no idea how that could be. There was water in the dirt and the air. There had to even be some moisture in the blackened trees, or they'd just be a pile of dust, I thought. But no mahier, no tilium, no mereum.

An idea hit me. It probably wouldn't work, but it was worth a try. Nothing else had worked, so why not? I reached my hand out over a blackened bush, standing about knee high. My mahier and tilium charges were still full, and I was close enough to the green to draw mereum from there. I focused on long, slow, and even breaths, and felt my heartbeat settle down from the long run. I started to pull in mereum. Suddenly, I got a buzzing feeling in my head—not painful, but not comfortable. Once before, I had mixed my mahier and the tilium I took from the Farro. It had purified their dark tilium into something new—my own pure tilium.

My idea was something I had never tried before. I didn't know what would happen if I pulled my mereum into that pure tilium. I was the only dragon who could use mereum who wasn't a mermaid. I couldn't use it well, but I could gather it in with my other powers, at least.

I felt the three powers swishing around inside me, and I stretched my hand out over the blackened little shrub and closed my eyes. With my mahier senses, I could still see the bush in my mind's eye, a gray outline against a field of white. In the healthy jungles, all I would have seen was green. I thought the white might mean that the land wasn't poisoned by adding something new, but instead, it may have just been stripped of every kind of energy.

Slowly, I reached out with my mahier, the power of dragons, the power of Truth. Then, I reached out with my purified tilium, the power of life and nature. Nothing happened, and the little bush stayed black.

It was time to try my idea. I thought about my mereum flowing out of me, through my hand, and into the plant. Mereum was the power of water, the irresistible force that could even carve away rock over time.

I felt it mix with mahier and tilium, and as soon as they touched, the mereum was absorbed into my tilium like water into a sponge. Water and life were so closely related, I didn't know if I was even surprised at the reaction.

Then, my mahier begin to wind its way through the new energy, whatever mereum and tilium became together. Tendrils of mahier spread through the bush, like fiberglass holding two sheets together and making both stronger. Then the new energy mix flowed around the bush. It settled over every leaf, and I could feel it going down into the roots, and then into the dirt and roots under it. I kept the energy flowing, but I opened my eyes to look.

My eyes went wide with surprise—the bush was green again! I didn't need my dragon senses to see that the leaves had turned green, then the stems turned from black to properly brown from the top to the bottom, and when it touched the soil, black and gray vanished. All that was left behind was rich, brown, healthy soil. Even the fallen leaves and other debris that covered the dirt weren't blackened anymore. They went from black to brown, like dead leaves should be, but then they turned green again! My jaw dropped as I felt dead bugs and earthworms twitch and come to life.

I wished Eva were there. It was incredible, stunning, and totally cool. *I could restore balance to the Earth!*

J.A. Culican

Chapter Eight

I stood looking at the little bit of green, the tiny island of life that I'd restored. My heart pounded in my ears from the excitement of realizing the world wasn't doomed. Somehow, I'd gathered all three kinds of power. Maybe the energy harmonized and made the whole thing stronger, different—like a fourth power no one had ever seen before.

And it could save a dying world!

I heard people rustling behind me, but in that almost lifeless place, I could sense their energy clearly. It was Jericho, with Eva and Cairo. I didn't turn around, too thrilled at the little patch of life to care about getting chewed out.

Footsteps, and then Jericho shouted at me with iron in his voice, "What are you thinking, Cole? Do you have any idea how worried we were or the danger you put yourself in? You put all of us in danger, too. We had to chase you through the blackness. Reckless! Do you have any idea what happens if they kill you?"

I turned to face them, but I just couldn't wipe the grin off my face. I think it surprised them all because they looked stunned. Eva's face went from just mad to both mad and smirking.

"What are you smiling at, fool?" Jericho shouted at me, his eyes glowing red and smoke puffing from his nose. "Don't you get—"

Still grinning, I cut him off. "Look," I said, and stepped aside to show the green life I'd brought back. "See what I did?"

His eyes went wide as he realized what he was looking at. Stunned, he looked up into my eyes. "You did that?"

Cairo's mouth was open, both eyebrows raised high on his forehead, and Eva stepped around us to get a look at the green island in the ocean of black all around it.

"Yes," I replied, and grinned even wider. "It's not too late for the world. I figured out how to save it. I had to use all the magic I could—dragon, Elven, Mermaid. I don't know why, but it worked."

"By Aprella's eyes, this is a miracle," Jericho said, and his nose stopped puffing smoke. "You can heal the plants? How did you know what to do?"

"It just came to me. I poured all my energy into it and willed the plant to heal. And even the dirt went back to a normal, healthy brown."

Jericho shoved his fist into the air for a second, like he'd just scored a touchdown. "Yes! I can't believe it, Cole. You figured it out! The Keeper of Dragons will save the world, just like the prophecy says." Then he fist-pumped the air again.

He clapped me on the shoulder, and Cairo shook my hand, both grinning like fools just like me, but Eva said, "That's great." I could tell from her tone that there was a "but" coming along with it.

Sure enough, she continued, "But there's a huge difference between sprucing up this little plant and healing the Earth."

The three of us went silent and turned to stare at her like she was a Martian, or like she'd grown another head.

She shook her head at us. "Look at me like that if you want, but Cole is just one dragon. Maybe he can keep Paraiso green, but the blackness is *spreading*, and faster than he can heal it. So, it's just not going to be enough, is it?"

She froze, waiting for him to reply, and I think she was desperate to hear she was wrong. The problem was, she wasn't. How long had it taken me to heal one plant? The black had to have covered more area on Earth than I healed, just in the time it took me to do it.

At last, Jericho shook his head just a little bit and looked down at the little plant. It was already less green than it had been when I healed it. It would be dead again soon. He finally said, "Come on. We need to get back to Paraiso and share the news. Maybe Gaber or the fairy queen will have ideas on what to do once they learn about this. There's got to be a way we can take advantage of this discovery, even if we don't know it yet."

We walked side by side through the black, dead Congo, talking mostly about happier days ahead once we figured out how to cure the world. It was a nice thought, at least.

***

As we were walking back, Eva and I found ourselves side by side at one point. She looked so sad. I walked next to her, to be there for her if she wanted to talk, trying to simply give her silent support.

After an awkward minute, she said, "You know I'm sorry, right? Everyone was so happy, maybe I should have just waited to say anything. I feel bad."

That was my friend Eva. She was as strong as anyone I ever knew, and it always surprised me to hear her doubts when she was usually so fearless. "Hey, don't apologize. Nothing you said could take away how awesome it felt to bring that plant back. So it won't heal the whole planet. It's a start, right? We know more now than we did before. Someone will have an idea how we can use it, so cheer up," I teased her, smiling so she knew I wasn't upset. "For the first time, I really feel like maybe things are looking up, like Fate didn't make some horrible mistake picking us."

She didn't say anything. She just slid her arm around my waist as we walked, and I thought she looked a bit happier. More relaxed.

It wouldn't last.

To my right, there were sudden noises in the black jungle, like trees falling. I stepped away from Eva, putting myself between her and the sounds just by reflex. I reached out with my senses, then felt something out there. I focused hard on it, but I couldn't get a solid impression. It was like catching glimpses of a light through trees, never there long enough to see what it was. "I can't feel it," I said, looking at Jericho. "Something is out there, but I can't get a grip on it."

He nodded, staring out into the jungle. He was concentrating, too, but the noise was getting closer. When he drew his sword, so did the rest of us. "Be ready, and if that's not just a herd of duikers, run."

I got ready to run. That seemed likely, since the deer-like duikers didn't travel in herds and, being dog-sized, wouldn't knock over even blackened trees. "Eva, I'll follow you if we have to run for our lives."

Interestingly, we all moved into pairs without anyone telling us to. Jericho and I stood back to back, while Eva and Cairo did the same. We had barely gotten into position when whatever was crashing through the jungle reached the edge of the little clearing we stood in. They didn't even slow down—at least half a dozen Carnites burst from the tree line.

I didn't have time to think about it because the Carnites reached us in only a few of their giant steps. In the daytime, here in the open, the things looked just as terrifying as they did at night, but none of these had their usual tree-trunk clubs. Instead, four had what looked like nets, while two had long, thin trees stripped of any branches which they held out with the tips toward us like spears. They broke off into two equal groups, forcing each of us to face a Carnite with a net, and each pair had a spear guy. The way they surrounded us made it impossible to run. Usually, Carnites just charged right at anything that moves, but not these.

My Carnite threw his net at me, but I knocked it aside with my mahier shield. Then one with a spear stabbed at me. The blunt tip hit me in the shoulder and sent me spinning to the ground. It felt like a massive hammer blow. I couldn't believe how strong one Carnite was.

The net came again, spreading out as it flew toward me, and I frantically rolled aside. That left me and Jericho both fighting alone.

As I scrambled to my feet, Jericho was spinning out of the way of another net, and we made eye contact for a split second. I glanced at Eva and Cairo; they had also been split up. This wasn't going well. At this rate, they'd kill us all.

Eva faced another Carnite, ready to knock aside its net, but she didn't see the one behind her. I sprinted toward her and, holding my mahier shield out in front of me, leaped through the air. I knocked the big net away enough that it missed her, and when I hit the ground, I tucked my chin and rolled into a somersault, then came up on my feet again.

"I can't hold them off!" Eva cried.

No kidding. It was pretty clear we were done for. I just couldn't get close enough with my sword to get at them, not with the spear-wielding Carnites keeping us away from the ones with the nets.

Then Jericho's clear warrior voice rose over the noise of battle. "To the north. Run! I'll make an opening."

I dodged another net, leaping aside and landing on my shoulder with a thud. It hurt, but I got to my feet without missing a beat. "What about you?" I couldn't leave him there, and I didn't want him to do something stupid. Of course, staying there to get killed or caught sounded pretty stupid, too.

He shouted, "By Aprella, do as I say, kid. Follow me!"

I turned and headed north, sprinting. It wasn't time to argue about being called a kid. Cairo ran next to me, and Eva was just behind him.

Jericho was five steps ahead of all of us. As we headed north, only two net throwers attacked us, the other two being somewhere between us and freedom, but both spear Carnites were to either side. One thrust its tree at me, but I ducked and the spear passed inches over my head.

Just before Jericho reached the two surprised-looking Carnites ahead of us, he leaped into the air and summoned his dragon faster than I had ever seen anyone do before. With his wings spread out, he crashed into the giant Carnites, and all three went down to the ground in a tangle of arms, legs, and wings.

The rest of us leaped over the twisting pile and then reached the tree line. We ran into the jungle. We were clear! "Keep running!" I shouted.

I didn't look to see if they were following me, but I could hear footsteps behind me and was glad they listened. As I ran, I began frantically thinking about how best to gather up a rescue party. I had to find Gaber first, and then we could—

I saw a shadow to my left and felt the air move, but I didn't have time to realize what was happening before a Carnite, still chasing us, backhanded me like he was swinging at a golf ball. I flew through the air until I hit a tree and bounced off, only to land on the ground on my back. I went into panic mode, not thinking at all, just rolled over and used my hands to push up enough to get my feet under me. Then I was off and running.

A second later, I risked glancing around me but I didn't see Eva or Cairo. I was alone, and we had been scattered in the jungle, being chased by Carnites. It didn't look good. I had to find them.

"Eva!" I shouted as loudly as I could while sprinting through a dense, dark jungle. There was no reply, but right away, the crashing sounds of two Carnites changed directions and then grew louder. Argh! I'd drawn their attention, but maybe it would give the others a better chance at getting away.

The Carnites were getting closer, even though I was siphoning my mahier into running. No human could have kept up, I think, but Carnites were big and fast. A net flew at me from my right, and I knocked it aside with my shield, but sprinting as I was, the movement knocked me off balance. I tripped and the ground rushed up at me. I landed hard, but I was already scrambling to my feet by the time I slid to a stop.

I never got the chance to take off running again. Another net came at me from the other side, and there was nothing I could do to avoid it. It hit me dead-center and knocked me to the ground. I struggled, but yet another net landed on me and I got completely entangled.

I only hoped Eva had escaped.

Chapter Nine

I struggled to find the nets' edges to escape, but before I could, one of the giant Carnites sprinted right at me. I thought it was going to trample me. I curled into a ball and covered my head with my arms. It didn't stomp on me, though. Instead, at the last minute, it bent down and swooped up the net in one hand, bringing me up with it like potatoes in a weave sack. It held me up in the air and brought the bag close to its face. I wanted to jam the Mere Blade into its stupid, ugly eyes, but the net had me pinned so I couldn't get the sword free.

The hideous thing had two long, sharp tusks jutting up from its mouth, which was as wide as its pig-like face, but its skin was sickly pale like moonlight and looked kind of like cottage cheese with the way it puckered and bunched up into rolls and pits. I could see little open sores all over its body, and it smelled bad enough to knock over a horse.

As it looked at me with its beady little eyes, its nostrils—just two holes in its face, really, since it didn't have a nose to speak of—flared open, and it hit me with a gust of breath as it snorted. The hot, foul breath smelled like rotting meat in a sauna, and I had to fight not to retch. It opened its mouth and lowered me, net and all, snapping its teeth at me.

That's when I panicked. Even more than I had before. All I could think of was getting away as I struggled inside the net, desperate, but the ropes were too thick and tight. It was going to swallow me, net and all.

I shrieked, screaming at the top of my lungs.

The Carnite pulled the bag away from its face and made a disgusting, wet-sounding grunting noise over and over, and I realized it was laughing at me. I stared at the monster, wishing I could somehow get to it with my sword.

The other Carnite walked up to it, and the two beasts sniffled and snorted at each other. They sounded angry, at least to me. I didn't know if Carnites were ever anything but angry. After a moment, though, they both turned west. The one holding me tied the sack to its belt, really just a few ropes woven together and tied at the waist. Every time it took one of its long steps, I was bashed around, bouncing off its thigh. I grabbed onto the net and held on for dear life, even though there was no way I would fall with it tied to the belt.

Where were these brutal Carnites taking me? From what I heard, Carnites weren't good for anything but fighting and breaking things. To them, every problem was a nail, and they were the hammer. Using nets, leaving people alive, even working in a team the way they had was all just so weird. The only explanation was that somebody was controlling them, and it wouldn't take three guesses to figure out who was doing it.

The trees went by as the monsters calmly walked away, tearing me from my life with the Elves and dragons. Who knew how my friends would do without me, without the Keeper of Dragons? I felt certain that King Eldrick would win, and the Earth would be lost. All the Elves and dragons, Trolls and Fairies—everyone who believed in Truth—all would soon be dead or slaves.

My eyes watered up and overflowed, and I quietly cried for the first time in I didn't know how long.

The giant Carnite had taken half a dozen pounding, bone-jarring steps when I heard a high-pitched scream. Then the monster began to fall, toppling like a tree, and the ground rushed up at me. I barely had time to throw up a mereum cushion to soften my landing, but it still knocked the wind out of me.

As I lay bound inside the net, trying to get my breath back, I heard the other Carnite fighting someone. It only lasted a few seconds before that monster roared in anger, then that scary noise got cut short mid-scream. My first thought was that the other Carnites had started a fight with my two, trying to get more spoils to take back to Eldrick, but then a familiar face came into view above me, peering down at me.

"You okay?" Eva asked. "I don't see any blood on you. We need to go save the others. Can you get out of that net?"

I shook my head, feeling light-headed from not being able to breathe. I was just able to sip the air a bit, but at least it was coming back to me. She took out her dagger and furiously worked to cut through the thick ropes of my net. It didn't take long to cut enough to let me wiggle my way out.

Thankfully, my breath was coming back, too. It wasn't the first time I'd had the wind knocked out of me, and I hated it every time. It hurt and it was a little scary. "Thanks for coming to my rescue," I said, looking at the two dead Carnites. At least she'd finished them off quickly. They might have been monsters, but I didn't like to see even them suffering

Eva grinned. "I guess that makes you the damsel in distress, huh? Cairo and Jericho both got captured, and their Carnites headed off that way," she said as she pointed west. "I don't know why the monsters split up, but I think they just didn't want to share the credit for capturing us."

I stretched my arms and rolled my shoulders a couple times to make sure I wasn't hurt worse than I'd thought. Then, Eva and I ran the way she'd pointed. She set a fast pace, but not sprinting. It was a speed we could keep up for a few miles and still fight. Maybe fifteen minutes later, I caught sight of the black trees up ahead swaying, like in that old movie about cloned dinosaurs getting loose and running around on a jungle island.

"There they are," I said, panting.

She nodded, then put her head down and ran faster, pulling ahead. I sped up, too, and drew the Mere Blade as we approached. Neither of us said a word before we jumped into the fight, and we dropped two Carnites before they even knew what hit them. The other two backed off, probably just surprised, but that was a mistake because the two we had taken out first were carrying Jericho and Cairo. We cut them out of their net in seconds, and then the two Carnites faced four of us. They turned and ran.

Eva started to run after them, but Jericho shouted, "Leave them."

Frustrated, she stomped back to us shouting, "Rats! Do you realize this is, like, the third time someone tried to catch us? Why aren't they trying to kill us? I wanted to question those two."

Jericho didn't flinch or step back from Eva raging in his face. Calmly, he said, "Do you speak Carnite?"

She paused, and I watched her closely. I wasn't sure if I should be amused or concerned about what she'd do. But instead of shouting again, she looked away and shook her head.

I asked, "Do they even talk?"

Jericho smiled at me but didn't take his eyes off of Eva. "Yes, a little bit. You heard one talk a long time ago, the first time you met one. But even if any of us knew their language, I don't think they'd trust us with any useful information. Eldrick's forces seem like they're trying to kidnap dragons. Not just us, but every dragon they find."

My eyes went wide in surprise. "What? Why would they do that?" My mind raced, but I didn't come up with anything that made sense. I also didn't know why he'd kept that news to himself.

Eva clenched her jaw and, between her gritted teeth, she asked, "What purpose does that serve? It's the Keepers they need to stop if they want to win, and Eldrick already started the dying Earth by killing Trolls. I doubt dragons dying would do that, or you'd know it."

"Well, that is indeed a question, isn't it? But I may have an idea. I need you kids to go—"

Eva cut him off. "What idea? You can't say that and then just send us back to camp without telling us what's going on. And we aren't kids anymore."

Jericho paused like he was thinking about it, but then he gave her a faint shake of his head. "No, not until I know for sure. And I know you aren't truly kids anymore. Children don't defeat Carnites. But you can't help me with this one. I need to go look into some things, then I'll tell you."

He turned to Cairo and said, "Get the Keepers back to Paraiso safely. Don't let them wander anywhere else alone, got it?"

Cairo gave him the dragons' salute, but Jericho was already mid-shift into his dragon form, rising into the air, and he left us behind. I couldn't help but smile a little bit when he left, too.

"All right, let's get back to camp," Cairo said. "We have to warn everyone about the Carnites, and my telepathy hasn't been working well in all this black stuff."

We walked in silence toward the Elves' home. Eva was angry still at being called a child, but I was too busy thinking to deal with that, and she wasn't the only one with hurt feelings. Plus, Cairo had been right about the mind-talk not working well out there. I tried sending my thoughts to Eva, but if she heard me, she didn't respond.

Chapter Ten

Jericho was gone, which made me happy, even a little giddy. Good riddance. In my head, I knew how important he was and how much he did for Ochana, but I didn't always *like* him. Lately, he'd made it pretty hard to remember he was on my side. It sure didn't feel like he was.

The black jungle was giving into gray, which boosted my mood a bit more, too. "So, what do you think that was all about?" I asked as we made our way between some ashy-looking trees.

Eva grunted, climbing over a log in our way. "Good question. I hope he's okay. I don't know, though."

I didn't care if he was okay or not. That wasn't really true, I did want him to be okay. But I was still mad at him. Maybe if he just got some scrapes and a bruised ego...

Cairo said, "I don't know, but if he can get Eldrick to quit trying to capture you two, I'll be thrilled. I don't like not knowing what's going on. At least if they attacked us, I could understand that. Killing each other, I get. Kidnapping? It's just weird. Carnites don't take prisoners."

"They do now," Eva replied. "While he's gone, we should try to figure out the source of whatever spell is killing everything. Maybe we could deal with that, one problem at a time."

I snorted. "Jericho is the problem. He treats us like kids, then leaves us alone in the jungle while he runs off chasing his tail. Are we kids, or aren't we? Make up your mind, Mr. High-and-Mighty. How are we supposed to fix anything if he doesn't tell us what's going on?"

"Oh, behave," Cairo said. His voice sounded like eyes rolling. "Jericho puts Ochana before everything else, including himself, and it's not right for you to forget that. He's gruff and mean, but he has a lot of weight on his shoulders. I know he's hard to deal with, though." His voice pitched higher a bit at the end.

"Yeah, I guess. But he doesn't have to treat everyone like that." I kicked a little rock, and it went flying into the gray, dark underbrush.

Eva said, "No, he doesn't have to, but we have bigger things to worry about. Like where the magic is coming from. Any idea where to look?"

My ears perked up. Adventure sounded better than sitting around waiting for Jericho! "No, not really."

Cairo said, "The Earth started getting black spots when Eldrick killed the Trolls, so maybe King Evander knows where to start looking."

I clenched my jaw and took a deep breath to squash my frustration. "The Troll King isn't here, plus I don't think he'll talk to us. Dragons let his Troll-kin get captured, then let them get killed."

"Evander isn't the only Troll left. I bet we can find others in Paraiso. They can't *all* blame us for Eldrick's actions, so maybe we can get one of them to talk to us."

As soon as we got back, we started looking for Trolls. The first man I spoke to didn't even reply, he just kept walking like I was invisible. Eva tried with the next one we saw, but that troll said she didn't know anything. She also kept looking around, like she was afraid to be seen with us.

After she had walked off, I said, "Let's go by the lake. Trolls liked to hang out on the shore sometimes, away from the training grounds."

We pushed our way through the underbrush to the water, then worked our way around the shoreline. Eva was the first to spot another troll, a woman sitting on a rock near the water with her knees tucked up to her chin and her arms wrapped around her legs.

Eva walked up, smiling. "Hi, how's the water?"

The Troll didn't smile back. "You know we don't swim in it. That's Elf Ancestor water."

I stepped up beside Eva and waved. "Of course. Eva's not good at breaking the ice, so I'm sorry about that. It's just a figure of speech anyway."

She nodded, then looked back out over the water and said, "No offense taken, dragons."

When she didn't say anything else, I blurted, "Why won't you Trolls talk to us?"

Cairo shot me a glare, but the Troll looked sideways at me. "You know why. Just because we know you didn't hold the knife yourselves doesn't mean things are okay between our people. The Trolls are hurt, scared, and angry. Maybe you know how that feels?"

Actually, I did know how that felt. The memory of meeting my parents, Rylan and Sila, came to mind. I hadn't been very easy on them at first, for the very same reason. "I can understand that. But you're talking to us, at least. Thanks for that. You know, I was wondering—"

Eva elbowed me in the ribs. "We."

"*We* were wondering... Do you have any idea what kind of spell is making the jungle turn black? I know how Eldrick started it, but do you know why it worked or why it kept going after the rest of the Trolls were rescued?"

She stared over the cerulean water, utterly still. In the water, the reflection of her and her rock under that sky was like a mirror image. It was beautiful. "I never thought about it. I figured if anyone knew why, they'd say so. Haven't you been out there to look?"

Cairo said, "Yes, we have. It just didn't work. Since you're a Troll and it started with the Trolls, do you have any ideas?"

She took a deep breath, then stretched out her legs before hopping off her rocky perch. "I guess we should start by going out there. Maybe if I look at it, since I'm a Troll, I might see something you missed, or feel something different."

I nodded. That was a good idea. Even if it didn't work, it was still better than sitting around waiting for Jericho to get back to bellowing orders at us. And it was time we could spend trying to mend things between dragons and Trolls.

She led us all away from the lake, but not the direction I'd expected.

I said, "The black jungle is that way."

"Actually, it's all around us. There's a patch over here that's closest."

"Cool," I said, and we followed her. A couple minutes later, I saw the blackness ahead. It looked thick, like oil covering everything instead of just color fading out like in the other places. "I didn't know this was here."

The troll shook her head. "It wasn't here until this morning sometime. It just popped up. I've stayed away from it since then." She walked to the edge of the black, then stopped and closed her eyes. After a moment, she said, "I don't sense anything in there."

"Same for us," I said. "Inside the black, it's not just like something is missing. It's more like the nothing is its own thing."

She nodded and snapped her fingers. "Yes! But it can't really be empty. Maybe if I step into it and then try to sense it."

I held out my arm to the black, inviting her to try. What could it hurt?

She took a couple steps beyond the edge until she stood entirely within the blackness. She bent down and closed her eyes, then reached her fingertips down to touch the black, leafy jungle floor. "I'm not sure, but I—"

She shrieked and fell to the ground, then kept screaming. Her eyes rolled up in her head, and she started to convulse. Her whole body shook.

Just as my shock wore off, I took a step toward her, but she shrieked again and her whole body went rigid. Her back arched so badly that she only touched the ground at her heels and the back of her head. That scream sounded like my worst nightmares.

Before I even thought about the risk, I wrapped one arm around her and lifted her off the ground, and ran back to the green. She shrieked the whole time. Cairo grabbed her feet and we carried her out of the dead spot.

We set her down on the green jungle floor just as Elves arrived. They must have heard the screaming. How could they miss it, though, when she was still shrieking?

The Elves coming through the jungle took one look at what was happening and their leader pointed a spear at us. "King Gaber's hat! What have you dragons done?" His pupils were wide open, taking in every bit of jungle light, and his lip curled back to bare his teeth at us.

"Nothing! She went into the dark spot, and when she touched the ground, she collapsed. Help her!" I didn't care about being blamed. The Troll needed help.

Four more Elves poured around the first, two shoving Cairo and me aside while the other two grabbed the Troll. Her body was flopping like a fish out of water when they got her arms around their shoulders and rushed back toward Paraiso, dragging her between them.

As the leader turned away, I asked, "Will she be okay? I only—"

"Silence! I don't care what you were *only* doing. Gaber was a fool to trust you."

I stepped forward, ignoring his spear tip, determined to follow the others. "Forget about that. Will she be okay?"

The Elf blocked my way with his spear. "Stay away from her, *dragon*. We'll take your latest victim to the medical ward. Get back to your quarters and stay there! If you try to leave, Keepers or not, I'll have you in chains. Gaber isn't here to save you." His face was a mask of snarling anger, and I could only nod once, shocked. He spun on his heels and stormed after his companions.

What else was there to do? I looked at Eva and shrugged. "I guess we had better do it," I said. "But if they think I'm staying there for long, they're out of their minds. I'm going to wait until dark and sneak into the ward. I want to make sure the Troll is okay. She's like that because of us. Everyone on board with that?"

Eva nodded. Cairo didn't, but he looked away and didn't argue. A few minutes later, we were in my guest treehouse, where we waited. And waited. No one came to see us, or even question us. By the time the sun went down, I think we were all ready to get out of there.

I gathered us by the door and then as we left one-by-one, we each shifted into our dragons to get to the jungle floor, just in case the Elves could sense it when we "blipped" down. Then, we made our way to the medical ward. The Elves had grown it from the living trees themselves, like much of Paraiso, and it was just as beautiful.

Inside, through the openings where windows would be if it ever got cold in Paraiso, I saw three glowstones on each wall casting just enough light to see by. We had to wait a few minutes for the only person inside to leave, but then we were able to walk right in without even trying to hide.

I made my way to the Troll's bed and looked down at her. She was pale, and her breaths were quick and shallow. The sweat on her face shone in the glowstone light. Everything about her expression told me she was in agony. She looked like she was dying, and it was my fault.

I sat on the edge of the bed and put my hand on hers. The hair on my arm stood on end, moving like a wave from my hand all the way up to the back of my neck, and I shivered. I could almost feel her pain radiating out of her.

Her eyelids fluttered open, then. At first, she seemed to be staring right through me, but then I saw her eyes focus on mine. "Colton," she whispered.

I wanted her to speak up or tell me she was okay. I wanted her to get out of bed and get better. Instead, the effort from just saying my name seemed to make her shrink into herself, like it took away from whatever energy she had left in her.

"Yes, it's me. Tell me what I can do to help you, please," I whispered, and I felt my voice cracking. This was my fault.

"... closer ..."

I leaned down and put my ear near her face. "Tell me how to help, I'll do it," I said, more loudly than I should have.

"... the source ... in the land ... Fairies."

I shook my head and found myself clutching at her arm. "Forget the source, forget Fairies. How do we help you?" I cried out.

She didn't answer me, and even before I sat back upright, tears were streaming down my cheeks. The Troll would never cry again, which only made me cry harder.

J.A. Culican

Chapter Eleven

I blinked and looked at Eva helplessly. If even dragon and Elven healers couldn't do anything to save the Troll, what chance did I have? None.

Eva put her hand on my arm lightly. "It's not your fault, you know. I know you're going to blame yourself for this, but I'm telling you, don't. We had no way of knowing what would happen. Really, we don't actually know what *did* happen. But it had to have something to do with the reason Eldrick killed the Trolls and started the Earth to dying in the first place. This time, it was just one Troll. What if it had been a whole group? Now we can let them all know that the Trolls have to stay out of the black areas."

I shook my head, more to myself than to her. Of course, she would try to cheer me up, she was my friend, but no matter what she said, it was my fault. For this Troll, this time, she touched the black area because I asked her to. Maybe knowing it was deadly to them could save lives down the road, and maybe it would even give the big thinkers some new clue on how to solve all of this, but none of it made a difference to the poor Troll lying dead on the bed in the medical ward.

Cairo had been silent since the Troll died, so of course, he picked that moment to start talking again. "Eva is right. You probably saved lives. Plus, I'm thinking it might give the people back in Ochana something to think about. Maybe they can connect the dots in some new way and figure out what's going on."

I shouted, "No!" Then I tried to get myself under control. I took a breath and said, "Look, thanks for trying, but it's not going to make me feel better, and it's not going to bring her back, is it? She's dead, and no matter how you spin it, it's because I asked her to go into the black zone. Everything else is just what ifs and maybes, not facts. Not only that, she was the only Troll who would even talk to me, and now she's dead. Because of me. You think the others will want to talk to me after that? Yeah, probably not."

Eva frowned and scrunched her face, irritated. "Why do you care whether the Trolls like you or not? You're not a Troll, and that doesn't change our mission. Does it?"

"No, of course, it doesn't change our mission. But they don't like me, and I don't like that. What's it matter if it's important to the mission? It's important to me."

Cairo said, "If Jericho were here, he'd say—"

"Forget Jericho," I snapped, interrupting him. "He doesn't have any feelings in him to get hurt. He's a robot. Boo-hoo, his best friend died. A lot of people's best friends have died, and if this war keeps going, a lot more are going to lose best friends. He should get over it, but either way, I got my own problems to worry about, starting with an innocent Troll who died just for trying to help us."

Eva shook her head. "I know you're mad, but you aren't alone, and it isn't just happening to you. I'm here with you."

Of course, Eva was with me. She would have my back no matter what. I said, "Look, it's not that I don't appreciate that. I know we're all in this together. But she still died because I'm the Keeper of Dragons. I never asked for this, and I don't want it."

"What do you want?" Eva looked up at me and the concern in her eyes made me start to feel bad. Maybe I was being hard on her.

"Sometimes," I said with a heavy sigh, "I just wish I could go home. My real home, the people I grew up with. Not all of this." I waved my hand around, taking in Paraiso, Ochana, all of it.

The door opened and an Elf I didn't recognize stepped in. He wore the colors of Prince Gaber, though. When he saw us, he stopped suddenly and saluted. Then, standing as tall as he could and staring straight ahead, he said, "Prince Colton of Ochana. Prince Gaber and the Elven leaders request your immediate presence. I am here to escort you back at your soonest convenience."

It seemed pretty clear by his tone that he really meant right now, not whenever it was convenient. I clenched my fists and let out a frustrated huff through my nose. "It seems I'm being summoned. You're going to have to get along without me for a bit. Please see if we can do anything nice for that poor Troll, would you?"

Cairo snorted. "I'll give you one guess what Gaber and the other Elves want with you."

"Yeah," I said, staring at him, "it looks like they agree with me about who's responsible for all of this."

Before they had a chance to answer, I spun on my heels and stormed out the door, my Elf guardian rushing to catch up behind me. I kept going until we were out of sight, then I stopped and looked at him. "What am I walking into? I mean, how bad is it?"

"I'm not sure what you mean, Prince Colton."

"Please, just call me Cole. And I mean, how deep is the trouble I'm about to get in when I walk in that room?"

His face was blank. "That's not something they have told me... Cole. They just told me to bring you to them, but they didn't say why. It did sound rather urgent, though. Now, if you'd please come with me, they're waiting for you."

I held my hand out. "After you." Then, I fell into step beside him. We walked through Paraiso until we got to the Council room tree.

The escort saluted me. "Prince Gaber and his council await you. Good luck, Cole."

"Thanks."

I blinked up to the walkway, just outside the council chambers, then knocked hard three times on the door. I didn't want to seem timid and afraid at an important moment like that. If I was going to be in trouble for the poor Troll's death, I had to keep the situation under control so that it didn't cause any problems to affect the alliance. Without that, the Earth didn't stand a chance. I didn't know if it stood a chance even with the alliance.

The door swung open on its own, startling me a little bit. I gathered myself up and straightened my shirt, then marched inside. Prince Gaber and his sister were there, along with three other Elves. I had seen the other three around Paraiso and knew they were important, but I didn't know who they were.

I looked at Gaber directly and said, "You asked for me to come see you. I'm here, of course. How can I help you?"

"Yes, thank you for coming. I'm sure you know why we've called you. The death of a Troll after touching one of the black spots. It has all the Elves and Trolls frightened. The black areas have been expanding unpredictably, and new spots are still appearing. We haven't figured out any pattern as to how or when they will appear. It means that one could very well pop up right here in the middle of Paraiso. If Elves and Trolls die the instant they touch the black spots, I'm sure you can see why they're afraid."

When Gaber mentioned the Troll who had died, I could see the blame in his eyes. It matched the guilt I felt. He stared at me, but I couldn't meet his eyes. Instead, I glanced from Elf to Elf, trying to look stronger than I felt. I said, "Yes, I get it. I understand why they're afraid, and they should be. We don't know why it killed the Troll when she touched it. I've touched it and it didn't harm me."

Gaber gritted his teeth. "I hope you see now how reckless that was. What if it had killed the Keeper of Dragons?"

"Then a black spot would have done what King Eldrick couldn't," I snapped.

Gaber shouted, "Don't you mention his name here!" He took a deep breath, trying to calm himself. He said,

"My brother is a traitor, not a king. And touching the black spot was reckless."

"I know," I replied, "and I had no idea what it was, but I touched it anyway. Worse, I sent someone else to go do the same, but I didn't know it would kill her."

"That's right, you didn't know. You cost a good Troll her life. I knew her, Cole, and I'm not the only one who will miss her."

I looked down at the floor. I just couldn't look him in the eyes. "I know. Because I was fine when I touched it, I assumed everyone else would be, too."

One of the other Elves said loudly, "Aha! So, the dragon admits he is at fault."

My head snapped around to face him and I hissed, "Don't twist my words. My fault? Did I plunge a dagger into her chest like your king's brother did? No. I asked her to do something I had already done myself. I don't ask people to do things I wouldn't do. Can you say the same?"

Oh, no. Too late, I realized what I'd done. He had just made me so angry by blaming me for the Troll's death as if I was the killer. Eldrick did it, not me. In the middle of the stunned silence, I said, "I'm sorry. That was disrespectful of me, and I apologize. I know that everyone is tense, and we're all upset over her death. She seemed like a good person, even though I barely knew her. I feel her death like a heavy weight. The truth is, I blame myself just as much as you do."

The Elf opened his mouth and leaned forward, gripping the arms of his chair, eyes shining like he finally had me where he wanted me, but Prince Gaber cut him off, slamming his fist down on the arm of his chair.

"Silence! Cole, taking responsibility for what you did surprises me. I have not come to expect that from dragons. I have one question. Why did you ask her to touch it? What did you hope to get out of that?"

Well, they couldn't judge me any harder than I was already judging myself, so I shoved my irritation aside. It didn't really matter what happened to me, anyway. The only thing that really mattered was the war, the Time of Fear. It's not like Gaber would let them execute me. I didn't think they could, even if they wanted to.

But, if I wanted to beat Eldrick and push back the blackness, I needed a strong alliance. If that meant apologizing to a scared and angry elf who snapped at me, I could handle that. I said, "We were hoping that she might discover something about the spots that we'd missed. Maybe she could smell something, or maybe the black spots had something to do with Trolls. I mean, we know it had something to do with them in the beginning, when…"

"When my brother killed so many of them."

"Yes. I thought maybe there would be a connection between the Troll and the spot, and we might be able to learn something and we could use it against it."

"I see how you might think that." Gaber shot a hard glance at the Elf I'd insulted, like a warning to be silent. I think they were talking telepathically, but I wasn't part of the conversation, so I couldn't be sure. "And what did her death teach you? Did you learn anything that you might use against Eldrick and his spots?"

I took a deep breath and let it out slowly. "No. We didn't learn anything from her death. It was just one more pointless murder by your brother and his forces. But there's more we *have* learned."

Gaber shook his head. His eyes were narrowed, looking at me. "You make no sense. What do you mean that you didn't learn anything, but you did? Explain yourself."

So, I told him and his Elves all about what I'd done— seeing the light, talking to Ancestors, pumping every ounce of energy I could into the bush and bringing it back to life.

They sat silently, and the expressions on their faces told me they were as surprised as I had been. That was a relief because I'd have lost my mind if I thought they knew something like that and kept it from me just because I was a dragon. The only thing I'd left out was the ring. I kept that to just me and Eva, and her only because she'd been there to see it. It was our secret. I don't know why, but it felt important to keep it private between us.

At first, they weren't fully convinced about bringing the bush back to life, but when they had a black leaf brought in by a glove-wearing Elf, I closed my eyes and did my thing, and when I opened them, the leaf was green again. They were shocked and stared at it a long time.

Then I said, "And my Troll friend said one last thing before she went to her Ancestors. She said, 'The source is in the land of the Fairies.'"

Gaber stood up and started to pace in front of his chair, walking back and forth with his hands behind his back, looking at the floor. Then he stopped mid-step and looked up at me. "Then it's settled. Although the Troll's death is on your hands, I think you feel remorse, and I am pretty sure you'll use your head before you risk someone else's life on a whim the next time."

"Yes, I—"

"It wasn't a question. One more thing is settled, too— you have to go to the Fairy realm. Maybe we should have sent you there in the beginning, I don't know. The Fates don't ask me how things should happen."

I said, "I'm sure you don't mind the fact that it takes me away from Paraiso."

He ignored the comment. "Find the source of this cancer in the Earth, and cure it. Only you can stop the land from dying, Prince Colton."

It was the first time I felt like he'd said my name without a sneer in his voice since I'd met him. I could almost feel his desperate hope sitting on my shoulders, and I didn't like it. I'd have rather had him sneering at me than inspiring unrealistic hope. What could I really do? Heal one spot. Not exactly legendary.

But I'd wanted to go to the Fairies in the beginning, before we went to the Mermaids. If I had, I wouldn't have learned to use mereum, and I wouldn't have been able to turn the black green again. So maybe Fate had planned that part out, and maybe it still had some new surprises in store for me among the Fairies. There was only one way to find out.

Chapter Twelve

"I'll go." I tried to stand tall, looking confident. I didn't really feel it, but they didn't have to know that.

You can do it, though. Eva's voice was in my head. I hoped she was the only one listening in.

Gaber gave me a quick nod. "Then it's settled. But be aware that after what happened with the Troll, you aren't welcome back in Paraiso. You're just too dangerous to have around. Besides, your quest is out there, not tucked safely here with us. When you've cured it so the blackness no longer threatens the world, then you'll be welcome back with open arms."

I was stunned. Exiled from Paraiso! I loved Paraiso's jungle paradise. I understood the decision, but I felt like part of me had been cut off. If I wanted it back, I had to save it first. "I understand. I won't let you down. As long as I'm still breathing, I'll be out there fighting for you and all the other races of Truth."

Hey, it sounded good in my head, even if it came out a little melodramatic.

Gaber nodded, then raised a small wooden staff from where it leaned against his chair and banged the metal-tipped bottom against the floor three times. It made an impressive booming noise. It also made it clear I was dismissed, so I turned and left without another word.

Outside, Cairo and Eva waited for me. She was the first to speak up when they saw me. "How did it go? Are you in trouble?" She looked really worried, biting her bottom lip.

"It wasn't great. They blame me for the Troll dying. They think I'm too dangerous to have around. So, I'm being kicked out."

"What! They—"

"They'll let me back in when we fix the planet. No biggie."

Cairo's eyes went wide as his cheeks turned red. "That's not fair! How were you to know what would happen? Let me go in there and tell them—"

"No," I said, cutting him off. I put my hand on his shoulder and looked right into his eyes. "Thank you for standing up for me. But they're right. My place is out there fighting Eldrick, not hiding here, where it's safe. That's an illusion anyway, because not even Paraiso will stay safe. Not if I don't fix this."

Eva slid her arm around my waist and nudged my shoulder with her cheek. "You mean until we fix this. I'm in. Where are we going?"

"Me too," Cairo said. "I go where Eva goes, but I'd come with you anyway. We're in it together, right?"

A voice behind me made me jump. "You weren't going to leave without me, were you?"

I spun around, startled, and saw Jericho. "You're back! Where did you go?"

"I had some things to look into, and some people I had to question."

"And did you learn anything?"

"I didn't find out anything new, unfortunately. Give it time. We'll see where it leads. I won't say more until I have something worth sharing with the Keepers," Jericho said with a nod to Eva, his eyes still on me. "Where are we going, and when do we leave?"

"I was just getting to that," I said, grinning. "I'll be a lot happier with you coming with us. We need to head to the land of the Fairies. We only have one clue, and it says we'll find the source in Greece."

Eva pulled her arm out from around my waist. She stepped up beside Cairo and looked up at Jericho. "Well, you get your wish after all, Cole. Maybe we should have gone there first."

I laughed since I'd had the same thought. "No, you were right. Fate works however it wants to. If we hadn't gone to see the Mermaid queen first, I wouldn't have learned how to turn the blackness green again."

Jericho let out a bark. His eyes flared brightly as he said, "You can fix this? How? Tell me everything."

I tried not to laugh at his reaction. "It turns out that if I focus mahier, tilium, and mereum at something, it comes back to life and the black goes away. I don't know how long it lasts, and I sure can't do it faster than all the black spots grow, but it's a start."

Jericho clapped me on my shoulder hard enough to sting, grinning. "You can say that again. That's one fine start, Cole. I would never have even thought to try, but then again, you're the only one of us who has more than one power. Aprella is smiling on us."

I grinned right back, but said, "Don't sing my praises, yet. We have to get to Greece and talk to the Fairies. I'm not sure what 'the source is in the land of the Fairies' means, but we'll find out when we get there."

"A wing of dragons will follow us and meet us there," he said. "Now, everyone, go grab your stuff and meet me back here in fifteen minutes. Actually, make that a half-hour so we can eat before we leave. I'm hungrier than I realized."

So was I, actually. I left the group and got me a fat cow to eat, then went and got my backpack.

The others were already at the clearing by the time I got there. Cairo said, "What kept you, slowpoke? I'm ready when you are."

I gave him a thumbs-up, then turned and leaped into the air, shifting into my dragon. They were right behind me, and the four of us rose up and away, leaving beautiful Paraiso behind. I hoped I would get to see it again, someday.

As we rose high above the Congo jungles, I could see for miles. The blackness had spread, that was for sure. It seemed like there was more black than green now, wherever I looked. It made me sad to think of all the poor animals and plants that were dying.

I sped up. The miles streaked by, and I let myself zone out. It was nice to just let everything fade away and focus on the feel of the wind on my face, the way the clouds tickled my wings when we flew through them. We flew like that, hour after hour.

When the sun began to sink into the horizon, I felt Jericho's thoughts in my mind. *We need to stop for the night. I know a dragon living in this area who will take us in. Follow me down, and I'll introduce you to him. Then we can get something to eat.*

I tipped my wings to let him know I heard him, then banked slowly to the west, following him down at a lazy speed. I wished he'd hurry up since I was practically starving, but I thought he might have a reason for going so slow. Maybe the dragon we were seeing wouldn't like a bunch of us streaking down from the sky at almost the speed of sound.

We landed in a rocky clearing surrounded by a big stretch of palm trees. That meant we were still in Africa, I figured, which kind of surprised me. We had been flying pretty fast. Then I remembered how I lost track of time daydreaming.

Anyway, I shifted into my human as we landed, then turned to Jericho. "Where is your friend? I don't see any houses, here."

He started walking toward the tree line. "He lives in a hut in the palm tree forest. There's a trail to his hut, but unless you know it's there, he has hidden it with his mahier."

We followed Jericho and he headed directly toward a tree. I thought he would go around it, but he didn't even slow down. He walked right through it! That must be the trail, I realized—and then it appeared to me. Trees shimmered away, revealing a nice trail that had been well-maintained. Somebody took the time to clear away all the weeds and underbrush regularly, too.

We must have walked for half an hour because it had become nearly dark. Jericho pointed up ahead, and I turned to look. I had to squint to see it, but there was a log house in the distance. Calling it a hut wasn't really fair, because it looked big. It was only one story high, but even from our distance, I could tell it had room for several bedrooms. I had been picturing a little hunting cabin, not a full-sized log house.

When we got about a few hundred feet away, Jericho stopped and held up his hand. "I think you should wait here. He doesn't know you, and he's out here because he wants his privacy. I'll go talk to him and then I'll come get you."

Eva and Cairo nodded, but for some reason, the hairs on the back of my neck stood up and I felt goosebumps down my arms, despite the heat. "No, I don't think that's a good idea. You've seen how Eldrick's people have been following us. If we separate, it's just that much easier to catch us. I think we should stay together, especially with the blackness so close."

Jericho said, "There's blackness everywhere you go. I'll be fine. Just wait here."

"Say what you want, but I'm coming with you unless you want to stop me."

A little puff of smoke drifted from his nostrils, but he didn't say anything. He spun on his heels and stormed toward the hut. I had to scramble to catch up.

As we got closer, we found a small, rock-lined path up to the house itself. Jericho didn't slow down until we were almost to the front patio.

"Is it normal for him to have all the lights out?" I asked, "I mean, it's dark already. Maybe he's asleep."

Jericho stopped mid-stride and I almost walked right into him. He held his arm out to keep me back. "No. If he's home, there should be lights on, and he's always home. I hope he's okay. We need to check it out. Stay close and keep your eyes open."

We headed to the house, my eyes darting everywhere, trying to see everything at once. When we got to the patio, what we found only made me more nervous. He had beautiful, hand-carved chairs and a table on his patio, but they had been tossed around. One of the chairs was smashed into pieces. The door wasn't closed all the way, either, and hung from its top hinge.

I whispered, "Let's check inside. He might be hurt."

Jericho shook his head and pushed me back away from the house. "No, I've seen enough. We need to get out of here. Someone knew we were coming and may still be in the area. It could be a trap. I'm sad to say it but the Keeper of Dragons matters a lot more than my friend, or even me, right now. Move out, Cole."

I didn't argue. I'd had enough close calls with Eldrick's people to know how bad things could get and how fast they could get there. We hurried back to where Eva and Cairo stood waiting for us.

I said, "He's not home. This could be a trap, so get to the air."

Without waiting for a response, I turned and jumped into the air, summoning my dragon. I poured as much mahier as I could into disguising us and hiding our presence, hoping not to be seen by anyone on the ground.

The others followed, and I could feel their mahier pouring over me as well, making the disguise even stronger. They'd had the same idea.

I projected my thoughts at Jericho. "How would they have known we were coming here? That had to have happened recently, right? Otherwise, your friend's illusion would be gone already."

I heard Jericho's deep, rumbly voice in my mind saying, "You're right. I don't know who knew we were coming or how. It's something we should definitely be worried about. Maybe a spy, or maybe they're tracking us again. I guess we're flying through the night, Keeper."

After an hour, Africa's coastline gave way to the Mediterranean Sea. At night, it looked like a giant hole of inky blackness, much like the black spots, but I knew it was just an illusion. There weren't any cities in the ocean, after all, so no light at all. We didn't even slow down to eat before we flew out to sea.

We must've been about halfway to Europe when I noticed the wind picking up. At first, I just thought it was the ocean breeze, but I kept having to put more mahier into keeping the wind from bothering us. When I had to concentrate even harder, I thought out to Jericho, "What's wrong with the wind? Are we in a storm?"

I didn't understand how it could be a storm, though, because there weren't any clouds. The stars all sparkled brightly above us. And I hadn't felt the wind like that since I learned to keep it off me while flying. We were going way faster than a hurricane.

"Not any storm I can see," his voice echoed in my mind. "I feel it, too."

Something was terribly wrong.

J.A. Culican

Chapter Thirteen

A burst of wind slipped through my mahier screen and blew me sideways, sending me almost crashing into Cairo. He dodged out of the way at the last moment, but then he caught a gust of wind as he lifted his wings to turn away. It carried him like a kite, up and away, sending him a hundred yards in an instant.

We struggled to get back together and keep formation. Being close together made it easier for us all to pour our mahier into shielding the whole group, layering our powers on top of each other for more protection, but my wings were getting tired from the struggle. When we got hit by another windy hammer, fear radiated from Eva, slipping through her mental screen as she focused everything on her windscreen instead.

She wasn't the only one afraid. I was having a hard time keeping my thoughts to myself, too. I think we all were, and that storm or whatever it was seemed to still be getting worse. We tried to keep together, but I think we spent more of our energy doing that than we did moving forward, toward land.

Then the clouds appeared, but not just any old normal clouds. They didn't just blow in with the storm. At first, they rose up like a thick fog, but soon, we had ugly, black rolling clouds everywhere around us.

Lightning flashed deep inside the clouds, the thunder booming like some terrifying war drums. Every time it flashed, it turned the wicked black clouds red. They looked like fire and anger. I don't know how I knew it, but I felt like those clouds were hunting us.

It was no natural storm! I could *feel* dark tilium practically oozing from the clouds, I suddenly realized.

The lighting had been distant, deep inside the clouds around us, but just when I realized they were dark tilium, they burst into the biggest, scariest display I'd ever seen. Half a dozen bolts shot from the clouds, one bigger than any I'd seen before. Each bolt forked ten, then twenty times, and even more! When they all flashed at once, the huge storm lit up like a candle in a paper bag, and I could have sworn I saw Eldrick's face coming through. A face of red fire-clouds and lightning. An angry, insane face...

The bolts started to get closer and closer, moving toward us. At the same time, we got hit by even stronger hammer winds, swatting us down like bugs. The blows came at us from above, and I think I lost a thousand feet of altitude in seconds. The lightning was herding us, keeping us from going back up—we couldn't fly above the storm if we couldn't survive the trip up there.

"We have to land!" I shouted my thoughts to the others. My fear and tilium worked together like a bullhorn, making my thoughts stronger and louder.

I couldn't hear their answers over the noise of the storm and my own projected thoughts, echoing in my mind. I could only feel their agreement and their fear.

We didn't have much choice, though, because the hammering winds pushed us down and down, throwing us at the water below. What a way to end.

"Lights," Jericho's voice came into my mind from the darkness, but he sounded far away. I didn't see, him but I looked down and saw a town lit up. He was right. It was land!

I swept my wings back and fell like a dart, dropping away from the lightning and wind. I aimed for a spot just outside the glow from the town lights. Just before I hit the ground, I stretched out my wings and tilted them back. The sudden resistance brought me to a stop so fast my teeth clicked together so hard that I thought they might break.

I dropped the last ten feet to the ground, summoning my human as I landed, and fell to my knees. I didn't think anything broke, though, so I struggled to my feet, calling for the others as loudly as I could. I didn't hear any reply, even in my head. I tried again, but there was nothing. They were gone.

I heard a faint cry high above me. I looked up and saw wings flying my way, pumping against the terrible wind. I couldn't tell who it was until I heard the voice in my head again. It was Eva!

"Cole, I'm coming!" she cried.

A bolt of lightning came at her with a flash and a roar. Instinctively, I flung my hand out toward her. I felt mereum stronger than I'd ever used before, making a shield around her. The lightning hit it and was knocked aside! The shield cracked into a thousand shards of mereum, which dissolved back into the storm as they dropped.

A moment later, I was catching Eva as she crash-landed in human form, and we fell to the ground together, hard. It knocked the wind out of me but probably saved her from getting hurt from her fall. We lay there for a moment, gasping for air and praying not to get hit by lightning.

I didn't have to worry, though. As soon as she touched down, the storm lightened and then faded away to nothing in a matter of just moments. The tilium I'd felt everywhere was gone, my senses told me. Eldrick was gone.

"Are you okay?" I asked Eva.

She slowly untangled herself from me and climbed to her feet, then helped me up. "Yeah. Bruised, but not broken. Do you feel the others close by?"

I frowned. "I'd hoped you did. No, I can't feel either of them, and I know there was a Woland realm flying after us. I don't feel them, either."

She was silent, lips pursed. I understood the feeling perfectly well.

I said, "They must have been blown somewhere else. We could fly around looking for them. It seems the storm faded as soon as we landed, so you must have been the last to touch down."

She turned suddenly to face me and narrowed her eyes as she shouted, "No! Until we know for sure it's safe, we're walking. And we can't waste time looking for them, not when we have a mission to finish. Where would you even look?"

I took a step back, surprised by how fierce she was about it. "Fine, okay. No flying. We'll walk. I don't know where we'd look. I just thought you would want to. Cairo—"

"—knows where we're headed! You need to use your head more, Cole. We could spend months trying to find them, only to learn they did the smart thing and went to the Fairies. Just like we should be doing."

She stared at me for a few seconds, and then I saw the tension leave her shoulders and her eyes stopped being all squinty at me. "Sorry. That storm was terrifying, and I'm scared for the others, too. But we can't spend time looking for them. If they're alive, they know where we're going. They'll head there."

I stepped up and wrapped my arms around her. I thought maybe it would help her because I knew she wasn't saying everything. She had to be nearly panicked about Cairo, after all. She struggled for a second, then just let me hug her. Finally, she hugged me back.

After a moment, she stepped back, wiped her cheeks with the heels of her hands, and sniffled. "Fine, you big goof. Ick, feelings. Can we go now, please?"

I grinned at her and then turned north. "I figure we're in Greece," I said over my shoulder. "Fairies are here somewhere, right?"

"Yeah." She rushed to catch up, then settled into step next to me. "The grove ought to be a few miles that way." She pointed northeast.

It only took a half an hour of walking to find the grove. It wasn't as big as the Congo jungle, of course, but it was still pretty big. I could tell from the tilium in it that it would look like something else to a normal human, shielded like Paraiso was.

I felt my heartbeat rising in excitement at the thought of seeing our friends again soon and picked up my pace. Eva was grinning as we entered the grove.

"Fairies! Eva, can you feel it?" She was about to say something in reply when her eyes went suddenly wide, looking at me. I felt something cold, hard, and sharp against my throat. "What the...?"

"Silence, dragons," a high-pitched voice said from behind me. Another figure stepped out from behind a tree next to Eva. Well, it looked like it stepped out from *inside* the tree. Either way, Eva got a knife held to her throat, too.

My stomach sank. Fantastic. Held at knife-point by Fairies, the very people we'd come to see. What had I done this time?

Chapter Fourteen

"Get your hands off her! How dare you? We're the Keep—
"

The fairy holding me at knifepoint yanked my hair, dragging my head back. "The Keeper of Dragons. Yeah, we know who you are," he hissed into my ear. "And you'll get what's coming to you, too. Come quietly and get it a few minutes later, or struggle and you'll get it now."

Eva cried out, "No! We'll come. I swear, no fighting. Cole, stay calm."

I wasn't trying to freak out, not with a knife digging into my neck. "We'll come, take it easy. I have no idea what you mean, but—"

"Shut up!" My Fairy swung me around to face down the path. "Walk," he commanded.

I glanced at Eva and started walking. If we could just stay alive long enough to talk to someone in charge, I knew this could all be cleared up. I wasn't sure what the misunderstanding was, but I was totally certain that our lives depended on us finding out and fixing it.

The Fairies dragged us deeper into the grove. After a few minutes, I saw buildings ahead, and my heart beat faster. The Fairy realm, at last! But as we got closer, my excitement turned sour.

The destruction I saw there was enough to make me want to cry. Every building was smashed or burned; every garden was black with many still smoking, just as many of the homes still did. The windows everywhere had been stained glass, and I could just imagine how beautiful it must have been there with daylight streaming through a thousand colored windows. But no more. The windows had been smashed and destroyed, just like the village itself.

My jaw dropped. I looked at the Fairy holding me prisoner and saw tears welling up in his eyes, and his jaw was clenched so tightly that the muscles stood out on his cheeks. "What happened?" I asked.

The Fairies didn't answer me. They just kept dragging and prodding Eva and me to keep moving. We came around a corner in the road and saw the main village square. It was wrecked, too, and lots of people were wearing bandages. Eldrick would pay for what he'd done here. I promised that much.

I saw people on their knees in the middle of the village square and realized it was Jericho and Cairo. Some of the missing Woland Realm that had followed us into the storm was there also. They were alive! But many were missing. They all had their wrists tied in front of them, and my mahier told me the ropes were enchanted. I guessed it was to keep Jericho and the others from summoning their dragon forms.

"What on Earth is going on?" I asked, trying again. My kidnapper still didn't answer.

When we got close to Jericho, Eva and I were shoved down to the dirt next to him. All around, armed Fairies stood guard over us, staring with angry eyes. I was pretty sure someone had ordered them not to hurt us because they looked like they would have enjoyed running us through with their swords and spears.

Jericho's eye was swelling shut. Someone had kicked him in the face, I could tell because the bruise was shoe-shaped. He saw me looking at his swollen eye and shrugged.

I tried to keep my voice low enough for him to hear it, but not loud enough for the Fairies to, and asked him, "Do you know what happened here?"

It didn't work. One of the guards shouted, "Shut your mouth, *Dragon*." The way he said it was like dragon was a bad word or something.

"Actually," a woman behind me said, "let's hear what these monsters have to say before we give them the justice they deserve. We're civilized, here, unlike you people. We let defendants have their say first, and *then* we execute them."

I craned my neck to see her. I didn't recognize her. She carried herself with perfect posture, though, like someone used to being in charge. She had elegant features but the effect was ruined by the red-stained bandage wrapped around her head.

Then what she'd said registered in my head. "Wait. Execute us?" My eyes popped and I shouted, "On what charges?"

One of the guards behind me kicked me in the back, knocking me down. "Mind your tone."

The woman sneered at us while I got back up to my knees. "Do you really want to go through with this game? Fine, we'll pretend you don't know."

Through her clenched jaw, Eva said, "We don't know. There's no pretending. So maybe you could humor us with an explanation before you murder us."

The Fairy leader rolled her eyes. "Fine. You stand charged with being dragons, the same fiends who attacked this sacred place—our *home*—destroying it and killing our people. When we beg for mercy, you ignore our pleas, but you want us to show you the mercy you denied us?

"That wasn't us, it was—"

"You dragons have become mad beasts! No one can reason with you. You're destroying everything around you. Where was the mercy you ask for when you were attacking us?" She'd gone from talking with ice in her voice to shouting, full of fiery anger.

I was stunned as I heard myself shouting back, before I realized what I was doing, "Impossible! Maybe dragons don't get along with most other races, but we aren't killers. We don't attack another True being for no reason."

There were about two seconds of total silence as everyone stared at me, shocked. I crossed my arms over my chest and added, "I never heard any such thing from my father, or from anyone in Ochana. Never."

The woman's eyes flashed. "Liar!"

Jericho spoke for the first time. "Prince Colton is no liar, Fairy, and he's the only one who can heal your grove."

Her eyes flicked over to look at me. "Heal it? And yet, here we are, having captured the dragon prince himself after he came to our grove to spread more chaos. Proof that you dragons are working against us now. What do you have to say to that, boy?"

The guard who had kicked me said from behind me, "Speak quickly, while you still can."

I only had one shot. I had to make it good. The fairies were scared, hurt, and angry, and they weren't looking for reasons to talk things out. "Dragons like me use the power, mahier. Some of you know how I also can use purified tilium."

The guard said, "That's nothing new. You're stalling."

"No! What you don't know is that I use mereum, too. When I use all three powers together, I can bring your grove back. It even works on the blackness spreading everywhere."

I was kind of proud of all that but tried not to sound like it. I kept my eyes looking down at the ground and hoped I didn't seem like I was bragging.

"The blackness! You dragons brought that, so of course, you're the only ones who can fix it. You destroyed our grove, and you turned the rest out to rot. You only left us our village, and now you've destroyed that, too." She looked like she might burst into tears, but I saw steel in her eyes.

"None of us here did that, but I really can fix it. The blackness is everywhere, not just here. If you left your realm to help the rest of the world, you'd know this. Eldrick created the blackness when he killed the Trolls."

The village leader stopped and stared at me, and I felt like she was trying to see into my aura for lies. She probably was, but must not have found what she expected, because then she let out a long, frustrated sigh. "The Trolls are gone?" she asked at last.

Eva blurted, "Many of them. Where their blood hit the ground, the black spots started. He killed them all over the world, and the dark spots are growing on their own. The Trolls that Cole and I rescued"—she nodded to indicate me—"are taking refuge with the Elves in Paraiso."

I saw the guards look at their leader. They looked tense and ready. This was it, the moment of truth. They'd either buy it, or they'd be playing "stabby-stabby cut-cut" with us really soon.

"Very well, if the Keeper can heal our grove, then I'll know you're telling us the truth. We'll go from there. But if you've lied, killing you won't bring our grove back, but it'll be some small justice."

I got to my feet and squared my shoulders. I looked her in the eyes and said, "Then we should get started. Where do you want me to begin?"

Chapter Fifteen

As the Fairies led me to the center of their grove, I kept stumbling from the chains and shackles they'd put us all in. It also made it hard to catch my balance, and I probably got more than a few bruises from falling down along the way. Each time I fell, Fairy guards helped me to my feet. Some were gentle, some were rough. It was obvious that I hadn't convinced them all, not yet.

But that's what we're on our way to do, right?

I glanced over at Eva and gave her a quick nod, but before I could think back at her, my foot caught on a root and I fell face-first into the blackened, dead soil. I let out a sharp, frustrated breath. We'd been walking longer than I thought we should have, but the growth seemed larger on the inside than it had looked when we were flying in. The chains might have been slowing me down, but it still felt like we should have reached the center faster. Eventually, though, we got there more or less in one piece.

The Fairy Queen was already there, waiting for us. After she'd been told what happened, the chains had been her idea, despite everything we went through together in Paraiso. The chains weren't the only thing frustrating me. The fact that she believed the nonsense about dragons attacking them showed me just how low people's opinions of Ochana had gone during my grandfather's reign as king.

She said, "We are in the heart of our sacred Grove. You swore to heal the land, and so I am giving you the chance to do so. You are in the enviable position of holding your fate in your own hands. Most people don't get that chance. Certainly, the Trolls didn't. I wish you luck, Prince Colton."

I turned to face her, then gave her a deep bow. She looked surprised, but it didn't hurt anything for me to show her respect in her realm, after all. I knew I could cure the blackness, so I figured I would score some brownie points at the same time. "I need the chains off my wrists, Queen. I have to have clear flow for my energies to work right."

When she narrowed her eyes, I hastily added, "But you can leave the ankle cuffs on, of course. It's just my hands."

She motioned to one of the guards and nodded. He came over and unlocked both cuffs.

I rubbed my wrists, grimacing as the blood flowed back into my hands, setting them to pins and needles. Then I took a few long, slow breaths and focused my will. I channeled my mahier and tilium through my hands, down into the soil, while I drew mereum from the air and guided that into the soil, too.

With my eyes still closed, I heard gasps of surprise all around me. I cracked one eyelid open enough to glance around; the queen had both hands over her mouth and stared at her trees with eyes as wide as saucers.

I tried not to grin and focused on keeping the energy pouring into the grove. I could *feel* the life returning, and as the plants and insects came back, I felt the grove's deep tilium pool coming back, too. Bigger and bigger, the circle of life grew all around us. Some of the Fairies even started laughing with joy to see their home returning to them.

I wasn't sure how long I'd been working at it, but eventually, I felt the very last of the blackness vanish—in this place, at least, the curse upon the Earth was completely gone.

The queen put one hand on my shoulder, looking me in the eyes, and smiled. "Prince Colton—Cole, as you like to be called—you have kept your word. You and your friends are free, and I name you Friends of the Grove. Will you stay for a banquet tonight? We need to celebrate the return of our grove! It would mean a lot to me if you would join us."

Before Eva could blurt out something to ruin the moment, I agreed. Besides, I was really hungry after the flight we'd had.

***

That night, just as the brightest stars began shining up above, my friends and I were led to the Fairies' Great Hall. I saw barrels and barrels of wine and ale open, but I wasn't interested in those things. After using so much energy earlier, the only thing I had eyes for was the huge feast that filled up a dozen long tables laid out end-to-end. I had never seen so much food in one place. My mouth watered.

Nearby, costumed Fairies played music on instruments that glittered every time the strings were plucked or a key was pressed. They played strange music, but it was beautiful. Whatever they played, there were always four main chords but if I strained hard enough to listen, I could almost hear a fifth note. It was like the four tones together made a new one.

At the head of the table stood the queen. When she spoke, her voice reached every corner of the hall though she seemed to be talking in a normal voice, not shouting. "My people, we have our grove back. Eldrick tried to take it from us, not the dragons, but it was the dragons who gave it back. It may be the last thing we expected, I know, but the truth is easy to see all around us. Our power returned with it, and so tonight, we celebrate! Let's rejoice in our home and our new friends. "

The Fairies all around clapped, so I did, too. I was led to a seat close to the head of the table, while my companions were seated farther away, but still close enough to the queen to be in places of honor. Fairies were masters at politics, it seemed. I raised a cup of cider to the queen, and she smiled and raised hers to me.

I didn't care where they sat me, just as long as I could get to all that beautiful, beautiful food. There were meat and fish, both roasted and fried. Mushrooms sautéed with shallots. Every kind of plant, even many I couldn't recognize, baked, fried, raw, or pickled. Basically, they had food in every delicious way there was to eat it. Okay, I wasn't sure about the pickled stuff, but I wasn't going to complain. I'd never been to a Fairy banquet before, and Jericho had told me that very few outsiders were ever invited.

As the party went on into the night, after I'd eaten all I wanted to and more, I was having a great time. Even Jericho didn't bug me as much as usual. I hadn't realized how badly I needed to set aside all the danger and fear and drama going on in the world, even if I knew it would only be for a night.

As it turned out, my vacation from all of that didn't last very long.

J.A. Culican

Chapter Sixteen

I was about to dig into another helping of some weird-looking but deliciously roasted bird when a horn sounded outside, and then another horn blew even closer. The queen jumped to her feet and cried, "To arms! We're under attack."

I rushed outside, drawing my sword, and found Jericho at my side. A nearby building was burning, its walls smashed by a big red dragon, who still stood in front of it. When he turned to look at me, I almost panicked-- the thing reminded me of a wild beast. He had crazy, red eyes and smoke poured from his nostrils. He snarled and drew a deep breath, getting ready to unload fire again.

"Get the queen back!" I shouted to Jericho, then sprinted at the rampaging dragon. How dare he stoop so low as to work with Eldrick! I wanted nothing more than to punish that traitor. When I got close, I drew my sword. I wasn't going to let him harm our allies.

The dragon ignored me and blew a cone of fire at Jericho, who was leading the queen away, but Jericho threw up a mahier shield and the flame parted harmlessly around them. "I know him!" he shouted to me. "He's an old soldier."

Something wasn't right, I just had a strong feeling about it. I couldn't put my finger on what it was, though. I stopped myself from skewering him with my sword, and instead, jumped over the dragon's lashing tail. I shouted back to Jericho, "When did he turn traitor?"

He raised his hands over his head, then brought them both down in the dragon's direction; faintly glimmering mahier threads as thick as ropes appeared and draped themselves over our attacker. "He didn't turn traitor! He was too rational for that. I saw him last week—"

He was interrupted when the dragon flexed his heavy wings, shattering the ropes, and the back-blast channeled back to knock Jericho to his knees.

"Let's see how you deal with something new," I muttered. I imagined new cords over the dragon, willing them to appear, and wove them together by moving my hands over each other. This time, though, they were made of tilium, not mahier.

Eva and Cairo arrived and flanked the dragon so one stood on both sides of him. I saw them throwing more mahier bonds over the creature. I was glad they figured out what Jericho and I were trying to do because I didn't want to kill the thing. You can't question a dead dragon, after all.

Jericho scrambled back to his feet and, raising both fists over his head and then swinging his arms down to his sides, he placed a mahier dome over the dragon, adding to the threads.

It thrashed and roared and growled, but never once used words. The only thoughts I got from it weren't in words either, but more like picture-thoughts. Lots of angry red hues. The more it thrashed, the harder we all concentrated on keeping it bound.

"Ropes!" I yelled. "Get this thing tied up. I'm using tilium like crazy, but it isn't slowing down." That was strange, but the creature really didn't seem to be getting tired at all, no matter how hard or how long it fought. I realized we were getting tired faster than it was, even with five of us. It would have been a lot easier to just kill him, but we needed information.

Thankfully, no one else got hurt while our crew of dragons—Jericho, Eva, Cairo, and I—all fought to get the invading dragon tied up with real ropes. When that was done, I put my hands on my knees, and sweating, and let my tilium cords fade away.

The queen walked up to me, but her eyes never left the tied-up dragon. She said, "Why didn't you kill it?" It sounded more like an accusation than a question.

I stood as tall and straight as I could when I replied, just out of respect, though I still hadn't caught my breath. "Something's wrong... It's not... acting right. We need to... question the thing."

She nodded but looked relieved. Maybe she'd thought we were just being nice because it was a dragon like us. That was a little bit true, I suppose, but it wasn't the main reason we'd tied him up instead of killing him.

Jericho said, "You made a good choice not to kill him, Cole. I knew that man, and he was a very sensible person, a methodical warrior, not some crazy berserker. He shouldn't be acting like this. And did you notice, when you try to talk to him, it's like he's not listening?"

"Yeah. And the thoughts I read from him were in pictures, not words," I replied. "A lot like how I think animals would do it."

Eva tapped her lips with one finger while she looked over at our new prisoner. He was still trying to fight his way loose, though he could hardly move an inch with all the chains and ropes we had tied him up with. "We need to study him. Somewhere with labs and doctors, I think. We—"

Trumpets blared from above, cutting her off. I looked up and saw two dragons, a man and a woman dragon judging by their sizes, with banners of Second Realm, Ochana's recon force. They spiraled down toward us, slowing a bit with each circle, but they were moving faster than they should be as they rushed to land. When they touched down and summoned their human forms, they staggered from the speed, but neither one fell. They both bowed to Queen Annabelle, then knelt in front of me with their left hand over their chest, saluting.

The man said, "My prince, I bear a message from your father."

My father! It felt like I hadn't heard from Rylan in quite a while, but that was probably just because of how busy we all had been. Everyone had more to do than time to do it in. I looked at my friends, unsure of what to do, and said, "Very well. Thank you for coming all this way. What message does he send me?"

The other messenger looked up at me, and I saw concern in her eyes. She said, "King Rylan instructed us to tell you that he needs you back in Ochana, urgently.

Dragons are vanishing all over the world, and he needs you at his side if we're to keep the order and peace in Ochana."

The man added, "They're scared, my prince. We are to bring you home immediately, and hope it is in time."

J.A. Culican

Chapter Seventeen

It took a couple days, but we were finally close enough to see beautiful Ochana, home and safe at last. Its enchanted waterfall, flowing forever into the clouds below, still mesmerized me every time I saw it. My thoughts drifted to when I'd first learned to fly, spending hours zipping in and out of those falling waters or just letting them carry me down into the clouds. I'd fall through and just drift down, until I got bored and spread my wings, ready to fly back up and ride the waters down again. Nice times that felt like they were in another lifetime.

I shook my head, clearing my thoughts, and glanced behind me. Dragon eyes could see a long, long way, like an eagle's. The Woland Realm was flying as fast as they could but were still a couple miles behind us. It was hard for them to keep up since they had to carry the tied-up, freaked-out, psycho murder-dragon. That guy still hadn't calmed down. I was surprised he hadn't summoned his human because if he had, he could have escaped the ropes easily. I guessed he hadn't thought of it.

Jericho's voice rang in my head: "Pay attention to where you're going, Cole. You almost ran into Cairo. Don't worry about the dragon back there. Our people will figure out what's wrong with him, I'm sure. We're almost home."

I looked ahead again. We were getting close enough that we had to slow down, which was why I'd almost hit

Cairo when I wasn't paying attention. We turned and decelerated, circling as we came down toward the landing area. People were gathered there, waiting, and Rylan and Sila were with them. They stood to one side, waiting for me to land. I was actually excited to see them again.

Jericho insisted we keep circling to let the Second Realm land first with the crazy dragon. Only after the Realm touched down and were human again did we finish our own descent. I summoned my human just as my feet hit the stone pavement, shifting smoothly.

Just as I'd imagined, my mother was right on top of me when I landed, wrapping me in her arms before I'd even come to a full stop. I put my arms around her, too, grinning. She kept it going just a little too long, so I started to feel kind of awkward.

Rylan said, "Enough, my love. Let our son go, you're embarrassing him." Then, when she grudgingly stepped back, he grinned at me and shook my hand. He was always the more proper of the two. I grinned back, thinking he would have tried to hug me if people weren't around.

Then Jericho was barking orders, getting the prisoner on the way to where they could safely study him. Maybe they had dragon-sized rubber rooms somewhere. I asked Rylan, "Where is he going? Something's really wrong with that guy."

Rylan nodded, watching Jericho and the others as they hauled the prisoner away. "Let's talk over lunch. I know you must be half-starved."

Sila added, "We have plenty of food set out in the great hall for you four, though Jericho will just have to take what's left. That man won't even sit down until everything is in order. He's quite diligent."

That was one way of putting it. I nodded but kept my smart-aleck comments to myself. I didn't want to wait even one more second to dig into the mountain of food that no doubt waited for us in the great hall. My stomach rumbled loudly, but my parents pretended not to notice. Eva, on the other hand, jammed her elbow into my ribs. "Well, let's get going before this one wastes away to nothing."

"Gee, thanks," I said as we followed the king and queen toward the castle.

An hour later, I sat in the great hall surrounded by a dozen empty serving trays that had once been mounded high with all sorts of meats, eggs, potatoes, and even a few veggies. I liked the carrots they grew in Ochana; they were the sweetest ones I'd ever tasted, but most dragons considered them to be just food for horses. I think Eva ate even more than me. Jericho was just getting started on his second platter of bacon and sliced ham as my meal settled.

My head was finally clearing from the hunger-fog, and I felt human again. Or dragon. Whatever. My mahier was coming back up to normal levels, too. Flying across Europe and half the Atlantic Ocean without being seen took a lot of energy! I was grateful my parents let us eat before the questioning began.

"So," I said at last, patting my full stomach, "I'm sure you heard the reports we sent ahead, right?"

Rylan, sipping at a glass of wine but not eating much, nodded. "I'm frankly amazed. You've learned to use mereum and brought the Mere Treaty to life. You can cure the blackness, at least in a small area—which is a great start—and you uncovered the reason the Fairies attacked the Realm of dragons we'd sent to help guard their lands while you were gone."

"True," Eva said, "but then you summoned Cole home again all of a sudden. What is going on?"

Rylan sighed. "You'd think I'd be happier than I am."

That got my attention. I hadn't grown up with my father, but I knew enough to recognize an opening when he presented it. "Yeah, I would have thought so."

He replied, "Jericho has already heard this, but I wanted to tell you myself, not through a report. We have some very bad news to share with you, my son. As Prince of Ochana, dealing with this will fall on your shoulders, too."

"Ooo-kay..." I raised an eyebrow at him. Why was he taking forever to get to the point? "Dealing with what, exactly?"

"We know why the Carnites and Dark Elves have been trying to capture you. It is not *you* they want, but all dragons. They have been catching as many as they can find, and then they're using dark magic to brainwash them. Eldrick is turning them into crazed monsters that only he can control through his mind powers, even halfway around the world."

My jaw dropped. All the times they'd tried to catch us, and failed... I could only imagine how many times they had succeeded if they were going after everyone outside of

Ochana. "How many of the brainwashed ones have we saved?"

I wasn't sure why that was my first question, but I caught my mother's approving nod again.

"It is good that your first priority is our people's safety, son," Rylan said. "The truth is that we haven't been able to capture any, much less save them. We've been forced to kill a few, but most of them are attacking our allies, wreaking havoc, then flying away before anyone can rally the defenders. Your prisoner is the first anyone has captured. I think we may be able to catch more now, though, since you've found out how to do it."

Between big bites of meat, Jericho said, "We still haven't had any success breaking the connection between the prisoner and Eldrick. I do not know if we will ever be able to bring their minds back. Our people will keep working on the problem, of course."

Rylan nodded. "Of course. In the meantime, all of this has created another problem for us all, especially you, Son."

Sila said, "Any Prince of Ochana has duties to the people. The fact is, our people are in the middle of a full-blown panic. There's fear in every heart, as much as it pains me to see that. Our allies are in a panic, too, but our immediate problem is Ochana itself."

Rylan stood from his heavy chair and began pacing back and forth with his hands behind his back. His shiny boots clicked on the tile floor with every step. "Fear is what will tear us apart. As long as the people fear to stand up and do what's needed, we're going to have a hard time fighting this war, or even protecting ourselves."

"What can we do to help?" Eva asked. "We don't have any concrete plans, right now. We were supposed to 'find the source in the Fairy realm,' but I don't think we did that."

Rylan glanced at me and kept pacing. "Right now, the people of Ochana need their prince to lead them by his example."

"What can I do?" I asked.

"We need you to stay here and rally them." He turned to Eva and added, "He'll need your help, even if it's just to stand by his side so he has the strength to face them all."

Eva nodded. Of course, she would do that. I was relieved to hear she'd be staying with me.

Rylan stopped and turned to look me in the eyes and said, "You're not just the prince of Ochana. You are the Keeper of Dragons. If you go among them and tell them that everything will be well again, our people will listen to you."

I pursed my lips. I wasn't sure that was true. "And what do I tell them if it isn't well again soon? We don't know that we're going to win the war. Maybe we should at least be ready with a backup plan, just in case their prophecy is the one that turns out to be true. What will we do if we lose this war?"

Sila put her hands together on top of the table, lacing her long, slender fingers together. It made her look like a beautiful statue, the way she sat so straight and confident. She said calmly, "The people already know we could lose this. They feel it in their bones. Sometimes, as a leader, you must tell your people what they need to hear, not what they already know. It may be true we could lose, but it's also true we could win."

Rylan said, "That's what they are forgetting."

Sila continued, "Yes, and you must remind them of that fact, Son. Eldrick might have a prophecy about ruling the world, but Aprella gave us a different prophecy, the one where the Keeper of Dragons saves all True beings. I have faith that we will win."

Everyone stared at me, waiting for me to reply. I didn't really have much of a choice, though. My mother was right. I stood from my chair and put my hands on the table, leaning forward. "Ochana deserves that hope. As my father just said, we have a lot to be happy about, too. A lot to give us hope. Yes, of course, I'll stay and rally our people the best I can."

Rylan grinned, looking relieved, but Sila just smiled as though she knew there had never been any question what I'd do. I hoped I could live up to her faith in me.

J.A. Culican

Chapter Eighteen

I wanted to get a good feel for how my people were doing, but I couldn't do that just listening to my parents. Having a bunch of bodyguards following me could have kept me from getting people's honest thoughts, so I ditched them after lunch. I wanted the unfiltered truth.

Now I walked through the streets of Ochana, trying not to be too obvious as I eavesdropped on people talking. I blended in by wearing jeans and a gray hoodie—the hood kept people from catching on to who I was, but it also meant I had to get closer to overhear what people were talking about through the hoodie's fabric.

First, I went to the Great Library of Ochana. It always had lots of people sitting on the stone steps out front or laying around on the well-kept grass fields to either side. Most of them were my age or maybe a bit older, so it had a vibe like what I imagined a college campus would be like.

Since I couldn't eavesdrop on the people out in the grass—it would be too obvious—I focused on the stairs. I pretended like I was waiting for someone, leaning against the wall running up one side of the steps, halfway up. Just below me, two men and a woman sat together, leaning back and taking in the sunlight while they chatted. The first thing I noticed was that they weren't smiling. Shoulders hunched forward, looking down a lot, they seemed tense. The younger of the two men kept turning his head back and forth, scanning around him while they talked.

"We never should have gone back down there. The king made a mistake trying to help the Elves," the woman said.

The older guy said, "Are you kidding? If we'd been down there all along, like we should have been, this never would have happened. You want to blame a king? Blame the last one, not Rylan."

"Don't let anyone hear you talking about kings like that, you two," the younger man replied. "None of that matters, though. What happened can't be changed I'm just glad the prince is back. The Keeper will fix all this, you'll see. Aprella herself said so."

The woman, sitting between the men, nudged the younger one's arm with her elbow and said, "You mean if he is the Keeper at all. I mean, what are the odds the Keeper came right when we needed him? And what are the odds that our prince himself just so happened to be the Keeper? I think it's a PR stunt to keep us all from freaking out."

"No way, he's the Keeper. I heard he can use tilium *and* mereum. And there's a rumor he can kill off the black spots that Elf traitor created. Only the Keeper could do that, and the oracles have always said the Keeper will fix the Time of Fear."

The older man snorted, laughing and mocking the younger one. "You mean the king's pet oracle? Of course, she'll say what he tells her to, that's her job. They just don't want us freaking out, if you ask me."

The woman sat up and wrapped her arms around her knees. "Well, I'm plenty freaked out, so it didn't work. Ochana is next, you know. And stop talking about King Rylan like that. It's treason, and wrong. He's our leader, and way better than the last one."

I had heard enough. It was pretty much what I expected to hear, except for the part where one of them thought Rylan was faking the prophecy just to keep people calm. If one person said it, how many more people just thought it?

I wandered toward the market zone, hoping to hear more from an older crowd. Extra centuries of living might have given them a different perspective. I wandered down the steps and then crossed the main boulevard. Ten minutes later, I was in the market, surrounded by throngs of people. I was wrong about them all being old—there were plenty of younger dragons, too, and more than a few who must have been ancient.

But young, middle-aged, or old, the conversations I overheard were mostly the same. Everyone was terrified, and some were even scared enough to look at their king, feeling the need to place blame somewhere.

Just then, I bumped into a young man carrying packages, which he'd almost dropped when we walked into each other. "Oh sorry," I said and turned to move on.

"Prince," he said, startled. "I should be the one to apologize."

A woman nearby must have only heard part of our conversation because she turned and said, "Prince

Colton? Pah! He's trying, but he's too young to do this. Keeper of Dragons, indeed."

A merchant with a wagon stand handed the woman a paper-wrapped package and said, over the market noise, "He may be the Keeper, but the trouble came too soon. He doesn't have the experience to protect us. He can't help us now. You should stock up on food now, because who knows how long it'll be here."

More people spotted me. Some shook my hand, but most stayed back a little. They seemed unsure how to approach me. Was it because I was the prince, or because I was the Keeper? Maybe both. But as word spread, more people pressed toward me until I had a crowd around me. They called out questions. They begged me to protect their soldier sons. They asked more questions than I could answer.

But mostly, they simply doubted I could save them. I could *feel* how strong their fear was. It was stronger than their faith in their king, stronger than their common sense, even. So much fear from so many people... Their auras washed over me like a wave, and I started looking for a way out. Coming to the market had been a mistake. My father was right. Blending with them wasn't the way to lead them. I thought about calling everyone together to talk to them all at once from the king's audience platform, a grand stone ramp that stuck out from Ochana Castle so the king could address all his people. It would work just as well for a prince.

But then I stopped, mid-step, realizing that I wasn't really thinking about the best way to talk to them. No, I was just making excuses to justify running away from so many people who doubted me. I couldn't run away, not if I wanted those same people to follow me. Why follow a leader who talked *down* to them from some platform? I had to talk to them where they were, right where they lived. It was the only way to lead them, and leading them was the only way to banish all that fear that made them doubt their future. They needed hope more than they needed a speech.

I moved through the crowd, hearing people murmur as I went by them, and headed to an empty auctioneer's platform off to one side. It'd be high enough for people to see me, but close enough to actually talk to them, not talk down to them. I climbed the ladder and walked to the front of the platform.

From the crowd of market shoppers and merchants, someone shouted my name and pointed to the platform, and a murmur went up as a hundred heads turned, every eye on me as they wondered what I'd do and why I was there. The cry carried beyond the crowd, too, and more and more people began coming to see what was going on. Two hundred people were staring at me, but in minutes it became three hundred. I wanted to shrink under so many eyeballs! I was terrified, really, but I couldn't show it. They didn't need to see me scared like everyone else—they needed a leader. That's why my father had brought me back to Ochana, after all. I'd just have to do it my way, not how he'd wanted me to. I wasn't a leader, but I could fake it for them.

Plus, if I messed up, it wasn't like the whole island would see it the way they would if I choked on a speech from up in the castle's platform. Up there, a thousand cameras would be on me and every dragon in Ochana would see it. The more I realized that it could be a practice speech, the more confident I felt. I squared my shoulders, looked out over the sea of faces, and smiled. Giving a speech was also kind of exciting, even if it was terrifying.

Someone shouted, "Silence, the prince wants to speak," but the noise didn't die down. If anything, it got louder as people started arguing about what I'd say.

I took a deep breath and stepped up to the railing, ready to shout out to them, but I paused. I really wanted it to seem like I was talking to each one of them, not just to a crowd. An idea hit me. Mereum was everywhere—Ochana lived up in the clouds, and the mist from its never-ending waterfall was a light fog. I had all the mereum I could ever need.

I focused my will on the mereum, not gathering it up like normal but channeling it, using it to carry my words to each person in the crowd. With that, I could talk normally. Plain old Cole having a pleasant chat. Yet, they'd all hear me like I stood next to them. Kind of impressed with my idea, I grinned, and saw the people up front grinning back at me. That helped take my stage fright away, too.

"Yes," I began, and adjusted how the mereum carried the sound so it would be a little louder, "I'm Prince Cole. Whatever rumors you've heard otherwise, I am the Keeper of Dragons. You hear me now like I'm standing beside you because I'm controlling mereum in the air to bring my words to you without having to shout. I want to talk to you, just one dragon from Ochana to another."

I had things I needed to tell them, but with my stage fright barely under control, I wasn't really sure what I was saying. The words just spilled out, almost like I was on auto-pilot. After that, I just sort of let my mouth do its thing.

I told them about the things I'd seen. I talked about fighting at the side of an Elven prince and a Fairy queen, a Troll king and a dragon chimera. I told them about the evil I'd seen Eldrick do, the people he'd killed.

But I also told them about how we rescued the Trolls from him. I almost shouted when I told them about the fight with the Farro, and how it felt to take their tilium from them and then defeat them. Permanently!

I pulled out the Mere Blade itself, letting it shine brightly over my head so they could see the awesome magical sword glowing.

I told them about fighting Carnites hand-to-hand, and how it felt to crush them. I talked about my personal fight with Eldrick, who tried to kill me with his visions, and how I not only survived but used the connection *he* created to help defeat his plots one after another.

I told them how it felt to bridge the rifts we dragons had created, bringing back our old alliances with other races of Truth. Together, they were all stronger than any crazy Dark Elf madman, and coming together, mighty Ochana could face any challenge. It was the *only* way we could ever win; it was the best way we'd always won before.

By the time I finished, the crowd was cheering my name. It had gone from being a speech to feeling like a school rally as they pulled together!

That was when I realized there were way more people around me than when I had started. The sun was lower than it had been. I must have been talking to them for an hour or more.

But the biggest shock came when I turned around to climb down the ladder. Suddenly, I saw myself displayed on the inside of the magic dome protecting Ochana as if it were a huge screen. I stared at it, frozen. I had totally forgotten the city had technology that was years ahead of anything I'd seen growing up among humans. I'd been televised on that jump screen to everyone, all over the island. My practice speech had been the real deal!

And judging by how the crowd here was cheering me, it must have worked. I'd spoken from the heart, and they responded. The jumbo-screen faded away, but the cheering didn't. I slid down the ladder to the waiting crowd. I shook hands and answered questions until long past dusk, well into the night. Ochana's whole aura had changed, and mine with it.

It was a long evening, but despite how late it was when I got to bed, I still had a hard time sleeping. I was just too excited, too wired up. Somehow, I'd made a difference to Ochana's people with one heartfelt speech. It was a lesson I swore I'd always remember.

Chapter Nineteen

Shortly after breakfast, three days after my weird and amazing speech, Jericho summoned me to a council meeting. The messenger let me know the king and queen, Eva, and Cairo had also been summoned, but he didn't know what the meeting would be about.

I thanked him, then looked through my dresser for more appropriate clothes. I'd been wearing jeans and hoodies for the last few days, which I'd been spending out among the people, talking to them where they lived and worked instead of on a jumbo monitor. Obviously, Jericho had something important to say, and I could practically hear his commander voice barking orders at me about how "playtime was over."

I let out a long sigh as I put on a set of clothes that looked remarkably like a uniform, yet wasn't. Rylan once told me that looking like a leader was half of actually being one, and I didn't really look forward to Jericho ordering me around like usual. Maybe if I looked like I outranked him, he wouldn't be as bossy. Come to think of it, I really did outrank him. That had never seemed to help me much before, though.

I was the last to arrive. The only elder present other than my father was Jericho. I'd expected the other councilors to be there, which could only mean that this would be a military meeting. A war council. But then, why were Eva and Cairo there? I'd find out soon enough.

I stepped into the room, waved at Eva, nodded to Cairo, then sat next to my father and faced Jericho across the table.

The wily general smiled and said, "Thank you for coming. I'll get right to the point and tell you why I called this war meeting." So, it was to be a war meeting, after all.

"You're welcome," I said, enjoying his irritated glance. He hadn't expected a response.

Instead of sparring with me, though, he got right back to what he wanted to talk about. "Eldrick seems to be gathering his troops. Reports show them moving all around the world, heading this way. Since most of his troops are on foot, it will take them at least a month or two to gather, but I think he's getting ready to make his move."

Rylan frowned. "What are we doing about this?"

"I've had my staff working around the clock preparing for our final stand. They'll keep doing that until time runs out, however long that may be." He paused to let that sink in, looking each of us in the eyes one at a time. "It is my belief that we should ask the other races to form an accord with us, *before* Eldrick attacks—"

"Wait." Rylan interrupted him.

My father was larger-than-life, always standing straight and proud like a king, or like a conquering general. He was used to being in charge, and history had shown he was right far more often than not. He was also the kind of person others naturally followed, even in battle. A born leader. So when he interrupted, he hadn't even had to raise his voice to silence the room. We all turned to look at him.

He continued, "I think your plan is too risky, old friend. The peace we've created with them is still fragile. It hasn't been long enough to start asking for their help, not like this. They have fresh memories of us refusing to come to their aid when my father ruled Ochana, and they have their own battles to fight."

Jericho bowed his head in respect. "Yes, my king. But times are different from when your father was king."

"Yes, they are. The peace is delicate now, and it wasn't then. Not until we turned our backs on them. If we'd come to their aid then, Eldrick would never have survived his attempt to take over the Elves. And every other race knows that."

Jericho's eyes burned red. "Yes, the new peace is fragile. I know asking for help might send *some* of them running to look after themselves. But the rest will honor the accord."

Rylan growled. "How is sending some of our allies running away what you want us to do? Give the alliance time to set! Then ask for help."

"Because some won't run! I'm telling you as plainly as I can, my king, that if Eldrick attacked us right now, he'd win. He'd push through our defenses in hours, and it would all be over for us. That is what we've been analyzing these last couple days."

Rylan shook his head and put both hands flat on the table, his thumbs touching, and looked into Jericho's stony eyes without flinching. "Eldrick may not attack today or even this year. If you pull in our half-hearted allies, some will stop being our allies. And what of the rest? Should they just sit in Ochana until Eldrick gets around to attacking us?"

No one would interrupt the king, of course, but I really wanted to cut in with a dozen questions. Yet the more I thought about those questions, the more I realized I already knew the answers. It was weird, when I'd first learned I was a dragon, I would have asked anyway. I wouldn't have had any confidence in my own answers. I had come a long way in the last few months, it seemed.

"Cole!" Rylan snapped.

I spun to face him, feeling my face grow warm. "Yes, Father?"

"I asked you a question. Well?"

I wanted to run and hide. I hadn't even heard his question! I was too deep in my own thoughts when he asked. "Um, what was the question?"

Rylan rolled his eyes, but my mother put her hand on his, stopping him from snapping back. She said, "You're the prince of Ochana, someday our king, and you're the Keeper of Dragons. What do you think? The two best military minds in Ochana disagree on what to do, and maybe the Keeper can help us find the way. He asked for your decision."

"My decision?" I wanted to shrink away and hide. I'd just been thinking about how much more confident and capable I'd grown. It was ironic.

Rylan let out a deep breath. "She's right. You must make the final decision. You are the one who keeps the balance. Do we shatter our new alliances without a second thought, or do we do the smart thing and wait for them to get stronger before we ask for their help?"

I recognized that stubborn tone. It was the same one I'd used a hundred times before. It was kind of interesting in how many ways he and I were so similar even though I'd grown up among the humans, not on Ochana with him.

I already knew my answer, though.

"If the final decision is up to me, then I say it's best that we ask for help now, while we still can. Eldrick won't wait as long as you hope, Father. Anything else is wishful thinking. He knows how weak we are because he's the one who made us that way. He's coming as soon as he thinks he has enough troops, not waiting for every last Carnite to get to Alaska."

Jericho nodded, and he looked at me like he was seeing me for the first time. Before Rylan could snap back at me, Jericho said, "Very well, Prince. Eva and Cairo will go to the Fairies and ask their help. Clara and I will go to the Elves and Trolls and see if we can get Gaber and Evander to see reason."

Sila said, "We should send Luka, Jules, and Allas to the Mermaids. They'll respect us more with them going to ask."

Jericho smiled and inclined his head to her. "Yes, excellent thinking. Cole will stay here and continue to rally the people. After that speech he made," he said, grinning at me, "he'll be of best use here."

Rylan slowly rose, but he didn't look as angry as I'd feared. "I don't think this is a wise plan, Cole. But very well, so be it. Each group will also take a battalion of dragons to escort those who ally themselves with Ochana. They'll need help getting here. Aprella only knows how you expect Eldrick to get an army here when our own allies need help to get here themselves."

I shook my head at him. I wasn't going to let him talk us out of this. "It may be risky, but it's safer than sitting here hoping Eldrick doesn't find some way to get into Ochana. He did it before, and if he's gathering his troops, it's because he has a plan to do it again. This is the only chance we've got."

I sounded more confident than I felt, just like with my speech to the people. The truth was, I wasn't sure we had a chance at all. I couldn't just sit back and wait for the end, though. It was better to go down fighting.

Chapter Twenty

I stood on my balcony high above Ochana, looking out over my beautiful city. I wasn't sure when I had started to think of it as my city, or when Paraiso had started seeming like a vacation. Glorious, beautiful, natural, but just a vacation. Those are never meant to last forever. As much as I wanted to help Paraiso, Ochana now felt like where I *belonged*. Getting exiled had been the swift kick in the pants I needed to realize it, that's all.

The sound of my sliding glass door opening dragged me from my thoughts. I recognized Rylan's presence behind me. "Father. It's beautiful, isn't it? Ochana, I mean."

"As it has been for more centuries than I can count," he said, almost whispering. "I stand on my balcony, too, when things are bothering me. It helps me put it into perspective. So what is troubling you today?" He stepped up beside me on the balcony and leaned against the railing, looking out as well.

"It's just easier to be alone when I'm up here like this," I said. I wasn't sure that was exactly right, but it was close enough to how I was feeling.

"Your friends have been gone a few days, but you're hardly alone."

I shook my head. Rylan was wrong about that. I felt alone in a crowded room, sometimes. "I've kept busy doing all I can, preparing our people for war if it comes to that, but when I stop for the night, I do feel alone. These are my people, but they don't truly know me. Like I don't really know them. It has only been a few months since I thought dragons and Elves were myths and humans were the top of the food chain."

Rylan was quiet for a long moment, and we just stood together on my balcony and looked down on the beautiful city. At last, though, he said, "A king is always lonely. Every one of these people is our responsibility. Even our friends. There will always be that part of you that knows your friends are also your burden and responsibility. But that doesn't make them any less your friends, Son. It makes them the motivation I use to keep going, to keep fighting and putting my people ahead of myself. Maybe they are for you, too."

"Wow. That's deep. I wonder if that's why your father turned his back on the world. Maybe he just couldn't bear the thought of something bad happening to any of his people."

Rylan's hands gripped the railing a little tighter. "I had never really thought of it like that. I guess our friends do more than give us a reason to put others ahead of ourselves. Maybe they also give us the perspective we need so that we don't make the mistakes my parents made when they ruled this kingdom. They... didn't have a lot of friends outside the family."

Maybe he was right. I didn't know what to say, so I just nodded.

"Cole, I want you to know that I'm proud of you. The role you've taken isn't what I had in mind for you, but it suits you. In the time you were away from here, traveling, you somehow found the strength and courage to become a leader. Your friends and your people, they all follow you now. It's not because they have to, and not because you were born in charge, but because of who you are. I think you may become a better leader than I have been, if you aren't already. Don't tell your mother I said that."

I snorted, but then I paused. Was he wrong? It didn't feel like I had been a good leader. So many people had died, and I couldn't save them. Sure, we saved some of the Trolls, but not enough to save their kingdom or the Earth. Dragons were supposed to lead all the races of Truth, but so far, my track record with that hadn't been great.

I found myself fidgeting with the ring that the spirit Prince Jago gave me. I wished he hadn't chosen me. I didn't think I deserved it, and there was a shadow in my mind that kept telling me I wasn't good enough, I wasn't going to save them, and I wasn't going to save the world. I was pretty sure I was going to fail at that, just like I'd failed to save the Trolls.

And I had to try anyway.

I didn't tell my dad any of that, though. We talked about nicer things for a while, maybe the first small talk I'd had with him, but eventually he had to go. He was the king, and he had duties he couldn't ignore.

When he was gone, I felt just as lonely as I did before he showed up. My responsibilities were heavy on my mind. One of those responsibilities was to our wounded.

There weren't many, not yet, but the dragon we captured was one of them. Almost without thinking about it, I found myself heading directly to Ochana's hospital wing. I just needed to see if there had been any change in his condition. He was a monster now, but he'd been a good dragon before that.

When I got there, I went up to the front counter. The administrator had been looking at her monitor, but when she saw who I was, she blushed. "I'm so sorry, Prince Colton. I didn't realize it was you, and I have more work to do than time. I should have paid better attention. What can we do for you?"

I put a smile on my face, mostly for her benefit. "I didn't mean to interrupt. I wanted to come see the dragon I brought with me from the Fairy realm. Has he gotten any better?"

When she flinched and set down the notepad she'd been holding, I thought the answer was going to be bad. When she stepped out from behind the counter and put her hand on my arm, I knew it was.

"I'm sorry. We haven't figured out yet how to cure him. We have people working on it twenty-four hours a day, though. The king made sure of that. But we're starting to think that there is no way to save him. If the magic is strong enough, only Eldrick's death can save this dragon, or the dozens like him who are still out there suffering."

"Can I see him?" I didn't know why I felt like I needed to, but I did.

"Yes, of course. You can't go into his cell, but we have a one-way glass set in the wall. You can see him, but he won't see you. It's for our safety."

"Of course. Thank you." I followed her to the cell and then could only stare at the monster inside. His body was a dragon's, but his mind felt like a wounded animal's to my mahier senses. Part of me hoped his mind really wasn't in there somewhere, watching himself like an outsider, even if that meant there was hope to save him. I wasn't sure which would be a worse fate.

I stayed there with him for hours, watching him, wishing that my being there was enough to help, somehow. I knew it wasn't, though.

When the facility's visiting hours ended that night, I headed back to the castle. I locked myself in my room and for once, I was glad my friends were gone. I needed to be alone after seeing the prisoner. I needed time to come to grips with it.

Hours later, I drifted off to sleep.

I dreamed of explosions. When I awoke, sweating, I sat bolt upright in bed and put my hands over my ears as I focused on slowing my heartbeat. I waited for the sleep fog to fade away so I could get back to sleep—

Then I heard more explosions. It was no dream, I realized with a sinking feeling in my chest. I ran to my balcony and looked out. That view had once given me a bit of comfort looking out over the beauty of Ochana. Now, it was full of smoke and fire, not comfort. All over the city, dragons swarmed, carrying Dark Elves and even Carnites on their backs. They landed and dropped off their cargoes, then rose into the air again. Fires raged and lightning forked the sky, and dragons flew through the air, thick as a swarm of bees.

Eldrick was attacking with so many forces, I couldn't begin to count them. So many dragons carrying so many soldiers... We didn't have months, after all. I felt my stomach flip-flopping. Ochana was doomed.

Chapter Twenty-One

I slapped myself a couple of times to wake myself up. With the sounds of battle coming through the window, I ran across the room to my gear. Most of it was in a wall locker, except my armor, which was displayed on a mannequin. I hated taking the time to put the armor on, but it was no time to be running around unprotected.

The breastplate looked like scales, and I'd been told they were actual dragon scales tied to hardened leather—immune to fire, almost impossible to cut. Smaller bits, also scaled, went over my shoulders and covered my upper arms. My shins were covered by engraved black metal plates, called greaves. There was also a skirt-looking thing made of a lot of long leather strips, covered in scales like the breastplate. The scaled, leather strips hung down from a belt I could wear over my clothes, protecting everything down to my knees without limiting my movement at all.

I threw on a pair of boots, grabbed the Mere Blade, and at the last minute, put on my helmet. It was made of engraved black metal, like the shin greaves. It covered not only my head but also the back of my neck. It had metal flaps hanging down to cover my cheeks, and a thin strip of metal hung down between my eyes to protect my nose. It was just as uncomfortable as it sounded.

When I opened my door, I came face-to-face with two Wolands. They wore full plate mail armor, heavier than mine, and their helmets covered their entire heads and faces, like medieval knights.

"My prince," one said, "the entire west end of Ochana is under attack. We have to get you to the safe room. Jericho gave us orders to protect you at all costs. King Rylan and Queen Sila are there already."

I stared at them in disbelief for a second. They wanted the prince to hide while the kingdom burned. Um, no? I'd been through too much to run away and hide now. "I can't run and—"

"Sir, we have to go *now* if we have any hope of getting you there at all. The attackers are pushing through our defenses already!"

My mind raced. From the safe room, all I could do was wait until Eldrick killed every defender and then he'd blast the royal family out or blow us up. The protection of the safe room would slow him down, but it wouldn't stop him from getting to us forever.

The thought struck me once again that I outranked Jericho. Maybe not when it came to defending Ochana, but I could bully my way through the guards... maybe. Plus, at the moment, Jericho wasn't in Ochana to give them other orders. Well, it was time to take my authority as prince out for a spin.

"No. I order you to come with me. Go to the safe room if you're too afraid to fight, but I won't run while our people are out there dying. I don't know about you, but I'm tired of running anyway."

I pushed my way past them and then ran down the hall, whether they followed me or not. Thankfully, they didn't try to stop me by force and instead ran with me.

As we came around a corner up ahead, there were other people rushing toward us, wearing hooded cloaks. They were dragons, but were they friendly or were they more of the crazed ones? I pulled my sword, and my guards did the same as they stepped in front of me.

The lead oncoming dragon stopped ten feet away and pulled back the hood covering his face. It was my Uncle Zane! I let out a whoop of joy.

"Cole," he said, saluting me, "I came right away. We can't let Eldrick capture you. The Keepers have to get out alive for the prophecy to come true. We have to get you out of here."

I shook my head as I slid my sword back into its scabbard. "No. If you want to make sure I stay alive, then you'll just have to come with me and do what you can to protect me. Bring your guards."

"What? Why? By Aprella, we have to get to the safe room." Zane's left eyelid twitched.

"No, we have to alert the east end of the island and rally our people out there. They may not yet even know we're under attack and they'll be sitting ducks."

"But Cole—"

"I'm going. You can stay here or come with me, whatever. It's been good seeing you, Zane, but my people are waiting for me." I took off running down the hall.

My two guards called after me, but I didn't slow down. I heard many boots behind me, clomping on the stone floor, and I smiled when I realized Zane was coming with me, along with our eight soldiers—my two in plate mail and his six armored in breastplates like Zane and me, but with chainmail everywhere else. I hoped eight soldiers would be enough to do what I had in mind, even with Eldrick's troops pouring in fast.

The ten of us ran east, dodging the enemy troops, who seemed to be scattered across the west end of Ochana. I used my mahier to keep anyone from seeing us, but that meant the good guys didn't see us, either. Only once we were well away from the fighting did I let the mask fall, and then we got busy raising the alarm and rousing everyone.

I wondered why Ochana's main alarms weren't going off, and suspected sabotage.

We went house to house after splitting up to cover ground faster. Every time I found someone home, after they got whatever battle gear they owned ready, I had them run off to find yet more people. And so on. The crowd quickly grew.

In less than half an hour, we had most of Ochana roused and dressed for war. Once that was almost done, I had to start gathering the troops, though. I took a deep breath and then focused my mind on sending a message to all my nearby people. "Join me at Rylan Square. To arms!" I concentrated on sending that message out, over and over. I wasn't sure whether my telepathy would be strong enough, but when mobs of armed dragons began coming to the square, I knew it had.

Rylan Square was a beautiful place, like a park, and I was told they changed the name every time a new king was crowned. If we survived the day, the park would someday be called Colton Square, but first, we had a job to do.

In the distance, the sounds of battle got more intense as Eldrick ferried fresh troops down. I didn't know how he had gotten through our defenses, but I suspected Zane had something to do with that. Hopefully, it was from back when Zane once pretended to join the enemy. We'd done a lot of damage to Eldrick's allies because of it, eliminating the Farro and taking their tilium, but Eldrick had learned more than Zane intended. He'd clearly saved some of that information until he was ready to attack Ochana with everything he had.

The alternative was that Zane really was a traitor, and had only pretended to be on our side again. If that was the case, I figured we were all doomed, so I really hoped he wasn't a traitor still. I hoped, but I wasn't going to turn my back to him just yet either.

My thoughts were interrupted when a dragon came swooping in from the west and a hundred of my dragons drew weapons at the same time. When he landed, though, he summoned his human form and saluted. So, he wasn't one of Eldrick's crazy, brainwashed dragons.

Zane said, "What news, soldier?"

The soldier's eyes were wide with fear, and he had a cut on his left cheek. He looked dirty and tired from fighting. He saluted and said, "Prince Colton, I spotted a company of Carnites coming this way. They went around us, going to the island's north end to get past our defenders, and I saw you in the distance so I came to warn you. Thank Aprella you got these people together already, or it would have been a slaughter."

I put my hand on his shoulder firmly, nodding. "Good job. So, we have a dozen Carnites headed our way? Um...Take a dozen of these dragons and go cut the Carnites off."

"Prince, these aren't trained soldiers. What can they do?"

"They'll fight. Listen, there are sleepers, children, and those too old to fight still hiding in these houses. I won't leave until they're safe, so I need time. You have to buy me time. Figure out how to make it work."

He grit his teeth, saluted me, then began collecting whatever dragons looked strong enough, whatever their color. Every dragon was a warrior today.

I turned to Zane and said, "Start getting the rest of these people into squads and send them west."

"Any instructions for them?"

I thought for a second, then said, "By the time they get close enough to join the battle, someone in HQ should see them and give them orders telepathically, right?"

"HQ has their hands full, or they'd have done the job we're doing."

He might have been right, so I said, "If they don't get orders when they get to the battle, make sure each unit has someone in charge to decide where they should go fight. Things look really chaotic out there, so they might need to come up with ideas on the fly. But if nothing else, they can fight their way toward Ochana Castle or the HQ."

Zane grunted and then started barking orders to the dragons we'd gathered. They looked terrified, especially the ones who weren't Wolands, but when he started telling them what to do, they listened. What else could they do? Hide? The war would come to them one way or another, so hiding wasn't an option. We had to keep Eldrick in the west end if we wanted to keep the kids and elder dragons as safe as possible. Most of the dragons actually looked relieved to have someone telling them what they should be doing.

Another messenger showed up, a woman in battered armor. She told me about a new enemy break-though. I grabbed four of the latest squads Zane had organized and sent them off with the messenger.

Then another dragon showed up, needing more squads. And another messenger, and another. We kept sending out units as fast as we could organize them, rushing to keep up with the demand. Ochana was being overrun. We needed to figure out a better plan, but I was kept busy dealing with enemy units breaking through our lines faster than I could get new units organized. It was frustrating. We started to get sloppy with our orders because things were happening too fast to think it through before just throwing units at them.

A real battle, I realized, was uncontrolled chaos. I was quickly learning what leaders did in battle, and it wasn't running off to fight. That would have been a relief, but as much as I wanted to go fight, I was doing more good for Ochana where I was.

All around us, more and more small battles were breaking out. A dozen dragons fought Dark Elves here, fifty fought Carnites over there. Angry roars, shouted orders, and the clanging sounds of swords hitting shields echoed through the city.

Then, I heard a high-pitched cry of pain behind me in the distance, carrying over the noise of battle. I turned to look. A few blocks away, I was horrified to see a big group of stooped, old dragons, along with kids in what looked like white paper robes. For a moment, it felt like time slowed to a crawl. I zoomed in with my mahier and dragon eyes, and realized the robes really were paper because they were actually hospital gowns. A Carnite had two of the kids, one in either hand, but when it threw one down like it was spiking a football, the kid's high-pitched scream stopped suddenly. I felt like throwing up. My people were getting mowed down, even the helpless elderly dragons and sick children.

I didn't hesitate—I was already sprinting toward the massacre, running past Zane as he turned to see where I was going. I heard him roar, outraged, but my only thought was to help the terrified, helpless dragons and punish the foul things that were hurting them.

Chapter Twenty-Two

I hit the nearest Carnite like a freight train and cut him down. The magical Mere Blade went through him like a hot knife through butter, and he toppled to the ground, dead before he hit.

The other Carnites, seeing their buddy go down, turned to me and roared. It was terrifying to look up at those giants and their spiked tusks, all of them staring at me with hatred. Their faces shifted from anger to fear, which confused me for a moment, but then I heard dragon roars and heavy footsteps behind me. A wave of armed dragons—red, blue, green, and even silver—surged past me, flowing around me as they charged the Carnites.

The Carnites were big and mean, but they were cowards. Before the armed dragon mob reached them like a swarm of ants attacking a beetle, the Carnites fled. The helpless dragons who had been the Carnites' victims cheered wildly.

I didn't feel like cheering, though, because when the Carnites fled, it revealed half a dozen dragons who were killed before I could save them. It could have been so much worse, I knew, but it still felt horrible.

The survivors all turned to look at me, desperate for someone to give them orders. I could see the panic written on their faces. My mind raced, but I didn't know what to say or do. The only thing I knew for sure was that I had to get them moving away from here. Doing *something* was better than standing around trying to figure out the *best* thing. Waiting around would only get more people killed.

So, I went with the first idea that hit me. "Zane, we've already cleared a path in the north end, right? Let's bring this mob that way. If we can get these kids, sick, and elderly dragons into the caves behind the waterfall, they can hide and wait out the battle." I pointed toward the beautiful mountain that had been the very first thing I'd seen in Ochana my first time here. It had a special place in my heart because of that, and it was kind of ironic that the same mountain might now save a lot of lives. But only if we could get them to it safely.

Zane said, "We'll have to fight our way through, but we'll have to fight if we stay here, too. Are you sure that's the best place to take them?" He looked tense, ready to burst into action as soon as I gave him the go-ahead.

I looked up, but all over the sky were far too many crazed, mind-controlled dragons to have my people risk trying to fly out. Most of the older ones didn't look strong enough to carry the kids on their best day, much less on a crazy, desperate ride for their lives.

"No, I'm not sure. But I *am* sure that if we stay here, we're done. Get them moving." I didn't wait for him to reply. I grabbed a couple squads of our assembled dragons, too young or too old to be soldiers but not to fight for their lives, and ran north with them. I had to trust Zane to get the rest of the mob moving, which I didn't like, but someone had to make sure the path was clear. I had told him it was, but I couldn't be sure it had stayed that way since the first messenger had come through there looking for reinforcements.

We ran through block after block of little dragon houses, corner parks with empty playgrounds, and small shops no one had opened today. They were all empty, and everything was creepy-silent except for faint battle noises from the west.

When we got closer to Ochana's north edge, we turned left, hoping to go around the worst of the fighting. The rest of the mob was only a hundred yards behind me, which was good. Zane had organized them quickly, so they wouldn't get too far behind.

A shadow fell over me and I ducked. It was pure reflex, but it saved my life as a huge, spiked club whooshed by me where my head had been. Carnites! Two dragons behind me had already jumped onto the one who attacked me, and they put the Carnite down. Two other Carnites were also quickly killed, though we lost one dragon who was too old and slow to dodge the Carnite's huge war club.

"Keep them moving!" I shouted without wasting any time. When Zane gave me a thumbs-up sign in reply, I ran ahead again with the ones I'd gathered, who included the guards who had started out with us—the few real soldiers we had. We made our way through the north neighborhood thick with small old houses and narrow, winding alleys. It gave us lots of cover, and before long, we came to the mountain.

My dragons started assisting the helpless people Zane and I waved through, rushing them to move faster into the caves behind the waterfall. It took a few scary, tense minutes to get everyone inside, and I felt like I didn't breathe again until they were out of sight inside.

From the entrance, Zane shouted, "Stay out of the council chambers. It doesn't have a roof, remember. The enemy will see you in there."

I recalled one tunnel I'd walked with Rylan which had spears and swords in racks lining both walls. I told Zane, "Gather up whoever is healthy enough to swing a sword or carry a spear, and get weapons from the displays by the council chambers. If Dark Elves get into the tunnels, you'll be the last line of defense and you'll need every armed dragon you can get."

He saluted sharply. "You can count on me. I wish we'd met under better circumstances, Cole. Your parents talked about you, always—I want you to know that."

I understood. This was our goodbye moment. The odds seemed pretty good that one or even both of us might not live through the day. I saluted back, then stuck out my hand.

He shook his head and wrapped his arms around me in a bear hug. In my ear, he whispered, "Aprella be with you out there, Nephew."

When we pulled away, we looked each other in the eyes. I nodded. There was nothing left to say. He turned and started organizing the civilians, and I gathered what few real soldiers we had.

Near the cave entrance, I looked them over. Eight red dragon soldiers, armed and armored better than any soldiers in all of history, especially the two in plate mail. As bodyguards, their armor was enchanted with mahier like mine was. I knew we wouldn't all make it through the battle. They knew it, too, but I could see steely determination in their eyes and I felt proud to be a dragon like them at that moment.

"Listen up," I said, and paced back and forth in front of them.

They snapped to attention, heels together, arms straight down at their sides with their thumbs lined up with their pants seams, standing tall. "Yes, Sir!" they all said together.

"You already know it's total chaos out there, so we have to stick together above everything else. Fight side by side, covering the dragon next to you with your shield while they do the same for you."

"Just like we trained," one said.

"Yes, nothing is different. Now, if you checked with your mahier to sense the battle, you already know we need to get the Realms organized if we want a shot at winning. Eldrick hit us by surprise, so our defenses weren't set and now they're scattered all over the battlefield. We have to get them fighting together and falling back toward HQ so we can get our front line back to being a line. Any questions?"

One stepped forward and said, " What do we do if we're attacked by those crazy dragons? Any one of them might be a friend, a brother, a sister. What then?"

I knew that question was going to come up because I'd been thinking about it, too. Even if they were mind-sick because of Eldrick, those were still my people. I'd been trying to think of something to do besides killing them, but judging by the way the other dragons were looking down at their feet, they all knew what my answer had to be.

With more confidence than I felt, I said, "We'll try to take them out of the fight without killing them. Focus on the Dark Elves and Carnites, instead. Remember, if Eldrick dies, we think his control dies, too. Killing him is going to be the only way to save them, or ourselves. Until then, you know how battle is. You don't always get to decide who you fight, and if it comes down to you or them..."

"Make it them."

"Yes," I said, "and when this is over, I swear to you, we'll give every single one of them the hero's funeral they deserve. Now, let's get out there, rally our brothers and sisters, and push these rats off Ochana, once and for all."

There was no cheering, but I hadn't expected any. There were quiet nods all around, and I gave them a few seconds to come to grips with the reality we all had to face if we hoped to win the battle.

Then I let out a long, deep breath, turned, and walked out of the caves. We snuck as far away from the waterfall as we could, as fast as we could. I felt dark tilium and mahier all around us as dragons overhead and Dark Elves all around us scanned the battlefield for enemies. It took a lot of my own mahier to keep us hidden, but I spent it happily to let my soldiers keep as much of their energy as they could. I had tilium and mereum to fall back on when my mahier ran out.

I had noticed that most of the fighting was in or around the huge plaza where dragons flying in usually landed. There were just too many enemies running around everywhere around us, though. Every dragon unit I sensed with my mahier was fighting two or three times as many dragons and Dark Elves. Ochana's troops were split up, which made it worse because it was like they each fought their own little battle. It wasn't two armies fighting each other, but one army fighting scattered mobs of defenders. We'd never win like that. Every time I saw a unit of dragons, I focused my thoughts at them, sending messages. Fall back. Gather together. Rally at the castle.

I led my little group of soldiers around the plaza's edge. We came out of an alleyway at the far end. I was startled half out of my skin when we practically tripped over a cluster of six dragons dressed in the blue uniforms of Realm Four. When I realized they were ours, I grinned and felt a flood of relief.

One of my soldiers called out, "Hail, Realm Four. Follow Prince Colton! We're pulling everyone back to get our defenses organized around the castle."

The Realm Four dragons, hearing him, turned and headed our way. Another six dragons wouldn't make much of a difference out there, in the grand scheme of things, but they'd bring my group up to fourteen. That would be enough to give me an advantage if we ran into a squad of Dark Elves or crazed dragons.

I grinned at the first one when they were about twenty feet away. "We sure are glad to see you guys."

The dragons didn't reply. They kept walking toward me. Something wasn't right... Their weapons! They didn't have any. Soldiers had weapons. I opened my mouth to shout an alarm, but never got the chance as the first one suddenly sprinted. I didn't even have time to bring my sword up before he crashed into me, shoulder-first, and it felt like I was hit by a truck. As I flew through the air, I heard the fight begin. I landed on my back and skidded a few feet before I came to a stop. The blow had knocked the wind out of me. I was thankful for my training, though, because I found myself already climbing to my feet, and I had somehow kept my grip on my sword.

I saw one of the dragons in blue kneeling on one of my dragon's backs, grabbing his hair in one fist. The dragon in blue had summoned enough of his dragon form to grow a big claw from the top of his other fist, like a dagger. He was about to stab that into the back of my soldier's head.

I roared and reached out with one hand, using mereum to hold his claw-fist back. He struggled against me with insane strength, and I immediately broke into a sweat from how much effort it took to hold him back. He was stronger than me, though; his wicked spike got closer and closer to my soldier's head. Desperately, I focused everything into stopping him, but my control was slipping fast and the dragon hadn't weakened at all, yet.

A sword seemed to grow out of the crazed dragon's chest, covered in his blood. The skewered dragon had a split second where I saw the light come back into his eyes, and he looked down at the sword sticking out of his chest with a confused look. A moment later, he toppled to one side and fell to the ground. He didn't move again.

Breathing heavily, I looked up at my soldier who'd killed him. He put his foot on the fallen dragon's back and pulled hard on his sword, muscles flexing, trying to get his stuck blade free. A moment later, it came loose suddenly and he staggered back a step.

As I climbed to my feet again, I saw that only six of my eight dragons were still standing. The other two soldiers and the four crazed dragons in blue lay on the cobblestone road. My mahier senses told me that none of the fallen ones had heartbeats. I wanted to scream. Or cry. Maybe both. I'd just lost two loyal, good dragons at the very moment I had thought we were getting reinforcements. There was safety in numbers, but now I had fewer dragons with me, not more.

I glared at the closest soldier and snarled, "Why were those dragons dressed like our soldiers? Answer me!"

I knew he didn't deserve to be yelled at, and that he probably felt just the same way I did, but I couldn't help myself. I felt my eyes well up and tears fell, crawling down my cheeks. I'd never wanted to kill Eldrick more than I did at that moment, with fire in my veins.

The soldier looked at me, first with irritation written on his face, but then his expression melted into a sympathetic look as he spotted my tears. Instead of snapping back or saying anything to embarrass me, he turned to the other soldiers and shouted, "Grab their dog tags. All of them, even the ones we killed. We'll make sure those tags get back to HQ with us, understand? That's our mission. Now, move it, our prince can't wait all day for you lazy dragons!"

The others quickly knelt down by whichever body was closest. In a few seconds, they had all the tags, and they handed them to the one who had barked orders.

He then turned to me with the fistful of dog tags, gripping their thin chains so the tags dangled down and tinkled as they bumped one another. He held them out to me and said, "Sir, as you ordered, here are their IDs. Now we can give them a proper burning ceremony even if the enemy takes their bodies, or if we have to retreat from Ochana without them."

He gave me a faint smile as I took the tags in one hand and wiped my cheeks dry with my other hand. "Thank you," I said, feeling kind of ashamed for snapping at him. My thanks was for more than the dog tags, but also for his understanding, and because I felt a weird kind of relief to be around people whom I had fought beside when our dragons died. It was as if so long as we remembered them together, they weren't actually dead. Not truly.

For the next hour, we made our way through Ochana, hiding and running. We did find more soldiers to join us, and we lost more, but by the time I'd gotten the plaza cleared and our scattered army to fall back to get reorganized, I had two squads with me.

Unfortunately, the enemy had also reorganized and they were pushing hard at us. Ochana's defenders were doing better than before because I'd given HQ actual units to send orders to instead of scattered individual units. It helped us to react better and faster to new threats, but we were still far too outnumbered. They were pushing us back as fast as we could back up, and I knew it was only a matter of time.

Most of Ochana's army had been pressed back until they were in a thick line around HQ, but some units were cut off by the enemy line—including mine.

My squads and I finished off the last of an enemy squad of dark Elves—thankfully not our mind-controlled brothers and sisters—when I looked up in time to see more coming around a corner at the end of the block. I turned to lead my soldiers the other way, but more Dark Elves were already coming around that corner, too. We were trapped between them. The only way out would be a mad dash off the street and through empty houses and their tiny yards.

I flung my mahier senses out all around us to find the safest path, but all I saw were more Dark Elves in every direction. There wasn't a way out.

"All right, dragons, listen up! We'll run south from here, through that blue house across the street. I'll kick in the door, and don't wait for me before you start running through it. Go out the back, then hightail it for HQ." After a moment's thought, I added, "And good luck. It has been an honor fighting by your side."

They nodded, some giving me grim smiles. They were soldiers, and we'd given it the best fight we could. Now, I just wanted to make it to HQ so I could see my parents before they overran us completely. Maybe I'd make it there, I thought as I glanced up into the sky, but—

Oh no. More dragons were streaking down at Ochana from the clouds high above us. Dozens of them, no, *hundreds*, each carrying two riders, some with three. They came at us fast, like falcons diving for prey. "Incoming dragons! Get ready!" I shouted, pointing up at the sky.

Well, we'd done our best, I supposed. There were worse ways to die.

Don't be so dramatic. Did you miss me?

It was Eva's voice in my head! I threw the last bit of my mahier at the diving dragons, extending my senses out to them. Elves, Trolls, even Mermaids, all riding on dragons! And among them flew a swarm of Fairies.

Eva, Cairo, Jericho, and the others had come back with help, at last.

Chapter Twenty-Three

As new dragons and our allies came streaking down, the thick line of Dark Elves, Carnites, and mind-controlled dragons was slowly marching toward Ochana's defenders around the castle and HQ. I had helped rally our troops together to rebuild a defensive line there, but that line looked so thin compared to Eldrick's. The coward hadn't even bothered to come lead his troops himself, he was so confident he'd win. So far, it looked like he had a point.

But then a warning cry went up from his battle line, many of them turning to look up into the sky and point. I even heard a couple panicked screams. Eldrick's battle lines first shuddered, then came to a sloppy halt, though their mind-controlled dragons kept right on going toward the castle defenders. Whatever the crazy dragons were up against, they just kept advancing thanks to Eldrick's mind control.

Our fresh reinforcements plowed into Eldrick's battle line from behind. I saw flashes of light as tilium and mahier flew back and forth. People screamed. In moments, it was hard to tell where Eldrick's line ended and our new troops began. My heart soared with hope! The dragons around the castle could probably handle the mind-controlled dragons still coming at them, without the Dark Elves and Carnites with them.

Then I realized that Eva and our allies, even all fighting together, were still greatly outnumbered. They had the advantages of surprise and hitting the enemy from behind, so it wasn't necessarily hopeless for them.

I was still cut off from the castle, though. "Come on," I shouted to my two squads, "we can't get to the castle, yet, but we can go help our friends out there. They came for us, now let's go help them!"

My soldiers must have been as excited to see reinforcements as I was because for once, they shouted back and raised their swords and spears in the air.

I could see the enemy line getting pushed back, and the buzzing horde of flying enemy dragons in what looked like airplane dogfights with the dragons who came back with Eva, but it wouldn't be long before the bad guys got their act together and hit back. There were just too many of them. I wanted to attack them from the side, or flank them as Jericho called it, when they started pushing back. I shouted for my soldiers to follow me, and we ran up the huge plaza's edge.

Two dragons with wings stretched wide flew toward us from up ahead, coming in low and fast. I couldn't be sure what side they were on, but when I led my squads down a side street, the fliers changed directions.

Enemies, then. "If you have mahier, still, get ready for shields," I said. A few of our people were already out of mahier, and they stepped behind those who still had some. I started pulling mereum together to hit the oncoming enemy with a big downdraft when they got low enough.

Then ten more dragons joined the two coming in, and I felt my heart sinking. Twelve dragons. Once they got closer, I saw that each had two riders, dressed all in black--Dark Elves. We had only seconds left.

When they were fifty feet above the cobblestone roadway, I threw every bit of mereum I had into making hurricane-force winds slam down on them from above. I wanted to plow them right into the pavement! I felt my heart race as the mereum flowed through me, and I could see a faint glow around everything—my eyes radiating mereum-blue due to the amount of energy coursing through me. It was a total rush.

Until nothing happened. The winds were there, I could sense them, but the dragons didn't dip, much less crash. I felt a familiar tingling at the back of my neck. Dark tilium was shielding them. I stared at them in disbelief. It couldn't be him. Why now? Why here?

Before I could think it through, the wing of dragons flew into us. I had to dive to the ground to avoid getting slashed by the claws of dragons flying by at two hundred miles per hour. Their riders leaped off as the dragons hit my squads, using their tilium to land safely, some in front and others behind us. They crouched to one knee to absorb the landing shock. I had hoped they'd hit the ground and go splat, but no such luck.

I dodged to one side as a Dark Elf slashed his sword at me. My counter attack broke his sword near the hilt, just before one of my dragons swung his sword across the Dark Elf's belly and then spun away like a deadly top, still swinging his sword around.

More and more Dark Elves landed among us, and then the dragons started to turn around for another pass.

I felt that tingle again, suddenly, just before a deep rumble came from nowhere and everywhere at once. I could feel it through the ground under my feet. The daylight faded a bit as if a cloud blocked the sun. I glanced up... and paused. The white, pretty clouds of Ochana had become suddenly dark and menacing. More clouds gathered, moving on fast-forward and growing thicker and thicker as they came together over Ochana.

I started to see a red haze around the very edges of the clouds, where daylight would have hit them. The Mediterranean! They looked just like the clouds that hit us when we were flying to Greece from the Congo. I hurled the thought at Eva, though I didn't know where she was, and just hoped she could hear it. "The storm is evil, get down!"

Something was coming through the clouds, something huge. The massive black clouds seemed to expand from inside—a huge face was coming out from within the storm bank. No, it was made of the storm clouds themselves. The mouth opened wide, and I froze in sudden fear as I remembered my dream, the one where Eldrick's giant face chomped on me and I was stuck inside his mouth.

When the mouth opened into a wide grin at the same time thunder boomed with a sound so deep that I felt it in my bones. Vast forks of red lightning shot from Eldrick's cloud-mouth and slammed into the plaza all along the battle lines in the fight between Eldrick's troops and our allies. Wherever the bolts hit, bodies went flying, dragon and Carnite, Elf and Dark Elf. More of Eldrick's troops flew across the battlefield aflame, but he had the troops to spare and we didn't.

I dove for cover, and just in time. Bolts crashed into the ground where I'd been standing. My squads, and the Dark Elves and dragons they had been fighting, scattered in every direction as lightning and thunder pounded both the main battle and its miniature copy where my squads fought his dragon riders.

The lightning stopped, its last rolls of thunder echoing across the plaza. I was half blinded by the lightning's after-images burned into my eyes, but though the lightning had stopped, the face kept coming. Cloud-Eldrick's mouth grew wider and wider, and as I stared down its throat, just before the face smashed into Ochana, I saw a lone figure coming from the cloud-throat, riding on a huge black cloud-dragon. The figure wore a crown and carried a long staff in his hands. I knew that had to be Eldrick, finally coming to his own battle, and he was flying straight at me.

My mind wouldn't accept what I was seeing. I muttered, "No," over and over, and backed away.

Eldrick's voice boomed in my head, loud enough to drop me to my knees with pain. "Keeper. I'm coming to end you," he said simply.

I drew mereum faster than I ever had before, pulling it from the clouds themselves, and hurled it at the cloud-dragon rider. My attack broke apart over him harmlessly, only making the wings seem to flap a little before I was drained. He was almost on me.

I turned and ran. The thing followed, coming on faster and faster. I cut to my left, running between two houses, hoping to lose him in Ochana's maze of homes and alleys.

As it turned out, that was a big mistake. When I came out the other side from between two houses, I found myself in a big courtyard with a high wall along the outside edges, surrounding it on three sides. The only way out was to fly or to go back the way I came, and I wasn't about to fly up with Eldrick's evil magic clouds throwing lightning everywhere and a swarm of crazy dragons attacking everything that moved, so I turned to run back the way I'd come.

I skidded to a halt after only one step. The cloud dragon, almost on top of me, shifted its wings back like an airplane landing, then it burst into a thousand black, snake-like tendrils that collapsed in on themselves in the center until it vanished with a loud pop and only Eldrick remained. His staff, I saw now that he was close enough, was really a huge mace. It looked big enough for a Carnite, I thought, although maybe that was my panic talking.

With his eyes flaring black as if they were made of a shadow-light, he walked toward me and laughed. "Prince Cole, the mighty Keeper of Dragons. Ha! Fight me, Cole. It's time to die."

I sprinted to one side, hoping to get around him and out of the courtyard trap I was in, but he was faster than me even using my tilium to move like a blur.

"Not good enough, dragon." He raised his mace over his head with only one hand, and my eyes bulged in surprise. I couldn't have picked that thing up with two hands, I was pretty sure.

I looked around, frantically, hoping to see friendly soldiers, but there were none there. I was alone with Eldrick in a courtyard, and no one knew it but us.

Eldrick brought his mace down at my head, a wicked grin painted on his face.

I leaped out of the way at the last instant, somersaulted back to my feet, and ran. He struggled to stop his heavy mace, and I ran past him. Freedom!

He pointed two fingers at me and flicked them to one side. I was yanked back like a stuntman in a movie, tied to a train. I flew across the courtyard, landing in a heap in the middle.

Dazed, I scrambled to my feet and drew mereum from the clouds, again, restoring my pool of energy. There was so much mereum that it threatened to overwhelm me in only moments. I snarled and ran at Eldrick. If I couldn't escape, I would have to fight, but I had a trick up my sleeve. As I drew close, he swung his mace again. I used my mahier to deflect it to one side, and it buried itself into the cobblestones.

I poured pure tilium and every bit of my mereum into my sword. My magic sword! The Mere Blade flared cobalt-blue, blindingly bright. It shone bright enough to turn his shadow-glowing eyes blue, even. And by swinging his mace, there was no way he could block my sword.

My heart soared as I leaped through the air, spinning. I passed him on my right and slashed straight out with all my might as I went by. I kept spinning and brought the blade down across his back, diagonally. Two fatal wounds! I landed in a crouch, one knee touching down on the pavement, my arms held out for balance. I felt the explosion of mereum and tilium flare out from Eldrick like a concussion behind me. I calmly stood and turned, grinning.

And froze. My attack had almost cut his shirt off of him, but where my first strike landed, there was only a faint trickle of blood. As I watched, the thin wound closed up completely. I was staring where he should have been nearly cut in half when a mountain smashed into my right side. That's what it felt like, at least, when his giant mace smacked me. I streaked through the air and smashed into the courtyard's stone wall faster than I could begin to throw up any kind of shield. The wall cracked from the force of my impact, and I bounced off. When I landed on my back on the cobblestones, I couldn't get up, no matter how hard I tried. I could move my arms a little bit, but not enough to swing a weapon. Anyway, I didn't have my sword anymore. I didn't know where it went, but I couldn't have reached it even if I knew.

Eldrick strolled up to me, the mace over his shoulder, and my eyes went wide. He smirked at me, the heavy-weight prizefighter looking down at some chump kid who never had a chance.

"Nicely done, Cole. If you had another one of those attacks in you, it's possible you could actually hurt me. You drained most of my tilium with that attack. But it was too little, too late, kiddo. Unlike Doctor Evil, I don't think a quick, painless death is too good for my enemies. I'd love to stay and chat, reveal my big plan, and give you a chance to escape, but instead, I think I'll just kill you. Tell Jago I said hello when you see your Ancestors."

"I'd rather... you... tell him." It was hard to get the words out. So much for my witty last words.

He snorted, still smirking, but didn't waste any more time. He raised his mace up with both hands and it cast a shadow as big as me. I couldn't rip my eyes off it as he began his deadly swing.

J.A. Culican

Chapter Twenty-Four

Time slowed down almost to a stop. I noticed the strangest things, like the way the sunlight shone off the black clouds in a red hue that almost looked like they were on fire from inside. Or the thick gash in Eldrick's mace, and how dirt drifted away from it from when he'd smashed it into the plaza's cobblestone floor. I noticed his eyes were wide with excitement, thrilled at the idea of smashing my head into that same floor.

I threw my arm up to protect myself, purely by reflex since there was no way that would save me, but then my eyes were drawn to my hand. The ring Prince Jago gave me was on my index finger, now risen to the surface and pulsing with a pure, cobalt glow. Hadn't it become invisible when I put it on? Hadn't it merged into my skin? Not anymore, though. Now it was brightly shining, gleaming in the sunlight.

Eldrick swung his huge mace down at me with his face twisted into a furious snarl, lips curled back to bare his teeth, mouth open in a roar I couldn't hear in the silence of that slow-motion moment. I looked away from him and back at the ring. I wanted the last thing I ever saw to be something beautiful, not him and his ugly face. From the corner of my eye, I saw his mace looming over me, blocking out the sun like it was about to block out my life.

The ring pulsed brighter, twice. There was a huge flare that made me close my eyes, but it stayed painfully, blindingly bright even through my closed eyelids. The light felt cool and comfortable on my skin, though, like it knew me and was brushing its hand over my arm tenderly.

I heard a scream. I opened my eyes as the flare faded away and saw Eldrick flying backward across the plaza. He landed hard, on his back, and the air between us shimmered like heat rising off a long, empty road on a hot day. I almost thought I saw figures in the shimmer. I blinked.

When I opened my eyes, I was *sure* of it; people started as just outlines, then filled in from the edges inward. There were four of them, all shades of white even when they finished becoming visible, like someone had taken a cell phone picture with a photo-negative filter.

One looked over his shoulder at me, and I jumped halfway out of my own skin in surprise when I realized who he was. Jago! The Ancestors! The ones who had given me the ring, which I'd forgotten all about. They had said it would make itself known when the time was right.

The four Ancestors sprinted toward Eldrick as he climbed to his feet. The way their robes and clothes and long hair blew back, they looked like they were running into a heavy wind, but to me, the air was perfectly still. Their weapons, the same white-cartoon color as the Ancestors themselves, flashed in the sunlight as the four struck Eldrick at the same time.

The force knocked him back down to his knees and I thought I saw him flicker. They hit him with their swords again and again, and each time, he flickered more and seemed to grow weaker until I could almost see through him.

But I didn't see any blood.

Then he burst into motion, leaping to his feet and sending the four Ancestors flying back in every direction. He jumped through the air at Jago, who had landed on his back, and smashed his mace down. It passed through the Ancestor harmlessly, though, cracking the plaza floor. He struck again, but it went through Jago just like the first time.

Then another Ancestor struck Eldrick from behind. Eldrick flickered and staggered, going down to one knee. The Ancestors surrounded him again and continued striking him with their swords, moving in a blur of speed.

I scrambled to my feet while I stared. I didn't know what to do. They were doing more than I could, already. With every sword blow, Eldrick looked less and less solid, but he didn't fade away to nothing, even after a dozen more blows.

Jago shouted into my head, "We can't kill him! Feel his dark tilium—it's sustaining him. We can fight him off, but the dead have no power over tilium. Run, Nephew."

Tilium was keeping him alive? I opened my dragon senses and reached out, looking at Eldrick. They were right—he had so much tilium in him that it was leaking out where the Ancestors' swords hit. It was like blood that I could only see with my dragon-sight, but there was so much tilium inside him that he'd never bleed it all out.

I felt a tingling in the middle of my chest, from my heart. The tingle spread from there, growing down my arms, down my body. I'd felt this before, I realized, in the jungles of South America with the Farro.

As the tingles reached my ankles and wrists, I felt myself rise up into the air like a marionette on strings, arms and legs dangling behind me. Glowing silver tendrils, like a thick mass of spider webs, shot out of my fingers and toes.

The tingle flowed up through my neck, too. I threw my head back, and the silver threads burst out of my mouth and even my eyes. The tendrils had a mind of their own. They did what they wanted. I could feel their urgent need as they raced to Eldrick. I heard him scream, and he sounded afraid.

Good. That thought strengthened me, and when I stopped struggling against them, even more threads came out of my mouth, my hands, my feet. They struck him and wrapped around him, a fly in a spider's silk cocoon. He thrashed wildly, but my energy was too strong for him to resist.

Then the threads drew tight. They pulled back into me slowly, at the same time dragging Eldrick toward me just like the Farro had when I took their dark tilium. I was going to devour Eldrick. I was going to be stronger than anyone had ever been, with all that tilium inside me. All the tilium in the world, it felt like. It was all mine, and all I had to do was take it from Eldrick.

Jago's voice inside my head said, "Colton. You must stop. If you draw him in, he'll poison your soul. Stop!"

I couldn't, though. I wasn't in control of the threads now any more than I had been when this happened before. "I don't know how!" I screamed.

Eldrick was halfway across the plaza. In seconds, he'd be with me. I didn't know what to expect, but I knew it was going to be bad for me.

I focused everything I could, all my willpower. "Stop!"

The threads kept pulling him toward me, ignoring my command. He was only feet away from me, thrashing and struggling with fear-filled eyes, trying to get away from me.

The ring...

I had an idea. I sent my mahier out to Eldrick and it wrapped around him like a second skin. Then I sent my purified tilium at him. It wrapped around him in cords thick as cables, binding him tightly. And lastly, I pulled mereum from the water vapor in the air, the humidity, even my own sweat. The mereum blob's edges moved outward over him, *tick, tick tick*, each bit stretching out over him like a potter moving clay with his thumbs. Finally, it surrounded him completely.

That was when the tendrils and my mereum fought each other. One tried to pull Eldrick into me, and the other I willed to pull him into the ring instead of me. It took so much effort, two drops of sweat fell off my chin. I couldn't keep that up, I realized.

But as panic threatened to overcome me, I felt a hand on my shoulder. Somehow, I knew Jago stood beside me. I grew calmer. I could do it. The Ancestors had faith in me.

Slowly at first, but then faster and faster, the tendrils lost their grip. They turned thin and frail, and one after the other, they snapped in half. The broken tilium ends slithered back into my body, leaving only the mereum. I knew what I had to do, then.

I tried again to will my mereum to pull Eldrick's power into the ring. He had so much of it! But the ring, I knew somehow, was strong enough to hold even Eldrick. Eldrick began to stretch out like silly putty. The instant part of that stretched-out soul touched the ring, it began sucking him in. First, it pulled what looked like his actual shadow out of him. It stretched thin as it was sucked into the ring.

I realized that, without his tainted tilium, there would be no Eldrick left. His power had long ago overwhelmed him, destroying every other part of himself until only that evil remained. He was made of the dark tilium I was forcing into the ring.

At the end, there was a whooshing noise that started low and deep, but then rose higher and higher until it was shrill and piercing, like the winds of a tornado blowing all around us. All of a sudden, the shrill train-whistle noise was cut off in one abrupt moment.

The air grew still. The black angry clouds above paused, paled slowly to white, and then faded away entirely.

I staggered and fell to my knees. I didn't have to look around to know the Ancestors were gone, just as Eldrick was. They left when he had. I silently thanked them for saving me until I discovered how to defeat our enemy.

As my strength returned, I climbed back to my feet. I looked for the Mere Blade and found it lying in a corner. I held out my hand toward it. It rattled, then flew through the air to me. I caught it in one hand and felt the ring grow warmer.

I had wanted the blade and it came to me. I could feel the almost unlimited power I possessed. The dark tilium called to me. It told me to do things. I could end everything if I wanted. All of it. Dragons, Dark Elves, darkness. I could destroy it all and go home to my human parents.

I shook my head. Those weren't my thoughts. The ring's stored power was calling me to use it. Fine, I decided, I would use it—just not the way the corrupted tilium wanted me to.

I raised my hands out to my sides, palms up, until they were at shoulder height. Then I turned my hands over and swung them toward the ground. "Down!" I shouted. Above, the swarm of thrashing, fighting dragons stopped in mid-air, then streaked toward the ground as though yanked down, hard.

"Stay!" I yelled. The rain of dragons stopped just before hitting the ground and then stayed there, immobile.

I had the power to end the war. At last, I could save the world, and I'd use Eldrick's own power to do it. I loved the irony. I stormed out of the plaza, heading toward the fighting.

A block away, I saw maybe two dozen Dark Elves and a Carnite fighting half a dozen Woland warriors. I flicked my hand to one side, and the Dark Elves and the Carnite flew up, away, and over the edge of Ochana, screaming the whole way.

The dragons turned to look at me, confused. I ignored them and kept walking. Every time I saw a crazed dragon, I could almost see the knot of dark tilium in its head, binding its thoughts. It was child's play to flick those away, and when they were gone, the dragons were free. Confused about where they were, but free.

I saved all the crazed dragons I could. I killed whatever Dark Elves and Carnites I saw. None had a chance against me, not with the power I had in the palm of my hand. It didn't take long for the fighting to stop, because there was no one left to fight. My dragons were safe, while Eldrick's army went on the run or died.

The battle was over. The world and Ochana were safe once more. But all I wanted was to find Eva, Cairo, Jericho, and all my other friends. I had to make sure they were safe.

After pausing and debating it, I pulled the ring off my finger and put it in my pocket where it couldn't cause any mischief.

Chapter Twenty-Five

The Congo was beautiful as we walked through the little pathway the Elves had grown, stretching from Paraiso to the clearing. The shoulder strap on my kilt dug into my neck, and the sweat from jungle heat didn't help.

Eva swatted my hand aside. "Knock it off. You'll wrinkle it."

"I never wore one before," I said.

Ochana's formalwear was a ceremonial kilt, like the ones Highlander Regiments wore in Scotland. Which kind of dragon one was made for determined the dominant color, except for the silver dragons. Theirs were all black fabric with lots of silver highlights and lines. I actually thought theirs looked way better than mine.

"Well," Eva said, "I think you can deal with it long enough to sit through Gaber's coronation. It's not every day the Elves get a new king, and it's kind of surprising we were invited."

We arrived at the clearing just then. It was the same clearing I'd spoken to the Ancestors in when they'd given me the ring. I was surprised the coronation wasn't being held at the lake in Paraiso, the source of their tilium, but then I saw the huge crowd and the choice made more sense. There wouldn't have been enough room for everyone by the lake.

"Look, there are your parents," Eva said, bouncing on the balls of her feet and pointing. "They're with Queen Annabelle of the Fairies and Queen Delsa of the Mermaids."

I said, "King Evander and Princess Clara, too. Did you ever think you'd see all of them sitting together and actually laughing?"

Cairo, standing on Eva's other side, chuckled. "Never did think it would happen. This is the first time I've ever seen it. I hear Gaber has a special announcement to make during his coronation, too."

He winked at me, because I was in on it, too. We all knew he was going to announce the Crowns' Accord. King Rylan, as king of the dragons, would normally have that honor but times had changed. Dragons changed it when we turned our backs on the world. Gaber announcing the new accord would go a long way toward healing those old wounds.

Jericho's voice, right behind me, made me jump with surprise as he said, "Rylan is more generous than I'd be."

Eva and Cairo grinned at me when I jumped. Embarrassed at being startled, I snapped, "That's why he's the king and you're the warrior."

"Truth." He put his hand on my shoulder and joined our little circle, ignoring my outburst.

Zane stepped up on my other side. He didn't say anything, but nodded to everyone, greeting us. Then we made our way to our seats, Zane sitting with us instead of with his brother. I wasn't sure what that was about, but I didn't complain. After the battle, he and I had become a lot closer.

All around us, the clothes were impressive. Everyone had on their very finest outfits, most of it newly-made and all very formal. It still made me uncomfortable. I was used to jeans and sweats. Worse, the coronation itself wouldn't happen for another hour, and I fidgeted the entire time. First, the kings and queens made their speeches praising Gaber, swearing to protect each other always. I guessed that was to set the stage for announcing the Crowns' Accord later.

After the boring speeches, the coronation was done. As amazing as the ceremony was, it only took a few minutes, which was disappointing. And then Gaber's speech afterward, while wearing the ancient Elven crown and looking rather impressive, took another twenty minutes. I thought he did a great job. It had to be kind of scary standing in front of so many people, even kings and queens, and trying to remember the speech he wanted to make. He did well, though, and there was a lot of applause when he finished.

After that, Gaber left the stage and went to his throne, and then came the part I didn't want to sit through. Everyone with any authority at all got the chance to make a speech and be seen with the new king, and none of them passed up the chance.

Cairo said, "Poor Gaber. We aren't going to sit through this whole thing, are we? They're going to open the buffet soon. A dragon's gotta eat, you know."

"Actually," I said, "I have something I want to talk to you all about. I need your help, though. Will you come with me?" I looked at my friends, but I also included Zane. Jericho was gone, since he also had to make a speech, and had disappeared after the crowning.

When they all nodded, I said, "Okay, follow me."

We made our way through the crowd, trying not to bump into men in tuxedos or step on the beautiful dresses. Finally, we got through them and were able to go deeper into the jungle, away from the clearing. As we walked, amazingly, my kilt made it easy to climb over big roots, logs, and so on. And it had pockets! Our little walk in the jungle gave me a new appreciation for kilts.

We reached a smaller clearing in the Congo jungle. In the center was a tree stump. Some human must have recently cut it down with a chainsaw, because the cut was flat and smooth, and the wood hadn't yet aged gray. It was perfect for what I had in mind.

I pulled out the ring the Ancestors had given me, the one with Eldrick's evil soul trapped inside. Just looking at it made me want to put it on. The ring, it called to me. I had to count to ten with my eyes closed to keep myself from doing it. And that was the reason I'd brought them all out to the middle of the jungle.

"Eva, you're my best friend. Cairo, you've become a friend, even though I didn't like you at first." I paused, grinning, and they chuckled politely. I continued, "And Zane, you proved yourself during Eldrick's attack on Ochana. I doubted you right up until then. I'd like to get to know you better, now that this is all over with, and to be friends with my father's brother."

Zane nodded, half-smiling back at me. He was always hard to read.

Eva said, "What's with the ring? Did you learn something else it does? Hurry up and show us!"

"Actually, I did learn something else. The thing is evil now that Eldrick is in it. I feel my blood drawn to it, if that makes any sense."

"Not really." Eva smirked at me.

"I feel a constant urge to put it on, and then to do bad things with it. You have no idea how much power the ring has—how much power it gives me."

Cairo said, "I kind of do know how much power it has. I was there. I saw how you marched through the battlefield smiting Dark Elves and Carnites like a god. It was amazing. No enemy could ever stand up to Ochana again, not with that ring on our side."

I shook my head, my lips pressed tightly together. I set the ring on the tree stump and said, "That's the point. I felt like a god. I don't think anyone should have so much power. It's too tempting. And Eldrick's spirit is in there, calling me."

Zane said, "What are you trying to say?"

I took a deep breath. "I think we should destroy it. We're safer destroying it than using it."

Cairo's jaw dropped. "You can't be serious. With that ring, Ochana is unbeatable."

Eva was opening and closing her fists, shifting from one foot to the other. She said, "I agree with Cole. What if someone put it on and the ring overpowered them? Cole's saying it's hard to resist the urges it gives him, and if he has a hard time, out of everyone I know, then we should get rid of it. Anyway, it gives me an eerie feeling. I don't like it."

Zane stepped up to the stump and looked down at the ring. Everyone turned to see what he'd do. Would he go for the ring? I had a barrier of mereum ready to go, just in case.

"Cole is right," he said, his gaze still locked onto the ring. "I felt it calling to me as soon as Cole said we should destroy it. It wants me to put it on. I could be the king, it says. I don't want to be the king, but it makes me want it. Or it brings out something in my subconscious."

"Either way, that's bad," Eva muttered.

"Either way. And one more thing is that you can't watch it twenty-four-seven. What if someone stole it? I could steal it right now, you know..."

As his voice trailed off, I knew I was right and the ring had to go. I looked at Cairo and tilted my head toward Zane; Cairo stepped up and got between Zane and the ring, pushing him back gently.

Zane's cheeks got red and he grinned sheepishly. "See what I mean?"

Yes, I did. I got everyone to stand in a circle around the stump. Once I made the decision for real, I suddenly just wanted to get it over with. Before I could talk myself out of it.